And Then She Was Running

Giselle, almost blind in her panic, did not see the young nurse. She threw the door open with such violence that it banged against the wall.

"You'll wake the baby!" Julie called after her, her own voice rising in panicked response.

Giselle plunged across the room to stand by the empty crib. An envelope lay on the small satin pillow. Giselle ripped open the envelope and read the brief note.

"If we tell anyone, ANYONE, they'll kill him," she said.

Giselle placed one hand, palm down, on the indentation Benjamin's head had left in the pillow. The satin was as cold as the window glass. Her son was gone.

Also by Dona Vaughn

Rivalries

Available from
HarperPaperbacks

The PRICE of EVERYTHING

Dona Vaughn

HarperPaperbacks

A Division of HarperCollinsPublishers

This is a work of fiction. The characters, incidents, and
dialogues are products of the author's imagination and are not
to be construed as real. Any resemblance to actual events or
persons, living or dead, is entirely coincidental.

HarperPaperbacks   *A Division of* HarperCollins*Publishers*
10 East 53rd Street, New York, N.Y. 10022

Cover illustration by Michael Sabanosh

First printing: January 1993

Printed in the United States of America

HarperPaperbacks and colophon are trademarks of
HarperCollins*Publishers*

❖ 10 9 8 7 6 5 4 3 2 1

For Janie—
Vivian Jane Vaughan

CECIL GRAHAM: What is a cynic?

LORD DARLINGTON: A man who knows the price of everything and the value of nothing.

Oscar Wilde,
Lady Windermere's Fan, Act III

1982

PROLOGUE

The butler had been with the family so long only the mistress remembered his first name. To everyone else he was simply Halloran, a bandy-legged, creaky old relic of uncertain temper. On the butler's bad days, the newer members of the staff—those who had been with the mistress for less than his thirty-six years of service—gave Halloran a wide berth. Today had soured earlier than most.

Opening the Palm Beach house for the season on a fine October morning like this usually put Halloran in the best of moods. From its site on the crest of the beach ridge, Casa Durand rose like a stucco-walled mountain from the pancake flatness of the world's most elegant sandbar. Designed by Addison Mizner, the mansion had been built for the mistress's father-in-law. When Giselle Durand acquired the house by paying the tab from her own pocket, she renamed it after herself with the help of a magnum of Dom Perignon. But today, Halloran's pleasure at reopening the villa had

vanished before he finished unlocking the wrought-
iron gates, and not even the memory of the lovely
smash the champagne bottle had made against the
stone steps could bring it back.

As always, Halloran's first act upon entering the
mansion had been to slide open the plate-glass walls
of the great tiled loggia. Now, as he stood framed in
one of the arches and gazed across the terrace, the
ocean breeze—and what fool preferred the chill of air-
conditioning when he could have God's free wind
from the sea—ruffled what remained of his hair. From
his vantage point, he saw that the cause of his foul
mood still lay peacefully beside the swimming pool,
soaking up the semitropical sun.

Halloran snorted in disgust and retraced his steps
to the kitchen. There, with his permission, the maid,
Ruthie, and the cook, Joyce, were enjoying a quick cup
of coffee between chores. The rest of the staff would
arrive tomorrow. Long years ago Halloran himself had
been hired as a chauffeur by the mistress's husband—a
nasty specimen of humanity, was Halloran's opinion of
the man, and the world better off for Charles Vale's
absence from it. These days he was a working butler,
doing house chores when necessary but still doubling
as a chauffeur for the white Rolls in New York and its
twin here in Palm Beach. Other residents of this tiny
island might have traded their chauffeurs and their
Rolls-Royces for the dubious pleasure of driving their
own Mercedes or BMWs, but Giselle Durand was fully
aware of the publicity value of the showy gesture. She
had put that same knowledge to work in the business
of making creams and paints for ladies' faces.

When she arrived in a few days, the mistress
would be accompanied as always by two uniformed
security guards. Some thought that gesture fully as
pretentious as the Rolls, but when the guards took
their places at the entrance to the villa, no one had to

read the Shiny Sheet to know Giselle Durand was in town. And *that* was the source of Halloran's foul temper on this fine morning.

The figure beside the swimming pool intruded on his thoughts for the hundredth time since her red Mercedes had pulled up in the drive behind him as he was unlocking the gates of Casa Durand. Miss Lilli should not be here today. Not without the guards. But the mistress would be too softhearted to scold her granddaughter when she found out the girl was not in school where she belonged. When he called the mistress this evening to report the situation, Halloran knew he—not the truant—would receive the reprimand.

On that black thought, Halloran entered the kitchen. At the sight of his face, both the maid and the cook dropped their coffee cups and scurried back to their chores.

In a two-piece swimsuit the same shade of scarlet as the roses in the bed beyond the pool, Lilli Rawlings lay as still as a corpse on a white mat beside the aquamarine water of the swimming pool, one arm flung across her face. Her long legs and lean flanks, topped with minimal breasts and a tangled mane of sun-lightened hair, gave the girl a more vulnerable appearance than most seventeen-year-old heiresses to great fortunes.

She gave no sign she heard the arrival of the yardman's truck in the service area behind the wall. Nor that she heard, a few minutes later, the *snick-snick* of the garden shears as a dark-complexioned young man, dangerously handsome, wearing a T-shirt, jeans, and cotton work gloves, appeared and, incomprehensibly, began to clip away the Bougainvillea vines on that same wall.

Leaving a trail of ruin behind him, the handsome young man worked his way closer to the pool area, until he came to a row of oleander at right angles to the wall. He snipped the bushes idly, letting the leaves drift like snowflakes onto the grass. As he worked the shears the sleeve of his T-shirt rose and fell over his right biceps, rhythmically revealing and concealing the smiling devil's head tattooed there in vivid red.

The girl turned onto her stomach and reached behind herself to unclasp the top of her swimsuit. As the straps fell away she raised her arms above her head, mashing her small breasts against the mat.

Exhibitionist, he thought. He had intended to clip his way down the entire row of oleander, but now he felt an intense desire to get on with it. He dropped the shears in the grass and strode back toward the gate.

On the side of the panel truck parked in the service area was the logo of the lawn-service company: a fist with a grotesque green thumb extended. The man gave it a salute in kind as he passed. He opened the back of the truck, ignoring the bound and gagged figure in a neat green uniform with the same green-thumb logo on the sleeve. The figure squirmed helplessly in the gloom and mumbled something against the gag as the man reached across it and took a tarpaulin and a length of rope out of the truck. The man gave the figure the same salute he had given the truck and slammed the door.

He tossed the tarpaulin and rope onto the seat, on top of the sealed envelope he had placed there earlier. Still wearing the cotton gloves, he got behind the wheel. He started the motor and sat there idling it for a few moments. Then he gunned the engine.

The truck hurtled through the open gate in the wall and onto the precisely manicured lawn, leaving tire tracks across the flawless green as it plowed toward the pool. It was halfway to where she lay when the girl finally scrambled to her feet, clutching the swimsuit top to her breasts. She stared, wide-eyed, as the truck stopped a few feet away, and the man got out. In one hand, he held the tarpaulin; in the other hand, the rope.

The swimsuit top fluttered to the ground as he advanced. She looked like a kid, he thought. Even with the breasts. Especially with the breasts. Twelve years old with breasts to match, that was what she looked like.

"Wait," Lilli Rawlings cried. Her glance darted toward the scrap of scarlet fabric on the ground a few feet away and then back to the man. "Please wait."

"No." He tossed the tarpaulin over her like a fisherman throwing a cast net. As it settled around her he grabbed her and secured it with three quick loops of the rope around her torso. Scooping her up, he threw her over his shoulder in one swift movement.

The girl cried out as his shoulder punched into her stomach, but the tarpaulin muffled the sound. As he jogged toward the truck, her head banged against his back, but she made no further protest. When he reached the rear of the truck he opened the door and lifted her in beside the bound figure. Then he slammed the door on both of them.

As the man climbed behind the wheel of the truck once more, a woman's voice rose from the loggia in a jagged scream. Ignoring the maid's alarm, the man took the envelope from the seat beside him and tossed it out the open window. As it fluttered to the ground he threw the truck in reverse, arcing back until the rear tires hung poised on the very edge of the pool. Then he stepped on the gas, leaving black streaks of rubber across the tiles before the front wheels churned back into the lawn. A second set of tire tracks a car's width from the first scored the turf all the way to the service gate.

The tires squealed as he hit the service drive and cornered sharply. "Rough ride, little rich girl," he muttered. With another screech of rubber, he accelerated down the drive and through the wrought-iron gates.

When Halloran heard Ruthie's scream, he snatched one of the pristine tablecloths stacked beside the table where he had been polishing silver and wiped his hands as he hurried through the house to the loggia.

Still shrieking, the maid stood in one of the arches, staring out toward the pool, her voice both amplified and made shrill by the tiled surfaces. As soon as she caught sight of Halloran, Ruthie stopped screaming, her mouth closing with almost comical swiftness on her terror.

Halloran stepped around her and halted, shocked beyond belief. Worse than the vandalism of the vines and shrubs was the scarred lawn. Then he spotted the small rectangle of white in the green beyond the pool.

Forgetting his years, Halloran clattered down the steps. The maid followed as he galloped across the terrace and around the pool. One dark tire track slashed diagonally across the mat where he had last seen Lilli Rawlings sunning herself. Halloran hurried past, intent on the envelope in the grass. As he stooped to pick it up, his knees popping painfully, the maid gasped. He rose slowly and turned her way. She held up a scarlet scrap of fabric.

Once before someone had held a piece of cloth aloft like that. Only then the red that colored the fabric had been the rust of dried life's blood. The memory smote Halloran with such force he nearly staggered.

The sea breeze snapped the swimsuit top like a flag. The maid dropped it and started toward the house.

"Where do you think you're going?" Halloran challenged.

Ruthie clasped her hands. "To call the police?"

"No." Halloran hefted the envelope in his palm as though its precise weight were a matter of vital importance.

"But Miss Lilli! She—"

"No police. Tell Joyce that I said both of you are to keep your mouths shut. Don't talk to anyone. Understand?"

The maid nodded and backed away.

"Go and tell her now," Halloran said.

Ruthie turned and ran toward the house, her ample rear bouncing ludicrously beneath the uniform.

Halloran followed more slowly. When he entered the loggia, he heard the two females sobbing in the kitchen. Ignoring them, he went into the library. He took his time opening the envelope and reading the note inside. Then he picked up the telephone and dialed New York.

"Mistress?" he said when she answered. "It's Halloran, mistress." His voice broke as he remembered the unbearable pain Giselle Durand had suffered. The women's sobs rose from the kitchen. He was near to weeping himself.

"Patrick? What's wrong?"

Her soft voice undid him. "Mistress," he said through his tears. "Giselle. It's happened again."

GISELLE

1946

ONE

Just inside the doorway of his brother's kitchen, Patrick J. Halloran paused. His stomach recoiled from the greasy smell that still seasoned the air—and from the strain of biting back the words he knew he should speak before he spent another night under his brother's roof.

Keefe, not one to be put off by the odor of last night's fish, pushed past his younger brother and sat down at the table just as the bacon began to sizzle. Halloran took the chair next to his niece, three-year-old Doreen. He removed his chauffeur's cap before he leaned over to ruffle Doreen's red curls.

Halloran's sister-in-law, her handsome face ringed by the same red curls as her daughter's, poured each of the men a cup of coffee. Halloran, winking at his niece, snatched her glass and poured some of the milk into his own cup. Then he shoved the milk back to Doreen, and made a great show of whistling in innocence as Doreen giggled wildly.

11

Keefe snorted, as close to a chuckle as he ever came. This morning Sheila did not turn to wink at Halloran. Her strong back to her family, she labored over the stove. Halloran wondered what his brother had done now.

The odor of frying bacon finally blotted out that of last night's meal and Halloran found he could watch without his stomach lurching as Sheila poured a bowl of beaten eggs into the bacon grease in the big iron skillet.

When Sheila dished up her husband's portion of the scrambled eggs, she said, "Would you look at the clean shave on our Pat. He hasn't primped like that for us, Keefe."

"I think he looks pretty," young Doreen crowed.

"I think so, too," Halloran told his niece. His chauffeur's uniform was not as elaborate as most—no leather leggings for him. No white scarf tucked stylishly around his neck to strangle him in the city heat when summer finally arrived. Just a simple double-breasted jacket, topped with a jaunty cap. That was Halloran's style, and Charles Vale, Halloran's employer, had not seen fit to change it. Not that it was the men who inflicted plum-colored jackets and other such nonsense on the hired help. But the mistress was not one of the upper-crust snobs who dressed the help like dolls to amuse herself.

"Looks like he's going to see a sweetie, doesn't he?" Sheila said as she set her brother-in-law's plate on the table with a clatter.

"Now, Sheila," her husband objected, "It was you who sent him for the job in the first place."

But Halloran's sister-in-law was not through with her ragging. "Giselle! What a hoity-toity name!"

"Keep your tongue leather off the mistress," Halloran said mildly. The game was one they had played since the first of January when he hired on as the Vales' chauffeur.

This morning Sheila dealt a new card. "Keefe, I do believe our Pat's in love with Mistress Vale."

The razor's edge on her words caused Halloran to glance up. What he saw in Sheila's face made him focus on his plate again. Just then young Doreen tipped over her porridge. Sheila's cuff set her to howling. The child's racket roused Mum, confined to her bed in the next room these two weeks just past, and the old lady began to call for Sheila to bring her pot.

Thankful that the moment was lost, Halloran bolted the rest of his breakfast, jammed on his cap, and hurried out of the apartment. Most nights he slept in the chauffeur's room provided by his employer. But his family expected him home once or twice a month.

It had been a blessing when Keefe married Sheila just before Pearl Harbor. Otherwise who would have stayed with Mum when one of her boys went off to win the war and the other worked night and day on the home front. Sheila was a tireless worker, and not so cowed she wouldn't give her husband a good scold. And not averse to giving Halloran himself a taste of her tongue leather, which was why he had found himself bright and early one January morning on his way to Riverside Drive—near enough in terms of distance on the little island of Manhattan, but a world away from the slums of the Middle West Side—to apply for a job as driver for a rich man.

Sheila had learned of the position from her own employer, Charles Vale's older sister. High time, Sheila had told her brother-in-law, that he brought a decent wage into the house. Halloran had no desire to be a rich man's lackey, but he was ashamed to tell Sheila so. The money his sister-in-law earned as a lady's maid had tided them over many a rough spot in the days after the war when there were more men than jobs. These last weeks that Mum's illness forced Sheila to stay at home had put a strain on the family finances that Keefe could not remedy.

Halloran's swift passage down the stairs made an unholy clatter in the echoing stairwell. This Hell's Kitchen tenement was a far cry from the lung blocks of the not-too-distant past, dark and fearful places in which Death in the form of tuberculosis had been no respecter of race or creed, age or virtue. Halloran knew that cruel life well enough. It had taken his own sweet dad. Keefe's apartment had four rooms, a washtub, and a sink. No hot water, but that could be heated on the stove. The public toilet was—praise God for Mum's sake while she was still mobile enough to use it—on the same floor and just down the hall.

Halloran reached the sidewalk and felt the bite of the damp March wind whistling down the street. Something made him look up the grimy brick face of the tenement. The curtain at his brother's window fell back into place. Halloran knew Sheila had been standing there, waiting for the sight of him. He shoved his hands deep into his pockets and trudged toward the corner.

His plan had been to strike out for California as soon as spring arrived to stay. A man could make money there, and live all year round in the sunshine to boot. He could double the amount he was contributing to his brother's family and still have plenty of money left for himself. He had only hesitated this long for fear it would break his poor old mother's heart if he left her. But Mum was drifting in and out of her head so much these days that she was unlikely to notice his absence. Her latest tack was complaining of Sheila's care. For all Sheila's labors, his mother had taken such a dislike to her daughter-in-law that Keefe had to have Father Flannagan in twice last week to counsel with her. The old woman wept like a baby and complained that her daughter-in-law was trying to murder her, when truth was his darling Sheila treated Mum with the same care she did young Doreen. And there was the problem,

Halloran told himself. She was not his darling Sheila at all, but his brother's wife.

He had decided to take the job Sheila located for the same reason he was planning to go to California: because it would keep him out of the house and away from his brother's wife. Otherwise he knew he would be bedding her.

He should have told them his plans last night, he thought. There was enough money under the mattress in his cubbyhole at the Vales to pay his fare, and had been for weeks. But he was no longer as keen to leave the city behind as he had been before he hired on as Charles Vale's chauffeur. Before he met the mistress.

This damned house, Charles Vale thought. He lay in bed listening to the click of metal on tile as the butler laid out his shaving equipment in the bathroom. Every morning for three months short of five years Charles had awakened in the spacious bedroom of his four-story house on Riverside Drive with the same feeling of rage.

The butler emerged from the bathroom and glanced toward the bed, but he did not speak. No one spoke to Charles in the morning unless Charles spoke first. After a moment Charles sighed deeply. "Mrs. Vale and I will be down for breakfast in a few minutes, Fry."

"Very good, sir. I'll tell Cook." The whole staff knew how abruptly the master's moods could shift; the bedroom door closed behind Fry before Charles's feet touched the carpet.

Charles wore only the bottoms of his maroon silk pajamas. He stepped out of them, leaving them where they fell. Two inches past six feet, with a compact, well-muscled body, he was an impressive sight in the faint dawn light. He stretched—and winced when he felt the soreness in his right shoulder.

Removing the robe the butler had laid across the foot of the bed, Charles went into his bathroom. Still nude, he began to shave, ignoring the ache in his right hand as he grasped the razor. Ever since boarding school, the dark, soulful eyes beneath his shock of black hair, combined with the elegant grace of his movements, had made him the target of frequent homosexual advances. His swift and brutal answer with his fists to those advances was out of all proportion to the cause. Last night had been no exception.

Charles flexed his fingers and then gripped the razor more tightly, urging his mind to grapple with the problem of a misplaced invoice, one of the petty details of the Vale shipyards that fell under his supervision. Charles's father, Truman Vale, had inherited the shipyards from his own father, along with the rest of Vale Enterprises. At twenty-seven Charles worked as a glorified clerk in those same shipyards. Not like Tru Junior. Charles's older brother had come back from the war with a chestful of medals to a cushy job just below the old man. Charles grimaced as the phrase returned like a few bars from a familiar song, blotting out everything else: This damned house!

Charles stared at his lather-covered face in the mirror. When Truman Vale announced his gift at his youngest son's crowded wedding reception and handed the keys to the new bride, Giselle had stood on tiptoe to kiss Truman Vale's cheek and gushed her thanks. Charles doubted she had given the matter a second thought from that day to this.

Charles himself, his jaw tight with anger, had remained silent. Riverside Drive! It was an address for the nouveau riche, the parvenu. Not him. He belonged on Fifth Avenue like his parents. In an apartment, of course; one of the prewar vintage with twelve-foot ceilings and a dozen or more rooms. Truman Vale knew that as well as he did.

Charles's sister had known it, too. Five years older, Alexandra was Tru Junior's twin. To Charles she had been part sister, part mother, and something else, not as easily defined. As soon as Truman Vale announced the address of his gift, her dark eyes, so like Charles's own, had met his glance from across the room, and she immediately pushed through the crowd to grasp his hands in hers. "You'll show him," she whispered. In that moment vague longings that had tormented Charles all of his life, had coalesced into a need, and he understood why he had chosen a bride as unlike his sister as he possibly could—and why, for that very reason, his beautiful blond wife would never satisfy him. He had hugged Alexandra to him, feeling the heat of her body through the thin silk of her matron-of-honor dress. That heat stayed with him the rest of the night, delaying the actual consummation of his marriage until the dawn.

Charles looked down at his erection and laughed. What would the old man think of that? Then he sobered. Release was a good eighteen hours away. He completed his shave with reckless strokes.

By the time Charles finished dressing, it was half past six. He went down the hall and rapped softly on his wife's bedroom door.

Giselle opened the door at once, already dressed for the day. The burnished gold of her hair, soft and gleaming, was caught at the nape of her long neck by a tortoiseshell comb. Her skin at twenty-two was as smooth and radiant as a child's, requiring only the lightest touch of makeup, the faintest hint of mascara to darken her long curly lashes. Although she had done nothing to emphasize it, her mouth was a shade too strong for his taste. However, he realized that strength was a vital component of her overall beauty, necessary to balance her best feature, the piercing peacock blue of her eyes. But the pink shirtwaist dress she wore—

Charles frowned, and Giselle's expression grew wary. "That dress . . . I see copies of it everywhere."

Giselle retreated a step, her beauty spoiled by the tiny furrow between her brows. "I'll change."

"No. We don't want breakfast to get cold, do we? Just be more careful when you're shopping."

"Of course," she said, but to his annoyance the wrinkle between her brows remained.

He extended his arm and she rested her hand on it lightly, as though he were leading her out onto a dance floor. Charles was conscious of how well her blond coloring set off his own dark good looks. Every man he knew envied him. So why couldn't the damned fags keep their hands off him? he wondered as they descended the stairs.

Charles paused in front of the large mirror in the downstairs' hallway, remembering the one last night, outside the men's room at El Morocco, whose hand had grasped Charles's ass in an unmistakable invitation. If Bryan hadn't pulled me off, I'd have killed the son of a bitch, Charles thought with satisfaction. He'd thrown a couple of punches at Bryan at the time, he remembered. Maybe tonight he would apologize. "Dinner tonight at the Rawlingses," he reminded Giselle.

Still studying his own reflection, searching for the faint scratch on his temple left by the faggot's diamond pinky ring, Charles Vale missed his wife's blush.

When Charles left for the shipyards, Giselle sighed with relief. Now her day could begin. She went back into the dining room and rang for Alice to clear the table. As she waited she frowned at the untouched food on her plate. A waste, but she couldn't help it.

"Yes, Mrs. Vale?" Alice said.

"Tell Cook I'll bring Zandra down in a few minutes."

"Oh," Alice began, and then stopped, red-faced.

"What is it, Alice?"

"Nurse Pritchard already sent for Miss Zandra's breakfast, madam."

"Not again!" A small pulse of anger began to beat in Giselle's temple. Zandra would be four this year. She was growing so fast Giselle could almost see the days spiraling by. She longed to hold her daughter close, to be with her every minute of the day. But as Charles was quick to point out, that just wasn't done. Not by a woman of their social class. One removed oneself from the daily care of one's children. That was the pattern set by the British royal family for all society women. A pattern Nurse Pritchard exploited as she ruled her domain in her starched cap and uniform, making no secret of the fact that she considered mothers a nuisance, best kept out of the nursery.

At the door to the nursery, Giselle hesitated, knowing Nurse Pritchard would prefer that she knock before entering. She compromised by reaching for the doorknob with one hand while she tapped once with the other.

Zandra was in her bath. The remains of her breakfast were on the table by the window. "Good morning, Zandra," Giselle said, but the three-year-old was more interested in the bubbles in her bathwater than her mother. "Nurse Pritchard," Giselle said, with a stiff little nod. "I thought you understood that I wanted Zandra to eat downstairs every weekday morning."

Nurse Pritchard looked up without a hint of emotion on her face. "You know it disrupts our schedule to wait until Mr. Vale leaves before the child eats. Mrs. Mainwaring feels that it's important we keep to our schedule."

Giselle took a deep breath. She had no real power in the nursery and they both knew it. While Charles signed the nurse's checks, it was actually his sister,

Alexandra Vale Mainwaring, who had employed Nurse
Pritchard, and to whom, ultimately, the nurse had to
answer. "But Zandra likes to have breakfast downstairs." Zandra glanced up at her name, but was distracted by the rubber duck Nurse Pritchard squeaked
at her. "And I'm going to take her for a stroll around
the boating pool." Riverside Park was closer. But the
children of Millionaires' Row went to Central Park for
their exercise and so must Charles Vale's daughter.

"Mrs. Vale," the nurse said reprovingly. "You know
Mr. Vale prefers I do that." Giselle did know that.
Charles worried how it would look to have his wife
walking with their child like a hired nanny. Charles
worried how everything looked. "Besides, Mrs.
Mainwaring called earlier to say she would be picking
Zandra up at eight. That's why I ordered breakfast for
her up here." The nurse paused. "Will there be anything else, Mrs. Vale?"

When Giselle did not reply, Nurse Pritchard
picked up her washcloth again. Her daughter, cruising
the rubber duck through the bathwater, did not look
up as Giselle left.

In her bedroom, Giselle unbuttoned the pink shirtwaist with trembling fingers. "Damn you, Alex!" she
whispered aloud. "Why don't you take care of your own
children and leave my daughter alone?" Alexandra Vale
Mainwaring's sons, nine and eleven, were both in
boarding schools, but Giselle knew it would have made
no difference in her own life if Alex's children were at
home in their mother's Fifth Avenue apartment, since
neither possessed what Giselle's father-in-law called
the "Vale look." Good-natured, sandy-haired, and freckle-
faced, Alex's sons both resembled their father, Neville
Mainwaring, who had died somewhere in France in the
last days of the war.

It was Giselle's bad luck that her daughter had
been born with the same black hair, black eyes, and

ivory skin as Charles and his older sister—as Truman Vale himself. While Giselle was still sleeping off the effects of eighteen hours of labor, Charles had christened the newborn Zandra, his childhood name for his beloved Alexandra. Alex had reacted as though that name were a tag on a gift.

Giselle tossed the shirtwaist aside and slipped on instead a blue silk dress from Bergdorf Goodman. With its heart-shaped neckline and side-draped skirt, the dress was far too dressy for the day ahead of her, but Charles would approve. He had bought it for her.

As she sat down in front of the dresser Giselle thought of the last time she had tried to defy her husband, shortly after Zandra's birth. Dressed for dinner at his parents', she had ignored his curt command to go back upstairs and change the lovely gray silk dress she was wearing for a strapless black gown he had purchased himself.

Two hours later, her ribs taped tightly and her eyes glazed by the effects of the painkiller the doctor had given her, she had attended Truman Vale's dinner in the strapless black gown. Giselle rubbed her right side, feeling the two small bumps where her ribs had finally knitted. She had learned that night there were no small battles where Charles was concerned. If she did not obey him, instantly and without question, he would punish her with his fists. "The next time it will be your face," Charles had promised her before the doctor arrived. Giselle, remembering the rage she had seen in her husband's face as he brutalized her, had believed him.

Her thoughts darted ahead to dinner tonight at the Rawlingses' and for the second time that morning, Giselle blushed. In sharp contrast to Charles, his best friend, Bryan Rawlings, was the most kind, the most gentle man, she had ever known. She wondered if Florence knew how lucky she was to be married to someone like Bryan. Or how much Giselle envied her.

If it weren't for Charles's fists, the murderous rages he was capable of, she would tell him she wanted a divorce, Giselle thought. But she knew he would never let her go unmarked. Didn't that make her a coward?

The question troubled her as she leaned forward to look into the reflection of her own gaze. She remembered what her mother had told her repeatedly over the years, "A woman's beauty is her only weapon." If Charles took her beauty from her, she would have nothing else.

Giselle reached for the jar of homemade face cream on her dresser. She unscrewed the lid, and the faint scent of roses brought back memories of watching her mother concoct lotions and creams for herself. What had her mother felt in the last moments of her life? Giselle wondered. What frantic thoughts raced through Lillian Durand Hauser's mind as she knelt on the damp earth floor of a German cellar, clasping her husband's hand? What was left for her to believe in when she finally realized that her beauty was not enough to save her?

At least her mother had had her husband's love. Giselle wondered how she had ever mistaken for love Charles's desire to possess one more beautiful object.

Florence Rawlings enjoyed nothing better than unearthing a secret about another woman's marriage, and something in Giselle Vale's manner this evening made Florence certain a secret was waiting to be discovered. "More brandy?" she asked her guest as their husbands strolled out onto the terrace for an after-dinner smoke. She hoped to get Giselle just the least bit tipsy before the men finished their cigarettes.

When she glanced up from refilling Giselle's glass, Florence found Giselle still eyeing the men moodily, and she almost laughed aloud. How many of her friends had warned her when Bryan Rawlings returned to the States that it would take a secure woman indeed to socialize with Bryan's best friend because of Charles Vale's incredibly beautiful wife.

Florence herself was no beauty. Something about her thin face and alert brown eyes combined to give her, in repose, a faint foxlike expression. But Florence, a pragmatist, had learned early that she could get her way as easily as a prettier woman. Marrying Bryan, for example. She knew Bryan had only dated her in the first place to please his family. But when Florence learned he had enlisted in the RAF just because he had been in London on business when the bombs started falling, she knew exactly what to do. She immediately wrangled an invitation from his youngest sister to stay overnight at the Rawlingses' home. The first time Bryan's name was mentioned at dinner, Florence fainted dead away. While Bryan's mother and sisters tried to rouse her by bathing her face with wet cloths, she had murmured his name. Once. Then resolutely refused to say another word.

Bryan arrived back in the States on a brief leave to find his family expected him to wed Florence Prestwood. Bryan Rawlings was a gentleman; Florence had counted on that. They were married at once. Luckily she had managed to get herself pregnant before he left for England again; she knew she would have a special place in her in-laws' hearts as the mother of their first grandchild.

Giselle sipped her drink absently, her gaze still on the terrace. When she finally spoke, it was a topic Florence had not expected. "Do you ever wish you could see more of your children?"

"You're lucky Charles's sister takes so much of the burden of Zandra out of your hands." Florence ignored the slight shake of her guest's head when she raised the brandy bottle and poured Giselle another drink. "I'm simply counting the days until Bry and Elizabeth are old enough for boarding school. There are so many other things to do in a day." A match flared in the evening gloom on the terrace; the men were starting on their second cigarettes. There was still time, Florence thought.

"But aren't you ever lonely?"

Florence laughed. At the merry sound, Bryan turned their way and smiled. Charles Vale continued to stare out over the city, the night wind whipping the hair back from his face. He looked positively Byronic. Florence preferred her husband's looks. Bryan's blond hair, rugged build and his angular, suntanned face were more appealing to most women than Charles Vale's almost feminine beauty, and what other women thought of her husband was quite important to Florence. "Why, I believe I've guessed your secret," she said brightly. Giselle paled, but Florence plunged right ahead. "You want another baby, don't you? Isn't Charles in a cooperative mood? Perhaps I'll tease him about it."

"No, Florence!" If Giselle had been pale before, now she looked ashen. "Don't! Please!"

Florence leaned over and patted Giselle's knee. "Why, of course I won't if you don't want me to. But if there's anything wrong, you'll tell me, won't you? You know I'm your friend."

"I know," Giselle muttered. To the astonishment of them both, sudden tears trickled down her cheeks.

At that inopportune moment, the men rejoined them. "What's this?" Charles asked.

Bryan extended a clean handkerchief. Giselle took it with a murmured, "Thank you," and blotted her eyes.

"I'm afraid we've helped ourselves to too much brandy," Florence said with quick smile. Damn, damn, damn, she thought. Why couldn't they have stayed outside a few more minutes? Then she relaxed as she watched Giselle compose herself. She knew she would uncover Giselle's secret if she kept digging long enough.

Driving the mistress and her husband to the Rawlingses' was a chore Halloran particularly hated, for Bryan Rawlings was a man who could make Giselle Vale smile as though she hadn't a care in the world—smoothing out the pinched frown that lingered longer on her face these days than when Halloran had first entered her husband's employ. Besides, any evening spent in the Rawlingses' kitchen was a long and uncomfortable one. The mistress of the house was the perverse, silver-counting type who begrudged someone else's man a bite or a sip of anything, and terrorized hospitality right out of her staff.

But the worst came still later in the evening. After the mistress was deposited back at home, the master called Halloran out again. Charles Vale made a point of giving Halloran the address, as if he might have forgotten it, seeing as they only made this drive three times a week.

This time the master must have called ahead. When they pulled up outside the apartment-hotel, the long-legged, ivory-skinned brunette was waiting beside the doorman, wearing a fur coat—"the wages of sin," Father Flannagan would call it. When she climbed into the car, a glance in the rearview mirror told Halloran there was nothing else beneath the skins of the small animals except her own.

"Drive," Charles Vale said.

"Where to, sir?"

"Anywhere. Just don't . . . stop until . . . I tell you." He slid the panel shut, but Halloran had already seen that the slut had her head in his lap.

He drove. But this was the one time of day he would not allow himself to think of the mistress. It wouldn't be proper. Last night Sheila had pumped him for every snippet of information he would divulge about the life of the Vales. This was the only one he hadn't shared.

Halloran grinned to himself and pressed the accelerator just hard enough that he came up too fast on a changing traffic light, then braked abruptly. If God had any sense of justice, then the little slut would have a full set of teeth in her otherwise empty head.

The yelp from the backseat made him grin. Then he heard the sharp sound of a slap followed by Charles Vale's curse. The girl began to sob.

Patrick Halloran hunched his shoulders as though against a blow as he pulled away from the light. As God was his witness, he had not meant for the girl to suffer. He drove with care the rest of the evening.

TWO

Charles Vale lurched against Giselle as they entered the foyer of his father's Fifth Avenue apartment. Waving the butler away, he leaned forward to take her wrap himself. "I wonder what new honors we're going to heap on the war hero tonight," he muttered, and the subtle fragrance of her perfume was lost in his whiskey-scented breath. He hung her jacket in the closet, sending half the hangers clattering to the floor in the process.

When he turned back, his gaze swept over her, taking in every detail of her dress, her hair. Giselle's heart raced with panic as it always did when he looked at her this way. "Make yourself useful tonight," he told her. "Talk to the war hero. Keep him away from Father long enough for me to tell the old man an idea I have for the shipyards."

"Why would Tru be interested in anything I have to say?"

"He'll enjoy the view down the front of your dress. That's why I picked it."

27

Giselle felt warmth spread up her neck to her cheeks. "Please, Charles. Let's just enjoy this dinner."

Charles grasped her arm roughly. "Let's see if Father's too stingy to offer us a drink before dinner."

In the drawing room, Sylvia Vale greeted her son and daughter-in-law with kisses. Slim, silver-haired, still lovely, she lived within the limits of her marriage, vivacious when Truman Senior wasn't present, reactive when he was. In Giselle's worst moments, she feared she would become just like her mother-in-law. Sylvia stepped back from her son, frowning. "Charles! You reek of alcohol!"

"Where's Father?"

"In his study. He doesn't want to be disturbed until dinner."

"And Tru?" Charles asked.

"Out on the terrace." She glanced uneasily at Giselle, and then back to her youngest son. Charles didn't often inquire after Truman Junior, Alexandra's twin.

Alex herself arrived just then, tall as a man and as self-assured. Giselle sometimes worried that Zandra might have inherited the Vale height as well as the Vale look. Charles hugged his sister close and kept her trapped against his hip for a moment. "Someone's already offered you a drink," Alex said, amusement dancing in her dark eyes.

"Liquid courage. I'm going to brave the lion in his den." Charles released his sister and turned to Giselle. "Go entertain the war hero," he told her, and his words had the snap of a command.

"Charles!" Sylvia protested as Giselle walked away. "You know he doesn't like for you to call him that."

"Then tell him to give back the medals."

Giselle hesitated in the open terrace doorway, gazing at her brother-in-law's back. She had never been able to sort out her feelings about this man who was so much like her husband and yet so different. The first time Giselle met Truman Vale, Jr., at the dinner party the Vales gave to announce her engagement to their son, Tru's angry gaze had followed her everywhere, although she had no idea what she had done to stir such strong emotions in this stranger. She had thought at the time he hadn't believed her worthy of his brother. Her father had been inordinately pleased with the match; Dieterich Hauser had worried that his wife's impeccable pedigree had somehow been sullied by her marriage to a German industrialist. In the rush before the wedding—hurried because Giselle's parents were on their way back to Germany to straighten out problems with her grandfather's estate—Giselle hadn't given her husband's brother that much thought. After the wedding, she and Charles had seen him infrequently. Then, just after Pearl Harbor, he enlisted in the Marines, something Charles found amusing at the time.

Tru had come back from the war thinner, quieter, but with more authority in his voice. The anger Giselle sensed in his manner toward her had been transformed into something else. What it was she could not name, but it made her uncomfortable in his presence. As though she could see something about him he would prefer hidden from the world. Not that she would ever share such a silly thought with Charles, she thought, rubbing her side absently. The bumps where her ribs had knitted made her remember the mission her husband had given her.

"On Iwo Jima," Tru said so softly that Giselle thought for a moment he was talking to himself, "I brought down a sniper who had decimated my platoon. No one else could find him. He would crawl in and wait, and then take out two or three men at a time before he vanished back into the jungle again. It was the smell of gunpowder that gave him away." Now he turned. "Lovely perfume you're wearing, Giselle. What kind of dirty work did Charles dispatch you to do?"

Giselle joined him at the terrace railing. "That's the most you've ever said to me, Tru."

"Definitely here on Charles's orders. Otherwise you'd have taken to your heels." His glance strayed over her body. "Did he pick out that dress for my benefit? I must say I'm appreciative."

"Why are you being so nasty?" Giselle asked in honest bewilderment. "I've never done anything to you."

Tru turned back to the skyline so quickly that his cigarette left a trail of sparks in the air. "Poor Giselle. Whatever scheme Baby Brother is planning, it won't work. Father's planning a little intrigue of his own."

"What kind of intrigue?"

"I don't know, but I'm sure Charles won't like it."

"Will you?"

"A good question. Probably. We both know that in my father's eyes, I can do no wrong. After all, as Charles is always pointing out, Father pulled all those strings to get me my medals." The mockery in his voice hurt her, she wasn't sure why.

"You should be happy that your father loves you so much."

"Should I? I wonder. I think he loves me for the part of himself he sees in me."

"What's wrong with that?"

"Haven't you known us Vales long enough to be able to answer that one yourself?" He turned around again. "I'm ready," he said, tossing the cigarette over the edge of the terrace.

"Ready?"

"For you to ply your feminine wiles. Isn't that what your husband ordered?"

"Even if he were that kind of man, I'm not that kind of woman."

"I don't think you know what kind of woman you

are. You remind me of a fairy tale. Sleeping Beauty, I think. I wish I could be there when you finally wake. But that would break Father's heart. He really admires you, you know."

"Your father?" she said, astonished. "Why?"

"Because he thinks you're like him." Tru chuckled at her expression. "And you are, in a way. You're strong, Giselle. Stronger than you realize. Stronger than Charles, that's for sure."

"Stronger than you?" she asked, not believing this nonsense for a moment, but enjoying it, nonetheless.

Tru's hands moved. The breath caught in her throat, but he was only reaching for a cigarette. He lit it. In the flare of the match she could see the expression in his eyes. "I wonder what you think of me, Giselle."

"That you're no gentleman," she said promptly.

"And is Charles?"

She remained silent.

"Do you really think a gentleman is what you're looking for, my dear little sister-in-law." He moved closer. She had the strangest feeling that she should turn and run, but instead she stood there as he reached out and touched her cheek with the back of his hand. "I wonder," he said. "Do you have a particular gentleman in mind?"

She jerked away, her cheeks flaming. "Of course not."

"I had the fairy tale wrong, I think. Not Sleeping Beauty, at all. It's Little Red Riding Hood. And I'm the wolf." This time she did turn away. He chuckled as she hurried back into the drawing room.

Truman Vale tapped his wineglass with his knife. The sharp ring of the crystal made all conversation around the dinner table cease. As Truman Vale sur-

veyed his family something glinted in his eyes that
Giselle recognized, a flash of cruelty that made her hug
her ribs protectively. "Pour the wine," he boomed. "I
want to propose a toast."

As the butler hurried to comply, Giselle watched
her husband and his sister. Their faces reminded her
of the moment at the circus when the ringmaster
snapped his whip, earning the hungry interest of the
big cats. Across the table, Tru's mocking gaze warned
her this was the intrigue he had predicted. Something
Charles would detest.

"I'm stepping down," Truman Vale told his family.
"Time for the next generation to shoulder the load." He
lifted his glass. "Here's to Truman Junior. You have the
reins now, son."

Charles's gaze fastened on his father's face. "But
what about me?"

Truman Vale looked at his younger son in a way
that made Sylvia Vale grasp her daughter-in-law's hand
beneath the table. Alex's face was as pale as Charles's.
"You?" Truman Vale said. "That will be up to Tru."

Charles bolted from the table. As Giselle rose to
follow she realized no one but Truman Vale had toasted his eldest son's succession, not even Tru himself.

When the mister came barreling out of the Fifth
Avenue apartment building in one hell of a hurry,
Halloran knew that the dinner with his folks had been
even less to Charles Vale's liking than usual.

The master stuffed the mistress into the car before
Halloran could climb out himself to hold the door.
Then he stepped back and slammed the door on her
soft cry. He gave Halloran a hard look over the car's
hood. "Take her home."

"Shall I come back for you, sir?"

"No." Charles Vale spun on his heel and strode

down the street. That was a man with drinking on his mind, was Halloran's guess.

He climbed in the car and looked in the rearview mirror. To his surprise the mistress's glance had not followed her husband's departure. Instead, she was looking back toward the door from which they had just emerged.

From the terrace, Tru gripped the railing as he watched the scene below. Charles, foreshortened, half a block away, climbed into a taxi, just as his car with Giselle inside pulled away from the curb in front of the building.

"Father sent me to fetch you," Alex said.

He turned with easy grace, shoving his hands in his pockets. "Oh? Did he want me to rattle my medals again?"

Alex went dull red for a moment. Then she threw back her head and laughed. "Poor Charles. You know he truly believes that's what you do."

"If he's so sensitive on the subject, why didn't he try for a few himself? And don't give me that bullshit about him staying out of the service for Mother's sake."

"He's not like you."

"You've done your part to see to that, haven't you?"

"Think what you like," Alex said. "You will anyway. I think that's why Father prefers you to Charles."

"And why you prefer Charles to me?"

"Why are you in such a foul mood tonight, my twin? Did Charles's little wife say something to upset you?"

"Leave Giselle out of this!" he snapped, and was immediately sorry because his response kindled a glittering interest in his sister's eyes.

"Oh-ho! I'll bet Father doesn't know that."

"I wouldn't bet on anything where the old man is

concerned." Tru looked down at the street. The lights of the Vale car had already disappeared.

"I hope I did right to call you," the bartender said.

"Of course you did," Bryan Rawlings assured the man. "Where is he?"

"Over there."

Thank heavens Charles had chosen a bar where the two of them were known, Bryan thought as he picked his way through the crowd to his friend.

Charles, usually an impeccable dresser, looked as though he'd rolled in the gutter. His jacket was open and he was tieless. The first three buttons of his shirt were missing, as though he might have jerked it open, rather than taking the trouble to unbutton it. He sat, legs sprawling into the narrow space between his table and the next, and as Bryan watched he took a gulp of his whiskey, spilling half the glass down his front in the process.

"'Lo," Charles said when Bryan sat down beside him. "Where'd you come from?"

"Home in bed. Where you should be."

Charles gave a clownish wink. "Busy making little Rawlingses, were you?"

"None of your business, is it, old man?"

"I love it when you go all British on me," Charles said delightedly. "It usually means I've scored. You're the last man in New York who still makes love to his wife." He signaled to a waiter. "Drinks for me and my friend."

Bryan sat back, willing away the dull thud of anger that pulsed in him. Charles had no way of knowing that every time Bryan tried to make love to Florence recently, she brushed him off. What had happened to her? he wondered. She had been frantic for sex when they were first married—when he was home on leave from the RAF—embarrassingly so.

"Drink up," Charles said as the waiter set their drinks before them. He followed his own advice.

Bryan sipped his drink and realized how tired he was. He had just arrived home when the call came from the bartender. That was another source of contention between him and Florence, the late hours he was keeping these days. He shifted wearily while Charles ordered another drink. He would like to walk away, leave Charles to his binge, but that wasn't something a gentleman would do—and the importance of being a gentleman had been drilled into Bryan from birth by his southern-belle mother. While his father was still alive Bryan had been able to make any romantic gesture he wished, including joining the RAF. But last December, his father had died in a freak construction accident. Bryan was only now beginning to realize how much his mother's philosophy contradicted his father's. His father had founded the small home-construction company the year Bryan was born, and no gentleman could have turned it into Rawlings, Ltd., with offices in both New York and Los Angeles, and contracts for everything from railway projects to pipelines.

And no gentleman, Bryan thought grimly, would succeed in keeping Rawlings, Ltd., afloat now that his father was dead. Perry Rawlings had allowed himself no margin for error on contract deadlines, knowing he possessed the ability to drive his employees past their endurance, working right beside them if necessary, to finish a project by a date chosen to cut his competitors out of the bidding. Now it was Bryan who must meet those deadlines if the company—and his family—were to survive. Bryan stretched wearily. He should be home in bed now, resting up for tomorrow's labors. "We have to leave, Charles."

"What?" Charles said groggily. "Are we going already?"

"We are," Bryan said as he pulled Charles to his feet and began to pull him through the crowd.

As they passed the bar Charles suddenly jerked away from Bryan and swung wildly at a man. It was drunkard's luck that just as Charles's fist reached his face the man turned and took the punch right in the mouth. Charles swung again, connecting with nothing. He would have lost his balance if Bryan hadn't caught him by the jacket. Charles's victim had his hand over his face. Bright red blood bubbled through his fingers.

"Come on," Bryan said urgently.

"He groped me," Charles muttered. "The fag. They're all fags."

The man beside Charles's victim launched himself at Charles. Bryan shoved him aside with his shoulder, and someone else threw a punch at the second man. Now four or five men were fighting. Bryan gave Charles a yank toward the door, but just as he did someone threw a heavy glass ashtray. It struck Bryan on the side of the head. The blood flowed immediately, blinding his right eye.

Bryan swiped at the blood with the sleeve of his jacket and shoved his way through the mayhem, pulling Charles after him.

In the taxi, Bryan gave the driver Charles's address and then took off his dinner jacket and held it to his head in an effort to stop the bleeding of the scalp wound. Charles slumped over in the seat, mumbling to himself.

The taxi driver observed them in the rearview mirror. "If that drunk throws up in my cab, it's gonna cost you extra, buddy."

"Just drive."

"Okay, but I hope wherever you're taking him, it's on the ground floor."

Bryan couldn't resist. "Why?"

"Because drunks is hell on stairs, buddy."

To his dismay, Bryan found the cabby was correct.

Getting Charles, scuffling, cursing, up his own stairs to his second-story bedroom, was the hardest physical labor Bryan had performed in the last few months. One of Charles's wild punches connected with Bryan's face, snapping his head against the stairwell.

When they reached the second floor, Bryan hesitated, unsure which closed door was Charles's bedroom. Charles took advantage of the pause and pulled away, trying to plunge down the stairs again.

Bryan grabbed him by the shoulders and turned him around, ungently. He reached for the first door, flung it open, and saw an extremely feminine room.

From behind him, he heard Giselle Vale's voice, "What in the world are you doing?"

Her husband and his best friend stood before the open door of her bedroom. Giselle tightened the belt of her robe, and then gasped as Bryan Rawlings turned her way and she saw the dried blood on his face and splashed down the front of his shirt. "We've had a little problem," he said. "Which room is Charles's?"

"This way," she said, and walked past him down the hall. She opened Charles's door and watched Bryan stagger toward her, supporting her husband's weight.

"I'll take it from here," Bryan said as he paused in front of the doorway.

"Don't be silly," she said, but when she reached for Charles's hands, her husband pushed her away with such force that she was shoved against the door frame.

"Let me." Bryan grabbed Charles around the waist and propelled him through the door and toward the bed, ignoring his flailing arms. He threw Charles down on the bed and then sat on top of him. Charles's struggles ceased almost immediately. He coughed once and then gave a snore so comically loud that Giselle almost giggled. "I think he's out for the night," Bryan said. He looked up at her and she saw fresh blood oozing from his hairline.

"You're bleeding!" she cried.

Bryan explored his scalp wound with his fingers. "A flying ashtray." He looked around him for a moment, searching for something. "I must have lost my jacket somewhere. Do you have anything I can mop it up with?"

"Just a moment." Giselle hurried into Charles's bathroom and returned with a towel.

"Thanks," Bryan said as he pressed it against his head. He stood, still holding the towel to his wound, and looked down at Charles. "He won't give you any trouble tonight, but he'll have a hangover tomorrow."

"I thank you for bringing him home. He had some bad news this evening. He didn't take it very well."

Bryan waited, but she did not expand on that. "I'd better be going."

"Not like this!" Giselle ignored the twinge of her ribs; Charles couldn't possibly object to a kindness extended to his best friend after a night like tonight. "Come down to the kitchen. I'll make you a cup of coffee and bind your wound."

Downstairs, Bryan paused in the kitchen doorway, struck by the lovely fragrance. Pots and pans covered the stove and small bottles and jars covered the kitchen table. "Did Florence mention my little hobby?" Giselle said as she put water on to boil.

"Florence and I haven't had a lot of time to talk lately." Not that they ever had, he thought.

Giselle spooned coffee in the pot. "This isn't a recent thing. I've always made face creams and fragrances for myself and my friends. It's something my mother taught me. When I can't sleep, I like to take over the kitchen in the middle of the night. It's so quiet and peaceful." She pulled out one of the chairs. "Let me look at your head."

Bryan sat, but his mind was on what she had just said. He wondered if her life was as lonely as it sounded. Charles never said anything about his wife. Bryan wondered if Giselle was happy in her marriage.

She stood close to him and parted his hair with gentle fingers. "Ah. That needs to be cleaned up." She retreated to the sink and returned with a clean, damp cloth. As she leaned forward and dabbed at the cut he was aware of her unbound breasts moving beneath her robe. He drew in his breath sharply. "Did that hurt?" Giselle asked.

"No." Bryan clenched his hands, trying to control the direction of his thoughts.

"This will," she said cheerfully, and applied something liquid to his scalp. He winced. She left the kitchen for a minute or two and returned with a blanket. "I can't offer you one of Charles's shirts. Your shoulders are too big. Put this on, and I'll rinse the blood out of yours."

Bryan handed over his shirt and sat there, the blanket around him, watching her at the sink, as she rinsed the shirt in cold water and then wrung it out. "At least it won't be ruined, but I don't know how quickly I can get it dry." She lit the oven and hung the shirt over a chair in front of the open oven door. Then she poured a cup of coffee and brought it over to the table. "Here you are. But let me look at that cut again, first."

When she took his head in her hands and tilted it so the wound was toward the light, Bryan was aware of the rise and fall of her breasts beneath the robe, his own bare chest beneath the blanket.

"That's better." Giselle looked down into his face and time seemed to stand still. Their faces were only inches apart. Bryan wondered what her mouth would taste like. He leaned forward as she bent toward him.

The sound of the kitchen door opening jerked them apart.

* * *

"I thought I heard a prowler," Halloran said brusquely. He did not like the look of the scene before him. Bryan Rawlings, half-naked, practically seducing the mistress.

"Mr. Rawlings brought Mr. Charles home," she said.

"Will you be wanting a way home, then, Mr. Rawlings?"

Rawlings stood. "Yes, I would."

Another man would have looked ridiculous wrapped in a blanket like a red Indian. Halloran was dismayed to see that Rawlings did not.

"You can't go without your shirt," Giselle cried.

Halloran moved before Rawlings could reply, gathering up the shirt and handing it over to the man. "It's dry enough," he said, although the fine cloth was still damp.

Rawlings made no complaint as he slipped it on. That angered Halloran as much as finding the man alone with the mistress. "Are you ready, sir?" he asked.

"Why are you rushing him so?" the mistress asked.

"He's right, I must be going," Rawlings said. The grin he turned Halloran's way did nothing to ease the chauffeur's anger. He ushered Rawlings out of the kitchen in a cold fury. If God was just, then Bryan Rawlings would catch pneumonia from this night's mischief.

But it was Mum who caught the pneumonia, so lost in her mental fog that she'd crawled out of bed somehow and opened her window to the night air after everyone else had gone to bed. The chill she caught settled in her chest and took her within a week. The master gave Halloran a day off when she died, and

Halloran spent it with his family. In the general sadness, it was hard to know how Sheila could pick up that there was something more than the death of his mum troubling him. Not that he told her what it was. Still, she had asked more than once.

As they sat around the table that evening Keefe said, "Sheila will be going back to the Mainwarings now that she's done with taking care of Mum."

"That's a nasty bitch," Halloran said with feeling. He'd seen the way Alexandra Mainwaring tormented the mistress. "She'd be better off with someone else."

"She likes the house and the money is good. If Mum hadn't passed away when she did, I don't know what we would have done, with money so tight."

"And who'll be taking care of young Doreen?"

"Tessie O'Connor."

Mrs. O'Connor's apartment, across from the pay phone, gave her the position of head gossip in the tenement building. "She'll be pumping Doreen for juicy tidbits," Halloran said.

"We've nothing to hide," Keefe replied.

That night, the thought of Bryan Rawlings with his sweet mistress tortured Halloran so that sleep was hard to come by. When the whisper of his name came in the dark of Mum's old room, it found him awake in Mum's bed. A body slid into the sheets beside him.

He tried to push it away, and encountered bare flesh. "For God's sake, Sheila," he whispered. "What do you think you're doing?"

"Trying to give you a little love and comfort. The kind you won't get from your precious mistress."

"What if Keefe should hear?"

"He won't. I gave him some of your mum's medicine. He'll sleep like a baby."

"And the child? What if she should wake?"

"I gave Doreen a dose, too."

"You gave her *that*. What if it was too much?"

"What kind of fool do you think I am. I only gave her enough to keep her asleep. Now come on, Pat. I've waited for this night long enough."

She took him in her hand and squeezed, trying to bring some life into what was normally not so flaccid. When that failed, she rubbed his manhood against her bush. Halloran knew, as well as if he could see in the dark, that her pubic hair would be dark and wiry. Not like the mistress. Giselle would be honey blond there, he thought, and felt his cheeks warm in the dark.

"Don't think of her," Sheila said harshly as though she could read his mind. "Think of me."

She burrowed her head between the sheets and put her lips on him. He shrank even more, if such a thing was possible. It was as though his manhood wanted to withdraw inside him, away from her touch, and he didn't know if it was because she was his brother's wife or because of the mistress, but whichever it was, there was no spark there to kindle a fire.

A few minutes of useless effort proved it to her as well. When she pulled away from him, he could see the faintest shape of her face in the shadows.

"You really do love her, don't you?"

"She's not for me, and we both know that."

"You could take her. Get her alone and have your way with her. You're a handsome man, Pat. She wouldn't report it. She would enjoy it, I think. And if she did cry rape, you could go to California like you planned." She felt his small start of surprise and chuckled. "Yes, I know that." She patted his limp manhood as though to comfort him. "Take her. Get it out of your system."

"It's not like that," he protested. "She's something finer than that."

"She's just a woman, Pat. Like me."

Not like you. The unspoken words hung in the dark between them.

"I love her," Halloran said, his pain clear in his voice.

"And I love you. Aren't we both a pair of fools." She slipped out of the covers. "Keefe will have a devil of a headache tomorrow. All for nothing."

Bryan had never shadowed anyone before. He wasn't really cut out for it, he thought. For one thing, he was too tall and too well dressed. Salesclerks kept coming up and asking if they could help him. With that distraction, he almost missed seeing Giselle leaving Saks's juvenile department, with her daughter's hand in hers.

He caught up with her on the sidewalk just as she climbed into her car. The chauffeur was about to close the door when she caught sight of Bryan and waved.

"Giselle," Bryan said, and then stopped. The expression on her face made his carefully concocted story fly right out of his mind. He hadn't been wrong, he thought. All those evenings, sitting across the table from her, staring at her face, he hadn't been wrong. "What a surprise," he said, and thought how phony that sounded.

"We've been shopping," Giselle said, as though the seats weren't heaped with packages.

"Have you had lunch?"

"I want to go home," Zandra wailed.

The chauffeur made as if to close the door, shutting Giselle in the car, shutting him out of it.

Miraculously, Bryan thought, Giselle caught the door with her hand and pushed it open. She was still holding her daughter's hand. She stared at their clasped hands for a moment, and then released the child's small one. "Take Zandra home," she told her chauffeur. "Nurse Pritchard will be furious if we don't keep to the schedule."

"But . . . But, Mistress . . . don't you want to come as well?" the man asked.

"No," Giselle said firmly. "I'm having lunch with Mr. Rawlings."

As the car pulled away with her child inside it, Giselle was staggered by the enormity of what she had done. "We can't go anywhere we'd be seen! You don't know what Charles is like! If he should find out we're together—"

"A hotel room," Bryan said as he took her arm. "We'll order lunch from room service. No one will see us."

They had leaped past the preliminaries, Giselle realized. "Have you done this before?"

Bryan halted in midstride, shocked by the question. "Of course not."

A real gentleman, Giselle thought. A gentleman at last.

Neither of them spoke again until the door of the hotel room was shut and bolted. Then it was Giselle who said, "I don't understand what went wrong in my life. I didn't want to do this. I'm not this kind of person. Neither are you."

Bryan didn't speak at all. He took her face between his two hands and touched his lips to hers. Her lips were warm and moist. Real. Not the fantasy that had pursued him ever since the night in the kitchen of his best friend's house.

"I love you," he said when they broke apart. He felt like weeping with joy when she opened her eyes and, looking him full in the face, said, "I love you, too, Bryan." This time she kissed him back with an urgency of her own.

"It's going to be all right," he told her as he unbuttoned her silk blouse.

Giselle reached behind her to unfasten her bra. "I don't care if it is or not," she said, and then she gasped as Bryan put his mouth to her breast.

*   *   *

Mrs. Mainwaring had a party for Zandra's fourth birthday and afterward sent her home in the car with Patrick Halloran. It was Sheila he had to thank for that favor, Halloran thought with annoyance. He knew from the smirk on his sister-in-law's face when she turned over the child that she had been the one to suggest summoning the Vales' chauffeur. "My mother should have been there," the child said from the backseat.

"She was shopping."

"She was with that man, I bet. I saw her yesterday, but Nurse didn't see her. She didn't even wave at me."

"What did you get for your birthday, then?" Halloran asked, desperate to distract her.

"She's always with him. Daddy's friend, Mr. Rawlings."

Halloran pulled the car over to the curb and turned to face the child. She had no idea the damage her childish tales could cause. She had no idea the kind of man her father was. "Shut your lying mouth about your mother. Or I'll stuff you in a tow sack and dump you in the river."

The child's face went dead white. She shrank back against the car seat and stuck her thumb in her mouth. He knew then he had won. For a moment Halloran was ashamed of himself. Then he remembered what was at stake.

Giselle was safe.

And though he despised himself for frightening the child, the mistress's safety was all that mattered.

1947

ONE

The third Monday in February, Giselle awoke with the sure knowledge that she was pregnant. Her heart fluttered in panic. It had been over a year since her husband had come to her bed. She would have no way to hide her unfaithfulness.

She lay staring up at the ceiling, one hand clasped over the mended bumps of her ribs. What price would Charles exact for the few hours of happiness she had seized for herself? Her life? Bryan's? Would Zandra suffer, too? A cold shudder of fear shook her entire body.

The butler's footsteps in the hall roused her. Fry was on his way to wake Charles. In a little while Charles himself would knock on her door. Giselle scrambled from her bed and hurried to the closet. What would please him today? She took far too long to decide on a turquoise wool.

Dressed finally, she stared at herself in the mirror, and the sight of her own face, of the slash of red lipstick against her paleness, terrified her. How could she keep him from guessing? she wondered as his knock sounded.

When she opened the bedroom door, she could tell from his shocked expression how awful she looked. "I'm ill," she blurted. "Would you mind if I don't join you for breakfast?"

He grimaced. Other people's illnesses depressed him. "I'll have a tray sent up."

"Don't bother," Giselle said, but he was already striding away down the hall.

When the breakfast tray arrived, Giselle couldn't gaze at the food without her stomach churning. She shoved it away and went to sit before her dresser. For herself, Giselle always used a lovely pink jar to hold the face cream her mother had taught her to make. Now she opened the jar and inhaled the familiar scent. The fragrance was too much for her stomach. She stood so quickly that her chair toppled. She barely made it to the bathroom.

Giselle had already changed into her robe when the maid came to retrieve the tray. She sent the girl to bring Zandra to her. It was Nurse Pritchard who returned, holding Zandra's hand. "Really, Mrs. Vale! I don't believe this is a good idea. You could pose a danger to the child."

Zandra gazed at her mother in real bewilderment.

"Don't talk like that in front of her," Giselle said. She forced herself to smile and patted the place beside her on the bed. "Come here, darling. Mother wants you to stay with her this morning." When Zandra complied, Giselle asked the nurse to hand her the comb and brush from her dresser and reached to loosen the tie around Zandra's single braid.

"You're not going to use your comb on her hair!" the nurse protested. "She has her own."

"That will be all, Nurse Pritchard." Giselle didn't look up when the door slammed. She began to comb out Zandra's midnight-black hair, so like Charles's. The Vale hair; the Vale look. It was as though she, Giselle, didn't exist. The comb found a tangle.

"Ow!" Zandra said, and tried to wriggle away.

"Sorry, darling."

"Nurse knows how to comb my hair better than you do."

Giselle regarded her daughter warily. "That's true. But she doesn't let you play with makeup, does she?"

Zandra's eyes lit with anticipation. "Makeup?"

"And while you put it on I'll tell you a story about your grandmother Lillian, how beautiful and brave she was."

"Like a princess?"

"Exactly like a princess."

Zandra was leaning forward, staring at herself in the mirror as she lavishly applied Giselle's best lipstick to her small mouth, when someone knocked at the bedroom door.

Nurse Pritchard entered without waiting for Giselle's invitation. "Mrs. Mainwaring will be here in a few minutes to pick up—good Heavens, Zandra! What are you doing!"

"She has my permission," Giselle said as Zandra dropped the lipstick. "Call Mrs. Mainwaring back and tell her I don't want Zandra to go out today."

"I'm sorry, Mrs. Vale. She's already left. She heard you were sick and didn't want Zandra to catch anything."

And I know how she heard about it, Giselle thought, watching the nurse's rigid expression. "Come here and kiss Mother good-bye," she told Zandra.

Her daughter came, but slowly, aware of the disapproval of the nurse. Then Giselle was left alone with her thoughts. And her fears.

Charles was reading in bed when he heard his bedroom door open. "What is it, Fry?" When there was no answer, he glanced up. His wife stood just outside the circle of light from the lamp beside his bed.

Giselle stepped into the lamplight. Her golden hair hung loose to her shoulders. She wore an ivory satin nightgown. The imprint of her body, from the small knobs of her nipples to the soft brush of her pubic hair, was plain upon the gleaming fabric. But beautiful as she was, she did not stir his manhood.

"Did you want something, Giselle?" When she didn't answer, he laid the book aside. "Are you still ill?"

She came closer and switched off the light. Then he felt the mattress give as she climbed into bed beside him. She reached out for him, pulling him closer to her. He could feel her nipples through the satin of her gown and the silk of his own pajamas.

"Are you trying to seduce me?"

She placed her head on his chest. "Don't you think Zandra needs a brother? A little boy," she said dreamily. "Blond like me and—"

"Shut up!" Picture her taller, he told himself. Long lean legs, lovely dark hair, eyes like your own. Beneath the sheets, he felt himself begin to grow, to stiffen. He turned to her, pulled himself over her. She gasped, but he did not notice. He grabbed the bodice of her gown and ripped it, spilling out her breasts.

"Charles!" she shrieked. "Please, don't—"

His slap cut her off. "I don't want to hear your voice." His tongue sought the hard bud of her nipple in the darkness, then, while his hand shoved the nightgown above her hips, he bit down, hard. She quivered, but no sound escaped her. In the darkness, he smiled, and then he plunged into her. Alexandra, he thought. Alexandra.

Back in her bedroom, Giselle clutched her ruined gown. Her breasts were covered with angry, red welts. Tomorrow they would be black and blue. Her cheek was swollen where Charles had slapped her. But when the baby came in October, Charles would believe it was his. What was a six-week discrepancy? Only a quirk of nature. Between her legs, she felt Charles's semen oozing from her. Her stomach lurched.

She dropped the gown and went into the bathroom. Turning on both taps, she let the water stream full force into the tub. Tears began to trickle from her eyes. She brushed them away. She didn't dare see or talk to Bryan alone again. He would never know what she had done to save him from Charles. The thought of her mother rebuked her. To save myself, she thought.

She hugged herself around the waist as she watched the water level rise in the bathtub. "You'll be mine." Her voice made an eerie sound as it echoed from the tiles. "The only thing in the world that belongs to me alone."

Bryan spent a long lonely morning in the small furnished apartment he had rented for the meetings with Giselle. Where was she? he wondered. For the third time the message system they had established—a note from a dressmaker requesting a fitting at a certain time—had failed to work.

This time he finally gave in and phoned her home. But when the maid came on the line, he hung up. How could he take a chance on compromising her?

Something has happened, he thought. Something has changed. But what?

"Bachelors out on the town," Charles said. Bryan could barely hear him over the noise of the bar. "I can't tell you how much I've missed you, old man."

"Work," Bryan said. "You should try it sometime."

"I have problems of my own," Charles retorted with drunken dignity. "Ever make love to a pregnant woman? I can tell you I don't care for it. Disgusting what happens to a woman's body when she's pregnant." Charles shuddered. "Now I have the 'honor' again, if I should so choose. I don't know why a beautiful woman like Giselle would go through with something like that. It's not as if she enjoys sex all that much. Oops!" Charles said with a clownish grin. "Shouldn't have said that, should I?"

"Giselle's pregnant?"

"Congratulate me," Charles said. "I'm going to be a father again."

This time Giselle herself answered the phone.

"I know about the baby," Bryan said.

"You shouldn't have called me."

"How else am I to get in touch with you?" he said. "You ignore my messages. You wouldn't talk to me last night—"

"In front of your wife and my husband? Don't you think they would notice if we had a long chat?"

"I love you, Giselle. I want to marry you."

"You're already married. So am I."

"You can divorce Charles. Marry me, Giselle."

Her laugh turned into a sob. "You don't know Charles very well, do you? He would never let me go."

"He can't keep you if you want to leave him."

"If I divorce Charles, I'll lose my daughter. You can't ask that of me, Bryan."

"But you love me."

"That doesn't matter anymore," she said, and hung up the phone.

Giselle waited as Charles handed her wrap to the Rawlingses' butler. They weren't the only couple here tonight. They seldom dined alone with the Rawlingses' anymore. For that, Giselle was grateful. In the months since she ended the affair, Giselle had discovered that just being in Bryan's presence racked her nerves. What if Charles should guess even now? The thought terrified her.

"There you are." Florence hurried over and grasped both Giselle and Charles's hands, pulling them into the dining room where Bryan was lighting the candles. "Let's tell them our good news before the others, darling." The candle Bryan was trying to light snuffed out. "Here," Florence said, "let me do that." When she had relit the candle, she turned to the Vales. "Bryan and I have some wonderful news we want to share. Giselle, you're not the only one expecting." Florence beamed at her husband. Charles clapped his friend on the back.

As the men moved away from them Florence said, "Aren't you happy for me, Giselle?"

"Of course," Giselle said. It was ridiculous that she should feel the shaft of jealousy in her heart. She was doing the right thing, she told herself. The baby turned a lazy flip in her stomach, and she was sure of it.

Florence smiled as she and Bryan followed the Vales from the dining room to join the other guests. She had thought for a moment Giselle might faint when she heard the news. Yes, you're beautiful, she thought. But you couldn't hold him. Now I've made sure you won't get him back. Bryan wouldn't desert a pregnant wife, not even for a woman as beautiful as Giselle Vale. Florence was counting on that.

The Vales paused to take a drink from the butler's tray, and Florence, seeing Giselle in profile, realized how much Giselle's slender figure had already swollen.

Florence's eyes narrowed. You would think she was a month or two further along than she claimed to be, Florence thought, but why would a married woman lie about a thing like that. Then understanding burst upon her. She clutched Bryan's arm so tightly that he halted and glanced down at her.

"Are you feeling all right, Flo?"

She forced herself to smile up at him. "I'm just so happy," she told him. "I want this baby so very much."

Her husband's face turned brick red and she knew her suspicions were right.

TWO

Giselle climbed into the car and waited until Benjamin's nurse handed him over to her. Then she leaned back against the seat, clasping the baby to her chest, almost intoxicated with the wealth of possibilities before her. Perhaps Zandra still belonged to Nurse Pritchard and Alex Mainwaring, but Benjamin was hers. That made even life with Charles bearable.

"Where to this morning, Mistress?" Halloran asked.

"Drive around Central Park," she told him.

Benjamin's small lips puckered into a smile.

"I do believe he understands," Halloran crowed. "Oh, look what a great fool I am," he exclaimed. "Holding open the door long enough to chill the lad." He closed it gently and hurried around to the driver's side. "Scold me all you want, Mistress," he said as he got in.

"Don't fuss so, Patrick." Giselle jumped in alarm as someone tapped on her window. Benjamin's nurse, her face white and tense, stood there wearing only a thin sweater. Giselle rolled the window down. "What is it, Julie?"

"Nurse Pritchard said I must go with you," the young woman said, and then bit her trembling lower lip. "I told her you didn't want me along. I—she said if you've taken a dislike to me, I must resign, Mrs. Vale."

"You're doing a fine job, Julie. I told you that this morning. Don't worry about Nurse Pritchard."

"But she said—"

"I'll speak to her when I get back."

If she climbed up on the window seat and stood on tiptoes to press her nose against the glass, five-year-old Zandra could see the car carrying her mother and the new baby as it disappeared down Riverside Drive. The new ugly baby. She had heard her father mutter that Benjamin looked just like a little blond monkey and he was right.

Zandra scrambled down from the window seat and hurried down the hall to her mother's bedroom. Carefully closing the door behind her, she went over to her mother's dresser and surveyed all the intriguing jars and bottles and tubes. The morning her mother had allowed her to play with all these beautiful things stood out in her memory. Although she had begged Nurse Pritchard to let her do it again, Nurse had told her first that her mother was too ill to bother with her, and then, that with the new baby, her mother had no time for a big girl like her. Zandra had begun to hope the new baby would disappear. One morning they would wake up, and the nursery would be empty.

Zandra climbed up into her mother's chair and smiled at her reflection. When Benjamin went away, she would be able to play with her mother's makeup all she wanted. She picked up a lipstick tube, opened it, and began to outline her small lips with total concentration.

Her mother had told her the story of her grand-mother Lillian and grandfather Dieterich that morning, Zandra remembered. She frowned at her reflection. Aunt Alex had warned her never to mention that her mother's parents had been killed by the Nazis. "Or they'll think you're a nasty Jew." Zandra didn't know what a Jew was, but she knew she didn't want to be anything Aunt Alex considered nasty.

"Zandra!" Nurse Pritchard shrieked from the door-way.

Zandra dropped the lipstick. It fell to the floor, and when she scrambled out of the chair, she stepped on it, crushing it into the rug.

The nurse grabbed her by the arm and marched her back to the nursery. "Perhaps a taste of the belt will cure your bad habits, young lady," Nurse Pritchard said.

Zandra began to sob. Benjamin's fault, she thought as the nurse pulled off the belt of her uniform. Why couldn't he just go away.

"It's just an ordinary baby after all," Keefe said at last, tired of hearing Halloran's tales of young Benjamin.

"Pay him no mind," Sheila said as she set their plates in front of them. "The child sounds like a charmer."

Halloran beamed. Sheila herself had been full of questions about the baby, and he had proudly recited every detail of the boy's habits, dress, and schedule to her.

"And when did you grow so fond of babies?" Keefe demanded of his wife. "You were all the time complaining of the care of young Doreen and passing her off to my mum. 'Here, she's spit up again,'" he mimicked.

"Where is my little darlin'?" Halloran asked to change the subject before an argument could burst forth.

"Mrs. O'Connor has her," Sheila said. "She'll bring her home in a little while."

"She sees more of Tessie O'Connor than us, while her mother goes out and works in another woman's house."

Sheila paused, hands on hips, and regarded her husband balefully. "If you cannot bring enough money into the house to keep us, then why turn your rough tongue on me?"

"It was enough money for a woman like my mum."

Halloran's heart lurched as Sheila turned back to the stove. How could Keefe treat her so?

A knock at the door broke it off, thank God. He leaped from his chair to answer and found Tessie O'Connor there with his niece. "Uncle Pat!" Doreen cried. "I didn't know you were here. You never come and see us anymore."

"That's God's truth," Sheila added from the stove.

"Perhaps he's thankful to be away from so much female society," Keefe said heavily.

The drink did Keefe in early. Keefe and Sheila had taken Mum's old room, and Doreen, theirs. Rather than dislodge his niece, Halloran had insisted on taking the small narrow bed that had once been hers. He lay in the darkness listening to the rasp of his brother's snores. The apartment was so quiet that when the mattress shifted, he heard that as well, and the soft sound of Sheila's footsteps on the bare floor. He tensed until he heard the creak of the hall door. She was going down the hall to the public bathroom rather than use a pot in her room. When he heard the door of her bedroom open, he had been afraid she was coming to his bed.

He thought of her body beneath her cheap cotton

dress. In spite of himself, his manhood stirred. If she does come to me, I'll push her away, he told himself, but he wondered if he would. Then, as the minutes stretched out, he admitted the truth to himself. If she came to him, he would welcome her.

Halloran sat up. The bare floor was chill against his feet. He pulled on his socks. Though he slept in his own skin in his room at the Vales, here he slept in his underwear. He put on his pants and shirt and, still in his stocking feet, let himself out of the apartment. Silently, he made his way down the hall to the public bathroom. But when he reached it, he found the room empty. He stood in the hallway and wondered where his brother's wife had gone.

Just before dawn, Sheila let herself back into the apartment. Halloran watched her through half-closed eyes. Her face had a flushed, just-kissed look. You've been with someone, he thought to himself. But who, my darling Sheila? And then, as he watched her disappear through the bedroom door to where his brother slumbered drunkenly, he thought, more fool me to have turned down what was offered.

At breakfast, Keefe snapped at young Doreen and cradled his head. "It's an ache I'm having like you wouldn't believe," he said with a moan.

"Too much whiskey," Sheila said.

Keefe shoved his plate away. "It's not whiskey that's made me feel like this. Perhaps I should go to a doctor. It's not right that a man should have as many morning headaches as I do."

"You've turned into a drunk," Sheila snapped. But over Keefe's head, her glance met Halloran's.

His blood chilled as he remembered her giving Keefe and young Doreen a dose of Mum's medicine that time after the funeral.

Sheila grinned, knowing as well as he that he would say nothing. When she set his own plate in front of him, she leaned close, and it seemed to him that he could smell the scent of another man on her. His manhood throbbed to life. He shifted his chauffeur's cap to hide his erection. Sheila caught the movement and laughed aloud.

"Have you no pity, woman?" Keefe asked with a moan.

"Not with a drunken fool," Sheila told her husband. "Now eat fast, the both of you. I have to be on my way."

"But who is she seeing?" Alexandra Vale Mainwaring asked her maid. The door to the balcony rattled from a gust of wind. Thank heavens in a few hours she would be on her way to join her parents at Casa Vale. Palm Beach was a world away from the December blizzard howling through the skyscraper-walled canyons of Manhattan. "I'm certain there's a man in her life."

"There was. I'm sure of it, though I could never get the truth out of my brother-in-law." Sheila Halloran poured her mistress another cup of coffee. "But for now she seems totally wrapped up in the baby."

"That will pass. When she starts seeing him again, you must find out who he is this time."

Sheila nodded, and Alex had no doubt the maid would do her best. Heaven knew she had been paid handsomely for every scrap of information she had delivered about Giselle in the past. "I'll get it out of him," Sheila promised now.

"Do that. I'll make it worth your while."

After Sheila left, Alex sat her coffee aside and listened to the sharp sounds of sleet pelting against the glass of the balcony door. She was certain that her brother was being cuckolded by his beautiful young wife. That child—she had taken one horrified look at it and realized immediately no Vale had sired it. But how could she tell Charles that awful truth. While he might seem strong to the world, Alex knew him better than he knew himself, knew how sensitive he was.

It had been a blow to Charles's fragile ego when their father turned Vale Enterprises over to Tru and left Charles in that simple clerk's job in the shipyards. And this—if she were right—this would be a hundred times worse. If he heard it from anyone, he should hear it from her.

It had been sheer genius on her part when she asked Sheila Halloran to send her brother-in-law to apply for the job as her brother's chauffeur. Patrick Halloran, though he never guessed it, had provided her with a perfect way to spy on her sister-in-law with no one guessing. And if Giselle were cuckolding Charles, Alex would find some way to make her pay.

1948

ONE

Giselle laid her hairbrush aside and reached for her face cream. When she unscrewed the lid, she was surprised to see how little remained in the jar. Time to make more. A memory surfaced of Bryan's startled glance around the kitchen the night he brought Charles home drunk.

Giselle smeared the cream on her face blindly, letting it soak into her skin. When she finished, the jar was empty. Bryan was not a subject she cared to think about. They didn't see Bryan and Florence socially anymore. Before Benjamin's birth, Charles had drifted away from his best friend. Giselle had been glad of that. She hadn't wanted to see Florence carrying Bryan's child, or to congratulate her over the birth last month of her daughter, Franny. But whenever she found the memories of her time with Bryan more than she could bear, the remedy was down the hall.

Julie, rocking the baby, looked up and smiled when Giselle opened the door to Benjamin's room.

Giselle crossed over and gave her son a kiss. His tiny hand flailed and found his mother's cheek. When he felt the cream on his fingers, his eyes squinted in concentration.

Giselle caught his hand before he could stick his fingers in his mouth and wiped the small fingers clean. At moments like this she was struck with sadness at all the moments of Zandra's life she had missed. She wanted very much to hug her daughter close and tell her how much she loved her. Tonight that wasn't possible because Alex had taken Zandra with her to Palm Beach to stay with her grandparents. Most other nights it wasn't possible because Zandra belonged to Nurse Pritchard.

Giselle took Benjamin from his nurse and hugged him close. She must remember to do this more with Zandra when her daughter returned from her visit with her grandparents. A five-year-old was too young to understand that her mother was angry with the situation and not with her. It had taken Giselle a long time to realize that. She handed the baby back to the young nurse.

"I'll be putting him to bed in a few minutes." Julie grinned wickedly. "Nurse Pritchard would complain if she knew how late we were up, wouldn't she, Ben, my boy? Five whole minutes past your bedtime!" She kissed Benjamin's chubby cheek and made him smile.

When Giselle went to bed, Charles had still not come home. Most nights he arrived just as the sun was coming up. She wondered if he slept during the day in his office.

Sometime after midnight, in the silent house, she heard Julie moving around in the nursery. Benjamin made a small sound. Giselle thought about getting up, but if there was a problem, Julie would let her know. She was a good, honest girl, and Giselle knew she was lucky to have found her.

Still, sleep would not come. Giselle sighed deeply, and then rose and put on her robe without turning on the light. She felt across the top of her dressing table until she located the empty face-cream jar and tucked it in her robe pocket. She knew the stairs well enough that she descended without so much as a creak.

In the kitchen she snapped on the light. But before she could kneel and open the cabinet where she stored her supplies, she heard a peculiar sound in the silent house, a dull thud, followed by a scrape, and then a thump, as though something heavy had fallen to the ground outside the house.

For a moment her heart raced with terror. Then she realized how ridiculous it was to feel so frightened. She was in a house full of servants. One scream would summon half a dozen people. Still, worry nibbled at her. What could have made such a sound?

Trying to dismiss it, she opened the cabinet door. She knelt, staring at the lanolin and bottles, but the worry wouldn't go away. She stood abruptly and leaned forward to clasp the countertop with both hands. The tile was chill against her fingers. Benjamin would need to be swaddled warmly against the February air when she took him out in the morning.

The terror was still with her. Giselle closed her eyes and visualized the house. Where had the sound come from? she asked herself.

And then she was running, stumbling in her haste, clawing at the stair railing as she mounted the steps, her robe tangling between her legs, threatening to trip her with every step, but she wasn't aware of that, or of her own gasping breath, the sound of a drowning woman, awash in her own terror.

Julie opened her own door as Giselle rushed past toward Benjamin's room. "Mrs. Vale?"

Almost blind in her panic, Giselle didn't see the nurse. She yanked open Benjamin's door and plunged across the room to the empty crib. An envelope lay on the small satin pillow. Behind her, Julie began to keen.

Giselle ripped open the envelope and read the note. She turned to the girl. "Shut up! You'll murder him if you do that."

Julie swallowed her sobs. She put her arms around her thin body and clasped herself tightly, as though to hold in her sorrow. "What do they say?"

"If we tell anyone, they'll kill him."

Julie hiccuped as she swallowed a sob. "The police?"

"No one." Still clutching the note, Giselle hurried to the open window. On the ground below, she could see a ladder. She pulled down the window and then leaned forward for a moment, letting her forehead touch the chill glass.

Julie sobbed aloud again, pointing to the foot of the crib. "They forgot his blanket."

Giselle came back to the crib and touched the indentation Benjamin's head had left in the pillow. The satin was as cold as the window glass. Her son was gone.

Halloran woke with a start to find the mistress herself bending over him in his tiny cubicle, and him without a stitch on beneath the blankets.

"Where is my husband?" she demanded.

"Mistress, I'm not—"

"You take him to that woman of his. I know you do."

"Mistress!" he cried out, wounded for her sake, that she should know such a thing.

"Go and get him!" she cried. "Bring him home at once! Tell him there's an emergency!"

How helpless a man felt without his pants! "What kind of emergency?"

"Go and get him!" She screamed it this time, and Halloran truly feared she had lost her mind. "Bring him home! Now!"

Worthless sot that Charles Vale was, he would be delivered to the mistress trussed like a chicken if necessary, but be delivered he would, Halloran thought when he kicked open the door of the girl's apartment.

The mister was a big man and strong, too, but Halloran, having grown up in Hell's Kitchen, had the advantage of him. Especially knowing that drunk as the man was, he would not remember the exact manner of his leaving.

The girl was a different matter. She cried out when Halloran punched the mister in the stomach. The look the chauffeur gave her made her shrink back against the wall. "If you tell him, I'll come back and do the same to you." At that moment he truly believed he would. He saw by the look on her face that she believed him, too.

"Bring a pot of black coffee to the study," the mistress said when Halloran steered Charles Vale through the backdoor and into his own kitchen.

The mister followed her docilely enough. But when Halloran took the coffee to the study, he found the mister swaying beside the door, threatening to leave. "I have unfinished business," he said so nastily that Halloran longed to punch the man again.

"Leave the coffee," Giselle told Halloran. "I'll call you if I need anything else." He took the precaution of remaining just outside the door.

When Halloran heard the mistress give a little shriek followed at once by the smash of crockery, he hurried back into the study. Coffee, hot and black, was splashed across the front of the mistress's robe.

"Listen to me, Charles," the mistress screamed at her husband, but Mr. Vale was having none of it. He tried to lurch past Halloran, slipped in the coffee, and fell heavily against the chauffeur. Halloran grabbed his arms.

"Hold him," Giselle told Halloran. "Make him listen."

"What is it, Mistress?" Halloran asked her. He kept the mister's arms pinned tight behind his back.

"It's Benjamin. They've kidnapped Benjamin."

"They're asking a ransom?" Charles Vale stopped struggling.

That was the mister, driven sober by the mention of money, Halloran thought uncharitably as he released the man's arms. Giselle took an envelope from the pocket of her robe and held it out. Charles Vale grabbed the envelope and opened it. Halloran read the note as well, over the mister's shoulder, and his stomach lurched.

"Goddamned thieves!" Charles Vale crumpled the paper into a ball and threw it across the room.

"We have to get the money as soon as possible. But no one can know why." Giselle looked at Halloran. "You have to make sure that none of the servants talk."

"Shall I call the police, then?"

"You read the note. No police," she said.

Charles lurched away and stumbled to his desk. He reached for the phone. Giselle reached it first and snatched it away, out of his reach. "Who are you calling?"

"Alex," he mumbled. "Got to call Alexandra. She'll know what to do."

"No," Giselle told him. "We're not calling Alex. We're not calling anybody. I won't risk my baby's life because you're not man enough to function without your big sister's approval."

Charles's face crumpled as though he had been slapped.

"I'm sorry," Giselle said immediately. "I'm upset, Charles. I didn't mean that. But you must see that the note says to tell no one. No one."

"Then how, dear wife, do you expect me to get the money?"

"We have money."

"Not that much. Not in cash."

"The bank?"

"On what collateral?"

"They'll give it to you if Tru says so."

"Ah, yes, the war hero. I wondered how long it would be before his name came up. I should have realized that it would be all right to tell the war hero, but not Alex. Oh, no, not Alexandra. You've always hated her, haven't you?" The mister's voice was that of a whining child. "Because she loves me more than anybody else does."

"Charles, please!" she screamed at him. "This is our son. Our baby. We don't have time for all this."

He leaned forward unsteadily and patted her hand. "You're right, of course. Don't worry your pretty little head." He started from the room.

Giselle followed and then, when she saw him mount the stairs, she called out, "Charles! What are you doing?"

"Why, as you can plainly see, I'm going upstairs, my dear."

"But the money?"

"I'm going to take a nap, shower, change clothes, and be at the bank when it opens." Charles looked at his watch. "Eight hours from now. You'll wake me, won't you?"

Halloran felt the blood rage stir in him, but he unclenched his fists and looked to his mistress. "He'll be the better for a nap. And if no one is to know, he can't be rousting the bank manager out in the middle of the night."

"Of course," Giselle said. "I understand." But her face was as pale and white as death itself.

Giselle leaned against the window of the study, her breath fogging the glass, and watched for the car to return. Charles had risen at 8:00 A.M., shaved and showered, and eaten a hearty breakfast, then departed with Halloran for the bank. Before he left, Giselle had flung herself into his arms. "I'm sorry for what I said last night," she whispered in his ear. "I was upset."

He patted her—almost impersonally, she thought with the faint corner of her mind that still functioned—and then he left, as though today was a normal day at the shipyards.

She ran her fingertip through the patch of fog on the window glass, writing the letters of Benjamin's name in the moisture. In the distance she could hear the wail of a siren. Other people's troubles, she thought. In this huge city, others were crying, waiting, hoping, dying, but she had no sympathy to spare for them. She could only think about the soft blue blanket folded so neatly by Julie this morning at the foot of Benjamin's bed. How cold it had been last night. Poor Benjamin. He hated the cold.

She laid her cheek against the glass. It was still cold this morning, but by now they would have him someplace that was cozy and warm. They would take very good care of him, she was sure. It was not just that he was worth so much money. They couldn't help but respond to his charm. She smiled to herself, remembering the feel of his small fingers against her face, and the soft cooing sounds he murmured as though he were telling her and her alone some special secret. Even the cold heart of a kidnapper would be moved by that soft coo.

Another siren, closer, reproached her. Surely everyone tried to bargain with fate. Not my child. Someone else's. Had her mother done that? she wondered. Had Lillian cried out in those last awful moments, "Not me, I'm beautiful. Life isn't supposed to treat me like this."

"Not Benjamin," Giselle murmured aloud. "He's too good. Just an innocent child. No one could be cruel enough to—" She broke off, staring down the street. Two police cars, sirens wailing, were speeding down Riverside Drive. She didn't want to see this. She didn't want to know about someone else's pain. Not today.

Her breath caught in her throat as she realized the first police car was slowing. With a screech of rubber, it stopped directly in front of the house. "No," she whimpered.

The second car pulled in behind the first, and now uniformed policeman were spilling out of both cars. Other cars were pulling in behind the police. These were unmarked. Someone began to bang on the front door.

Giselle ran out of the study and down the hall. Fry was about to open the door. "Don't let them in!" she screamed at the astonished butler. "They're going to kill Benjamin! Don't let them in!"

Someone caught her around the waist. Giselle spun in her captor's arms and saw that it was Julie who held her. "Let me go!" Giselle screamed at the nurse. "They're going to kill my baby!"

"Mrs. Vale, please. It's the police. They must be here to help get Benjamin back."

"No," Giselle wailed, jerking her arms free. When Julie reached for her again, Giselle slapped her so hard that the red imprint of her hand appeared on Julie's white face. Julie gasped, and began to cry.

Fry reached for the door once more. Giselle clawed his hands away from the latch.

"Hold her," Julie screamed at the butler. "She doesn't know what she's doing."

The pounding continued. Now the police were shouting. Fry tried to hold Giselle with one arm and open the door with the other, but she lunged at his eyes with her nails.

Glass shattered as one of the policeman used his club to smash the narrow window beside the door. Then he reached inside and unlocked it. When it swung open, half a dozen people pushed their way into the entry hall and stopped to stare at the struggling woman.

The first flashbulb exploded, and Giselle fainted.

The vacant lot was littered with trash. When the patrol car pulled up, carrying Halloran and Charles Vale, Halloran wanted to yell in protest. Little Benjamin was not a broken toy to be discarded without ceremony.

Across the way, someone held up a diaper soiled with a rusty-colored liquid, dried now. "Over here!"

The police officer, O'Rourke was his name, tried to take Charles Vale's arm to guide him across the stubble of weeds, but the mister shook off his hand. Charles Vale walked—no, strolled—across the trash-covered lot as though it was a park. Halloran followed, pain already clutching at his heart. A knot of men surrounded the first one. Halloran heard someone mutter, "Rats," and a sob caught in his throat.

Charles Vale reached the knot of men, paused, looked down. After a moment he shook his head. "How am I supposed to identify this?" he asked O'Rourke.

"Perhaps the clothes?" O'Rourke asked gently.

"Do I look like a nursemaid?" Vale asked. "Halloran! Get over here!"

Halloran took the last three steps that brought him beside Charles Vale and then looked down.

For a moment his stomach danced wildly out of control. He made himself concentrate on the cloth alone, a soft and fuzzy blue, soiled now with long-dried blood as the diaper had been, but still showing the decorative stitches of young Julie's needle. He groaned.

"Mr. Halloran?" O'Rourke asked. "Is it the Vale baby?"

"Halloran? Say something!" Vale demanded.

"It's the boy. Young Benjamin." Halloran stumbled away and knelt in the weeds, emptying his stomach of the little he had eaten this morning. The dry heaves passed at last. As one of the policeman helped him to his feet, Halloran saw O'Rourke's car pulling away from the curb with the mister inside.

Halloran took one faltering step in that direction, and the patrolman caught his shoulders. "It's all right, boyo. One of us will run you home." The patrolman stared after the unmarked police car. "Cold fish, though, isn't he? You'd think it was someone else's kid."

Halloran stared at the man wildly, his mind churning with a possibility he had never considered before. "No," he whispered.

The policeman squeezed his shoulders. "Take it easy, man. Monahan," he called to one of the other policeman. "Take this gentleman down the block to that hole-in-the-wall bar and get him a shot of whiskey. Then take him home."

Monahan came over speedily and took Halloran's arm. "No whiskey," Halloran told him. "Just take me home."

Monahan, a young lad, looked at Halloran doubtfully. "Are you sure?"

"Home." He would shower, wash the stink of this place off of himself, and then he would go to the hospital. The mistress, he thought. The poor, poor mistress.

When the mist finally rolled back long enough for her to perceive that she was in a stark hospital room, Giselle had no idea how long she had been in its grasp. She lay on the stiff, unyielding mattress and watched the rays of the rising sun bathe the curtains with light. Gradually she became aware of a rhythmic *click-click*. A nurse sat in the corner of the room knitting.

In the hallway outside, she heard the rattle of trays. A soft knock sounded at the door. The nurse laid her

knitting aside and hurried to the door on soft-soled
shoes. She opened the door and said something to the
woman outside with the tray. The smell of the food
made Giselle's stomach contract painfully.

"What day is it?" Her voice sounded rusty and
unused. Both the women jumped and then turned to
stare at her. "What day is it?" she asked again.

"Tuesday," said the nurse who had been knitting.

"What day of the month?"

"February twenty-fourth."

The next question caught on her lips, but the
women saw it. They dropped their gazes, unable to
meet hers. She turned her face to the wall.

"Go and call the doctor," the knitting nurse told the
other. Giselle heard her soft-soled shoes approach the
bed. "Let me help you fix your hair," the nurse said.

Clara Pyle took up her knitting again, her duty
done, her patient cleaned and prettied up so no one
would know that she had been in a virtual coma from
the sedatives.

The doctor had bowed to the husband's wishes on
that, and of course, the husband was paying her own
fees as well, but still Clara felt it wasn't the right way to
treat a bereaved mother. If they had only let her
scream it out of her system, weep wildly as any woman
would do for her dead child, then she wouldn't be lying
there with that numbed look of despair as though she
wished she were dead herself.

The husband arrived with the doctor, and Clara
thought again as she had the first and only time she
had seen him—the day his wife arrived at the hospital—that he was an odd one. Handsome as a woman,
yet cold and withdrawn. Perhaps that was the way his
private grief had taken him.

The doctor waited by the doorway just out of Mrs.

Vale's sight as her husband advanced to the bed. He couldn't hear the whispered conversation, but Clara could. She started to move, to give the couple more privacy, but then she realized that would only distract them in this moment, when they needed above all to concentrate on each other, so she kept her place.

Charles Vale sat down on the edge of the hospital bed. "Hello, Giselle."

"Who did it?" Mrs. Vale whispered. "Who told them?"

"I did," Charles Vale said.

Clara Pyle stopped in midstitch. She glanced the doctor's way, but he had not heard what the husband said.

Mrs. Vale grasped her husband's hand tightly in her own, half pulling herself off the pillow. "But why? Why?"

Clara, stirred by the pain in the mother's voice, shifted in her chair. Charles Vale glanced her way and his look made her sit motionless, her needles still as well.

He leaned over his wife, pressing her against the pillow, and whispered something to her, something only the patient could hear.

"No!" Giselle Vale screamed. "No!"

Then her husband held her as she flailed her arms, and the doctor, hypodermic already prepared, rushed forward. "Nurse! Help us!"

Clara dropped her knitting needles and caught one of the mother's arms. Giselle Vale's grief had given her almost superhuman strength. With one part of her mind, the nurse was thinking that the woman's body would carry the bruises of this struggle, but she was able to hold the slim arm still finally while the doctor stabbed in the needle. Only a few moments passed before Mrs. Vale went limp.

Clara released her and looked up. Charles Vale was staring down at his wife with the coldest expression the nurse had ever seen on another human's face.

TWO

Halloran halted when he recognized the man in the suit standing in the hallway outside his brother's apartment. "I see you've come to visit your family," the FBI agent said.

"Are you after them again?"

"We've talked to the families of all the Vales' staff."

"Not a person who worked for the mistress would harm that sweet child." Halloran, embarrassed by the tears that sprang to his eyes, turned his face to the wall. Still the sobs broke loose. "No more!" He punched his fist into the wood and felt the impact all the way to his elbow. After a moment he put his fist to his mouth, sucking his split knuckles. At least the shock of the pain had stopped the tears and he could look the FBI agent in the face once more. "Why don't you get out and find that poor babe's murderers?"

"I want them as much as you do. But something has to lead me to them." The FBI agent gave Halloran a searching look. "If the mother hadn't gotten up on a whim, the kidnapping wouldn't have been discovered until the next morning. Someone spoke out of turn, Mr. Halloran. Someone let slip something about the baby's schedule, or the house, or something. That's how the child was snatched so easily."

"Goddamn you! It wasn't my family," Halloran's voice echoed down the shabby hall. "Maybe we're poor and Charles Vale rich, but I loved that child more than he did!"

"Mr. Halloran, for what it's worth, I believe you," said the FBI agent.

Halloran stood sucking the blood from his torn knuckles, and listened to the *tap-tap* of the man's shoes down the stairs, like the sound of nails driven into a tiny coffin.

When Sheila let him in, Halloran found Keefe at the table, a water glass of whiskey before him. "I'll join you," Halloran said. Sheila took two more glasses from the cupboard and poured both herself and Halloran a healthy shot. She brought the glasses, the bottle, and herself back to the table to join the two men.

"They're treating us like criminals, Pat." Keefe reached for the bottle, but Sheila knocked his hand away and poured the whiskey herself.

"The same questions over and over," she said as she pushed the glass back to her husband.

"It's worth it if they find the baby killers." Raw and cheap, the whiskey burned Halloran's throat.

Sheila looked across at Keefe. "Our Pat thinks we're the kidnappers now. He would choose his Giselle over us."

"You know it's not like that," Halloran protested.

She drained her glass like a man and gave him a hard stare. "Do I, Pat?" She stood up and reached for the whiskey bottle.

Keefe snatched it first. "Leave it."

Sheila shrugged, but she left the bottle with them.

Keefe poured himself and his brother another generous glassful. "Are you staying the night, then, Pat?"

"He'll be wanting to rush back to the rich folks," Sheila said from where she stood peeling potatoes.

"I'm staying." Halloran drained his glass in one swallow and shoved it toward Keefe for another refill. He lifted his gaze to find Sheila staring at him. He couldn't keep his eyes from drifting down to where the bodice of her dress strained across her breasts.

Sheila snorted.

"What is it, then?" Keefe asked his wife.

Sheila shook her head. "Our Pat knows," she said, her eyes bright with amusement. Halloran felt his bones chill.

But Keefe, feeling the drinks already, said merely, "Women. Can you understand them at all, Pat?"

"Not me, big brother."

Sheila laughed out loud. "What are pair of drunken fools the Halloran brothers are." She dropped the potatoes into the pot, and the Halloran brothers had another drink.

When Doreen came in from her school, Halloran gave her bright red pigtails a playful yank. "I see an ink spot here on the end of this one. Some young man must be dipping it in the inkwell and writing love letters."

"We don't use inkwells, Uncle Pat!"

After supper, he played her two games of checkers and lost them both, the first on purpose and the second because his mind drifted to Sheila, in the corner with her mending.

When the child had gone to bed, Sheila got out the whiskey bottle again, without Keefe's asking. "Go ahead, then," she told them. "I know it's what you're wanting. Make sloppy drunken fools of yourselves." She went off to bed, and they did their best to follow her orders.

Long past midnight, Halloran lay in the darkness listening to his brother's rasping breath from Mum's old room, and wished that the drink would take him as it had Keefe. He could not get the memory of the baby's remains out of his mind. It came at him worst in the darkness as he waited for sleep. In the silent apartment, he heard the door of the apartment open and knew it was Sheila.

Halloran was still awake when Sheila let herself back in just as the promise of dawn lightened the curtains. She went directly into the kitchen and the normal morning sounds of a wife making breakfast for her husband and family began. Who was it? The blood lust stirred within him at the thought of another man's hands on his darling Sheila.

At the hospital, Halloran found more bad cess. Bryan Rawlings waited outside the door of the mistress's room as he had for all the days she'd been there. Halloran glared, but Rawlings, head sunk on his chest, did not notice.

"How is my lady this morning?" Halloran asked the night nurse just going off duty.

"Better," the woman said. "But she kept asking for someone in her sleep last night. Are you Bryan?"

Before Halloran could speak a word, Rawlings was on his feet. "I'm Bryan," he told the nurse.

The nurse turned her back to Halloran. "I think she would rest easier if she could see you," the woman told Rawlings, and left Halloran to cool his heels in the hall. God's curse upon you, you bitch! he thought. But the smile he gave the nurse when she returned was warm; she was the gatekeeper, after all.

When Giselle looked up and saw Bryan bending over her, she did not question how he had come to be there. She simply held out her arms. She clung to him, letting some of his strength flow into her, feeling the dampness of his stubbly cheek against her own.

They stayed that way, without speaking, just holding each other, until the nurse finally told Bryan he would have to leave. "I'll be back as soon as they'll let me," he promised as he stood.

"That man has been right outside your door for two solid weeks," the nurse told Giselle. "Tell him to go home and shave. You'll still be here when he comes back."

"She's right," Giselle told him. "I'll be waiting."

Bryan stopped outside the door and leaned his head against the wall. He felt as though a burden had been lifted off him, and he was almost dizzy with relief.

Halloran grabbed him by the shoulder. "Can I see her?"

"Not right now. They're—look, can you stay here while I go and shower and change?"

"Of course I can. You don't need to be rushing back. I can take care of her."

"I'm sure you can. But I will be back." When Bryan left, his step was lighter than it had been in days.

"Mrs. Vale?"

Giselle looked up. The man who stood in the doorway of her hospital room, a briefcase in his hand, looked vaguely familiar. "I'm sorry. I don't seem to—"

"Leonard Solomon. Your husband's lawyer."

She leaned back against the pillow. "I've already told the police and FBI everything I know. I'd rather not go through it again." The thought of repeating the details of that awful night made her eyes well with tears.

"It's not about the kidnapping, Mrs. Vale." He gestured at the chair beside the bed. "If I may sit down?"

Giselle flushed. "Of course. How rude of me."

"Not at all." Leonard Solomon sat and opened the briefcase. "Perhaps you would like to read through these before we talk," he said, as he took out a folder full of papers.

Giselle shook her head wearily. "I really don't feel up to it. Can't you just tell me what this is about?"

"Your affair with Mr. Bryan Rawlings, Mrs. Vale." He paused, judging the effect of his words on her. When she did not betray her feelings by so much as a blink or nod, he continued. "These are sworn statements by witnesses regarding said affair."

"My husband wants a divorce?"

"And what would you say to that, Mrs. Vale?"

"Fine. Tell him I agree. Tell him I wouldn't share the same house with him again if he were—" Giselle shuddered, gained control of herself. "Tell him, yes."

"I don't believe you understand the situation, Mrs. Vale. He doesn't need your agreement. If he chooses to seek a divorce. This—" The lawyer held up the folder of papers. "This will assure that a divorce will be granted if Charles Vale seeks it. And if he does choose to seek a divorce, he can do so in the messiest possible manner. You will lose custody of—"

"No!"

"Of your daughter, Zandra. You will never be allowed to see her or communicate with her again. In the eyes of the court, you will be adjudged the worst kind of unfit mother. Not only that, your story will be in all the newspapers. Your daughter will be made to suffer for your mistakes, Mrs. Vale. She will hate you for the stigma you will place on her young life. What is she now? Five years old? She will suffer the rest of her days from this."

"But why? Zandra is his daughter, too. Why would he want to hurt her like that?"

"I believe that Mr. Vale has assured himself that Zandra Vale is indeed his true daughter. However, he has some question about the child recently deceased, as to whether—"

"Don't!"

He stopped and looked at her. She wanted to scream, but she knew that if she did, the doctor would come to sedate her again. Above all else she needed to have her brain clear to think. A bargain was being offered. The prize would be Zandra. "I want my daughter, Mr. Solomon. What must I do to have her?"

"Its very simple, Mrs. Vale. My client could leave you penniless. He could take your daughter away from you. But he will do neither of those things if you choose to cooperate with him."

"Just tell me what he wants me to do."

"Give up your affair with Bryan Rawlings."

"I'm not—"

"And swear that you will never see him again."

"He can't ask that!"

"Mrs. Vale, he can ask anything he wants. He is the injured party."

"But Bryan and I—"

"If you wish to see your daughter again, there will be no more 'Bryan and I.' You must be perfectly clear on that. If you agree to Mr. Vale's terms, Zandra will be raised by Mr. Vale's sister."

"Alex? But she's—"

"Mrs. Mainwaring will take excellent care of the child. She will allow you visiting privileges with your daughter, as her schedule allows. In the Riverside Drive house, which you will be allowed to keep if you agree to Mr. Vale's terms."

The lawyer looked at her expectantly, as though she should applaud Charles's generosity. When she continued to lie there without moving, he went on. "Although you and Mr. Vale will live apart, you will keep up the public fiction that you are still happily married. You will make yourself available to attend any public, private, or family functions required to keep that fiction alive in the minds of others. Along with the Riverside Drive house, you will have the staff of that house, and also Mr. Vale will furnish you with a generous allowance."

Hysteria bubbled within her. She had lost Benjamin; nothing could bring him back from the grave. But Zandra was still alive. She refused to lose her daughter as well as her son. "All right."

"All right, what, Mrs. Vale?"

"I accept Charles's terms. Anything. Just let me have my daughter."

"For you, mistress," Halloran said shyly, holding out the roses. He had waited over an hour to see her. First Rawlings had barged in and then that lawyer fellow. But the mistress looked at him as though he were a stranger. What had that lawyer said to her, to leave her like this?

"Don't bother yourself about the flowers," Halloran told her. "I'll call the nurse to put them in a vase." Still the mistress looked at him with that same queer look, as though she weren't quite sure who he was.

When the nurse came, she said, "Oh, Mrs. Vale, that nice Mr. Rawlings is here again. Shall I have him come in?"

"No! He can't come in. Tell him that. Tell him to leave." Giselle began to sob violently.

The nurse caught her arm. Another nurse appeared at the door and then hurried off in search of the doctor. Halloran found himself in the hall.

Bryan Rawlings grabbed his arm. "What's going on?"

"You've upset her," Halloran told him bluntly as the nurse rushed past with the doctor and both of them disappeared into the mistress's room.

"How?"

"She doesn't want to see you. She said so. So go on with you." It gave Halloran such a great gust of pleasure

to say those words that he immediately felt small and
mean.

"What is this? Some trick of Charles's."

Rawlings tried to push past him, into the room.
Halloran caught the man's arm and swung him back
against the wall. Rawlings was taller than he, and mus-
cled, but Halloran knew a fine gentleman would not
use brawler's tactics in the corridor of a hospital. He
brought both fists up and slammed them into
Rawlings's solar plexus.

The doctor emerged from the mistress's room.
"Here now. Stop this brawling at once!"

Rawlings dropped his fists. "This man tried to keep
me out of Mrs. Vale's room." He started forward.

The doctor stopped him. "You can't go in."

"What's wrong with her? Is she—"

"She doesn't want to see you," the doctor said
calmly.

"That's what I told you," Halloran said with great
satisfaction. "Now get along with you. You have no
business here if she wants you gone."

"I have to see her," Rawlings told the doctor.

"She does not want to see you. If you don't leave
the building at once, I will have you ejected by force."
The doctor summoned one of the watching nurses.
"Call the police," he told her.

"You're lying!" Bryan Rawlings said. "I talked with
her this morning. She said—"

"I believe you, Mr. Rawlings, but the lady has obvi-
ously changed her mind." The doctor's voice softened. "If
you care for her, surely you see the great emotional strain
she has been through. She needs rest and relaxation. She
does not need you bursting into her room when she has
specifically asked that you not be admitted."

Halloran took Rawlings's arm. "I'll see you out."

Rawlings shook him off. "I'm going," he told the
doctor. "But I'll be back."

"No, you won't, Mr. Rawlings," the doctor said. "You will not be allowed on this floor. Her husband will have a guard stationed outside her door if necessary."

Rawlings looked at him. Then he turned, without another word, and marched away down the corridor.

"I'll just tag along behind him and see that he leaves," Halloran told the doctor.

"Do that," the doctor said. "And about the guard—she said nothing about that. I thought it would prevent more trouble. But tell your employer I think that guard might be a good idea for a few days. That man—just tell Mr. Vale, I believe that a guard outside the door would give Mrs. Vale a great deal of comfort. I don't want to see her suffer through any more emotional outbursts like this."

Halloran patted the man's arm clumsily. "Don't you worry your head about it," he said with satisfaction. "Guarding the mistress from that man will be my pleasure."

Sheila Halloran set the tea things down in front of her mistress. "Will there be anything else?"

"A moment of your time," Alexandra Mainwaring said as she poured herself a cup of tea. "Is your brother-in-law going to continue working for Mrs. Vale now that Mr. Vale is living elsewhere."

"Yes, madam." Sheila wouldn't tell this fine lady that Pat was so besotted with Giselle Vale that nothing would pry him from her side. Especially now when grief had left her pale as a lily and more beautiful in her drawn way than Sheila cared to admit. "And now that Mr. Vale has moved out, will you no longer be wanting to know what she does and who she sees?" If not, Sheila would miss the nice packet of money she got for the information she pried out of Pat.

"I'll want that information more than ever," Alex

Mainwaring said as she set her cup down with a clatter.
"I'm responsible for my brother's child now. I have to
assure myself that Zandra will have the right kind of
atmosphere when she visits her mother."

"Of course, madam." Dismissed, Sheila went to the
kitchen and made herself a cup of tea. Pat might despise
Mrs. Mainwaring, but for herself, Sheila admired the
woman. She had guessed that Alex Mainwaring would
not forgive the injury done to her husband by his best
friend. Mrs. Mainwaring had paid handsomely for the
information that young Benjamin was not her brother's
child. Giselle Vale might not know who Sheila Halloran
was, but Sheila Halloran knew more about Giselle Vale
and her daily life than even Pat himself might suspect.
None of the hoity-toity upper class realized how much of
their personal habits were known to their staff. Giselle
Vale's maid had furnished Sheila with the news that
when Giselle Vale shared her husband's bed for the first
time in over a year, she was already pregnant with another man's child.

Sheila added a dollop of whiskey to her tea from
the bottle she had pinched from the mistress's last
party. The other servants knew where Sheila kept it,
but none of them would dare touch it. Or report her to
the mistress.

From what Pat had let slip of his mistress's stay at
the hospital, Sheila realized that Alex Mainwaring had
used the information to arm her brother against the
woman. That made up a little for the other thing, which
had gone so sour, Sheila thought, and sipped her tea
with satisfaction.

"And what are you grinning about?" Cook said,
when she came into the kitchen to start lunch.

"I was just thinking how good life has been to a
poor Irish girl like myself," Sheila told her.

1949

ONE

The Easter basket was the biggest Giselle could find. It sat on the kitchen table of the Riverside Drive house as she filled it with the soft moss Halloran had fetched earlier from the florist. Halloran was fishing eggs out of the boiling water. Giselle glanced with alarm at her shirt-sleeved chauffeur. "Are you sure they're done?"

"I'm an egg expert, mistress," Halloran said proudly.

"Maybe she'd rather have colored them herself." It was so hard to make the right decisions. She saw Zandra so seldom and only at Alex's whim. At least she had not been compelled this month to play "wife," a role she hated. Charles had been in Paris for the past four weeks. But still it had taken all of Giselle's strength to argue Charles's sister into agreeing to let her have Zandra for Easter and the following week. "What if she doesn't think hunting them is enough, Patrick?"

"Of course she will, mistress. And we'll reward her with the chocolate eggs." Halloran brought the hard-boiled eggs to the table, where the cups of brilliant color waited. "Now watch the Easter rabbit do his duty." Before he could reach for the first one, the phone rang.

"Not this time!" Giselle exclaimed.

But when she picked up the telephone, the voice was that of Nancy Allen, Alex's social secretary. "I'm afraid Zandra won't be able to spend Easter with you. Mrs. Mainwaring has to fly to Paris to meet Mr. Charles Vale, and she will be taking Zandra with her."

"Tell Mrs. Mainwaring that I refuse—"

"Mrs. Mainwaring will let you know the moment she returns so you can schedule another visit."

"Tell her—" Giselle found herself holding a dead phone. The social secretary had hung up.

"Mistress? What is it?"

Giselle shook her head. She dialed the number of Alex's Fifth Avenue apartment. "This is Mrs. Vale. Put Mrs. Mainwaring on the phone."

Zandra was big enough to pack her bags alone now—she would be seven in August—and she was enjoying herself. Sometimes she wished her mother would make time for her in her life, like other girls' mothers did. But this time, she was to spend a whole week.

She was lugging the suitcase down the stairs when she heard the phone ring. It bumped down a few more rungs before she could stop it. Aunt Alex, on the phone, looked up at her and grimaced.

"Good-bye, Giselle!" Aunt Alex said, and slammed down the receiver. "That woman!" Aunt Alex stood up and called for her social secretary. When Miss Allen appeared, Aunt Alex said, "I'm not taking any more calls from Mrs. Vale today." Then she came forward and caught Zandra's hands. "I'm afraid I have some bad news, darling. Your mother has canceled your visit."

Zandra felt the tears sting her eyelids. "But she

said I could hunt eggs! She promised, Aunt Alex."

Alex hugged her close. "I know what," she said suddenly. "We won't let that woman spoil our Easter. We'll have a celebration of our own. In Paris!"

Zandra pulled back and looked at her aunt. "Paris?"

"Where your father is. I'll send him at cable right now." Alex stood, smoothing her skirt. "Nancy can have the tickets by this afternoon. Won't it be fun?"

She didn't wait for Zandra to answer. The truth was it wouldn't be fun at all. Whenever her father and Aunt Alex were together, they had no time for anyone else. No one had time for her, Zandra thought. Not even her mother.

Halloran lay in wait for the maid when she came down to the kitchen to get the mistress's lunch the Tuesday following Easter. "And how is she, then?"

"Still in bed. I asked didn't she want me to call the doctor for her, but she said no." Alice shook her head at the food on the tray. "I don't know why I'm bothering taking this up. She didn't eat breakfast and she won't touch this either."

"Should we call Mrs. Mainwaring?" Cook asked him.

"And why would you call that bloody bitch?"

Cook retreated, her wattles wobbling. "When the mister was here, he always—"

"The mister is gone, praise God in his infinite mercy. You keep your hands off the phone. And you," he said to the maid, "get that tray upstairs."

Alice's hands were trembling so much that coffee sloshed out of the cup. When Halloran reached toward her, she dodged, spilling more. "Hold still, you idiot. I'm only trying to wipe up your mess. See that you smile when you set it before her. That might help her appetite."

By the next morning Halloran had decided that if the mistress didn't come down, he would go up himself and knock on her door, though the thought of it made his palms damp. When he entered the kitchen, the cook looked up from the stove with a wide grin. "She'll be wanting the car."

"She said so?"

"Called down bright and early."

"And did she eat?"

Cook frowned. "Not enough to keep skin on her bones."

Halloran snagged a biscuit. "Did she say where to?"

"Shopping."

He halted in midbite. "You're pulling my leg."

"Life goes on," Cook said.

When the mistress came out, Halloran saw she had taken pains with her appearance that she hadn't done since the days when the mister was there to find fault with every pleat and button. The cold, lifeless look that had haunted her eyes ever since she returned from those long days in the hospital after Benjamin's death had finally vanished. Now she wore a look of determination. Halloran's heart faltered. What course had she decided on? he wondered. He'd guessed about the bargain between the mistress and Charles Vale's lawyer. If it had fallen through, would she be seeing Bryan Rawlings again?

He saw her safely into the car and then hurried around to take his place behind the wheel. "And where would you be going this morning?" he asked as he started the engine.

"Saks."

And why does a woman who hasn't shopped in a year go to Saks on a fine Wednesday morning? he asked himself fiercely. Without thinking, he turned the key again, grinding the starter against the already running engine. The protest of his pride and joy cut him to the quick.

"Is something wrong with the car, Patrick?"

"No, mistress." Mentally he cursed himself for treating a fine machine like that.

The threat of Bryan Rawlings loomed larger in his mind as he ferried the mistress from Saks to Bloomingdale's. Shopping for finery to wear for the man she was, and Halloran knew it. Yet she emerged from each store empty-handed. When they ended the day with no packages to show for her efforts, he decided she must be having them sent.

But the next morning, Cook told him nothing had arrived from the stores. "What did she buy?"

"None of your business," Halloran snapped.

"Don't be giving me any of your lip," Cook said. "Or I'll slip something in your food your tummy won't like." He glared, but his mind was not on her threat. "Better drink your coffee," Cook told him. "She's wanting you again this morning."

"For what? Did she say?"

"Shopping," Cook said, and shopping it was.

This time there were packages. But not dresses in their boxes, or silky things in bags. No, the clinking and clattering told him it was nonsense for women's faces—not that the mistress needed any such, Halloran thought with a glance in the rearview mirror. It had to be that bastard Rawlings who was giving such a glow to her—

"Patrick!"

Halloran snapped his glance to the front again, and turned the wheel to miss a taxi. "Sorry, mistress."

"I believe you're out of practice," Giselle said with a little laugh. "We haven't been out enough this past . . ." Her voice faltered to a halt and Halloran knew it was the poor dead baby her thoughts were on. "But now things will be different for us, Patrick."

"Yes, mistress." That bloody bastard! Halloran thought. He's back again!

*   *   *

"Rawlings, Limited," a female voice answered the phone.

"Caldwell Limousine Service." Halloran had written down the name so he wouldn't stumble over it. "We're to deliver a car to Mr. Bryan Rawlings at six tonight, but the girl forgot to get the address."

"I don't understand," the woman said. "You say Mr. Rawlings ordered a limousine?"

"Perhaps he wasn't wanting his regular car tonight," Halloran suggested. "And we are a reliable company. Only the stupid girl who took the—"

"But Mr. Rawlings isn't here," the woman said.

"I'll be calling his home, then," Halloran said. "And my apologies for bothering you. But we wouldn't want to leave Mr. Rawlings waiting for a car and then—"

"You don't understand," the woman said. "He's not in the country. He's been in the South Pacific since February. He won't be back for a least two more months."

"No harm done," Halloran told her. "The stupid girl must have gotten the name wrong as well."

"But did she give you this number?"

Halloran slammed down the phone and frowned. If Bryan Rawlings wasn't the cause of the past two weeks' activities, what was?

When Halloran drove the mistress home the day after he called Rawlings, Ltd., the car was finally full of the kinds of purchases he had expected from the first. Dresses and such. And if the finery wasn't for Bryan Rawlings, then who was it for? The next morning, he had his answer.

The dress the mistress wore when she came out to the car was a blue the same as her eyes, with a full skirt that flared around her shapely legs and a belt that showed a waist so small a man yearned to put his hands around it. But it was her eyes that startled Halloran most. She had done some trick with women's paints that emphasized them more than normal. While he was still trying to take in the change in her, the mistress told him to drive her to the offices of Vale Enterprises.

Her husband, then, Halloran thought, and his astonishment was mixed with disbelief. How could she think to entice the man who had been the cause of her son's death? "Are you sure, mistress?" he asked, his hand on the key.

"Whatever do you mean, Patrick?"

He looked at her reflection, and he couldn't bring himself to form the words. "Nothing, mistress."

It's going too fast, Giselle thought. She had expected to wait, to have time to compose herself. But no, the secretary had said she was to go right in. Giselle straightened her frivolous little hat and twisted her gloves in her hands. She stared at the doorknob. Should she put on her gloves again? No, she didn't dare hesitate or she would lose her nerve. She reached out with a bare hand and turned the knob.

He stood with his back to her, staring out the huge glass window that made up one wall of his spacious office.

"Hello," she said, when he failed to turn. She slapped the gloves against the palm of her right hand. "I'm glad you could make time for me today."

Truman Vale, Jr., turned and looked at her with an appreciation she could not fail to mistake. "I'd be a fool not to. Especially since my curiosity is aroused. I thought without baby brother to urge you, you wouldn't come voluntarily into my presence."

She shook her head. "That's—"

"The truth," he finished for her. "At least until now. So why are you here today, little sister-in-law? Why the formality of an appointment?"

Giselle took a deep breath. "I have an investment opportunity for you."

TWO

"**D**o you know what that woman's done now?" Charles's voice over the phone sounded tinny and far away, as though he were still in Europe instead of right here in Manhattan. "She's changed her name to Durand. Giselle Durand."

Of all her brother's possible complaints about his wife, Alex hadn't expected that. "I thought her maiden name was Hauser."

"Durand was her mother's maiden name. Don't you recall what a personality her mother was before she married that German? Lillian Durand? The toast of café society?"

"But why would Giselle change her name?"

"She's going into business."

Alex laughed.

"You may think it's funny. I think it's embarrassing."

"What kind of business?"

"She's going to peddle that cream she was always

92

concocting for herself. You should have seen the mess in the kitchen when she turned chemist!"

Alex doubted Charles had ever seen the kitchen of any of his residences. "So that's why she changed her name. Giselle Durand. It does sound good, doesn't it?"

"Apparently the war hero thought so, too."

"Tru? What did he—"

"Our dear brother is bankrolling her."

"You must have misunderstood the situation."

"And Father approves. He's as taken with her as Tru."

It took forever to get Charles off the phone. But when she did, Alex sat there for a moment wondering what she could do. After a moment, she rang for the maid. When the girl arrived, Alex said, "Miss Zandra's mother called, Mary. She'll be over in an hour to pick her up. Have her change."

The maid hesitated. "The last time Mrs. Vale called, she never came. Poor Miss Zandra cried all afternoon."

"She is the child's mother."

"But are you sure she's really coming?"

"Just give Miss Zandra the message, Mary."

Zandra, in a starched pinafore, sat in the entry hall of her aunt's apartment and waited for her mother. Not that she had anything better to do. Not since the Christmas holidays when her cousins, Aunt Alex's sons, were out of school. The whole family had stayed at Casa Vale in Palm Beach. Although Noel and Wesley were twelve and fourteen to her six, they tolerated her, letting her join in their play.

Zandra looked at her watch, a present from Grandfather Vale when she proved to him she had learned to tell time. Almost half an hour had passed. She squirmed on the bench. She wouldn't let herself think about the awful possibility that this time, like the last, her mother wouldn't come.

That reminded her of what Noel had said at Christmas. She had been watching the boys splash in the pool, and the thought of the lonely days after they left for school again had made her mad. She informed Alex's sons haughtily that they weren't Vales, but Mainwarings, and, worse, they didn't have the Vale look, the dark hair and ivory skin of Truman Vale himself—while she had both the name *and* the look. Noel had grabbed her and dunked her in the pool while Wesley screamed with laughter. The more she screeched and threatened to tell Aunt Alex, the harder Wesley laughed until he tumbled into the pool himself.

And Noel had said the awful thing to her then. "Don't bother telling Mother. She doesn't care about you any more than us. All she cares about is Uncle Charles."

Zandra knew it was true. She had scrambled away from the pool, running back toward the house. Wesley caught her. He put his arm around her and held her while she cried. Then he whispered, "It hurts us, too. But you've got your mother. Since Father died, we don't have anyone."

Zandra glanced at her watch and saw that over forty-five minutes had passed. Wesley had been wrong. She didn't have anyone, either. A noisy sob escaped her. Before she realized what was happening, arms encircled her. "Mother?"

"Poor Zandra," Aunt Alex said. "Go ahead and cry."

"She's not coming?"

"I can't believe how that awful woman treats you. I know," her aunt said. "I'll take you to the zoo."

Bryan Rawlings rubbed the stubble on his cheek absently as he leafed through *The New York Times*.

The bouncing taxi made it hard to read, but he had become used to worse modes of transportation during the past few months in the South Pacific. His glance fell on a photograph under the caption "Cosmetics Company Launched." "Giselle!"

"What was that, buddy?" the cabdriver said.

"Nothing." Bryan scanned the short article announcing the launching of Giselle Durand Cosmetics. Giselle had gone into business for herself? What on earth was Charles thinking of?

Bryan thrust the paper aside and leaned back. He knew that for all practical purposes Giselle and Charles were separated. Not that they mixed socially anymore, but he heard the whispers. But even if they were living apart, no gentleman in Charles's social position would allow his wife to go into business. Even a frivolous pursuit like this.

And why on earth would Giselle have changed her name? Bryan snatched up the paper again, but the article yielded nothing beyond the bare facts: Giselle Durand was entering the cosmetics market with an all-purpose face cream. A beauty cream concocted, so the article said, from an old family recipe handed down to Giselle by her mother, the famous beauty Lillian Durand. The article devoted a paragraph to Lillian Durand's café society days, her marriage to a German industrialist, and her execution by the Nazis during World War II. The kidnapping was mentioned briefly, but it was Lillian Durand the reporter had chosen to emphasize. She had handed down to her daughter both her loveliness and the secret of her beauty cream.

Bryan remembered the night Giselle had patched his wound in the kitchen. Pots and pans had been scattered about, and she had said something about making her own cosmetics. But he had been so overwhelmed by her that he had never given that a second thought.

Giselle Durand. It suited her. More than that, it

seemed to hold a promise. Perhaps she had finally decided to divorce Charles. He stared at the photograph. "Pull over here," he told the cabbie.

"Do you know what kind of neighborhood this is?"

"I want to make a call." Before the man could protest further, Bryan was already out of the cab, cutting through the traffic to the drugstore he had spotted. Inside, he searched through his pockets for change and called Giselle's home number.

"Mrs. Vale's not in," the Irish chauffeur told him.

"This is Bryan Rawlings. Would you tell her that I'll only be in town for two days. She can reach me at my office tomorrow or the next day." He gave the man the number and then hesitated. "Is she all right, Halloran?"

"She's fine, sir. Thank you for inquiring."

Giselle, Bryan thought when he hung up. I love you. What went wrong? She would call, he told himself as he left the drugstore. They would be together again.

Halloran stood beside the telephone, staring at the note with Bryan Rawlings's office number scribbled on it. He ripped it into shreds and pocketed the torn paper.

A noise on the stair made him glance up. The mistress was coming down. How beautiful she looked. If her face paints and creams would make ordinary women look like that, she'd have no trouble with the selling of them. "Who was that on the phone, Patrick?"

"No one, mistress."

"But I want to go to the airport. I want to see Daddy's plane leave," Bryan Junior protested.

One look at Florence's face told Bryan that would not be possible. "No," he told the nine-year-old, gently untangling the arms around his neck. "You stay here, Bry. Take care of Mommy while I'm gone. And your sisters."

"But when will you be back?" Bry asked him.

Bryan glanced at Florence in spite of himself. That was the question his wife had failed to ask. "Not for six months, I'm afraid."

"You'll miss my birthday again."

"Your mother will be here." He had hoped for a private word with Florence before he left, but she managed to keep herself surrounded by children and servants the whole time.

That wasn't entirely fair, he reproved himself as he climbed into the waiting cab. He hadn't insisted on their being alone together. Not after he had seen Giselle's photograph in the *Times*.

Momentarily, he felt guilty, remembering how stiff and unnatural his elder daughter, Elizabeth, had acted around him. The seven-year-old had spurned every advance he made to her. The only time he picked up the baby, even she had made it clear with her rigid body that she regarded him as a stranger.

At the airport, Bryan checked his luggage and headed toward the phones. "Any new calls?" he asked his secretary.

Dutifully she read him the list of messages that had accrued since he last talked to her three hours ago. "Are you certain that's all?"

"It's everything, Mr. Rawlings. You were very explicit in your instructions."

He hung up the phone and leaned against the wall. He should have gone to her house, banged on her door, until he had an answer from Giselle, he thought. But that wasn't a gentleman's way. The lady had given her answer by her silence.

Tru Vale's apartment was elegant but masculine. He took Giselle's wrap and kissed her bare shoulder.

She stood quietly, repressing the shiver of delight his lips tried to coax from her. Was this going to be the unwritten part of their agreement? If so, he might be surprised. Although Giselle had thought of this moment, she had yet to decide what she would do if he tried to coax her into bed. She'd had enough of Vale men in her life. An association with Tru was necessary only because of his money.

Tru moved to gather her into his arms. Giselle turned away gracefully and crossed the room to look out over the Manhattan skyline. "What a lovely view."

"Yes," Tru said. She turned and found he was gazing not at the view, but at her. "Lovely."

"I thought we were going to have champagne."

"We are." He pulled the bottle from the ice bucket and wrestled with the cork. It let loose with a satisfying pop. "You've earned it."

"It was the advertising that made the difference," Giselle said as she accepted the glass he poured for her.

"And your photograph."

It wasn't vanity that made her nod in agreement. She had understood as soon as Tru had broached the subject of her own photograph being used in the advertising. "My mother told me that a woman's beauty is her only weapon."

Tru lifted his glass in a salute. "Here's to a formidable weapon—Giselle Durand's beauty."

Giselle drank. "It's really a success, isn't it?"

"A wonderful success," Tru agreed. "I'm lucky to be in on the ground floor."

"But not for long." She had insisted on a clause in their agreement that allowed her to buy him out when she wished. He had argued furiously against it at first.

"Does that frown mean you're still afraid of me?"

He said it laughingly, but she replied in total seriousness. "Not afraid, no. But I no longer want to be dependent on a man. Any man."

"Even me?" Tru asked.

She rubbed her ribs. Especially Charles's brother. "Giselle Durand Cosmetics. Doesn't that sound wonderful?"

But he would not be put off. "Will you ask Charles for a divorce now?"

"Ask him?" She set the champagne glass down so hard it shattered.

"Giselle?" She was in his arms before she realized that was what he intended.

"Do you realize how difficult your sister makes it for me to see my own daughter? If I ask Charles for a divorce, he'll make sure I lose any chance to see Zandra."

"I'll speak to Alex."

"What do I have to do in return?"

"Nothing."

"I despise liars."

"Did you ever wonder why I'm not married? Because when I met the right woman, she was engaged to someone else."

"I'm still married."

"Do you really think that's going to make any difference to us?"

When Tru's lips touched hers, she knew he was right.

"It's Mrs. Vale on the line," Nancy Allen told Alex Mainwaring. "Shall I tell her you're out?"

"No," Alex told her social secretary. "I'll take it." As though she had a choice. Last night's conversation with Tru still made her boil. There were so many ways he could bring financial pressure to bear—not on her, but on Charles.

"I'll pick Zandra up at noon," Giselle said. "If there's any problem, I'll take it up with Tru."

"There won't be," Alex told her.

"Good." Giselle hung up.

"Bitch!" Alex said when she had replaced the receiver. She glanced around. Nancy had already fled the room.

Alex went upstairs in search of her niece. She found Zandra in her bedroom, playing with her dolls.

Zandra glanced up, and what she saw in Alex's face made the seven-year-old's own expression sober. "What is it, Aunt Alex?"

"I'm sorry, Zandra, but things don't always work out as we wish. You're old enough now to understand that."

Zandra looked frankly bewildered.

Alex sat down on the edge of the bed and put her arm around her niece. "I had planned to take you shopping this morning for that new dress you've been begging for, but your mother just called. I'm afraid she has other plans."

Zandra stiffened and drew back. "What kind of plans?"

"She didn't say." Alex stood. "Put on something else, dear. I don't want her to think we let you wear rags."

"She never comes when she says she will. I won't go!"

"Of course, you will. Your uncle Tru was pointing out to me only last night that she's your mother and should spend more time with you."

"But she doesn't want to spend any time with me."

"I'm sorry, darling. But it's really out of my hands. Do hurry and get dressed. She'll be here at ten."

Giselle glanced at her watch as she stepped off the elevator. A quarter after noon. She hurried down the hall to Alex's door. As eager as she was to see her daughter, even fifteen minutes lost in traffic galled her. When the maid admitted her, she saw Zandra sitting on a bench in the entry hall. "Darling! Sorry, I'm late." The sullen look her daughter turned her way chilled Giselle's heart. "I have a wonderful day planned for us," she went on, but less exuberantly.

"I'd rather stay here," Zandra said.

"Nonsense." Alex stood in the living-room door. "It's your duty to go with your mother."

Zandra's expression as she climbed down from the entry-hall seat and walked toward her made Giselle wonder if she was doing the right thing. Could her daughter really prefer Alex to her own mother? Of course not, she thought. But whatever the price, I must get her away from Alex's influence.

When the door closed behind Giselle and Zandra, the maid said, "It breaks my heart to see the way that woman treats Miss Zandra. To keep her waiting for two hours. Can't you do anything?"

Alex lit a cigarette. "She *is* Zandra's mother, Mary."

1950

ONE

"**D**on't complain, Noel." Wesley Mainwaring struggled with his tie. "Most funerals are only good for a day. We've stretched this one out for a week." At thirteen he greeted any excuse to miss a few days of school with glee.

Noel Mainwaring would be sixteen in May and stood at the head of all his classes. "It's ridiculous to have had the funeral in New York and the will read in Palm Beach."

Zandra, sitting cross-legged on one of the beds in her cousins' room, said, "Grandfather loved Casa Vale. That's why he wanted us here."

"Bullshit," said Wesley. "He just wanted to show he could still make everybody dance like puppets."

"Tell him not to swear," Zandra commanded Noel.

"Don't swear, Wesley." Noel winked at her. "Happy?"

"I think everybody is talking mean about Grandfather."

"That's because you've only known him seven years," Wesley told her. "The longer you knew him, the more you realized what a—"

Noel's hand on his mouth cut him off. "I think our little cousin is precocious enough without you adding to her vocabulary." Noel glanced at his watch. "Time to go."

Zandra scrambled off the bed. "Will it be fun to hear a will read? Like the Fourth of July?" She had been promised fireworks for the Fourth of July.

The two boys exchanged glances. "Exactly like the Fourth, if we're lucky," Wesley said.

Alexandra recrossed her legs. Leonard Solomon's reading of the list of minor bequests had dragged on and on. But more annoying was her mother's response. Sylvia Vale had tearfully expounded on each person's tie to the family.

Truman Vale, Jr., watched the proceedings with a polite expression that could mean anything. And how would her twin like it when he had to split his power three ways? Alex wondered.

Charles caught her eye; he knew what she was thinking. It was Charles who leaned forward at the exact moment she did, when Leonard Solomon said, "Now the main bequests. To my wife, Sylvia Vale, I leave the New York apartment, and the income from my portfolio of stocks. I'm sure her sons will continue to look after her in the same manner that I have."

Fat chance, thought Alex. I'll be the one stuck with her flutters and her moods.

"To Truman Vale, Junior, I leave my entire holdings in Vale Enterprises. He proved he deserves the helm."

"Tru?" Alex asked, although Charles's bloodless face told her she had heard right. "Tru gets it all?"

"Your father left you a sizable bequest, Mrs.

Mainwaring," Leonard Solomon said.

"But the company! What about me? What about Charles?"

"I'm sure Mr. Tru will find a suitable place for Mr. Charles. And as for you, your father felt your business was raising your children and your niece." The lawyer continued reading. The sizable bequests for her, for Charles, and for the boys and Zandra were all to be doled out by Tru as the spirit moved him. But Casa Vale went to her sons. "Although," Leonard Solomon pointed out, "he understood the house would be sold eventually. The upkeep—"

"He should have willed it to me!" Alex burst out. "He knew how much I loved this house."

"Of course he did," the lawyer soothed. "But he knew the upkeep would be prohibitive, and he felt you might be too sentimentally attached to it. While your sons—"

"Damn! Damn! Damn!" Alex screamed. "Charles! Aren't you going to do something?"

Charles stood. "I believe I'll have a drink, dear sister. Care to join me?"

Alex glanced around wildly. Zandra was staring with wide eyes. The faces of her sons and her twin wore identical expressions of amusement. As for Sylvia Vale, the widow looked as though she might swoon at any moment. Alex took a deep breath. "Perhaps, you could just get on with it," she told the lawyer.

"We're finished," Leonard Solomon said.

Charles set the brandy bottle down and lifted his glass in a salute to the rest of them. "All the way to Palm Beach to find out just how much the old bastard hated me."

"Charles!" Alex reproved, but what she meant was "hated *us*."

* * *

Tru arrived at Giselle Durand Cosmetics' new showroom at 5:00 P.M. Although it was his first time there, Tru paid only the scantiest attention to the elegant offices. Nor did he give his full attention to Giselle's excited chatter about the publicity for the new jar design: an opalescent oval with a pale gold top. *Harper's Bazaar* had just run a full-page photograph of the jar surrounded by gold coins.

But it was Giselle's own face that had the greatest impact on sales. To sell cosmetics, one sold a dream. In this case, the fantasy of being Giselle Durand. A dream even I can't live all the time, Giselle thought wearily as she left Tru in the showroom and went into her office to collect her purse. She had been on the road for weeks as a traveling salesman, visiting specialty and department stores, making personal appearances. The women whose faces and lives she touched with her cosmetics would never dream how lonely she was most of the time, how many nights of the year she spent playing solitaire in a hotel room. She had picked up the game as a way to concentrate her thoughts, to shut out her surroundings, and sometimes in the midst of it, she gained insights into new products, new techniques, new ways to train her growing sales force. But mostly, the cards served to shut out her awareness that she was truly alone.

Each time both she and Tru were in New York, each time their names were linked in the gossip columns, there was a corresponding jump in the sales of Giselle Durand products. When they were out in public, Giselle found herself observing the two of them from somewhere outside her body, acutely aware of what a handsome couple they made. That was part of the fantasy women purchased when they bought Giselle Durand products. She wondered if Tru realized that.

She was too weary to go anywhere tonight, but she could hardly tell Tru so on his first evening back from

Palm Beach. He would want to discuss the reading of his father's will—the last thing she wanted to hear. Soon, though, she wouldn't have to consider his feelings above her own. The cosmetics industry in America promised to do at least forty million dollars retail this year. Her own sales were climbing. If business continued to escalate, she could pay back Tru's investment before the end of the year, then the business would be hers alone—no more arguments. With Tru as a partner, expanding the business had been a constant battle. He bitterly fought her decision to branch out from skin treatments into lipsticks this year. She wondered if it was because he realized that this step would make her independent of him that much quicker.

The toehold at Saks Fifth Avenue that Tru's influence had gained for Giselle Durand Cosmetics the year before had been the start; and then the large-scale advertising his money paid for had made Giselle Durand Skin Cream a formidable contender with Arden and Rubinstein overnight.

Giselle went into the small washroom off her office and freshened her makeup. When she went out to Tru, she looked like the fantasy creation in the Giselle Durand ads.

As soon as they were settled in the back of his limousine, Tru said, "I've missed you." He pulled her close and kissed her.

When he finally released her, she said slowly, unwillingly, "And I've missed you."

"You don't sound very happy about it."

She wasn't. She had never expected to feel so strongly about a man again. Especially Charles's brother.

The car stopped. She was surprised to see that they were in front of Tru's apartment building. "Aren't we going out?"

"Later. First I want you to see something."

They took the elevator not to the eighth floor, where Tru's apartment was, but to the sixth. He produced a key from his pocket and let her into one of the apartments. "How lovely!" she said as she glanced around. "But this doesn't look like you, Tru. It's so feminine."

He pulled her to him. "Sell the house. Move in here!"

Joy coursed through her. To be free finally of the memories of Charles, of Benjamin's abduction, but— "I can't. Charles wouldn't approve, and Alex would make sure I saw Zandra even less. You have no idea how hard she's worked to turn my daughter against me."

"That's over now. Father made me the sole heir to Vale Enterprises. Neither Charles nor Alex will trouble you now. I need you here, Giselle. Near me."

"But, are you sure . . . ?"

He answered her with a kiss. She kissed him back as part of her mind calculated the price she would pay to see Zandra more often. The cost to her reputation. The danger of being under a man's thumb once more, subject to his whims. Or, God forbid, his rages. But what did that matter when it was her child for whom she was bargaining? Or was she lying to herself? Was Zandra only an excuse she was using to be with a man she had never planned to love?

"And what does our Pat think of his prissy mistress now? Of course, you'll be defending her, Keefe," Sheila reproved before her husband could answer. "A pretty face turns away criticism. I used to have that power myself."

"And still do," Halloran told his sister-in-law, although the years were beginning to sit heavily on her. "But the mistress doesn't deserve your scold."

"And what do the papers say about her?" Sheila demanded. "That man's 'constant companion.' Father

Flannagan knows what that means, if you don't. And now you tell me she's to live in the same building with him?"

"Did you expect her to knock around in that huge house all by herself for the rest of her life?"

"I'd say you're a softer judge of her than of others," Sheila snapped back.

Halloran reddened and glanced at his brother, but Keefe, having finished his beer, had dozed off, his chin resting on his chest. Sheila still stood there, and he could see the challenge in her eyes.

When he looked away, she laughed. "One of these days, I'll win, Pat. And then you'll be thinking of me. Not her. And something dead will stir to life again."

"She's moved into his apartment house. Did you know that little tidbit? Half of New York does. The half that counts." Charles rose and lurched toward the bar. "Father wasn't cold in the grave."

She should try to distract him, Alex thought, but her own anger and dismay mirrored his. How could Tru do such a thing? Surely he realized how embarrassing it was to the rest of the family. Even worse than his flaunting his brother's wife on his arm.

Her father's will still made Alex burn with resentment. He had known how much she wanted to be a part of Vale Enterprises. She had understood that it would not happen until after his death. But his betrayal had shocked her. All the more because Charles was included in it.

Charles mumbled something into his drink.

"What did you say?" Alex asked.

"The war hero knows the rules. Winner take all."

"Charles, be cautious."

"He's always had things his own way," Charles said, not listening to her. "It's time that changed."

* * *

The snippy secretary told him to wait. As he paced Charles was aware of the tremor in his hands. He needed a drink, but he knew if he succumbed to that desire, he would lose control of the rage that bubbled just below the surface. He swung around so suddenly that the secretary started. "Did you let my brother know I'm here?"

"Yes, sir, but he's on a transatlantic call." She looked back to her typing.

"You stupid bitch! You didn't tell him anything, did you?"

She gasped. "Mr. Vale!"

"Tell him again. Or better yet, I'll tell him myself." Charles strode toward the inner door. He threw it open with such force that it banged against the wall. Tru, behind his desk, waved a negligent hand in Charles's direction, as though his younger brother had entered in a normal manner.

Charles slammed the door, cutting off the secretary's babble. Alex's twin occupied what had been their father's office. Behind him, the view of Manhattan was spectacular. It should have been mine, Charles thought. Too bad you weren't killed in the war.

"Would you repeat that, Herr Geitler?" Tru said into the phone. "We had a little disturbance at this end."

Charles stooped beside the desk and yanked out the phone wire. Tru stood. Charles tensed, but all his brother did was lay the useless receiver on the desk.

"I assume that what you've come about is too urgent to wait for me to conclude a several-million-dollar agreement?"

The scorn in his voice raised Charles's temper another notch. "You know why I'm here, you bastard."

Tru grinned. "Now, Charles. You knew the old man

too well to imagine he would ever step out of line to the extent of fathering two bastards. So if I'm one, what does that make my twin."

"It's Giselle I'm here to talk about."

"What about her?"

"She's still my wife! I won't have her cuckolding me again!" That wasn't what he had planned to say, but he couldn't stop the words bubbling out of him. "I won't have you fathering another bastard on her. Once is enough! Keep away from her, Tru. If you don't, you'll be sorry."

Tru looked at him with hooded eyes.

"What's the matter, war hero? You didn't know that Bryan Rawlings got there first?"

Tru said nothing.

A chuckle escaped Charles. "You really didn't know, did you? I'll bet you thought she told you everything. Those big blue eyes will fool you, won't they?" He laughed with real amusement. "Big brother taken in. I never thought I'd see the day." The laughter took him again with such force that it brought tears to his eyes.

"Are you through?" Tru asked coldly.

"Oh, yes." Charles wiped ineffectually at his eyes. "I'll bet Father wouldn't have thought so much of you if he'd known how easily she could wrap you around her finger."

"I have work to do, Charles."

"I was just leaving." The laughter broke free again. Charles reeled out of Tru's office in the grip of it, and dropped into one of the chairs opposite the secretary.

The intercom on the secretary's desk buzzed. "Have someone come up to fix my phone," Tru's voice said.

Charles glanced at the secretary's face and laughed until he was weak. Then he went in search of a drink.

The limousine pulled up to the curb, and flash-bulbs began to pop. When Tru handed Giselle out onto the sidewalk, they were both bathed in the brilliant light. Truman Vale's death last month had changed everything. Now the fantasy woman, Giselle Durand, made her public appearances by the side of one of the richest men in the world, and sales of Giselle Durand products were climbing wildly. Giselle wondered if Tru realized that.

Or how Tru's wealth had changed the way the world regarded her. She could see it in the faces of the reporters and photographers crowding around them. It was all right, those faces said, to step outside the normal bounds of morality. Even the move to his apartment building had gone unremarked in the press. After all, she was the woman other women dreamed of being. That change in the press's perception of her had wrought some fundamental change in Giselle herself.

"Hold it," someone shouted, and Tru obeyed, turning a proud smile on her. Then they swept toward the door.

Soon, she thought. Soon she would feel secure enough in his—love?—to ask for the biggest thing of all: full custody of her daughter.

The reception was so packed Giselle could hardly breathe. But as she moved through the crowd, exchanging pleasantries with half of New York, she was aware of Tru's eyes on her. It was the strangest glance, as though he were weighing her, measuring her.

Afterward, when he helped her into the car, she said, "What is it, Tru? You want to ask me something. I can see it in your face."

"You're a very perceptive woman."

"And that's no answer to my question."

"Invite me to your apartment and ply me with champagne."

She chuckled. "All right."

She laid her head back against the seat as the car sped through the Manhattan streets. Rumors might fly, but Tru had been scrupulous where their apartments were concerned. They never spent the entire night together, although Giselle found herself longing for that more and more. Since the new glare of publicity had descended on them, he had been even more careful where her reputation was concerned.

When they entered her apartment, Giselle tossed her wrap aside. The champagne was ready, chilling. "You read my mind," Tru said as he opened it.

"I was hoping," she admitted. She went to him, and he let the bottle sink back into the ice.

"My hands are cold."

"I don't care." She lifted her face for his kiss.

His lips came down on hers, but she was aware that he was being careful not to touch her bare skin with his icy hands. She felt a moment's irritation. This wasn't the real Tru, treating her with such care, always worried how things would affect her, how things would look. She was reminded for a moment of Bryan, and the thought disturbed her. She didn't want to be treated with kid gloves. She had accused Tru once of being no gentleman, but now she knew it wasn't a gentleman she wanted. Her hand moved instinctively to her ribs, rousing the memory of Charles's fists. Not that either. Neither a fragile flower nor a punching bag. Just a woman.

She closed her eyes, trying to lose herself in the moment. But he was holding back, she realized, keeping a certain distance, as though there were something he didn't want to forget in the heat of their passion.

He released her and turned back to the business of opening the champagne. She moved away, looking at the dark windowed wall that showed her the New York skyline, until the pop of the cork called her back.

"To another successful evening," Tru said as he handed her a glass. The crystal sang when their glasses touched.

"For both of us. Giselle Durand Cosmetics should

pay you a fee for all the free publicity."

He drained his glass as though it were whiskey.

She stood there, her own untouched, waiting. Some blow was about to fall.

Tru poured himself another glass of champagne. "Charles came to my office today."

Her worst fear leaped to life. "Is it Zandra? He's not going to let Alex take her out of the country again, is he? That's not fair, Tru! She's my daughter, too."

"Not Zandra."

His expression, so solemn, so frightening, cut off her emotions as though a switch had been pushed. "Then what? Don't keep me dangling like this, Tru. Whatever it is, it's troubled you all evening."

"Yes, it has. Perhaps you ought to sit down."

"If he didn't speak to you about Zandra, then what—"

"Bryan Rawlings."

She did sit down then. Abruptly. "That changes things between us?"

"No, but I think it answers a riddle that's troubled me for a long time."

"Are you wondering how I could be unfaithful to my husband?" The pain was so sharp that it cut like a knife. "Just as I am now?"

He dropped to his knees before her and took both of her hands in his. "Was Benjamin the child of Bryan Rawlings?"

The memory of her loss was so strong it blotted out every other feeling for the moment. She felt the tears well up in her eyes and begin to trickle down her cheeks. "Yes."

"Did Bryan know?"

"Yes."

"Why didn't you leave Charles?"

"Because of Zandra." The sobs choked her for a moment. "I knew he would never let me have her. And I

was afraid of what Charles might do to me . . . To Bryan
. . . And then . . . and then I lost Benjamin . . . and I
agreed . . ." She was crying hard now. ". . . agreed I'd
never see Bryan again and they said they would let me
see Zandra . . . but they didn't. They didn't." She jerked
her hands free of Tru's grasp to cover her face.

He waited, kneeling before her, until her sobs
eased. "There's something else you need to tell me."

Her face still covered, she shook her head.

"Someone leaked the information about the kidnapping to the press."

"Yes," she whispered.

"Charles told them, didn't he?"

She nodded as fresh tears sprang to her eyes.

Tru's voice went on, as calm as a judge pronouncing sentence. "I think my father knew. That was why
he wrote his will as he did."

Giselle remembered the few times after Benjamin's
death that she had seen Truman Vale at the Vale family
gatherings. Yes, she thought. He had known. That
explained the way he'd looked at his youngest son.

"How did you find out it was Charles?" Tru asked her.

"He told me," she said, her voice muffled by her
hands. "In the hospital."

She felt his hands grip her upper arms, but it was
the past she saw. "What did he say?" Tru demanded.

The words were burned on her heart. "He said it was
too much money to pay for another man's bastard."

His hands released their grasp. She looked up then,
through the curtain of her tears. What she saw in his face
terrified her. She grasped his arm. "He's your brother,
Tru," she cried, uncertain as to whether her intention was
to save Charles—or Tru himself—from Tru's anger.

Charles had never had a worse hangover. When
Tru's secretary called, he tried to put her off, but she

would have none of it. "He said now, Mr. Vale." Then she added the magic words that brought him out of bed. "He said it was something to do with your income from Vale Enterprises."

That brought him running quickly enough. Damn the old man anyway, for giving the war hero the purse strings and leaving Charles to beg for his rightful inheritance.

This time Charles was gratified that the secretary showed him in with no waiting. At least his message had gotten through. He was as important as the war hero, whatever this little bitch might think.

Tru sat in his chair, facing the windowed wall. Charles heard the door close behind him. Gloves off time, he thought. Let the war hero know that he couldn't be shoved around. "What was so important that you had to call me down here this morning?" he said testily.

Tru swung around to face him. "I know what you did."

TWO

Alex woke to darkness and the maid's screams. The bed sagged beneath a man's weight. Someone shook her shoulder. "Wake up, Alex," Charles cried.

Alex sat up and ripped off her sleep mask. "That's all right," she told the screaming maid. When the door closed, she turned to Charles, who was sitting on the edge of the bed, shoulders hunched. "What's wrong?"

"Tru's sending me out of the country. He called me to his office this morning. What could Father have been thinking of? He never understood anything. That house. On Riverside Drive. I knew then that he—"

"What did Tru say?"

"If I want my income, I must live in Europe."

Alex knew her twin. There would be no appeal. She put her arms around Charles and pulled him close.

"Everyone will know," he wailed like a little boy. "They'll know she cuckolded me with my best friend. That she had his baby. They'll think I'm not a man."

"Tru won't let it come to that. Family is important to him."

Charles jerked back. "You didn't see his face when he looked at me. He hates me. He thinks I'm a coward."

"He's wrong," Alex told him.

"What will I do in Europe without you?"

"You haven't left yet. I'll think of something."

She felt Charles relax in her arms. "You're strong enough for both of us," he said. Of course he was right.

"You knew I would come," Alex said to her twin.

Tru nodded. "And you know I'll refuse any appeal you try to make on Charles's behalf."

"Why do you hate him so?"

"I don't hate him."

"Then why—"

"I despise him." It was said without heat, but with finality.

"You don't have any hold over me. You may control Charles's income, but Neville left me quite well off."

"The boys?"

"My sons?" She laughed. "You're too noble, Tru. You would never stoop to a revenge that would injure my sons." She saw by the flash of annoyance on his face that she had read him correctly. "But I can injure you."

"Don't threaten me, Alex. It makes me—testy. I might forget I'm a benevolent paterfamilias and turn out more like Father."

"I'm more like him than you or Charles," Alex told him. "Keep your mistress if that's what you want—"

"Don't you dare—"

"But don't let her divorce Charles. He couldn't stand losing her to you. It would crush him, and I don't intend to see that happen. If she tries to get a divorce, I'll see that every bit of her dirty linen is laundered in public. How long do you think that little company of hers would survive if everyone knew that the poor mother who lost her baby to the nasty kidnappers was actually—" His expression hadn't changed, but something about his stillness told her this was too dangerous to pursue. "Sleep with her all you want. Just don't try to marry her. Because if you let her destroy Charles, I'll make you pay."

Alex rose, and then she halted, looking into Tru's face. What she saw there made her smile. "I see now that I shouldn't have worried, Tru. You did just fine against the nasty old Japs. But you wouldn't take that final step against Charles. You're too noble to be responsible for your own brother's destruction."

"Don't be too sure," Tru warned.

"Oh, but I am sure, war hero. Charles is right about you. You're noble to the core." She smiled. "I do hope you'll furnish Charles with enough income to buy a suitable villa. I hate living in cramped quarters."

"You're going, too?"

"Of course I am, dear twin."

"You aren't taking Zandra."

"Do you want an eight-year-old in your love nest?"

Tru shoved back from his desk. "If you were a man. . ."

Alex's laugh mocked him. "Don't worry about my dear little niece. I'll work something out with Giselle."

Halloran was so worried about his own foul smell he could give no thought to the nasty bitch the mistress was on her way to have lunch with. He had been with whores before, and never had it made him feel as though he reeked with the odor of their bodies. But last night, after Sheila—finally Sheila, and in the backseat of the Packard at that, where the mistress herself sat now—Halloran feared he would never get her woman's smell off him or the car. He had driven around for hours last night with the windows down. "The smell of sin," he mumbled, and went crimson when the mistress asked, "Did you say something, Patrick?"

"Talking to myself like the fool I am."

"Don't be so hard on yourself," she said, kind as always, and he wanted to cry. It wasn't just his brother he had betrayed last night; it was his mistress as well.

Giselle ordered a salad and then waited impatiently while Alexandra Mainwaring had a long discussion with the waiter about the wine. She and Tru had had their first fight the evening before. She knew he was up to something, but he would only say, "My family owes you."

"All I want is my daughter," she had told him. *And my son back.* Although she did not speak the words, she knew he heard them as clearly as if she had.

Alexandra waved the waiter away. "I suppose you know that Tru is sending Charles to Europe? Charles is absolutely crushed. I don't know what will become of him."

"I didn't know, but I'm afraid I really don't care."

"You might when I tell you I think I should go with him."

"But what about Zandra? How will I see her?"

"Perhaps," Alex said slowly, as though the thought had just occurred to her. "Perhaps I could leave her with you."

Giselle's heart leaped. "Oh, Alex, if you only would."

"It would be another blow for Charles. Tru's done a wicked thing to him. At your request, I suppose?"

"I wouldn't do that, Alex. Surely after all these years you know that about me."

Alex gave her a long, wary look. "No, you wouldn't have thought of it. A Vale would."

"Perhaps you're right. It was a Vale who thought of separating me from my daughter in the first place."

"That's behind us now. We must think of what's best for Zandra. If I did leave her in the States, I would need some assurance that you plan to take care of her in a manner befitting a Vale."

"For heaven's sake, Alex! She's my daughter. Why wouldn't I take care of her?"

"Children have been used as pawns before."

Under other circumstances, Giselle would have laughed. "What proof could I give you?"

"Something tangible that will convince Charles you're sincere. We both know he has reason to distrust you."

Giselle felt the blood drain from her face. Her glass was in her hand. One more word from Alex and she would fling the contents of it in her sister-in-law's face. She took a deep breath. "What do you want?"

"A piece of your little company for Zandra," Alex said, and Giselle fought back anger. Little? Perhaps compared with Vale Enterprises. But it was her company. Vale Enterprises certainly didn't belong to Alexandra. "Stock," Alex went on. "Tie it up any way you want, but make sure it eventually goes to Zandra with no strings attached."

"And if I do?"

"I'll leave Zandra here with you."

Tru was waiting for Giselle in her apartment when she finally returned late that afternoon. "You don't have to do this," he said when she told him what Alex wanted.

"I don't mind. I see nothing wrong in giving Zandra something she will eventually inherit anyway."

"If Alex asked for it, she has some scheme in mind."

"There's no way she could use this against me,

Tru. I've already talked to my lawyer. A portion of the company stock will be put into a trust for Zandra. She'll begin receiving income from the stock when she's twenty-one, but actual control won't pass to her without restriction until her fortieth birthday. She'll only be eight in August. Alexandra wouldn't wait that long for revenge."

Tru shook his head. "You don't know the Vales."

"She called it my 'little company.' She'll be surprised when she finds out what a piece of it is worth."

"Don't let your pride blind you to—"

"It's not my pride, Tru! I want my daughter back."

"No," Zandra screamed. "I won't live with her."

"I'm sorry," Alex told her. "Uncle Tru said you must. That woman knows how to twist him around her finger."

"Can't Father do anything?"

"No, your mother is having your uncle Tru banish him to Europe. And me with him."

Zandra ran to her aunt and threw her arms around Alex. "Then I want to go to Europe, too."

"I'm sorry," Alex told her. "It's out of my hands. But I was able to do one thing for you."

Zandra, still clinging, looked up. "What?"

"I forced your mother to put a piece of her cosmetics company in your name. Eventually you'll have control over a very substantial portion of Giselle Durand Cosmetics."

"I don't care!"

"You will, darling."

"Should I be here when she arrives?" Tru asked.

Giselle stopped pacing the living room. "I don't know. What do you think?"

"I've given you my opinion on everything from her clothes to her bed sheets. This one is your decision."

Giselle smiled, in spite of the trembly feeling in her stomach. "Let me see her alone for a few minutes, I suppose. You can join us for dinner."

Tru glanced at his watch and rose. "I'll run up and change, then." He kissed her gently and departed.

Giselle decided to go and change herself, but just as she reached her bedroom the doorbell sounded. This is the happiest day of my life, she thought as she hurried back to the door. When she opened it, Zandra stood there, and behind Zandra, her hands on Zandra's shoulders, stood Alexandra Mainwaring.

"Good afternoon, Giselle," Alex said. "Here we are."

Giselle dropped to her knees and opened her arms. "Zandra! Darling!"

Zandra stared at her with a look of pure hatred.

"Go to your mother, Zandra," Alex said, shoving her niece forward into Giselle's open arms.

Giselle clutched her daughter's rigid body and stared up into her sister-in-law's face, at the triumph in Alexandra Mainwaring's eyes.

ZANDRA

1959

ONE

Mrs. Sheldon took the note from the senior girl who had just entered the classroom. "Zandra Vale is to go to the office of the headmistress immediately," she announced. "And take your books with you."

"What have you done now?" Maribel Quarters whispered from across the aisle.

Zandra shrugged. But as she followed the senior girl from the classroom and down the echoing hall, she searched her brain for the answer.

The senior girl, Felicia Hudson, was one of the most popular girls at Wellington. When Zandra first arrived at the exclusive Connecticut girl's school as a twelve-year-old—just as her mother and grandmother before her had done—she had dreamed that someday she, too, would be popular, and girls like Felicia would be her best friends. But after four long years at Wellington, Zandra still felt like an outsider here. Especially since she had become such a gawk.

After her mother inexplicably changed her last

name to Durand, Zandra had clung even more fiercely
to everything Aunt Alex had taught her about her Vale
heritage, proud of what her aunt called the "Vale look."
But she had never in her worst nightmare dreamed
that the "Vale look" would curse her with six feet of
height. She was taller now than even Aunt Alex, and
towered over every other girl in school. Felicia was
only five feet three, a perfect size. No one stared or giggled at her, or tried to trip her when she walked to her
desk. No one called her "Giraffe" or asked "How's the
weather up there?"

When they reached the headmistress's office, the
school secretary's desk was empty. Felicia motioned
for Zandra to sit in the wooden chair beside it. Zandra
took a deep breath as she stared at the heavy oak door
of Miss Agatha's office. Zandra had paid many visits to
Miss Agatha's office over the past four years, visits during which she had endured endless scoldings by the
headmistress for not living up to her mother's example
as a Wellington girl. Not living up to her mother's reputation as a scholar or a beauty was something to which
Zandra quickly grew accustomed at Wellington. But
then her mother had never been a six-foot-tall geek.
Zandra chewed nervously on a ragged fingernail and
wished the visit to Miss Agatha's office were over.

"Here she is at last," the secretary said when she
returned finally and ushered Zandra into the headmistress's office, as though it was Zandra's fault, and not
her own, that the headmistress had been kept waiting.

"Ah, Zandra, tardy as usual." Agatha Bamfield was
an imposing woman who seldom smiled. She advanced
with a binder in her hand. "I am losing my patience
with you, young lady. How stupid do you think your
teachers are?" She held out the report and Zandra recognized the flowery curved handwriting with its circles
for dots. Her roommate's report on the Inquisition.
Where Liz's name should have been, someone had

written Zandra Vale. "What have you to say for your-self?" Miss Agatha demanded.

Zandra studied her name. It was a good forgery, but Miss Agatha would never believe that. She shrugged.

"Really!" Miss Agatha cried. "I fail to see why the granddaughter of Lillian Durand, the daughter of Giselle Durand, would steal someone else's work and put her own name on it. The Durand girls have been something special at Wellington for as long as I can remember."

"I'm not a Durand. I'm a Vale."

"One week in your room. Starting now. Writing your own report will give you something to do."

It was Felicia who marched her back to her room. Felicia who said with a smirk before she turned away, "I guess this shows you what Wellington thinks of your kind."

"Who did it?" Zandra demanded when her room-mate returned. She and Liz Rawlings had only been roommates since Christmas, but Zandra was already tired of Liz's insipid blondness.

"I swear I don't know, Zandra." Liz stood just inside the door, as if she were afraid to come all the way in the room. "I tried to tell Miss Agatha it was a mistake, but she wouldn't listen. I don't know what happened to your report."

"Oh, for heaven's sake, come on in. I'm not going to hit you." Zandra threw herself down on her bed. "I don't see why everyone hates me so much."

"If you just wouldn't act like you're so much better than everyone else," Liz said.

"Is that what they think?" Zandra asked, astonished.

"And you should try to get along with Felicia instead of always making her angry. She saw those car-toons."

"They weren't cartoons. They were caricatures." This past year Zandra had discovered she had a gift, a talent of catching a likeness of someone in a simple line drawing. Last month she turned in a sheaf of drawings of both students and teachers to the editor of the school newspaper, hoping that some of them would be printed. Every single one was returned. When she asked the editor why, she was astonished to hear that the likenesses were "too cruel." Felicia had been one of the subjects. "You mean it was Felicia who forged my name on the paper?"

Liz backed up, shaking her head. "I didn't say that."

"You didn't have to." Zandra turned her face to the wall. After a few moments she heard the door close behind Liz, but she stayed where she was, thinking. How could showing what a person really looked like be considered cruel? she wondered. She sat up and reached for her sketch pad. Quickly she began to sketch a tall, storklike girl, with spindly legs and arms, and long dark hair. Then she ripped the sketch from the pad, tore it up into little pieces, and began to cry.

Silently Zandra slid open the window of her dorm room. The chill February air flooded in. Liz moaned in protest, but didn't awaken.

Zandra tossed the rope of knotted-together sheets over the windowsill and then leaned out. The rope of sheets reached from the fourth-story window to within ten feet of the ground. She dropped her suitcase into the snow, then boosted herself onto the windowsill. As she stepped out onto the narrow, ice-coated ledge her boot skidded, and she almost fell. Only at the last moment did she grasp the windowsill and pull herself back up. Her heart thudded in her chest and she almost gave it up. She had put up with three days of confinement to her room. Why not stay cooped up like a good girl for four more? The thought of Felicia Hudson's smirking face answered that question.

Carefully she grasped the knotted sheets and began to lower herself toward the ground, her boots scraping against the brick wall of the dorm. If she fell, the snow would cushion her, she thought as she scrabbled her way down to the end of the rope. She swung there for a moment, unable to force herself to let go, until she conjured up a picture of her cousins' faces one Palm Beach summer, taunting her to follow them off a diving board.

Zandra released her grip. She hit the snow and her boots crunched through the frozen crust. Staggering, she managed to keep her balance. Then she laughed aloud with sheer pleasure. Let the other girls treat her like a freak and refuse to speak to her. None of them would have had the nerve to do this! She reached for her suitcase.

"I see you've tired of our company, Zandra," the headmistress said from the shadows beside the building.

Zandra glanced up. Four stories above, Liz leaned out the window watching the scene below. When she saw Zandra looking at her, she ducked back inside.

Miss Agatha followed Zandra's gaze. "Elizabeth!" she called. Liz Rawlings appeared again. "Pack the rest of Zandra's things for her." Miss Agatha grasped Zandra by the arm. "Bring that suitcase with you. You'll sleep in the infirmary tonight. Tomorrow you'll be on your way home."

"Mother's in Paris."

"I have her number. I'll call her and let her know what I've decided." Miss Agatha stopped, and for a moment Zandra thought she saw the gleam of tears in the old woman's eyes. "It is a shameful day for me when I am forced to expel one of the Durand girls from Wellington."

"I'm not a Durand," Zandra said fiercely. "I'm a Vale."

The glint of tears vanished from Miss Agatha's eyes and she gave Zandra a small mocking smile. "My dear, I'm afraid that's absolutely true."

Giselle's hand trembled as she hung up the phone. She took a deep breath, trying to banish the feeling that it was she who was the schoolgirl, she who had just been called on the carpet by Miss Agatha. First Zandra had begged with all her heart to be allowed to go to Wellington when she turned twelve, even going so far as to enlist her aunt Alex's support, and then she had spent four years doing her best to get expelled. She had finally succeeded.

"What is it?" Tru asked from the other side of the bed.

Giselle turned to him, thinking as she did how out of place he looked in the lace-edged sheets. Why had she persisted in decorating this apartment with such heavy-handed femininity when she had known it would be a haven for the two of them in Paris? She leaned forward and laid her cheek against his bare chest. "After we make love, I can smell myself on your skin."

He tipped her head up so that he could look into her eyes. "Something about Zandra. I caught that much."

Giselle grimaced. "She's been thrown out of Wellington. She forged her name on someone else's paper."

Tru rolled away, wrapping himself in the sheet.

"What are you doing?" Giselle asked as he stood.

"You'll want to pack. I'll only be in the way."

Giselle lay back on the pillow. She still looked good; she could see that in his eyes. "I'm not going anywhere."

For the first time since she had known him, Tru seemed disconcerted. "But Zandra? You'll want to be there."

"Why?"

"To talk to her. To comfort her. She needs you more than I do right now."

"What makes you think she would accept any comfort from me, Tru? For nine years, she has rejected every overture I've made to her. And I'm not in Paris for three months just to sleep with you. I have several very important meetings this week. They've taken over a year to set up."

"Meetings more important than your daughter?"

"I don't have a daughter anymore. Your sister made sure of that. Oh, yes," she said before he could protest. "You saw to it that I have custody of her. But that's all. Your family stole her from me. Now all I have is my company. And I don't intend to let her schoolgirl escapades rob my time from my business."

"I can't believe I hear you saying this. You're not the woman I thought if this is what you truly believe. Go to your daughter, Giselle. She needs you."

Giselle stood and reached for her robe. "Let me ask you something. Why have you always refused to help me get a divorce from Charles?"

"That has nothing to do with this."

"It has everything to do with it. When you tell me to go to my daughter, I don't trust you, Tru. Maybe you don't realize it, but always, instinctively, you put your family first. That's why you don't want me to divorce Charles. That's why you do want me to throw away everything I've worked for this past year and rush to Zandra's side. Not because of me—or Zandra, for that matter—but because it would be best for the Vales. Well, I don't want what's best for the Vales. I want what's best for me!"

The phone rang again. Giselle stared at Tru. He

reached for his shirt and continued to dress. She picked up the receiver. "Orlena?" She glanced at Tru's angry face. "No, nothing important."

"I'm having a little party at my villa at Beaulieu next month." The countess began to reel off her guests' names.

Giselle listened to her with half an ear while she watched Tru gather up the rest of his things. He looked at her for a moment, then turned and left the bedroom. After a moment she heard the door of the apartment close.

Giselle wiped her arm across her eyes, but there was no trace of the tears in her voice when she told the countess, "Let me check my appointments and get back to you."

Halloran put his hands over his ears, but Sheila's screech bored right through them as did Keefe's booming bass. Added to that was sixteen-year-old Doreen weeping in her room, a sound to rend a heart in two, though neither of her parents gave it notice. "Enough," he shouted himself. "Neither of you is listening to the other!"

"And what's it to you?" Keefe shouted back. "If you had a daughter, you would understand, Pat."

"How can you object to a nice clean-cut boy like Javier?" Sheila demanded of her husband.

"He's a Puerto Rican. A foreigner. I can't even pronounce his name!" Keefe bellowed.

"She only wants to date the lad," Halloran told his brother. "He hasn't yet asked for her hand."

"What good's dating if there's no hope of marriage?"

"Father Flannagan thinks he's a nice boy," said Sheila. "Do you set yourself above a priest?"

"Shut your mouth, woman," Keefe roared. "In my

house, I'm above a priest, yes! It's the damn Puerto Ricans who will be driving us out of our home again."

"Surely you don't long for the old days, Keefe," Halloran interjected. The old Hell's Kitchen tenement had fallen to a slum-clearance effort, a fact that still angered Keefe Halloran. Like many of their friends, the family had moved into the Amsterdam Houses complex of apartments, but now the Puerto Ricans and rural Negroes from the South far outnumbered the working-class Irish.

"I do," said Keefe. "All Father Flannagan cares is that the Puerto Ricans will keep him well supplied with sinners while our kind flee to the suburbs. You don't live here, Pat. You don't hear their damn roosters crowing every morning. You don't see the street gangs."

"And the Irish boys are not in gangs?"

"Does that make it right?"

The ringing phone stilled Halloran's reply. Doreen poked her head out her bedroom door, a hopeful expression on her tearstained face, as Sheila picked up the receiver.

"If it's the boy, hang up," Keefe thundered.

"I'll tell him," Sheila said into the phone, and then turned on Keefe as she hung up. "Will you be quiet, you great ape. It was a call for our Pat." Doreen ducked back into her bedroom and the wails began anew.

"What was it, then?" Halloran asked Sheila.

"They want you at your mistress's apartment."

Ordinarily, Halloran would have called back to see why he was needed since the mistress was out of the country. But just now he was glad of any excuse to take him out of the apartment.

"Running out on us, are you?" Sheila taunted.

"He knows better than to mix in a man's business in his own home," Keefe shouted at his wife.

"I've been called back to work, and that's why I'm leaving. But I have to say you're wrong in this, Keefe.

Sheila has the right of it. It won't hurt for Doreen to date her little Puerto Rican friend. She's a good girl."

Keefe's face turned red. "Be gone with you then," he bellowed. "If you or Father Flannagan were married, maybe then I'd listen to one of you. She's only a good girl until some boy makes her otherwise!"

"And isn't that just like a man!" Sheila shouted. "You think every female is in heat like an alley cat!"

"Married to you, why wouldn't I have that idea?"

Halloran dodged for the door when Sheila hefted a cup. He heard the smash of crockery before he reached the stairs.

But when he got to the mistress's apartment, he found he was to be dispatched to pick young Zandra up at Grand Central Station. "And why couldn't you have told me that in the first place?" he raged at the maid.

"It was Mrs. Durand who called from France and said for you to come home. Miss Zandra called after that," the maid said, dabbing her eyes with a handkerchief.

Halloran recognized the lace. He snatched the linen square away from her and gave her a slap. "Don't be poaching from the mistress."

"She gave it to me," the woman wailed, but she made no move to grab it back.

Halloran ignored her, already on his way back to the garage. He dropped the handkerchief in a garbage pail on the way. He would not see it back in the mistress's possession, even laundered, not after that creature had blown her nose in it!

By the time he reached Grand Central Station, Halloran's rage had focused on Zandra Vale. A freak, the girl was, he told himself as he followed her out to the car, loaded down with her luggage. Not her mother's daughter in looks, though a man might find that dark hair and ivory skin attractive were it not on a six-foot-tall bean pole like this gawk. Still, she had a sly way of moving her body that made men turn and watch her pass, he noticed.

Not her mother's daughter in actions, either. She climbed into the car and crossed her long legs, without a thank you for his holding the door. Before he had put her luggage in the trunk and slipped behind the wheel, she was already puffing away on a cigarette.

Halloran turned to stare at the backseat. "And does your mother know about that nasty habit?"

She shrugged.

"Put it out. There'll be no smoking in this car."

Zandra gave him a long look, as though he didn't exist. She turned to the window, the cigarette still in her mouth. All the way back to the mistress's apartment, the smell of tobacco smoke fed Halloran's rage.

He had hardly gotten Zandra's bags unloaded when one of the maids came to tell him that he was to call his brother. "Was there no message?" She shook her head and retreated toward the door. "Pick up this, then, you useless thing," he said, shoving one of the bags her way.

It took two trips to carry all of young Zandra's luggage to her room. Before he arrived with the second load, she had already pawed through the first, scattering clothes everywhere, changed, and flitted out of the house.

Halloran watched grim-faced, but there was nothing he could do. For a moment he considered calling the mistress in France to report on her daughter's behavior. He would do it, too, if he did not dread adding to the mistress's load. She was seldom home these days. If she wasn't hawking her wares to department stores in the United States, she was off to Europe to oversee the start of the Paris branch of Giselle Durand Cosmetics. Every salesgirl in every store had to be trained to her standards. Every buyer had to be wooed personally by her. The mistress burned with such a bright flame Halloran feared for

her health. Two weeks ago she had been in Texas, then
on the train to Arizona and the West Coast, then back
across the country by train, and on a plane to France. She
lived like a Gypsy now, never in one place for more than a
few days. He had little enough chance to drive her and he
missed her dearly.

Halloran went down to the kitchen to phone his
brother. "Is that you, at last?" Keefe boomed.

"Don't shout. I can hear you," Halloran said.

"It's shouting I feel like. The next time a man and
his wife disagree, have the kindness to stay out of it!"

"What's happened now?"

"She's gone." Keefe began to weep.

Patrick Halloran's heart quivered. "Sheila?"

"No, you great fool! Doreen! Doreen has run off
with that greasy-haired boyo from Puerto Rico!"

"Run off?"

"To marry, the note says. And if not, I'll break her
neck, I promise you. You and Father Flannagan.
Meddling where you don't belong."

Halloran heard Sheila in the background, shouting
something.

"Shut up, woman!" Keefe roared. "And what could
he have done if he had been here, except cause more
trouble?"

The receiver slammed down, and Halloran sagged
back against the wall. Doreen. She was just a baby. She
had no business marrying. If he had been there, she
would have listened to her uncle Pat.

Halloran's face hardened. He would have been
there except for the summons to pick up young
Zandra. What an evil child, and now look what she had
done to his family.

Zandra lay on her bed. Three weeks after being
kicked out of school, she was beginning to regret it.

She had hoped that Wesley and Noel would have time for her, but they were too busy working for Vale Enterprises. When she was small, Zandra used to feel sorry for her cousins because their father died in the war. But now Uncle Tru seemed to regard his twin's sons as his own children.

Zandra had heard the gossip that Uncle Tru was having an affair with her mother, but she'd been with them a million times, and they seemed less interested in each other than in their separate businesses. Besides they were old. Mother was nearly thirty-six, and Uncle Tru was ten years older. So was Aunt Alex, of course, but she never seemed that old, even if she was Uncle Tru's twin.

If Uncle Tru hadn't sent Father to Europe, Aunt Alex would be here and Zandra could have some fun instead of staying in this dull apartment. Life was so unfair, she thought. Aunt Alex should have been her mother and not her aunt.

Zandra reached for the phone, not bothering to glance at the clock, and put through a call to the villa in the south of France.

"My God!" Aunt Alex said when the servant finally roused her. "Do you have any idea what time it is?"

"I want to come over there," Zandra said. "Send me the money for an airplane ticket to Nice."

Alex yawned noisily. "What about school?"

"Which one?"

"What?"

"The one I just left? Or the one I'm going to? I was thrown out of Wellington for cheating."

"For heaven's sake, Zandra!"

"It was a mistake, Aunt Alex. I wouldn't—"

"That's exactly what the boys used to say."

For some reason that gave Zandra a little thrill of pride. Then she felt called upon to defend her cousins. "They're not boys, Aunt Alex. They're men. Noel is going to be twenty-five and Wesley will be—"

"For heaven's sake, Zandra. I don't need to be awakened out of a sound sleep to be told I have children that old." She muttered something Zandra didn't catch.

"Is there someone with you, Aunt Alex?"

"I'll know you're a grown-up when you realize that's an improper question. Where is your mother?"

"Paris, I think," Zandra said sullenly. "But I'm not going to call her."

"No, I wouldn't think that was a good idea. And I definitely wouldn't ask her if there's someone in bed with her. Your uncle Tru might object."

Was it true, then? Zandra wondered. She could hear the hum of the transatlantic cable in the silence.

"I can see that you're at loose ends, darling. But I have a perfectly wonderful solution for you."

The false heartiness in her tone told Zandra that whatever it was, it wouldn't be something she'd enjoy. "Won't you send me the money for the ticket?"

"You know I want you here with me, but if I let you come, I would be selfish. Thinking only of my own best interests and not yours. No, what you need is right there in New York."

"Not a school here. No one goes to school in the city."

"I'll leave the chore of finding a new school up to your mother. No, I meant your mother's little company." Aunt Alex's scornful chuckle showed what she thought of Giselle Durand Cosmetics. "Thanks to my hard work, part of it is going to be yours one day. It's time you started learning something about it. I know you're not grateful now, but someday—"

"What do you want me to do? Peddle cosmetics door-to-door!"

"I want you to learn everything about Giselle Durand Cosmetics from the ground up. Someday you'll be running it. You need to be worthy of the responsibility."

"But—"

"Look at Noel and Wesley," her aunt said. "How interested could they be in building ships? That's more Tru's line. But they know that someday they'll inherit everything, so they're working hard to learn it all."

"Are you sure that you wouldn't rather have me there with you?" Zandra asked forlornly, although she already knew she had lost the argument.

"Of course I would. But I have to think of your future, just as I always have. You must promise me you'll make an effort to think of it, too."

"I promise."

"And today isn't too early to do something constructive, is it?"

"No, it's not. I'll make you proud of me, Aunt Alex."

"I know you will, darling. Now I really must go."

As soon as she hung up, Zandra bounced out of bed and began to rifle through her closet. What exactly would a rising young cosmetics' executive wear?

TWO

Still in her nightgown, Giselle walked out onto the balcony of her Paris apartment with a small mirror. Ignoring the view, she held the mirror at an angle that allowed her to examine the texture of her skin in the merciless sunlight. In a few short weeks she would be another year closer to forty. She was pleased to see that information was not yet etched into her face. The whole future of her company rested on the condition of her skin.

As always, the jolt of recognition that another year had passed made her think of Benjamin. He would be eleven now. Giselle pictured him as a chubby-cheeked, blond-haired boy in a baseball uniform; the image was from a magazine photograph she had seen of Bryan's son a few years ago.

She returned her mirror to its case and poured herself a second cup of coffee. The maid had left the door to the living room open when she brought in the breakfast tray, and Giselle could see the arrangement of red roses that had arrived last night still sitting on the table where the maid had placed them, the ivory envelope visible through the greenery. She had replaced the card in the envelope as soon as she read it, but it would require an answer. She took a sip from the cup in her hand and grimaced; the coffee had grown cold while she stared at the roses.

Henri Laud had planned every moment of this day, except the hour it would start. When he arrived at the building that housed the Paris branch of Giselle Durand Cosmetics, Giselle Durand herself was already there. A cool, competent Frenchman, Henri had spent five years working in New York before returning to Paris to take over this branch of Giselle Durand. He knew that his staff joked that his unruly curls gave him the look of a poodle although no one dared say that to his face. This morning he did indeed feel like a poodle as he hurried to greet his employer and then trailed behind her as she poked and pried into every detail of the Paris operation like a canny French housewife checking the operation of her household.

Finally she finished, and he was able to usher her into the private dinning room just off his office where a lavish lunch was to be served, complete with several wines. Henri was certain his budget would be approved for every penny after this luncheon.

Just as he drew out Madame's chair his secretary rushed in to inform her there was an urgent call for her from New York. Henri waved away Madame's apologies as she went to take the call, but he vowed to himself that his stupid cow of a secretary had worked her last day for him.

"Jessie?" Giselle asked her secretary when she picked up the telephone in Henri's office. "Is something wrong?"

"I hated to bother you with this," Jessie Fiedler said. "But the whole company up in arms."

The pause was so long Giselle thought she must have been disconnected. "Hello? Jessie? Are you there?"

"I'm sorry, I really don't think it's my place to tell you this, but everyone else seems to think—"

"Is it Charles Revson again? Are his salesmen—"

"No, that seems to be under control for now."

"Then what?"

"It's Zandra."

"Zandra?"

"She's here every day. Snooping. Prying. You know how delicate some of the egos are in this business."

Giselle chuckled. "Doesn't it make any difference that she'll own a sizable piece of the company one day?"

"It's her attitude. If she approached them with a little more respect, perhaps it would make a difference."

"Tell them for me that it does make a difference," Giselle said, a note of steel in her voice. "I'm glad she's showing an interest in the company. And I don't consider it snooping or prying."

"I will pass that message along."

The formality in Jessie's voice made Giselle soften. "It's only until the fall," she said. "Until I can get her into another school. Surely everyone can cope that long."

"Of course they can," Jessie Fiedler agreed, but the tone of her voice made Giselle wonder if that was true. "Oh, I almost forgot to mention the sketches."

"What sketches, Jessie?"

"Caricatures, really. Your daughter has a wicked talent. I've gathered up all the ones I could find and mailed them to you. I laughed out loud when I saw them. Even the one of me," she added ruefully. "You'll understand when you see them why the uproar has been so violent.

Especially the one she did of Ed Crown during the sales meeting." Ed Crown was Giselle's second-in-command at the cosmetics company. "She did have a good idea for a new product line, even though Ed was so furious about the caricature he wouldn't listen. Have you ever thought of marketing teen cosmetics?"

"Zandra thought of that?"

"Not only thought of it, but had facts and figures all prepared. If only she were a little more tactful, she might have gotten a hearing from Ed. As it was, the meeting ended in an uproar, with the two of them shouting at each other."

"Ed wouldn't behave like that in a sales meeting!"

"The two of them make an explosive mixture."

"He'll just have to tolerate the situation until I get Zandra into another school. You can tell him so."

Giselle hung up and turned to find Henri at her elbow, ready to escort her back into the dining room. "I'm sorry," she told her manager. "I really don't feel like eating now. I believe I'll just go back to my apartment."

"But . . . but the budget figures, Madame!"

"Send them over to me this afternoon."

After she departed, Henri marched back into his office and fired his secretary on the spot. Then he sat down with a pencil and began to whittle the budget figures down to an amount that a sober Madame would approve.

Giselle ignored the maid dusting the living room and walked over to the roses. She removed the envelope from the bouquet, took out the card, and reread the message. *If your business is finally finished, how about meeting me in Rome next week? You need some sun and fun in your life,* Tru had written in broad, masculine strokes.

She hadn't seen or heard from Tru for a couple of months, not since she'd gotten the phone call from Agatha Bamfield telling her Zandra had been expelled from Wellington. She hadn't meant to blow up at him, but nine years of waiting for him to declare himself had suddenly overwhelmed her. After Zandra was returned to her, Giselle had waited for Tru to say it was time to get a divorce from Charles, time they were married. Over a year passed before she finally realized that he didn't want her to divorce his brother, that he didn't intend to marry her. She wasn't sure if he thought she wasn't good enough to marry him, or whether he wanted to protect the Vale family from the stigma of divorce. Whatever the reason, it meant that he put the Vale family first in his life, just as his father had done, just as Alex did. A coolness had come into their relationship. They never spoke of it, but it was there, nonetheless. Tru came and went in her life, asking for no commitment from her and giving none in return—a very lonely life, Giselle admitted to herself. She was still young, still beautiful, but for how long?

She reread the card. "Your business," he had written. As though running a large corporation were something that could be concluded in a few weeks' time. "Your little business," Alex had called it.

Giselle ran her fingers through her hair. Actually, the corporation was doing fine without her moment-to-moment guidance. The meetings she had come to Paris for had gone well, especially the one with Ellefson, the perfumer. Ellefson's company was responsible for many of the finest perfumes in the world and the price for his cooperation was astronomical. But Giselle knew in her heart that it was time to bring out a fragrance. Otherwise, Giselle Durand Cosmetics, as well as it had done, was just one "little business" among many. The right perfume could do for her what Youth-Dew had done for Estée Lauder's line.

She had planned for this moment for almost nine years, but again and again she had let herself be talked out of it. This time she was going forward. Ellefson had come up with a fragrance that she knew was right for the company. Now the papers were signed, and the fragrance was hers. That was the reason she couldn't rush to Zandra's side when she was expelled from school. From what Jessie had told her today on the telephone, Giselle saw that if she returned now, it would look as though she were rushing to Zandra's rescue. Not a very auspicious beginning for Zandra with the company.

If she had told Tru the reason for her Paris meetings, he would have argued against sinking so much money into the launching of a new perfume—just as he had from the beginning. Only now he was no longer a part of the company. Buying him out had been the correct thing to do. She looked down at the card. "Sun and fun," Tru had written. Perhaps he was right.

"Does Madame desire anything?" the maid asked.

"Remove those roses," Giselle told her.

"But, madame, they are still beautiful."

"Get them out of here."

The girl gave a slight curtsy. "As you wish, madame."

When she was alone in the room, Giselle picked up the phone and called the countess. "Orlena? Yes, it's Giselle Durand. I know I turned down your lovely invitation a few weeks ago, but I find my plans have changed. Do you still have room to include me in your house party?"

"Of course, I do," Orlena said. "And I have some very handsome escorts for you to choose among. I hope you'll be able to join me on the yacht afterward."

Giselle hesitated only a moment. "I'd love to. Someone just told me I need some sun and fun in my life."

When the countess hung up, Giselle rang the operator

again and arranged for a one-word cable to Tru in Rome: *No.*

In the basement of the Giselle Durand building, Halloran stood beside the car, waiting for Miss Zandra to appear. It irked him to be at the girl's beck and call. He had bent the ear of the mistress's prissy secretary and gotten her to call Giselle in Paris when the girl first started her nonsense of working here, but it had done no good. The mistress could not see her daughter for what she was, a bossy bitch and a troublemaker besides.

His Doreen was not like that. His niece had gotten herself married after all, and now there was a little one on the way. November, Keefe was telling one and all, but Halloran was guessing October or even September. Otherwise sweet Doreen would not have defied her mum and dad.

With much giggling and chatter, the employees of Giselle Durand left for the evening. Zandra Vale's height made her stand out. Halloran had to admit there was something striking about the girl. She looked like a model from one of Doreen's women's magazines.

"Take me home," Zandra told him without so much as a thank you, sir, and opened the car door for herself.

Bloody bitch, he thought. Just like the aunt. A shame the mistress had been cursed with such as this.

In her cabin, Giselle glanced at the ship's clock on the wall and then sat down to read through the packet of mail she had brought on board with her. She had become a frequent guest on the countess's yacht as well as at her delightful villa in the hills above Beaulieu. This time she had flown from Paris to Athens at Orlena's invitation. One of Orlena's uniformed crew had met her and driven her down the coast to Vouliagmeni, where the countess's yacht was moored. Now they were anchored off Majorca in the aquamarine waters of the Bay of Formentor.

She pushed aside the mail and reached for her playing cards. Ed Crown kept importuning her to return to New York, and the truth was she had stayed in Europe far longer than she had intended. Not that it wasn't to the company's benefit. Her friendship with Orlena had blossomed into full-fledged membership in the society of international nomads known as the jet set. She was her own best advertisement and she emphasized it with free cosmetics samples for all her new friends. But that wasn't the real reason she had been reluctant to return to New York. Tru was there now, and she knew that when she returned, she would have to build a new life without him. The prospect of that was proving far harder to face than she had imagined.

She lost the hand of solitaire, but the cards had worked their magic once more, she thought as she scooped them up. She suddenly realized what it was she really wanted to do.

"I've decided to get a divorce," Giselle told Orlena. She and the countess were seated at the bar on the upper aft deck. Orlena signaled the bartender, a handsome Spaniard of twenty-four or twenty-five. "Thank you, Carlos," the countess said. "Would you mind fetching Hubert for me."

"Shall I tell him his presence is required immediately, Countess?" Carlos inquired.

"Not immediately, no." When the door closed behind him, she sighed. "Such a bad boy! Never sleep with the help, darling. It makes for discipline problems."

"Orlena! You didn't?"

The countess sighed again. "Unfortunately, yes.

And now Hubert is insisting I fire him." Hubert was the
yacht's chief steward. "Jealousy, I expect. I would never
make the mistake of sleeping with Hubert. He's too
essential to my well-being." She sipped her drink.
"Now, for your extraordinary announcement, my dear.
I must advise you not to get a divorce. No. No. No."

"But you know I haven't seen Charles in years. I'm
independent of him in every way, including financially."

"But to be a divorced woman? No. No. No."
Although they were alone in the spacious bar, the
countess leaned closer and lowered her voice confiden-
tially. "A husband, especially absent, is so handy for
avoiding entanglements. Say you find a charming man,
young like Carlos, but of our own class, a perfect
escort—"

"A gigolo?"

"I prefer the term *minet* for these young escorts.
Men always seek the companionship of younger
women. Why should we not do the same?"

"What has this to do with my getting a divorce?"

"When your baby-faced escort comes to you with
his protestations of undying love, begging for your
hand in marriage, then you pull your husband out of
your pocket and say, 'So sorry, my dear.'"

The countess's attempt at a sad face was so comical Giselle laughed. "And if your husband comes to you
for a divorce, Orlena?"

"Ah, no, my dear. Our husbands will never do that.
We serve the same purpose for them, you see."

"No, I don't see. What purpose is that?"

"Our husbands have a thing in common, do they
not?"

"Absent wives?"

"Is it possible you do not know?" For once the volu-
ble countess seemed at a loss for words. After a
moment she said, "You are a woman of the world, my
dear. Surely you know of men who love men?"

"You're saying Charles is a homosexual?" Giselle laughed. "Really, Orlena. Those kinds of rumors used to madden him, but I assure you he is not."

"I know you think that because he has slept with you that makes him something else. But he is what he is. And so, too, is Silvain, which is why I have this lovely plaything all to myself, and my houses, and my jewels, and . . ." The countess waved her hands. "And everything. And so will you, if you ignore this stupid idea of divorce."

"But I'm not getting money from Charles."

"He gives you something equally important. A distinguished name."

"Not one that I'm using, dear Orlena."

"Nevertheless, it is important to your social status, and that we both know." The countess looked over her shoulder. "Ah, Hubert, what are those awful things in your hand. Not more cablegrams."

The chief steward handed the sheaf of messages to Giselle. She riffled through them quickly and saw that half were from Zandra, and the rest, except for one, were from Ed Crown. The remaining message was from Jessie Fiedler and said simply, *Do something!*

"This child is driving me crazy," Giselle told Orlena. "For years I've wanted her to be interested in me and my life, and now that I've finally gotten what I wished for, I'm sorry for ever wanting it."

"Ignore all this," Orlena said with an airy wave of her hand. "Put the child back in school where she belongs."

Giselle put the messages aside. "Perhaps you're right."

Zandra glanced around the main drawing room of the Gold Coast version of an English Tudor manor house and wished she could sink into the floor. She turned slightly so that her back was to her date, and said to her friend Myra Hayworth, "A graveyard would be livelier."

Myra, short and delicate, with a pink face and curly hair, gave a horrified giggle. "Someone will hear you!"

"Not unless they remembered their hearing aids."

Ralph Martin, Zandra's date, tapped her on the shoulder. "What did you say?"

Zandra shrugged away from his hand. "Nothing to you." Why couldn't he get the picture? As hard as she tried to ignore him, he persisted in standing beside her, letting the whole room see that her date was shorter than she. Ralph groped for her hand. She snatched it away and clasped her arms across her chest. Surely, if she were rude enough, he would give up and wander away until it was time to leave. Zandra couldn't believe her luck. With one phone call, her mother had managed to destroy Zandra's whole life. First her mother had informed her that she was being shipped off this fall to some California school. In the meantime she would be tutored at home. "But what about all my ideas for the company?" Zandra had asked.

"They've caused quite a stir," her mother had said. "I heard the outcry all the way over here. I'm curious, Zandra. Did you really think I would fire Ed Crown on your say-so? He's a very good manager."

"He's rude and obnoxious."

"I haven't noticed that."

"You're not here. I am. He treats me like a child."

"Zandra, the man is in his forties. You are a child to him. You say you're interested in making Giselle Durand a better company. Try to understand that I need someone there I can trust to manage things when I have to be away."

"If you fire him, I can manage the company for you."

Her mother's chuckle made Zandra squirm.

"You're not quite seventeen. Don't you think that's a little young?"

"Noel and Wesley both started working for Uncle Tru when they were my age."

The amusement vanished from Giselle's voice. "What the Vales do or do not do doesn't concern me. I want you to stay away from the company. No more trouble with Ed Crown." Just the memory of the conversation made Zandra's cheeks burn, but that wasn't the worst of it. Her mother had gone on to tell her that she had engineered a double date for Zandra with Myra Hayworth to Cathy Freeland's party. Zandra liked Myra all right; they had known each other since grammar school. But Cathy had been one of Felicia Hudson's friends at Wellington. And Ralph—from Europe her mother hadn't been able to see that Zandra would be a head taller than Ralph Martin, the son of her mother's old school chum.

"May I get you some more punch?" Ralph asked.

Zandra turned and looked at him as though he were a stranger who had just wandered up. "Isn't there anything alcoholic to drink?"

"Zandra," Myra cried, horrified.

"You're quite a joker." Ralph reached for her cup.

"Zandra? Don't you want to go to the little girls' room?" Myra asked as her date left with Ralph.

"No thanks."

"I want to talk to you."

"Talk."

"Upstairs." Myra grabbed her wrist and pulled her toward the staircase.

An older boy was coming down as they mounted the stairs. He was good-looking, Zandra saw in a flash, a ruggedly handsome blond, but more than that, he was tall. If he were my date, I could have worn heels, she thought, and smiled as he passed her. The boy smiled back and her heart fluttered. Puzzled, she

turned to stare after him. She had seen his face somewhere. "Who was that?" she asked Myra.

"Felicia Hudson's date. He's in college."

Zandra halted. "Felicia's here?"

Myra jerked her arm. "Come on!"

"What's wrong with you?" Zandra said when Myra
pulled her into the bathroom. "I told you what Felicia
did."

"Just don't start anything here. I promised Cathy
you wouldn't do anything wild."

"You shouldn't have done that because I just
might. This is the most boring party I've ever been to
in my life." Zandra walked over to the mirror. She
looked more like twenty-one than sixteen, Zandra
thought. Watching the salesladies training at her mother's company, she had learned a lot about makeup over
the past few weeks.

Myra wasn't through with her yet. "I don't suppose
you realize the reputation you're getting. Being kicked
out of Wellington is the worst thing that could happen
to a girl. I don't know where in the world you'll go
next."

"There are always schools if your parents have
money."

"But not good schools," Myra said earnestly.

"I don't see what that matters," Zandra told her.

"You're really hopeless, aren't you? Well, I'm not
going to waste any more time arguing. Are you ready
to go back down?"

"You go ahead."

When Myra left, Zandra dug around in her purse
until she found the pack of cigarettes she had been carrying with her for weeks. She lit one and looked at herself in the mirror. Now I look like a woman and not a
teenager, she thought. She smiled at her reflection.

Coming downstairs again, Zandra paused on the
landing to take a drag on her cigarette and survey the

crowd. At the far corner of the main drawing room, Ralph, a cup of punch in each hand, waited patiently for her to reappear.

Poor Ralph. Stuck with a geek. Zandra took pity on him and started to descend the stairs again. Just then, she caught sight of the college man with the vaguely familiar face who had smiled at her as he was coming downstairs. He caught her glance, and raised one eyebrow in inquiry.

Her stomach contracted, but the chance to pay back Felicia was too good to miss. Besides, he was tall. Zandra nodded, and the college man grinned at her. She concentrated very hard on descending the stairs without falling on her face.

When she reached the ground floor, Ralph met her with a cup of punch in either hand. "There you are," he said. Then he spotted the cigarette in her hand. "Uh, are you sure you should be doing that?" He glanced over his shoulder toward the chaperons.

"Positive." She snatched the cup and quickly drained it. "It's so warm in here, I'm just parched. Would you mind getting me another?"

"Why, of course not," Ralph said.

When he disappeared into the crush, the college man came over. "Are you as bored as I am?"

She enjoyed the sensation of tilting her head back to look up at him. "Until this moment."

"Your friend is on his way back."

"What a pity I won't be here."

As they drove away from the Freeland house the headlights made the rhododendron-lined drive look like a cave ahead of them. "How did you ever end up with such a childish bunch?" the college man asked Zandra.

"Who cares about them? What's your name?"

"Bry Rawlings. What's yours?"

"Zandra Vale."

"Hey! Charles Vale's daughter?" When she nodded, he said, "I think our fathers used to be friends."

She shrugged. "So what?"

"So maybe I won't just love you and leave you like I do the rest of the girls."

"Rawlings?" That was where she had seen his face. In the family photograph on top of the bureau on Liz Rawlings's side of the room at school. "Your sister Liz and I were roommates at Wellington," Zandra blurted before she thought.

"You roomed with Elizabeth? But she's just sixteen."

"A couple of years ago," she improvised quickly. "I was an upperclassman."

Bry braked at the end of the long drive. When he turned to her, she could see his puzzled look by the dashboard lights. He was about to ask her how old she was. Zandra scooted closer, pressing against him. "I envy those other girls," she said.

"What other girls?"

"The ones you love and leave."

"Don't envy them." He touched his lips to hers. She let his searching tongue into her mouth.

"Wow," he said after a moment. "You're really something." He kept one arm around her, pressing her body close to his, as he pulled out on to the main road.

Zandra's heart pounded. "Where are we going?"

"You'll see."

When Bry turned down another drive between two granite pillars, she was disappointed. She'd hoped he was going to kiss her again, not take her to another party. But then she saw that the structure rising out of the gloom at the end of the drive was the charred shell of one of the old Long Island mansions. "Who lived there?" she asked as they got out of the car.

He opened the trunk and took out a blanket tied in a tight bundle. "Who knows. Anyway, they're gone now." He took her hand and guided her toward the edge of the cliff overlooking the Sound. "There are steps here somewhere."

They climbed down toward the beach where a boat house still stood. From a distance its walls, overgrown with vines, looked nearly intact. When they drew closer, she saw the shattered windows and rotting cypress shingles. "That's where we're going?"

"It's not as bad as it looks."

Inside, the boat house smelled of damp and decay. Bry released her hand and knelt to untie the bundled blanket. Something rustled in the shadows where the moonlight didn't reach, and Zandra took a step backward.

"Squirrels." Bry rolled the blanket open. Inside were a bottle of rum, several bottles of Coca-Cola, and two glasses. "Sit down," he said as he began to mix two drinks.

Zandra remained standing. "Was that for Felicia?"

"You know Felicia?"

"Was she your date tonight?"

"Why?"

"Was she?"

Bry handed her a glass. "Yes, she was. And she's going to be plenty mad that I left her at the Freelands."

Zandra took a sip. Lots of rum and very little Coke. She'd never had warm Coke before. Or a drink that strong. "Would you have mixed her drink like this?"

"No. She's just a kid. Not like you." He patted the blanket beside him.

Zandra sat and he immediately enfolded her in his arms. The thought that she had taken him away from Felicia made her cling to his lips longer than she would have otherwise.

"Wow," he said, when he pulled away. "You're some

kisser." He drained the rest of his drink. "Want another?"

By the time they finished the third drink, his hands were touching her under her skirt. She moaned with the feelings his fingers aroused.

When he suddenly rolled away, she reached to pull him back. "Did you bring anything with you?" he asked her, his voice hoarse.

"I don't—"

"A diaphragm?"

"No."

"I'll be right back." He moved away from her in the darkness and the floor of the boat house creaked. In a moment she felt him on the blanket beside her again.

"We shouldn't," she said as he reached under her skirt for the waistband of her panties.

"It's okay," he told her. "I've got a rubber."

When he entered her, she cried out. He only pumped for a minute more, then he moaned and collapsed against her.

"I'm sorry," he murmured against her neck. "You acted so—I didn't realize you were a virgin."

He was still inside her, although much diminished. "Don't worry about it," she said, hiding her face against his neck. "I'm glad it was with you."

He said, "Me too." He lay on top of her, not moving. After a moment he murmured, "It's my first time, too. I've carried that rubber in my wallet for three years."

She reached up and touched his cheek. "Bry," she breathed.

"That's nice," he said. He lowered his lips to hers, and she could feel him begin to grow once more. He began to move inside her, and she gasped with pleasure.

It was great that Zandra's mother was still out of town, Bry Rawlings thought as he let himself into his parents' apartment just before dawn. Making love in a bed beat the hell out of the floor of a mildewed boat house. He stopped just inside the door and slipped off his shoes.

"No need for that, Bry," Florence Rawlings said from the living room. "I'm awake." She switched on the light.

"Sorry, Mother."

"Shall I make you coffee?"

"I could use some sleep more."

"Where have you been, Bry? Out again till all hours."

Suddenly she was crying. Bry's stomach twisted. His father had made her cry; he had always promised himself that he wouldn't. He went over and put his arm around her shoulder. "Don't do that, Mother."

"What's happening?" his sister Elizabeth asked from the doorway. "Why is Mother crying?" Ten-year-old Franny stared at Bry with huge eyes, as though he were an ogre.

He ran his hand through his hair. "Go back to bed. Both of you. It's none of your business."

"Who were you with, Bry?" Florence demanded. "Some of those wild boys from school?"

"I was with a girl, Mother."

"What girl? Do we know her family?"

"I know," Elizabeth said. "He's been dating that awful Zandra Vale."

Bry felt his mother stiffen beneath his arm. "What do you mean 'awful'?" he asked his sister.

"She was the roommate I told you about. The one who got thrown out of Wellington."

"Go to bed!" Florence Rawlings told her daughters. Bry started to rise. "Just a moment, Bry. There's something I want to tell you."

When the girl called, Florence was not surprised. In fact she had instructed the maid that any female callers for Bry were to be referred to her. "Who is this?" she asked.

"Zandra Vale. Is Bry there?"

"He's gone back to school."

"Already? But—"

"He went back early because I asked him to. Because I didn't want him associating with a girl like you."

"Like—but you don't know me, Mrs. Rawlings."

"I know your mother, Miss Vale. That's all I need to know. Don't call my son again." She slammed down the phone. And smiled. How good she felt. At least she had saved Bry from the clutches of one of the Vale women.

Zandra cried the rest of the evening, until her eyes were swollen and ghastly. When the servant went to bed, she placed a call to Europe. "Aunt Alex?" she blurted when Alexandra Mainwaring answered the phone. "Something terrible happened," and then she began to cry again.

Alex waited until Zandra's tears had slowed and then pried the story out of her. "Poor Zandra. No one warned you. I should have, I suppose, but who wants to tell a young girl those things about her own mother."

"What things, Aunt Alex? I don't understand."

"I suppose there's no kind way to do it. I must be brutally frank with you. Florence Rawlings has good reason to hate your mother and to refuse to allow her son to associate with you."

"But Bry said that his father and mine were friends."

"They were. That was what made it more awful when your mother seduced Bryan Rawlings."

Zandra gasped. "I don't believe it."

"Neither did I at first. Until she became pregnant by Bryan Rawlings and tried to pass the child off as Charles's . . ."

"You mean Benjamin?"

"Your parents didn't separate because of Benjamin's death, Zandra. They separated because Giselle was an unfaithful wife. Will you forgive me for not telling you sooner? You were so young. I tried to spare you, and then to have you find out like this . . . I'm sorry." Zandra felt her cheeks burning. "Will you forgive me?"

When Zandra hung up, all she wanted to do was cry, but there were no tears left.

Giselle arrived home with a great bustle. Zandra found her in the entry hall, surrounded by dozens of suitcases. Her mother was gazing into the living room. "I'd forgotten how dowdy this place looks," she said by way of greeting. "The first thing I plan to do is get a new apartment."

"I thought you liked it here because Uncle Tru lives upstairs," Zandra said.

"Why would that make any difference?" She hugged Zandra. "We'll have dinner together tonight, and you can tell me how you're getting along with your tutor."

She swept on by, lovely, delicious smelling. Standing there, Zandra wanted to throw her arms around her mother again. To forget all the hateful things her aunt had told her. But then she thought of Bry, of what she had lost.

"It's all arranged," Giselle told Zandra at dinner that evening. "You'll be leaving for school the last week in August. That will give us plenty of time to refurbish your wardrobe." She paused while the maid brought the main course. "So what have you been doing with yourself?"

Zandra looked up. "I talked to the wife of an old friend of yours last week."

Giselle smiled. "Oh? Which old friend?"

"Bryan Rawlings."

Zandra was gratified to see her mother go pale. Thank you, Aunt Alex, she thought. The truth is a wonderful weapon.

1962

ONE

Keefe Halloran moved through the mourners crowded into his fourth-floor walk-up apartment, white and numb in his grief. After the West Eighty-fourth Street riot last year between the Negroes and Puerto Ricans, Keefe and Sheila had moved across the Brooklyn Bridge to the Heights. Doreen, her husband, and baby remained in their apartment on the edge of Spanish Harlem. It was there someone shot the couple for their small mite of cash and left the two-year-old to scream for a day and a night before someone noticed his cries.

Halloran caught Keefe by the shoulder. "Sit down," he said, and fetched his brother a whiskey. Sheila broke out in fresh sobs, and the women gathered about her. She would have the care of young Francis to see her through, Halloran thought. Poor Keefe had never reconciled himself to the marriage, and that only made today harder for him.

The little one began to wail. Sure enough, Sheila rose and went to him. Halloran looked into his brother's face and felt the same pain he saw there. Lovely Doreen with her red curls and her laughing face. Gone.

"And what will they be doing with the little one?" someone asked, but not so quietly Keefe didn't hear.

"We'll raise him, of course," he bellowed. "And any man who says a word against his father will taste my fists."

"No one will speak against the poor dead boy, Keefe," said Halloran. Young Javier had been the fine husband to Doreen the priest had predicted, but who could have guessed their life together would be so short.

"I'll light a candle for them," Mrs. O'Connor said.

"Fine," Halloran said. Perhaps a candle would ease her mind. He hoped the bottle would ease his.

Jessie Fiedler bolted through the door of Giselle's office and closed it behind her. Giselle looked up, amused. "Are you trying to keep someone out?"

Jessie leaned back against the door. "Zandra's here."

Giselle took a deep breath. "Not again."

"This time she says she's not going back to college. She wants a full-time job with the company."

"Really? That's not a bad idea."

"You weren't here the summer she decided she was going to run the company!"

"I keep hearing about it. She's nineteen now. Someday she'll control a substantial portion of the business."

"When she does, you won't have a single employee left."

"Jessie!"

"It's her attitude. She thinks she's better than everyone else. If you put her in any position of authority, you'll have wholesale resignations. And it won't do her any good to think she can just waltz in and start at the top."

"I'll keep that in mind. You know I value your opinion." That was the truth, although she felt Jessie was exaggerating. "Go ahead and show her in."

When Zandra entered, it was easier to believe Jessie's forecast. She was a lovely girl, tall and willowy, with the long dark hair and dark eyes that reminded Giselle so poignantly of Charles. But the scornful expression on her face was that of Alexandra Mainwaring.

Zandra backed away from Giselle's hug, dropped her knapsack on the floor, and plopped down on the sofa. "Jessie gave me the third degree before she'd let me in."

"She's my secretary. That's her job."

"To keep your daughter out?"

"She didn't keep you out. Here you are with your feet on my sofa." Giselle said it lightly, but the sight of Zandra's dirty-heeled boots on the pink damask made her fight to repress a shudder.

"I think you should fire her."

"For doing her job?"

Zandra shrugged. She pulled her feet under her and left a distinct black smudge across the damask.

"What do you plan to do with yourself now that you have so much free time?"

"Didn't she tell you? You say I'm going to be a part of this someday; well, now is the time."

"Then you should learn everything about the company. The hiring is done by Mr. Sanders. First floor."

"Mother!" Zandra said, and Giselle was struck by how infrequently her daughter called her that. How infrequently Zandra called her anything at all. "That's demeaning."

"I'm sure you wouldn't want any special favors just because you're the owner's daughter." Giselle ignored

Zandra's glare. "I'll give you one, however. I'll call Mr. Sanders and tell him you're on your way."

After the door closed behind Zandra, Giselle resisted the impulse to lean against it as Jessie had.

It wasn't often that the boss lady called down to Personnel. Mike Sanders wondered fleetingly if someone was pulling his leg. "I could have sworn you told me to give your daughter a job in the mail room."

"I did," said Giselle Durand. "I want her to have a position that's in line with her experience and education."

"You'll hear the fireworks all the way up there if I give her to Gordon. You weren't here the summer she decided she was taking over the company, were you?"

"Please, Michael. Just do what I asked."

Mike Sanders hung up the phone and wondered if he could resign and leave the country in the time it took an elevator to descend from the fifteenth floor. A knock sounded on his door. "Too late," he said aloud.

A lovely young woman with ivory skin, huge dark eyes, and long black hair opened the door. "What did you say?"

"I said, come in." She was a good four inches taller than he, but he liked tall women, especially when they were built like that. "Zandra? Wow!"

"My, my, little girl, how you've grown?"

"Right!"

"You called me the pain-in-the-ass boss's daughter the last time we met." The dark-haired beauty gave him a smile that almost broke his heart. "My mother said she was phoning you about a job for me."

Mike felt his face flush. "Ah, she just called."

"And?"

"The mail room."

Those lovely lips went from smiling to pouting.

"I'll try to change her mind," Mike said.

"Don't bother," she snapped.

"We could talk about it over dinner."

"Isn't there a rule about employees' dating?"

"Not that I know of."

"There should be," Zandra said sweetly. "I'll speak to Mother about it."

"I'll leave you two to talk over Miss Vale's duties," said Mike Sanders. "Good luck, Zandra."

Zandra felt a wave of embarrassment sweep over her as he left. She should have been nicer to him, but short men made her angry. So did the other employees of the mail room, she decided as she glanced around. The room had been full of laughter and jokes when she entered. When Mike Sanders introduced her to Gordon, the supervisor, all that died away, to be replaced with instant suspicion.

"Where shall I start?" Zandra asked Gordon. He had a small button of a nose that twitched as though he'd just caught a whiff of something unpleasant. If she were sketching him, she'd make him a rabbit, she thought, then realized she already had, the summer she was sixteen. Her cheeks warmed. She wondered if he'd seen the caricature.

"Why bother today?" Gordon told her. "Come in fresh tomorrow morning and I'll find something for you to do."

"Certainly," she said brightly, knowing that he intended to call around and find out just what was going on before he decided what to do with her.

After Zandra left on her way to Michael Sanders's office, Giselle flipped on the intercom. "Jessie? Call for the car. I'm going to knock off early today."

Jessie's voice came back loud and clear. "Good. You've been working entirely too hard."

"I'm glad someone thinks so." Funny how glamorous a life could look from the outside, and how empty and unfulfilling it could be in reality, Giselle thought. She was on the road twenty-six weeks of the year. Sometimes meeting with suppliers, sometimes with customers, sometimes mingling with the rich and royal of the jet set. No one seemed to understand that last was also a part of the job, and absolutely wearying at times.

And still, no matter how well the company did, everything boiled down to a fight with the money men. Each expansion, every need for new financing, brought all the old arguments out of the woodwork. She had thought that once she bought Tru out, everything would be smooth sailing. But after Ellefson presented her with the perfect fragrance, the arguments had started with her own people. No one liked the fragrance as much as she did. No one else thought it would be suitable for a wide range of women. By the time she browbeat everyone into accepting the fragrance itself, the name roused new animosities. She wanted to call it Lillian, for her mother. Too old-fashioned, had come the cry. It has to have a "young" word in the title, the ad agency had insisted; after all, you're competing with Youth-Dew. But on that she absolutely refused to budge. She was not competing with Youth-Dew, she told them; she was giving the women of the world her own special fragrance. It ended with her firing that agency after a particularly long meeting during which one of the men from the agency told the group that Giselle Durand knew nothing about women.

But that had worked out for the best, she thought as the elevator doors slid open on the ground floor. It had been Maury Austin from the new agency who convinced her the perfume should be marketed not under her mother's name, but her nickname, and Lilli was well on its way to becoming a legend in the industry. When the doorman opened the car door for her, Giselle was surprised to see Halloran behind the wheel. "I didn't expect you back so soon, Patrick."

"Would I be leaving you in the hands of a man like that a minute longer than necessary?" he said over his shoulder.

"Your family needs you now more than I do."

"They do not," he said as he pulled away from the curb. She knew him well enough to realize that was the end of it.

Zandra came and went from the apartment, tight-lipped and sullen. She made her own way to work each morning, refusing to ride with her mother. At the end of her first full week, she tried to complain of her treatment at the hands of the other employees. Giselle, remembering what Jessie had said, refused to listen. When Zandra retreated, Giselle thought perhaps she had succeeded. But by the end of the next week, she was complaining again.

This time Giselle lost her temper. "You have to fight your own fights," she told her daughter. "You have to be courageous. You have to learn that being beautiful and rich isn't enough. Your grandmother Lillian learned that. I learned it. Now it's your turn."

It was after six when Zandra arrived home. "Finally," Giselle said. "Cook's been holding dinner for us."

"I'm not hungry," Zandra told her mother, and stormed on into her bedroom, slamming the door behind her. She stared at her own angry reflection in her bedroom mirror. Why had she ever thought she wanted to work in her mother's company?

When she arrived in the mail room for her first full day, she could tell that the word had come down from her mother that she was to receive no special favors. The mail-room staff interpreted that decree liberally. The heaviest packages were hers to wrap. Any invoice with a problem was automatically hers. Missing items, billing problems, illegible handwriting—dump it on Zandra! But those things weren't as bad as the hazing. If she entered the ladies' room alone, the light was mysteriously switched off the moment she closed the stall door. When she started to pay for her lunch in the cafeteria the second day, she found that all the money had vanished from her purse. When she complained to Gordon, he told her she must be mistaken. But the incidents continued to escalate.

Zandra plopped down on the bed. She hated this room, she thought. Her mother had moved into this Park Avenue apartment three years ago, just after she shipped Zandra herself off to school in California. Everything had been bought new for Zandra's room, and she had never really felt it belonged to her.

Long past midnight, Zandra raided the refrigerator. Then she placed a call to her aunt at the villa in Nice.

"I don't understand your complaint," Alex said.

"They put me in the mail room. Packaging up shipments. Any moron could do it."

"Surely you didn't expect that woman to make it easy for you. Stand up for yourself, darling."

"But how?"

"You're a Vale," Alex scolded from half a world away. "Act like one."

The next morning, it was Gordon himself who sent Zandra to the storage room for forms. As soon as she stepped inside, the door shut behind her. The lock clicked.

She hammered on the door and screamed her lungs out, but no one came. If she hadn't found a discarded screwdriver behind a box, she wouldn't have been able to pry the door open. When she burst back into the mail room, Gordon looked at her and smiled. His button nose twitched, and Zandra suddenly realized that he had indeed seen the sketch of himself she'd done the summer she was sixteen.

Zandra walked over to her desk and picked up her purse. She went straight back to her mother's apartment and searched the rooms from top to bottom, taking all the cash she found and a pad of blank checks. She packed only what she could cram into her knapsack and departed without leaving a note or a message with the help.

By the time her flight landed at the Nice-Côte d'Azur airport, Zandra was tired and rumpled. Her mood was not improved by the first taxi driver she approached. He spat and muttered something about "the American flea market," before he turned away.

"It's your knapsack. He thinks you're one of us." An American by his voice, the boy had long stringy red hair and a sparse beard. On his back was a knapsack like hers and in his right hand he carried a guitar case. She had seen him boarding the plane ahead of her and ignored him.

"What exactly are we?"

He smiled. "He thinks we're beatniks. Actually we're free citizens of the world."

"And for that he dislikes us?"

"For that he can't stand us. Want a ride into Nice?"

Zandra looked around. The other taxi drivers were giving them hard stares. "Why not? It looks like you free citizens of the world have destroyed my chances of getting there any other way."

The group that met him was made up of three boys with the same stringy hair and straggling beards, and two girls in shapeless tunics with dirty blond hair that hung to their waists. Between them, they had two motor scooters, two more guitars, and a broken-down car that looked as though it couldn't limp its way into Nice. It was far too early to turn up at Aunt Alex's villa, so Zandra accepted their invitation to breakfast with them at a small café in the Vieille Ville, the old town, near the port. The meal consisted of hot black coffee, croissants, and plenty of butter and jam. Her appetite finally satisfied, Zandra looked around at the mixture of other young people, artists, and workingmen, crowded into the café this morning. A cinch Aunt Alex had never been in this part of Nice.

"A dive," said the boy from the airport. "But you should taste Vincent's bouillabaisse." The cook, an immense man with a gap-toothed smile, waved at him from the kitchen doorway. The boy leaned closer to her. "I saw you on the airplane," he said softly. "You didn't look happy."

"What's your name?"

"Dennis Norton. My friends call me Den. My father wants me to be a banker like him, but I have the soul of an artist." He scooted closer. "You look happier now."

Zandra glanced at the cook, who was still smiling from the kitchen door. "Does he bring the check?"

"He knows we don't have any money. We do odd jobs for him and we sing for our supper in the evenings."

"I have money." She pulled out her billfold. Den lunged for it, trying to push it below the table, but Vincent spotted the bills and hurried over. The amount they agreed on pretty well tapped out the last of the cash she had with her. Den saw that.

"Why didn't you wait? He wouldn't have asked you to pay. We have him trained. Now you're broke, too."

"It's all right. My aunt lives here."

"Family, huh. What a drag! If you decide to cut free, we'll be here for at least a couple more weeks."

"And then?"

"Then we'll be somewhere else."

"If I wanted to get in touch, where are you staying?"

The girl next to him put her arm around his shoulder and frowned at Zandra. "Do we still have a room, Paula?" Den asked the girl.

"Packed in like sardines, yes," Paula said with a Scandinavian accent. "Not for the likes of her." She kept her arm around Den's shoulder.

Den ignored Paula. "We're here every evening."

"Maybe I'll see you later," Zandra said as she stood.

Before she reached the door, Den was beside her, dangling a set of keys. "Want a ride to your aunt's place? Paula's loaned me her scooter."

Zandra glanced back at the table. Paula was glaring. "Sure," she said.

She shouted directions into his ear as she clutched his waist. They roared past the Cours Saleya where fruits, vegetables, and flowers were displayed in riotous colors. "If you hadn't spent all your money, I'd buy you flowers," Den shouted over his shoulder.

They turned on to the Quai des Etats-Unis, following its gentle curve until it became the Promenade des Anglais. The palm-lined avenue was already crowded with tourists from the luxury hotels, as was the beach down the steps. It was such a beautiful morning, with the wind whipping through her hair, and the blue Mediterranean stretching off toward the horizon, Zandra wished it could last forever.

When they reached the turnoff to the villa, Den pulled up. The house was visible ahead above the Italian pines. "You better walk the rest of the way," he told her. "Family takes a dim view of my kind."

She climbed off the scooter and shifted her knapsack to ease her shoulders. "Thanks," she said with a wave, and started up the road to the villa. When she got to the top of the hill, she looked back. Den still sat there, looking after her. She waved again and then forgot him.

The French she'd learned at Wellington was good enough to brush aside the maid's protests and get her inside the villa. "The bedroom of my aunt?" Zandra asked the girl.

The maid pointed.

When Zandra crossed the courtyard, she could hear the rhythmic sound of the mattress. So that was why Aunt Alex had been so distant. She had a new boyfriend. Forty-eight and still going for it! Zandra paused outside the door, listening to the masculine grunts and groans as she lit a cigarette. When Aunt Alex's cry of pleasure signaled the end of the festivities, Zandra ground out her cigarette with her boot heel and opened the door.

Her aunt's lover had his back to the door. "Fabienne, you stupid thing," her aunt cried. "Stay out until I call."

"Hello, Aunt Alex." Zandra grinned. "I see you're having fun." Her aunt turned first pale and then crimson.

The man beside Alex turned over. "Zandra?" said Charles Vale.

"Father?"

"It's not what you think, darling," Aunt Alex cried, but Zandra was no longer listening. She turned and fled.

Aunt Alex called her name, but Zandra kept going, out of the villa, down the hill.

Den was still where she had left him, smoking a cigarette, looking off into the distance, toward the

Mediterranean. He turned at the sound of the small avalanche of pebbles down the road before her. "Trouble?"

"Take me somewhere." Zandra paused only long enough to slip her knapsack over her shoulders. "Anywhere."

TWO

The Trastevere section of Rome was one of the poorest quarters of the city, a jumble of old houses and winding streets. It was late morning when the sun's rays finally penetrated the narrow alley and found the bare window of Zandra's room. When she got up, Den rolled over. She shook his shoulder. "Do you have any money for food?"

Den groaned and blinked. "Spent it all last night after the performance." He played his guitar two nights a week at one of the simple little trattorias so popular with tourists at night in the exciting old slum area.

Zandra bit back a reply. If she scolded or complained, Den would move out. For her entire life, she had always known Aunt Alex was there to serve as a lifeline. Now the lifeline was gone, and she was terrified of facing the future alone. She reached for her clothes.

"What are you doing?"

"Going out to earn some food money."

"You could earn a lot more if you'd fix yourself up."

"I told you I won't do that, Den."

"If I don't mind, I don't see why you would."

Zandra pulled on her tunic and turned to the mirror. "Sleeping with you doesn't make me a prostitute." She combed her hair with long angry strokes.

"Is that an invitation?" Den rolled out of bed and came to stand beside her. When he put his arms around her, she pulled away and reached for her knapsack.

"I'll see you this afternoon."

"Wait until I throw on my clothes," Den said. "I'll drop you off. I want the scooter."

That meant she would have to walk back from the Via Veneto. Tourists didn't visit the shadowy Trastevere in the daytime. Again she resisted the urge to complain, even though the Vespa was hers, bought and paid for by her earnings. She caught sight of herself in the cracked mirror on the far wall and turned away from the sight of the tall girl with long, lank hair. "Then hurry up. I'm starving."

When the museums and shops closed for the three siesta hours, Zandra thought about hiking back to the Trastevere in the broiling July sun, and then decided to eat first. The waiter at Doney's made her show him her money before he would allow her to pull up a chair at the outdoor café and order an enormous meal of spaghetti, meat, salad, and cheese. When she finished it all, she signaled for another glass of red wine. The waiter brought a large golden peach along with the wine, and she favored him with a warm smile so he wouldn't miss the tip she didn't plan to leave.

She looked up when she heard the scrape of a chair. "May I," said the sandy-haired man in the English-cut suit who stood there holding a sheet of paper in his hand.

"Wesley! Is it you?" She jumped up and hugged her cousin. "What are you doing here?"

Wesley Mainwaring sat down and handed her the paper he'd been carrying. "I've been searching all over Rome for you." It was one of her caricatures. A potbellied American tourist, complete with camera and leer, signed, as all of her drawings were, with a scrawled *Zandra*. "One of Vale Enterprises' clients, over from New York to visit the Rome office—that's me, these days," he added with a proud grin. "He was quite fond of this. I had to pay him four times what he gave before he'd agree to part with it."

"Wesley! You shouldn't have!"

Wesley Mainwaring looked down at the sketch. "You've underpriced yourself. This is really good."

"It's just something I do for food money."

"So that's how you've been keeping yourself since you dropped out of sight. Don't you realize that the whole family is frantic with worry? You've got Mother and Aunt Giselle speaking for the first time in years."

Zandra shielded her eyes against the sun and stared at the passersby. "They don't really care, you know."

"Noel and I do. We've talked about you a lot since Mother and Giselle started burning up the phone lines between Nice and the States." He fixed her with a long level look. "I don't know why you ran out on your job at your mother's company, kiddo, but it was a mistake."

"Says who?"

"Your betters. Me and Noel. We would be shirking our cousinly duty if we let you keep throwing your life away. When I told Noel I thought I'd located you, he hopped on the first plane from New York. He'll be here tonight. We'll spend however long it takes to argue you into accepting your family responsibilities."

"Which are?"

"To get in there and take over your mother's company."

Zandra thought of that awful morning she was locked in the storage room. To have bolted like a child seemed silly now. But if she'd stood her ground, she wouldn't have learned the truth about Aunt Alex and her father. Not that she could tell Wesley that.

"What is it, kiddo?" Wesley asked. "You look glum."

"They don't like me."

"Your mother's employees? Why would they? You're the snot-nosed upstart who's going to run that place one day. They don't just dislike you, kiddo. They hate your guts."

"Is this the way you plan to talk me into going back?"

Wesley's grin was so familiar it tugged at her heart. "When could you ever resist a challenge, Zandra?"

She thought about that for a moment. Then she ran her fingers through her hair. "I need to get cleaned up before Noel gets here."

"Want me to take you home?"

Den would have sponged a meal from someone and be back at the room by now. At four he would awaken ready to make love. Everything of importance to her was in the knapsack at her feet. She looked down at her shapeless tunic, her worn sandals. "No, I want you to take me shopping."

That evening Zandra felt as though she had stepped from one world into another. She had realized as she sketched American tourists in the daytime along the Via Veneto and American movie stars in the evenings, that it was the upper-class Italians who had become the best-dressed people in the world. When Wesley opened his billfold, she was able—her hated height and slimness didn't seem so bad now—to slip into a Valentino prepared for a showing. Why had she ever thought living in a single room with no toilet was tolerable? she wondered as she washed her hair over and over. When she was sure it was the cleanest it could be, she let it fall to her waist in a gleaming sheet of black. It dried long and straight and shiny, and when she put on the Valentino, no one would have recognized her as the same ragged free citizen of the world. When Noel arrived at Wesley's apartment, he took one look and kissed her hand.

Zandra fidgeted through dinner on the panoramic terrace of Wesley's apartment as her cousins discussed everything from the latest movies to Vale Enterprises' net worth. Finally she could wait no longer. She cleared her throat noisily and her cousins turned their full attention on her. "I thought you two were going to talk me into going back to Giselle Durand Cosmetics," she complained.

Noel shrugged. "Why bother? As soon as I saw you in your war paint, I knew you'd already decided to go back."

Wesley stood, drew a imaginary sword from an imaginary sheath, held it aloft, and yelled, "Charge!"

"You'll see," Zandra told them.

Wesley grinned. "I know we will."

Most of the furniture in her mother's apartment was shrouded with dustcovers. "When do you expect her back?" Zandra asked the maid who let her in.

"Not for weeks, Miss Zandra."

That would definitely slow her plans, Zandra thought. "Uncover these things and act like someone lives here."

"But Halloran said—"

Zandra turned and stared at the girl.

"Yes, Miss Zandra." She hurried to comply.

In her bedroom, Zandra tossed the knapsack on the

bed and looked around. I need to get a place of my own, she thought. She walked over to the dresser and looked in a drawer, at the clothes of a lifetime ago. She pulled the drawer out of the chest and upended it in the floor. One by one she did the same thing to the rest of the drawers. Then she turned to the closet, taking the clothing out in arm loads and adding it to the pile. When she finished, she called the maid. "Get rid of this," she said, pointing to the discards. Eyes wide with wonder, the girl complied.

Unpacking didn't take long. Zandra upended the contents of her knapsack into the first drawer. Tomorrow she would use her mother's charge accounts to buy the clothes for her new life.

Zandra talked on the phone with Wesley almost every day. "Mother's still traveling," she told him when she called the first of September. "If the maid hadn't shown me Mother's itinerary, I'd think she was trying to avoid me."

"When's she due back?"

"Not for weeks."

"Have you been down to look over the operation?"

"Not yet."

"Where's the daredevil who followed me up on the roof when she was seven years old?"

"This is slightly different."

"Is it?" That cool and cynical voice was Noel's.

"Are you eavesdropping on a private conversation?"

"I've taken over from Wesley since he doesn't seem to be accomplishing anything with his kid-glove tactics."

"What do you expect me to do?"

"Surprise me. That's what you've done in the past."

* * *

The first call came at 9:05 A.M. When Giselle Durand was away, Jessie Fiedler's life was more calm—and more boring. She filled her hours with crossword puzzles. But a little excitement on a Tuesday morning was a welcome thing, she thought after the second call. However, the situation quickly grew from a little excitement to wholesale hysteria. The fifth call was from Margo Hall, Ed Crown's secretary. "Did you know that Giselle's kid is back?"

"You're the fifth person to tell me that," Jessie said. She could hear the sound of raised voices in the background.

"Has anyone else told you that she went through the offices with two guys from shipping, seizing pieces of furniture?"

"Three people."

"How about this? She's had everything moved out of my boss's office and her booty moved in."

Jessie blinked. Ed Crown's office was next door to this one; the second-best location in the entire building. "You're the first person to mention that," she admitted.

"They're in his office yelling at each other right now." Margo dropped her voice to a whisper. "You should have seen his face when he walked in and found her already installed behind her new desk. It's about time someone gave that son of a bitch some grief."

"Don't get your hopes up. Giselle thinks Ed is her good right hand."

"That's because he doesn't try to pin her up against the filing cabinets. Oops!" Margo broke the connection.

As Jessie replaced the receiver she heard the clamor of raised voices in the hall. Then her office door crashed open and Ed Crown himself stalked in. "Do you know what's happening?" he demanded.

Jessie regarded him icily. He might be important

to the running of Giselle Durand Cosmetics, but she couldn't stand the man. "Is there a problem?"

"That stupid Durand kid just threw me out of my office!"

Giselle likes him, Jessie told herself. She made an effort. "That stupid kid's mother owns the company, Ed."

"I didn't take this job to run a kindergarten. Or to let some little bitch tell me I've lost my office."

"Hello again, Mr. Crown," said the "little bitch" from Jessie's open doorway. "Good morning, Mrs. Fiedler. When you talk to my mother, would you tell her I've settled in nicely and things are going well."

Ed Crown's face had turned an unattractive shade of red. He looked, Jessie saw with fascination, a little like a boar. Just as Zandra had drawn him three years ago. "Listen, you cunt! Get your things out of my office now."

Zandra turned to face him and gave him a slow, appraising, top-to-bottom stare. "You're fired, Mr. Crown."

"You can't fire me!"

Zandra turned to Jessie. "Would you please get my mother on the phone, Mrs. Fiedler. Mr. Crown would prefer to hear from her that he's fired."

"Oh, no, you don't, bitch. I quit!"

"Fine. You can pick up your check at—"

"I know where to pick up my check," Ed Crown said, and stormed out.

Zandra turned back to Jessie Fiedler, her voice still calm. "You can tell Mother this little tidbit while you're giving her my other news, Mrs. Fiedler. Tell her I'll send her my views of the operation here in a couple of weeks."

This wasn't the defiant young girl from this spring who'd disappeared without a word to anyone, Jessie thought. This was a calm confident woman, more than equal to confronting a man like Ed Crown. "Call me, Jessie. Your mother does."

Zandra sat down behind the desk in her new office and reached for the phone. Her heart was pounding as hard as it had the day she followed Noel and Wesley up onto the roof of Casa Vale. She would never forget the glory of that view, standing on the slippery red tiles, looking out at the Atlantic with the sea breeze twisting her hair into tangles and the thrill of it turning her blood into bubbles. She could feel that same exhilaration now. "Noel," she said when her cousin answered the phone. "I did it!"

Jessie Fiedler had a quizzical look on her face when the maid led her into the living room of Giselle's New York apartment. "Coffee," Giselle told the maid. "I'm still on French time," she said as she turned back to Jessie, who was gazing around the room with the same quizzical look still in place. "You noticed the bare spots?" Giselle guessed.

"Were you robbed?"

"You might say that." She sat down on the sofa and patted the cushion next to her. "According to the staff, Zandra took a 'few things' with her when she moved into her own place."

"My goodness," Jessie said faintly.

"Yes," Giselle said dryly. "Well, to business." She extended her hand for the reports Jessie held and skimmed through them quickly. "She really is amazing," Giselle said after a moment. "We're lucky she's not working for Lauder or Revson."

Jessie glanced around the room again. "Or maybe they're the lucky ones."

Giselle leaned back. "This is what we've needed,

Jessie. A breath of fresh air. Look how the sales for Lilli have already jumped."

"She'll be glad to hear you approve."

Giselle chuckled. "I doubt that. Besides, I'm only here tonight. I'm on my way to Palm Beach. Orlena has a big Christmas ball planned for next week."

"You're not coming in to the office?" Jessie asked, dismayed.

"I'd rather not, just now. I'm tired of the complaints from the 'old faithful' about every little thing Zandra has done."

"I don't know how you intend to stop the complaints if you don't see them yourselves."

"This will stop them," Giselle said.

Jessie read through the memo. "Giselle! This is—"

"No! I don't want to hear it. Just make sure that everyone in Giselle Durand Cosmetics sees it." She rose. "Now, I've got to get a little sleep before I leave in the morning."

"But you just arrived! Zandra won't be back from Los Angeles until tomorrow night. You'll miss her altogether."

"I know."

Zandra looked up when Jessie Fiedler entered her office. "Not more bellyaching from the troops."

"There will be." Her mother's secretary held a memo. "Your mother asked me to distribute this throughout the company. By now everyone but you has seen it."

Zandra felt a chill go through her. So here was where the house of cards fell down. "Why am I the last?"

"That was the way she wanted it."

And Jessie Fiedler would never deviate from what Mother told her to do.

"Merry Christmas," Jessie said as she handed it over.

Zandra skimmed the lines. "She's made me executive vice-president?"

"Second-in-command." Jessie was grinning. "I've got to get back to my office. The phone will be ringing off the wall."

"Complaints?"

"You're twenty years old and you've been here not quite four months. What do you think?"

"What do you think, Jessie?"

"I think your mother is the smartest woman I ever met. If she thinks this is the right thing to do, it must be."

After Jessie left, Zandra read through the sheet again. It gave her a funny feeling to find out her mother was essentially rewarding her for barging in and seizing control of the company. She wanted to call Aunt Alex so badly that she almost reached for the phone. Only the memory of that morning in her aunt's villa stopped her.

A soft tap on her door interrupted her thoughts.

Jessie entered, another sheet in her hand. "Another bombshell?" Zandra asked.

"Maybe. These are resignations."

Zandra took the list and read quickly through it. Five top people. "Fine," she said. "I'll handle it."

"Of course she had no trouble replacing them," Jessie told Giselle in her weekly phone call. She always managed to track her boss down, wherever in the world she might be. "Who wouldn't want to work here?"

"I think you're a little prejudiced," Giselle told her. "But if the positions are filled, then what's the problem."

"These people are loyal to her, not you."

"She had to hire someone to fill those positions.

She would have been a fool to hire someone who hated her," Giselle said, refusing to respond to Jessie's alarm.

"I'm not sure you should let this stand."

"But she didn't fire those people. They resigned."

"If you would only come home for a while. Let the employees here see you more."

"No," Giselle said. "Zandra's managing things now."

"And here's what Francis wore for Halloween," Sheila Halloran said, shaking out a tiny clown's suit.

"Wasn't our Francis a bit young to go trick-or-treating?" Halloran asked. The poor motherless tyke was not quite four.

"As if she cares for your opinion," Keefe said from behind his whiskey glass. "She won't even let me correct the child and he's my own grandson."

"He's had enough trouble in life already without your heavy hand on him," Sheila told her husband. "If it weren't for you, maybe Doreen and Javier would still be alive."

"Sheila!" Halloran cried.

"Give it up," Keefe said heavily. "I have. She cares for nothing but the boy now. Even Father Flannagan can't convince her what a little hellion he's growing into."

That he was, Halloran had to admit. Without a man's hand to steady him, the boy reacted to disappointment like a wild thing, screeching and bawling until he had his way.

"You're glum, Pat," Sheila said. "Missing your mistress, are you? No time for common folk like us?"

"Keep your tongue off him," Keefe told her.

"She was in Europe and now she's in Florida," Sheila snapped. "He's no duties at all, yet he never spares a day for us."

"I'm here now, aren't I?" Halloran asked.

"And it took Christmas Day to bring you," Sheila said, and stomped out of the room.

The whiskey bottled clinked against the glass as Keefe poured himself another drink. "She misses Doreen, that's all," Halloran told his brother.

"So do we all," Keefe said, and drank his whiskey in one swift gulp.

1964

ONE

The awards ceremony had begun to drag. Across the crowded ballroom, a man rose from his seat and wended his way through the narrow spaces between the tables.

"Too important to wait for the little guys to have their time in the sun," Mike Sanders said sourly. Thanks to Zandra's influence, Mike was now executive vice-president of Giselle Durand Cosmetics. Zandra had replaced her mother as president last fall when revenues hit $100 million. Giselle herself had taken the title of chairman of the board. Not that her mother had relinquished any control over the big decisions, Zandra thought. She absolutely refused to allow the company to move into men's cosmetics, although Zandra was certain the time was right.

The man making his escape from the ballroom looked vaguely familiar. He was tall, with blond hair, a rugged build, and an angular, suntanned face. "Who is that?"

"Bryan Rawlings." Taking her blank look to mean something else, Mike added, "Rawlings Construction?"

"Oh, yes," she said, but it was his son's likeness she had recognized in Bryan Rawlings's face. Her insides churned as she recalled the summer encounter with Bry Rawlings that had turned into a disaster because of her mother's affair with this man. She picked up her bag. "I'd like to leave."

"Can't," Mike said. "I've got an award to present."

Zandra stood.

"What are you doing?"

"I'll see you in the morning." She strode away through the crowded tables. Outside the banquet hall she searched for the nearest ladies' room and ducked inside. Dampening a paper towel, she pressed it against her face while her stomach gradually settled down. Then she combed her hair and freshened her makeup. Looking cool and unruffled again, she departed the ladies' room for the lobby.

Before the doorman could hail a taxi, a limousine pulled up. "Miss Vale?" someone said in a deep voice.

Zandra turned to find Bryan Rawlings beside her. "How did you know my name?" she asked when he introduced himself.

"I saw you present an award inside. Will your date be joining you?"

"He's not my date. He's an employee. And he has an award of his own to give out later."

"Then may I offer you a lift." Bryan Rawlings motioned toward the limousine.

"You were about four years old the last time I saw you," he said when she'd given the driver her address. "I was a friend of your mother's."

"And my father's?" Zandra couldn't resist asking.

A frown quenched his charming smile. "Yes. Charles and I were quite good friends at one time." He hesitated. "I'm sure you've heard family stories about me."

"Not a word," she said.

He relaxed visibly. "How is Giselle?"

"Fine. We keep in close touch because of the business, but I don't see her very often. She travels a lot. Is there any message you would like for me to pass on to her?"

Bryan Rawlings shook his head. "Here we are," he said as the car pulled up in front of her apartment building. He helped her out and then took her hand formally. "It was good to have met you again after so many years, Zandra."

She was almost as tall as he was. Some impulse made her lean forward and kiss him lightly on the cheek. For a moment they stared at each other in mutual astonishment.

"Zandra?"

"Thank you for the ride, Mr. Rawlings." Zandra turned and marched toward the doorman without looking back. Inside her apartment, she went swiftly to the phone and began to dial her aunt Alex's number. Before the call went through, she slammed down the receiver.

At times like this it was hard to remember that she no longer wanted to communicate with Aunt Alex. She was bursting with the news of what had just happened. Imagine running into one's mother's old flame and not having anyone with whom to share the news. It was at times like this she wished she had a close female friend. Tomorrow she would call Wesley, she thought. Noel wouldn't see the amusing part of it, but Wesley would.

Just before she drifted off to sleep, she thought of Bryan Rawlings's face.

Someone in the art department had come up with the idea of photographing the new ad campaign in a building under construction. Giselle Durand, out of New York as usual, had approved when she saw the sketches. But it was Zandra who stood on a creaking platform, her hands thrust into the pockets of her thick wool coat, watching the models shiver in the chill spring breeze twenty floors above Water Street.

"What one goes through for beauty," a deep voice said behind her just as she became aware of the delicious dark odor of chocolate. She turned. Bryan Rawlings, a steaming mug in his hand, stood there. "Hot chocolate," he said.

"Where can I get one of those? And for heaven's sake, don't let the models see it. They're on the edge of revolt as it is."

"This one's yours. I'll be your human shield." Bryan moved between her and the photographer, his broad shoulders blocking her view of the shoot.

Zandra sipped the hot chocolate greedily, holding the mug with both hands. "Thanks," she said as the warmth of it went through her. "I was really chilled. Do construction workers always drink hot chocolate?"

"When I found out what was happening here this morning, I made sure I was prepared in case you came along."

She raised the mug again to hide her expression and drank deeply.

"They're almost through," Bryan Rawlings said. "Would you like to go all the way up? The view is fantastic."

She stepped around him. "This kind gentleman has offered to show us the view from the top of the building," she called to the group. "Anyone want to go?"

The models groaned. The crew jeered. The photographer didn't even look up.

"Herd them down, will you?" Zandra told her assistant.

"You're not really going all the way up there?" Her

assistant made it sound like Mount Everest.

"Sure." Zandra turned to find Rawlings grinning.

"You like a challenge," he commented.

She thought of her cousins. "Always."

From the top of the building Zandra looked across the East River to the brownstones of Brooklyn Heights. "The poor bastards who end up working in this big box won't have this view," Bryan Rawlings told her. "They'll have slivers instead of windows."

"You ought to be ashamed of yourself," Zandra said as she leaned forward.

"That's the architect's department." He took her arm and pulled her back a step. "You're not frightened of heights?"

"I'm not scared of anything." Zandra turned to face him, the wind whipping her hair around her face. "Except . . ."

"Except?"

"This." She leaned forward and pressed her lips against his.

Bryan Rawlings took her face in his hands and kissed her back. As his lips moved on hers Zandra realized she was telling the truth. She was more frightened than she had ever been in her life.

When they broke apart, he said, "I'm old enough to be your father."

"I know."

"I'm married."

"And your wife doesn't understand you?"

"No, she understands only too well. That's why we've been separated in all but name for a long time."

"I don't care about all that," Zandra said, but she was waiting for him to say one thing more. How would he phrase it? When you were a child, your mother and I were lovers? I cuckolded my best friend? I fathered your little brother?

But he said nothing; instead he leaned forward and

took possession of her lips once again. Zandra forgot what it was she had been waiting for.

Zandra was in her bedroom packing her overnight bag when the telephone rang. She lunged for it, hoping desperately that it wasn't Bryan saying this weekend getaway must be postponed again. She was so startled to hear her aunt's voice on the line that she almost dropped the phone.

"I can't believe you're in New York in July," Alexandra Mainwaring said as if they had just spoken the day before.

"I work here, Aunt Alex."

"That's not the impression I get from the newspapers. What in the world are you trying to do, Zandra?"

"Do?"

"I told you what Bryan Rawlings did to Charles!"

"That was a long time ago."

"Surely this man can't be important to you. He's old enough to be your father."

"I don't think that's any concern of—"

"You've got to break this off. It hurts your father to see your picture in the papers with that man."

Zandra took a deep breath. "It hurt me," she said slowly and deliberately, "to see you and Father in bed together."

Zandra listened to the silence on the other end of the line, then she slammed down the receiver. She was looking forward to this weekend. The occasions when she and Bryan could slip away from their separate responsibilities for the hour-and-a-half drive to the weekend cottage he had bought on Long Island were few and far between. She loved the white clapboard cottage, sheltered by locust trees and overlooking Stony Brook Harbor. She'd had a moment's apprehension when he first took her there in March, wondering if this was where he and her mother had spent time together. She had been relieved to learn he had only purchased it the week before.

She had been expecting the call she just received, but not from her aunt. Zandra and her mother talked semimonthly about the state of Giselle Durand Cosmetics. When the gossip columns began to print items about Zandra and Bryan Rawlings, Zandra expected her mother to say something, but Giselle had yet to breathe a word. No way could she have missed the news, Zandra mused. Jessie Fiedler read the columns avidly, and Zandra did not deceive herself about where Jessie's loyalties lay. She would have reported whom Zandra was seeing to her employer.

Zandra repacked the last few items she had thrown into the overnight case. She looked down at the packet of birth-control pills she'd just placed in the bag. After a moment she tossed them in the wastebasket. Then she went on with her packing.

TWO

Bryan pulled off Las Vegas Boulevard and parked in front of a wedding chapel almost hidden between a motel and a Texaco station. "This one has to do," he told Zandra. "Any further and we're in the desert."

This chapel was no better or worse than the dozen others they had driven by. With its phony white spire, it looked like a quaint little New England church set afloat by some terrible mistake in the neon ocean of a Las Vegas night. At least they had managed to elude the photographers who had followed them both everywhere since word of Bryan Rawlings's divorce became public, Zandra thought as Bryan opened her door. How ludicrous pictures of a pregnant bride would have looked splashed all over the tabloids.

In the anteroom lobby, the proprietor went down the list of charges. "Twenty-five dollars for the chapel. Witness, six dollars. Rings? Black-and-white photos? Tape recording of the ceremony?" Another couple entered. The proprietor waved them to one of the vinyl couches as he continued. "Flowers? Perpetual plastic keepsakes of the occasion? Or maybe you'd prefer a live orchid?"

Zandra shook her head and walked on into the chapel, leaving Bryan to deal with the rest of it. She sat down on one of the wooden benches. She was feeling out of sorts. She hadn't realized how tiresome being pregnant would be. The chapel's own flashing sign made the fake stained-glass windows shimmer. In the light of the elaborate electric candelabra, the lavish arrangements of white plastic carnations almost passed for the real thing.

Bryan entered the chapel. Zandra was touched to see he had given in to the proprietor's sales pitch and purchased a small rose corsage for her and one white rose for his own lapel. He walked over and took her hand. From the anteroom, she could hear the proprietor, well into his spiel for the new couple: "Flowers? Perpetual plastic keepsake of the occasion?" The opening bars of "The Wedding March" from a speaker at the rear of the chapel blotted out the rest.

The minister beckoned them both to the front of the chapel. The professional witness joined them. The music stopped abruptly so that the ceremony, delivered in a low monotone, could begin. Before the minister reached the end, Zandra could hear the proprietor begin yet another spiel.

". . . kiss the bride," the minister said. Bryan's kiss was brief, apologetic. Zandra glanced at her watch as they left the wedding chapel. They had been in the building less than a quarter hour.

"Tacky," Bryan said as they got in the car. "I'm sorry about that. It was one way to avoid the press, but this is a poor place for a honeymoon."

"We've already had the honeymoon," she told him, patting her growing belly. She was sorry when she saw the hurt expression come over his face. Quickly, before she lost her nerve, she said, "We have to talk about my mother."

He paused, his hand still on the key in the ignition. "What about her?" he asked cautiously.

"We have to tell her about this in person."

"Why?"

"We both know why."

"You said your parents never told you about . . . me."

"They didn't. Someone else did." She shook her head before he could press her. "That's all past, but we both know that we owe my mother the courtesy of giving her this little piece of news in person."

"How can we get there before the gossip?"

"I already have our plane reservations to Paris."

Bryan looked at her. In the flashing light from the wedding chapel's sign, she couldn't read his expression. "Pretty sure of yourself, aren't you?"

"Yes," she said calmly, but when she clasped her hands over her stomach, they were icy cold.

It was almost 8:00 P.M. when the hired car crossed the bridge to the Ile St.-Louis in the middle of the Seine. As they turned down the narrow Rue St. Louis-en-l'Ile, Bryan peered through the gloom at the lovely buildings. "The whole place looks like it dropped straight out of the seventeenth century," he observed as the car pulled up in front of a mansion that had been converted to apartments.

"She said she had the top floor."

"Don't you think we should wait until morning? It's a little late to come calling."

"I called her from Las Vegas. She's expecting us."

"Us?"

"Me."

When they walked through the porte cochere, they

were met by the concierge, who directed them to the
elevator. The maid who met them when the elevator
doors opened, led them down the hall as Zandra looked
around with interest. She had never been in this apartment. Her mother had taken it two years before, just
after making Zandra executive vice-president of Giselle
Durand.

The maid stopped at the door to the drawing room.
A smile on her face, Giselle half rose from the pale
green silk-covered sofa as Zandra walked in. Then she
caught sight of Bryan. "Why, what are you doing here,
Bryan?"

Zandra turned. Her husband stood just inside the
drawing room, his eyes on Giselle. "I told him we
should come," she said gaily. "To give you our news in
person."

It didn't seem possible Giselle could become paler,
but she did. "What news?"

Zandra held up her left hand, flashing the engagement ring and wedding band. "I'm married, Mother."
The expression in Giselle's eyes was what she had
come so far to see. So why did unshed tears suddenly
prick her eyes?

"Giselle," Bryan began, and then faltered.

Zandra didn't wait for whatever else he might say.
"Meet your new son-in-law."

Giselle rose then. She came forward slowly and put
her arms around Zandra. "I'm so happy for you," she
said. She extended her hand to Bryan. "And for you,"
she told him.

"Oh, no!" Zandra cried. "You must hug him, too."

Instead Giselle stood on tiptoe to place a small kiss
on his cheek. "Welcome to the family, Bryan."

He grasped her hands. "Giselle, we didn't want you
to read about this in the papers."

"Of course not." Giselle pulled her hands free.
"Can I offer you some tea? What am I thinking of?" she

cried before they could answer. "We should have champagne."

"Giselle, don't," Bryan said.

Zandra flashed him a look he ignored. "We'd love to have champagne," she told her mother.

"I'll be right back," Giselle said.

When she left the room, Bryan turned on Zandra. "What are you trying to do?"

"Let her know we're married. Isn't that why we came?"

"Is it? I'm beginning to wonder exactly why we did come. What about Charles?"

"What?"

"Your father. Don't you want to tell him our news in person?"

"No."

"Good. He might decide to take a pistol to me."

"With good reason?"

He looked at her. "Perhaps."

Giselle swept back into the room followed by the maid, bearing a tray with champagne and glasses. As the bottle was opened Zandra begin to wonder if coming here hadn't been a terrible mistake.

Bryan sat in the dark in his suite at the Crillon, listening to the soft, regular whisper from the bed, the sound of his new wife breathing for herself and his child.

He knew where he wanted to go. But still he sat there, overwhelmed by a sick feeling that seemed to lodge in his very soul. It had been easy to justify cheating on his wife when that wife was Florence, with her moods, and her withholding of sex. But Zandra was so young, so vital, so eager to experience all the joys of their bodies. He felt like a monster sitting here, wanting with all his heart to go to another woman.

He looked at the hands of his watch glowing in the dark. He had adjusted the time when they landed at Orly. Just past midnight. He stood in his stocking feet and reached down for his shoes. Then he tiptoed quietly out of the bedroom. In the living room of the suite he sat down and put on his shoes. Then he let himself out.

Giselle's concierge was reluctant to let Bryan go up. It cost him a hundred francs. When the elevator doors opened, Giselle herself stood in the entrance hall.

"Please," she said. "Go back to Zandra."

"You know it's you I love."

"You married my daughter, and I've wished you well. What more do you want?"

"I thought you didn't love me. All these years and you wouldn't answer my calls or let me see you. But tonight I saw the truth in your eyes."

"You're wrong," she said, and turned.

Bryan followed her gaze. A man came out of the drawing room and walked toward them. For a moment he thought it was Charles. Then he realized it was Charles's older brother, Zandra's uncle.

"Where's your wife, Mr. Rawlings?" Tru Vale asked.

"At the hotel."

"Then I suggest you go back to her," Tru Vale said.

"Of course," Bryan said. He stepped back into the elevator. Before the door could close, Tru stepped in as well. As the doors slid shut Bryan caught a glimpse of Giselle's shattered expression.

Giselle stared at the elevator doors for a moment and then retreated into the drawing room. She sat down on the sofa, battling the urge to cry. But too much had assaulted her this evening. The tears came anyway.

Eventually, she rose and poured herself a glass of wine. Then set it aside and threw herself on the sofa as the tears returned. "Oh, Tru," she gasped aloud. When she had opened the door after Zandra and Bryan left and found Tru standing there, she had almost fainted. "I have news," he said as he stepped forward to take her hands in his. "About Zandra. She's married someone."

"I know. She and Bryan were just here."

Tru dropped her hands and walked past her into the drawing room. With an unerring sense of direction, although he had never been in this apartment, he found the bar and began to make himself a drink. "So I didn't arrive in time to cushion the blow," he said lightly.

"What made you think there was a blow to be cushioned?"

"I thought perhaps Mr. Rawlings was the reason you broke off with me." He brought her a drink and then lifted his own in a salute. "To the newlyweds."

She stood there without drinking. "It wasn't Bryan or anyone else who made me call it off, Tru. It was you. You thought more of your family than of us. Of me."

Bryan returned then, alone, interrupting them.

Giselle had known from the expression on Tru's face that he believed if he hadn't been there, she would have welcomed her old lover, her daughter's new husband, into her bed. That was why he had left.

Giselle woke to the chill light of dawn, still on the sofa, where she had cried herself to sleep. A terrible fear clutched at her heart. She hurried to the phone and dialed the number of Tru's hotel. "I'm sorry, madame," the desk clerk said. "He checked out last night."

"Did he leave a message for me? Giselle Durand?"

"I'm sorry, Madame Durand. No message."

She hung up. Tru had asked Bryan to leave not because of his feelings for her, but because he was once again putting the Vales first. Bryan had married Zandra, so Bryan must go back to his wife. "Another blow for the Vales," she muttered aloud. "Oh, Tru!"

Then something registered with Giselle, a thought she had been trying to hold at bay since the night before. When Zandra turned to Bryan, Giselle had seen the faint swell of her daughter's midriff. Zandra was pregnant with Bryan's child. Was that the real news for which Tru had rushed to her side to prepare her? Giselle looked down at her hands. Suddenly she felt so old.

She heard the door ring. The maid entered. "Madame?"

"No calls. No visitors. Just leave me alone."

"But there's a message from your daughter."

"Read it."

"My English is not so very—"

"Read it!"

"A wedding breakfast. She asks you to come to her hotel."

"Send back a note that I'm ill."

"Shall I ask her to come to you."

"No. I think she's already accomplished what she came to Paris to do—and more."

Zandra had never thought to plan beyond the moment of confrontation with her mother. But a bout of nausea over the Atlantic on the way back to New York had let her know that her body was proceeding on its course without any conscious instructions from her.

To add to her misery, she was furious with Bryan.

She'd barely had time to inspect the new salon, and he had given her no opportunity at all to shop. All she'd managed to do was pick up a couple of scarves and a few small items at the hotel boutique just inside the Crillon's revolving door before Bryan appeared and said he had just received a telegram from his ex-wife and must return to New York. He'd tried to leave her in Paris, but Zandra was having none of that.

As soon as they landed in New York, he'd tried to persuade her to go to their apartment, so new it didn't even have all the furnishings yet, but again she had refused. Just as he had refused to answer a single question all the long hours they were in the air.

In the car, Zandra asked, "Now that we've arrived, will you tell me what the telegram from Florence said?"

Bryan, his eyes on the back of the chauffeur's neck, didn't even register that she had spoken.

"Bryan!"

He turned to look at her, and the expression in his eyes was the same one she'd seen the morning after their visit to her mother's apartment. She had lost something on this trip, something she hadn't known she possessed. Worse than that. She had thrown it away in search of a vengeance that she hadn't really wanted after all. "You shouldn't have come," Bryan said, and then he turned back to the driver's neck. "Can't you go any faster?"

The driver hunched his shoulders and stepped on the accelerator. She wondered if he knew the nature of the emergency that had called Bryan to his ex-wife's apartment.

Bryan leaped out of the car as soon as it halted in front of the building and slammed the door behind him. He was already past the doorman by the time Zandra could scoot across the seat and open the door herself. The doorman took one look at her face and didn't question her right to follow her husband. In the lobby she saw Bryan hesitate before the elevator.

When she joined him, he didn't acknowledge her presence by as much as a glance.

The elevator door slid open on the fifth floor and Bryan plunged out. Zandra, following, slowed when she saw that a uniformed policeman was standing outside the apartment door he was approaching. Her stomach gave a sudden, queasy lurch.

"What's going on, officer?" Bryan demanded of the man.

"Are you Mr. Rawlings?" When Bryan nodded, the man said, "Have to be careful. The press has been nosing around. She's doing fine now. In the hospital, of course. There was some confusion initially because we thought she had been attacked instead of—are you all right?"

Bryan had gone pale beneath his tan. "She tried to kill herself?" he asked hoarsely.

"I'm afraid so."

"My children?"

"They're in the living room." He stepped aside. But when Zandra started to follow Bryan inside, the policeman put his hand on her arm.

"Let me go with my husband."

"You the second wife?" Zandra nodded. "They're pretty upset. Your name was mentioned in the note."

Her stomach gave another lurch. "I need to sit down."

"In here," he told her, and guided her down the hall and into the dining room. He left her and then reappeared in a few minutes with a cup of coffee. "Maybe this will help."

She eyed the coffee warily, unsure if her stomach would handle it well. "What happened to her?"

"Slit her wrists in the bathtub. The youngest girl called the police, said her mother had been murdered. There was so much blood she couldn't tell what had happened."

Zandra leaned forward and rested her face in her hands. From somewhere in the apartment, she could hear angry shouts. She looked up and started to rise.

"Sit still," the policeman said. "I'll let your husband know where you are when he's ready to leave. Can't figure why he brought you into this in the first place."

"I wanted to come," Zandra said. "He's my husband. My place is beside him."

"Not here," the policeman said. She was glad when he left the room.

The smell of the coffee was nauseating. She shoved it away and rose. Slowly, she walked around the dining room, looking at the paintings, nice ones, on the walls. Good old Florence, she thought. Salt of the earth. What a nice little wedding present for her ex-husband.

When she heard a man's footstep, Zandra turned, expecting to see Bryan. Instead she saw Bry.

"I can't believe he brought you to my mother's home," Florence's son said.

"He didn't bring me. I came."

"Was I the reason you went after him? Snatched him away from my mother?"

"I didn't snatch him away from anyone. He and Florence were quits a long time ago."

He walked closer, looming over her. "You're a bitch," he told her. "Just like your mother."

She slapped him as hard as she could.

He continued to gaze at her, the imprint of her palm red on his white cheek. "Just like your mother." Then he left the room.

By the time the policeman returned, Zandra was so bone weary she ached all over. "He's leaving now," the policeman said.

She followed him down the hall, braced for another

confrontation with Bry Rawlings, but instead she saw her husband waiting for at the door, his face impassive. They rode down the elevator in silence.

There was a slight wait while the doorman summoned the car. As it pulled away from the curb Zandra looked at her husband. In the light from the street, he looked drawn and haggard. His shoulders began to shake, and she realized he was crying.

Zandra leaned over and put her arm around his shoulders. Bryan shrugged her off and leaned against the car door, staring out the window into the night.

1965

ONE

Giselle kicked off her heels and in stocking feet padded over to the tall drawing-room window. Through the gathering darkness of the March evening, she could still see the massive towers of Notre-Dame on the Ile de la Cité, the other island in the Seine. The Ile de la Cité was the core of the original Paris, where twenty centuries before, near a village of the Parisii, one of Julius Caesar's men had set up his headquarters. The rents on the Ile St.-Louis were the highest in Paris, but well worth it, Giselle thought. Helena Rubinstein also had a home on the Ile St.-Louis—on the Quai de Béthune—but the two cosmetics queens had never met. Madame Rubinstein was now ninety-three, but there were rumors that she still had not recovered from the shock of being tied up and robbed in her New York home last spring, and that last summer's trip to Paris would be her last.

For the past two years, Giselle herself had made only one- or two-day stops in New York. Jessie kept insisting Giselle should spend more time there and take back some of the day-to-day decision making from Zandra. But the Ile St.-Louis apartment had become a refuge she was reluctant to leave. The seventeenth-century quays and streets had a sleepy provincial air Giselle found soothing. Like others on the island, she said, "I'm going to Paris," when she crossed one of the bridges. Here, in the middle of the Seine, she was a world away from the bustle of the Champs-Elysées and the new Giselle Durand Salon.

The twenty administrative districts—arrondissements—into which Paris was divided spiraled outward, with the lower numbers clustered around the Seine. Giselle's apartment was in the fourth arrondissement. Her salon was in the eighth arrondissement, where the *maisons de couture* and chic boutiques drew fashionable crowds. With Henri Laud's help, she had spent the last two years making the salon and offices into a showplace on the glittering Champs-Elysées. At street level was the retail shop where all the cosmetics and skin-care products were displayed and sold. On the floor above was the elegant Institut de Beauté, for manicures, pedicures, facials, and hair care in private salons. The third floor and above were given over to the offices. Business had been so good lately that Henri was suggesting they add additional boutiques in the first, seventh, and sixteenth arrondissements, and perhaps he was right.

When the phone rang, Giselle had no idea how long she had been standing there. She waved away the maid and answered it herself.

"I thought you'd like to know you're an official grandmother as of an hour ago," Jessie Fiedler said. Giselle's heart give a little flutter. "Giselle?"

"Is Zandra all right?"

"Mother and daughter are doing fine." The warm sound of Jessie's voice made Giselle's heart resume its normal rhythm. "I'd better get off the line so you can make your reservations."

"Reservations for what?"

"You are coming home?"

"She doesn't want me there. We both know that."

"She's a mother now. She'll change."

"When have you ever known Zandra to change her mind about anything. And photographers would be lurking behind every fire hydrant, trying to get a picture of me and Bryan together." Not long after Florence's suicide attempt, someone—it could only have been Florence Rawlings or one of her children—had leaked to the press the story of Giselle's relationship with Bryan. It had been a brief sensation, and Giselle had no desire to stir it up again.

"But you have a grandchild. Your first. Aren't you going to do anything?"

"Send her two dozen roses," Giselle said.

"How do you want the card to read?" Jessie snapped. "Best wishes from Giselle Durand Cosmetics?" The secretary hung up with a clatter, not waiting for Giselle's reply.

As Giselle fought the impulse to call Jessie back the rhythm of her heart was disrupted once more. After a moment she unclenched her fists and fixed herself a drink. Then she walked back to the tall window and her view of the Ile de la Cité. Paris was truly the City of Light: the lights were on at Notre-Dame and the Conciergerie, and would remain on until one o'clock in the morning. What had Zandra named her daughter? "My granddaughter." What a curious feeling it gave Giselle to utter those two words aloud. How strange life was. She had started her company as a way of getting Zandra back, and look how things had turned out.

"Time for her to go back to the nursery," the nurse said as she took the small bundle from Zandra's arms. "Isn't she a little beauty?"

She was, Zandra thought proudly. It was surprising what a pang she felt letting the baby go.

"Oh, and there was a message from your husband," the nurse said as she paused at the door. "He'll be here tonight. I'm sure you'll be glad of that."

Zandra nodded, though she wasn't sure if she was glad or not. Bryan had asked, formally, if she wanted him here for their child's birth. She had answered just as formally that his presence wouldn't be necessary. She had thought she was telling the truth until the contractions started and she felt so abysmally alone and vulnerable. Then she would have given anything to have him by her side.

He was getting too old for this hands-on stuff, Bryan thought as he slogged through the rain and mud toward the construction shack. A man pushing fifty should be behind a desk. Bry had come into the business after he graduated from college, but he was better with the paperwork, so Bryan found himself still out in the field more than he would have liked. Inside the shack, Bryan pulled off the borrowed boots and then stepped outside again.

"Anything else, Mr. Rawlings?" the foreman shouted over the roar of the bulldozers.

Bryan shook his head. He waved at the man in the nearest bulldozer and then climbed into the rental car, getting his shoes and socks wet in the process. His watch told him there wasn't time to go back to the hotel if he wanted to make his flight. Wearily, he crawled back out and hailed the foreman. "Can you have somebody pick up my stuff at the hotel and ship it to the New York office?"

"You're not going to travel like that? You'll have pneumonia before you pass Chicago."

"I've got a new daughter as of this morning. I should have already been there."

"Congratulations. We'll take care of it. Want an escort to the airport? The local cops?"

"I can make it," Bryan said with another glance at his watch. "Just." When the plane took off, he had dried off except for his socks and was ready for the stiff drink the stewardess brought. By the time he landed in New York, he knew he had the beginnings of a bad cold, but the alcohol was holding the worst of the achiness away.

He hadn't asked anyone to meet him at the airport since he hadn't been sure when he could get away. He shouldn't have left the site at all, but the birth of a daughter took precedence over a lot of things, he told himself. Even if he hadn't wanted another child at his age. When she was eighteen, he'd be sixty-seven. That thought made him detour for one more drink before he took a taxi to the hospital.

Bryan, with the stubble of a beard and mud-spotted trousers, entered Zandra's hospital room without knocking. When he leaned over to kiss her, she could smell the alcohol on his breath. "Sorry I wasn't here for the big event."

"I'm sure it's no longer as exciting the fourth time around," Zandra said, and then wished she hadn't.

"It wasn't that," Bryan told her. "All hell broke loose at the site—"

"And no one but you could straighten it out. The same old story." She wished she hadn't said that either, but this conversation seemed to be falling into a familiar pattern. "See all my flowers," she said in an attempt to change its course.

Bryan looked stricken. "Sorry. I didn't have a chance to get you anything."

"I didn't expect anything," she told him, and then realized how he would take that. She sighed. "I just wanted you to admire the flowers."

"Pretty roses." The two dozen roses were the most spectacular of all the arrangements. "Who are they from?"

"Mother." And that, too, was the wrong thing to say.

Bryan glanced at his watch. "Didn't mean to be so late. They'll be kicking me out soon. I better go and see the baby. What are we calling her? Have you decided?"

"Lillian."

He considered it in the slow, stolid way she found maddening. "A little old-fashioned, isn't it?"

"It should be. It was my grandmother's name."

"I know."

"We can call her Lilli. Like the perfume. Think what an advertisement she'll be." That wasn't the reason she had picked the name, but she couldn't seem to define the real reason, even to herself.

Bryan stood there a moment longer, then shrugged. "All right," he said, "Whatever you want." Then he left to see his new daughter.

Zandra wondered why he bothered. But of course he would; it was the gentlemanly thing to do. And the one thing she had learned about her husband was that he was always a gentleman.

Home, Bryan thought as he let himself into the apartment, but he didn't feel it. Zandra had chosen it, furnished it, fixed up the nursery, asking his opinion over every little detail, but through it all he had felt aloof, removed, as though he didn't really belong here in this apartment. Or with a woman young enough to be his daughter. The first thing he did was strip off the clothes he had worn for two straight days and shower.

Afterward, dressed in pajamas and robe, he fixed himself a stiff drink and then, halfway through it, reflected that it had been hours since he'd eaten, and an inadequate airline meal at that. In the kitchen he rustled through the refrigerator for sandwich makings, but settled instead for eggs and toast. The eggs were hard and rubbery and the toast singed, but another drink cured all that.

He left the dishes and skillet in the sink and carried his drink down the hall to the room Zandra had designated as the nursery. It had a bright, cheerful look about it, and the traditional child's furnishings she chose had surprised him. The name she had chosen for the baby was a surprise as well. She had never said anything about Giselle's mother that he could recall.

He had been surprised at the emotion that clutched his heart this evening when the nurse held Lilli up to the window. He had been expecting a miniature edition of Zandra. The baby's blondness had surprised him. She looked so much like the pictures of Benjamin reprinted endlessly in the newspapers that tears came to his eyes. The nurse mouthed something through the glass, but he had shaken his head and turned away.

Bryan closed the nursery door quietly behind him and went back to the bar. When he had refilled his glass, he took it to the study. He didn't have to look up the number he dialed. He had never called it but he knew it by heart.

"Durands' Residence," her man answered.

"Halloran?"

"It is. And who is this?"

"Bryan Rawlings. Is Giselle there?"

"She is not."

"Can you give me a number where I can reach her?"

"No, sir, I cannot."

"Can't or won't."

"It's all the same, isn't it, sir?"

"Call her yourself. Give her this number. Tell her I'll be here the next three days."

"Very good, sir."

* * *

And how the devil had Bryan Rawlings learned the mistress had flown back this very day from Paris? Halloran asked himself as he replaced the receiver. The man had a positive genius for being where he was not wanted.

Here she was sleeping in her own bed for the first time in Lord knows how long, and that man would have her awakened on a whim. Well, not while Halloran was here to guard her.

"Sweets," Wesley said, offering a huge box of chocolates. "Noel wanted to be practical and get baby things, but I told him this would be your last chance to indulge yourself before you went on a diet."

"You know me well," Zandra said, helping herself to two chocolates at once. "I don't suppose either of you would consider marrying and having kids of your own."

"Nope," Wesley said.

"Not after our childhood," Noel said, unexpectedly serious. "We had a telegram from Mother, by the way."

"We'd have brought it to show you," Wesley added, "but it went up in flames the moment big brother opened it."

"Didn't you realize she'd be hurt when you didn't send her word about the baby yourself?" Noel asked.

"You mean that she's forgiven me for not telling her I was getting married?"

"Now that she has a new gripe, yes," Wesley said. "Don't you think you should indulge the poor old thing?"

Zandra shook her head. She had never told her cousins what she had learned that afternoon in France when she entered their mother's bedroom. Did they suspect the true relationship between their mother and her father?

"Don't expect us to baby-sit," Noel cautioned. "We already put our time in with you."

When Wesley and Noel left, Zandra felt let down. A lot of acquaintances had visited her the past couple of days, but the truth was that she had no close friends besides her cousins. Her personality was too prickly to allow that, and for the first time, she was beginning to regret it.

"Hello, Zandra," a woman's voice said from the doorway.

No one who had just had a baby should have a mother who looked like that, Zandra thought. Giselle Durand was radiant, her eyes dancing. She crossed to the bed and gave Zandra a light kiss on the cheek.

"Have you seen the baby?" Zandra found herself anxiously waiting for her mother's approval.

"Yes." Something warm came into Giselle's face, something Zandra dimly remembered from a long time ago. "She's so beautiful. What will you name her?"

"Lillian. Lilli, for short."

"Oh," Giselle cried softly, and then fumbled in her purse. She came up with a handkerchief and blotted at her eyes. "This is so silly of me," she said after a moment.

"I think it suits her," Zandra said softly. She had never felt closer to her mother than she did at this moment. "She has your coloring."

"And your grandmother Lillian's." Giselle patted her daughter's hand. "I wish you could have met her."

"I almost feel as though I did. Do you remember when I was four and you told me all about her and Grandfather Dieterich?"

Giselle beamed with pleasure. "You remember that?"

"Giselle!" Bryan said from the doorway.

Giselle stood so rapidly that her purse slipped to

the floor and her compact and lipstick tumbled out. "I came to see Zandra and the baby."

Bryan had knelt and his hand closed on the compact just as Giselle's did. "I tried to call you last night. Your man said you weren't in the city."

Giselle babbled something about how protective Halloran was, but Zandra was no longer listening. She was watching her husband's face. He still loved her mother, Zandra realized. How could she have forgotten that? Wasn't that the reason she had been attracted to him in the first place?

The first Friday in April was not a day to which Giselle looked forward. Zandra had formally made an appointment with Jessie for a private conference, and Giselle feared she knew the subject about to be raised.

When Jessie knocked softly on her office door, Giselle glanced up. "Is she already here?"

"Not yet." Jessie, her face pale, clutched *The New York Times.*

"Is something wrong?"

"The end of an era," Jessie said as she laid the paper on the desk. "Helena Rubinstein died yesterday."

Giselle picked up the paper. The *Times* had given her rival four full columns on the front page. Giselle leaned back and rubbed her forehead. The depression she had been trying to hold at bay settled over her. "You'll see about flowers, won't you?"

Jessie patted her shoulder. "Of course. Shall I bring you some coffee? Or something stronger?"

"Ask me again after I talk with Zandra."

Zandra had never seen her mother so furious. "But Lilli is only three weeks old!" Giselle cried. "I can't believe Bryan would agree to this."

"Bryan has no say in a business decision regarding Giselle Durand Cosmetics. I would be an excellent representative for our products." Zandra knew she didn't look like a new mother. The diet Wesley predicted had taken place. She had lost every ounce she gained with the baby and a few pounds more. "I have a perfectly adequate situation set up to care for the baby." She smiled grimly at Giselle. "It's the same way you saw fit to raise me."

"Not because I wanted to," Giselle cried. "Because your father insisted."

Zandra couldn't resist one more jab. "And yet Aunt Alex always had plenty of time for me."

Giselle frowned. "Things were more complicated than that. Your father didn't—"

"This has nothing to do with Father or Bryan," Zandra interrupted, sorry she had let herself wander. "This has to do with promoting Giselle Durand Cosmetics."

Her mother sat down suddenly, her hand to her chest, as though she were trying to still a racing heart. "All right," Giselle told her daughter. "If that's what you want."

Zandra smiled, victorious. "It is."

But back in her own office, Zandra didn't feel quite so triumphant. Since Bryan left for the West Coast again, there hadn't been a single call from him either at home or at work to ask about the baby. Maybe he was sorry he had married her. Maybe he was having second thoughts.

If he was, that was just too bad. He was hers now, not her mother's. She didn't intend to let him go.

TWO

When Giselle answered the telephone, all she heard was a baby's screams. "Hello?"

"Mrs. Durand?" The voice was that of a stranger: female, young, frightened. The next words were unintelligible, lost in the frantic infant's cries.

"Could you repeat that?" Giselle asked. Whoever it was had called on the private line that went directly to her desk without going through Jessie. "I'm afraid that I didn't catch what you said."

"I said the baby is sick. Little Lilli. I'm all alone here and I don't know what to do." The girl, for that was what she surely was, began to sob almost as loudly as the screaming child.

"Who is this?"

"Kelley Winters. I'm Mrs. Rawlings's maid. She's out of the city and the baby is so sick that I just don't know what to do."

"Have you called the doctor?"

"I can't find the number. The nurse is gone on

vacation and the housekeeper is out sick with the flu and Mrs. Rawlings hasn't checked into the Dallas hotel yet. I tried to call Mr. Rawlings, but he's out on a construction site in Oregon and can't be reached until tonight." The girl began to sob again. "She's burning up with fever and I don't know what to do."

"I'll be right there," Giselle told her. When she finally got the girl off the line, she buzzed Jessie. "Have Halloran bring the car to the front entrance immediately."

"You're leaving? But you have a meeting in fifteen minutes. What will I tell them?"

"Tell them my grandchild is ill."

"But Zandra—"

"She's in Texas this week and some little maid is trying to cope."

"What about Mr. Rawlings? Did they try to contact him?"

"For heaven's sake, Jessie! You know that men are no good with sick babies. The poor little thing is less than two months old!"

There was silence on the other end of the line. Still holding the phone, Giselle looked up at the sound of the office door opening. Jessie stood there, grinning. She said, "I had to see it for myself."

"See what?"

"You don't look like a grandmother, but you certainly are beginning to sound like one."

"You're the grandmother?" Lilli's pediatrician was a rosy-cheeked, white-haired man with sharp blue eyes.

Giselle nodded. "My daughter is out of the city."

"I know. The nurse brought the child in last week."

"What's wrong with her?" When Giselle spoke, young Lilli looked directly at her face as though she understood the words.

The baby had stopped screaming as soon as

Giselle took her from the young maid. She hadn't begun again, but her small body seemed unnaturally warm.

"Nothing serious. Or at least nothing that antibiotics can't cure." The doctor gave her a sharp look. "Are you going to be taking care of the child?"

Giselle thought of her crowded schedule. Jessie would shriek if she heard that question. "At least until the nurse or the housekeeper return to work."

The doctor looked at her. "She needs more than that." He chucked Lilli under the chin. "Don't you, young lady?" The baby regarded him with wonder. "It's a rotten idea to leave a baby solely in the care of hired help. She needs her mother's love." He gave Giselle another long look. "Or perhaps her grandmother's."

"That hasn't been a very popular view in the past."

"No, women of your social class left their children to be cared for by others. I suppose you did, too."

"It wasn't my idea! My husband insisted."

"And are you happy with the results?"

Giselle thought of her daughter. She knew less of Zandra than of a stranger she might pass in the street. "No," she said softly. "I'm not."

In the car once more, Giselle looked down into Lilli's face. What perfect, tiny rosebud lips. And what delicate skin. Bryan's child, she thought. She was holding Bryan's child in her arms again. Lilli's blue eyes focused on her face. She tickled Lilli's palm and the small pink fingers clutched her own. Tears blurred her vision.

Benjamin was gone forever. But here was Lilli.

"Oh, Mother," Giselle breathed. "If only you'd lived to see your beautiful namesake."

* * *

Halloran glanced in the rearview mirror. What a pretty picture the mistress made as she cuddled the baby in her arms. "Where to, then, mistress?"

"I'm taking her home, Patrick."

"Now that's fine," Halloran said, as pleased as could be. "She's too sweet a babe to be given over to the likes of that silly girl we snatched her from."

Giselle laughed. "But we'll stop at Zandra's first and get what the child needs."

"And if anyone tries to stop us, we'll make him sorry," Halloran promised her.

"No one will try to stop us, Patrick. She's my granddaughter. Who would object to my taking care of her?"

Not Zandra, Halloran thought. That one had no motherly instincts at all. Think of it—to go off and leave a babe this young. But Bryan Rawlings, now that was another matter. The man may have married the daughter, but he was still sniffing around the mistress. Halloran glanced in the mirror at the scene in the backseat again and then smiled to himself. Let Bryan Rawlings try to interfere. If he had to, he would give the fancy gentleman another taste of his fists and enjoy it, too.

Zandra checked into the Dallas hotel, dead tired after a full day's work and then a flight from San Antonio. Her mother might believe that keeping her own name in the society columns was what kept the Giselle Durand line moving, but Zandra knew that wining and dining cosmetics buyers and training sales people in the correct way to use their products was also important. When she saw the message from her mother, Zandra phoned New York from the hotel lobby, not even taking time to go up to her room.

"I'm sorry you were bothered," Zandra told her

mother when she learned what had happened. "I'll see that the girl is replaced."

"Don't you do any such thing. I'm glad she called me. She was all alone and had no idea what to do with the baby. I was glad to step in. After all, she is my granddaughter."

"Giselle Durand a grandmother? Not a very good image for the company, is it?"

"It's what I am," Giselle said angrily. "I've decided to act like it for a change."

"What do you mean?"

"You're traveling all the time. I'm here in New York. I think Lilli should stay with me until she gets better."

"Really, Mother. I don't think—"

"So does her doctor. I'll call you again tomorrow and let you know how she's doing. And Zandra, if you're planning to fire someone, I think it should be the nurse. Imagine that woman not even leaving emergency numbers with the staff."

She could see through this, Zandra thought. It was a ploy of her mother's to edge her out of the business. "If I do fire the nurse, who will take care of Lilli?"

"I will."

"I suppose you'll stay in New York *and* stay home from the office?" Zandra said with heavy sarcasm.

"Yes," Giselle said. "I will." She broke the connection.

Zandra paced around the room angrily. Then she went over to the photograph on the bureau, the one she had brought with her from New York. She stared into Lilli's face and the hurt twisted inside her. The baby had been in the world for such a short time and already it was painful for Zandra to be away from her.

But if she did otherwise, Zandra knew she would continue to play second fiddle to her own mother for the rest of her life. If she didn't travel, make herself known to the customers of the company, then she didn't have a chance.

Zandra picked up the photograph. She could cancel the next day's meetings. Return to New York. See why the carefully vetted group she had assembled to take care of her daughter had failed to function. She could snatch Lilli back from her mother.

For a moment the urge to do just that burned stronger than anything else. Then, slowly, the memories returned. How often had she herself been left alone as a child? How many times had her mother said she would pick her up and then been late or else canceled out altogether because of business? The same business that her mother was castigating her for being so attentive to.

Become a housewife? Another Florence, she thought with a grimace. Wouldn't Bryan love that?

Why not let her mother take care of the baby? A sharp pain shafted through her, but Zandra ignored it. Let her mother immerse herself in the nursery and walks in the park. Let her worry whether the nurse would quit if you spoke sharply to her or simply suggested a more efficient way of doing things.

This could be the solution she was searching for, Zandra realized, the way to ease her mother out of the company altogether.

"Really, Giselle," the countess complained. "I hope you don't intend to make a habit of carting that child about with you." They were in the bedroom of Orlena's Palm Beach house, the bedroom that was always Giselle's when she visited—which was frequently.

"I told you I was bringing her," Giselle said, unruffled, as she settled Lilli into the crib.

"Other women have small dogs," Orlena told her. "They provide companionship with no problems and you can pamper them so. Lovely collars and little sweaters. I saw a tiny poodle the other day so small it would fit into your handbag."

"You're not suggesting I trade my grandchild for a poodle?"

"You twist my words," Orlena protested. "I'm telling you it is the mother's responsibility to care for the child. Not yours."

"She . . . doesn't have time."

"Doesn't make time. Were you able to push aside the demands of motherhood so easily?"

"Servants took care of Zandra. I've always regretted that."

"But how will you enjoy yourself?"

Giselle leaned down and kissed the baby's cheek. "I'll enjoy myself, Orlena."

Orlena sat down suddenly, an expression of distaste on her lovely face. "I cannot believe how the world is changing." She looked out the palm-shaded window to the red-tiled roof barely visible through the greenery. "And now I will have new neighbors, too. I'm sure they will be unsuitable."

"The Vale house is being sold?"

Orlena shook her head sadly. "It went on the market this week. The Mainwaring boys seldom visited Palm Beach anyway. Such a waste of a beautiful house."

After Orlena left to dress for dinner, Giselle walked over to the window and looked across to the stucco walls of Casa Vale, rising from the crest of the beach ridge. Her first visit to the Vales' Palm Beach home had been not long after her marriage to Charles, in early December 1941. She could still remember the song of the rails echoing back from the concrete of the Flagler Memorial Bridge. She had been eighteen and already pregnant with Zandra.

That first Sunday morning at Casa Vale, Charles

slept late and Giselle had refused to go down to breakfast on her own—unwilling to brave dining with his parents by herself. Sylvia Vale, the soul of discretion, sent
up a breakfast tray and delayed lunch. It was just after
2:00 P.M. when they finally sat down at the dining room
table.

Lunch finished, Truman Vale asked Charles to join
him in his study while he smoked a cigar. Before they
could rise, the butler burst in, babbling something
about a radio broadcast. The four of them sat in the
study all afternoon listening to the news of the
Japanese attack on Pearl Harbor.

Over dinner that evening, Sylvia Vale had kept up a
stream of chatter, although it was obvious that the
minds of the men were far away. Sylvia surrendered to
their mood at last and dispatched Charles to the library
to fetch an atlas and then spent a great deal of energy
trying to find out exactly where Pearl Harbor was located. Amused, the men finally shook off their gloom and
helped her find the island of Hawaii.

After dinner Giselle had gone up for a wrap and
then back down to the great tiled loggia whose plate-
glass walls were open to the night wind from the sea.
She remembered vividly standing in one of the arches
and looking out at the moonlit surf. In less than six
months her mother and father would be dead, victims
of the Reich.

"Giselle! You're not dressed!" Orlena cried.

"I've been standing here thinking about the Vale
place," Giselle said as she turned to the countess. "Is it
in good condition?"

"Excellent," Orlena said. "The Mainwaring boys
have kept it up. Their mother was furious that her
father left it to them instead of to her, you know. She
loved that house."

"I know," Giselle said. "How would you like to have
me for a neighbor, Orlena?"

The countess clapped her hands. "What a wonderful idea."

Halloran, cradling the magnum of Dom Perignon like a babe in his arms, stumbled in his haste to follow the mistress. "Come on, Patrick," she called impatiently. He had never seen her like this, giddy as a schoolgirl.

She paused when she reached the stone steps before the large double doors of the formal entrance to Casa Vale and turned to watch him approach. "Right here," she said. "Give me the champagne."

Halloran handed over the magnum reluctantly. "Are you sure you don't want me to swing it for you, mistress?"

"I'll enjoy doing it myself." She hefted the magnum of champagne. "You're no longer Casa Vale," she told the house. "I christen you Casa Durand." She swung the bottle with all her might at the stone steps where it shattered with such a satisfying smash that Halloran half expected to see the huge house slide down the beach and into the Atlantic like a newly launched battleship.

Giselle grabbed him and gave him a hug and a kiss. "It's all mine, Patrick!" she cried. Then she spun away, fumbling in her purse for the door key.

Patrick Halloran stood like a man in a daze, watching as she unlocked the door. It was not until she disappeared into the foyer that he moved to follow.

Fabienne brought the mail while Alex and Charles were still at breakfast on the terrace. "I have to go into Nice this afternoon," Charles said as Alex sorted through the envelopes, passing two over to him.

Alex said nothing. She knew from the tone of voice

he used that she was not invited on this expedition. Things were not the same between her and Charles, had not been, ever since that disastrous morning Zandra had walked in on them. She was positive that he had a woman in Nice. The thought made her tear into the first envelope with enough vigor to break a nail. "They can't do this!" she cried.

Charles raised an eyebrow. "Do what?"

"The boys have sold Casa Vale. They should have given me a chance to buy it. It should have remained in the family."

Charles snorted. "That immense pile of stucco would take more than you and me together have to simply pay the bills and taxes, let alone the upkeep. Whoever bought it will raze it and put up something more modern. Arabs probably. They're the ones with all the money."

Alex suddenly crumpled the letter into a ball. She stood up and tossed it over the retaining wall and down the slope.

"Alex?"

"It was that woman!"

"What—"

"Giselle bought it." Then she screamed the words, "Giselle bought it!"

Charles stared at her a moment, stupefied. Then he began to chuckle.

Alex turned on him in a fury. "It's not funny, Charles. That house was part of our family legacy. She's not a Vale. It should have gone to me." Her fingernails were digging into her palms, but she was hardly aware of the fact, so angry was she. "That woman! She renamed it Casa Durand. What will Zandra say when she finds out?"

"To us? Nothing, I imagine."

The cool tone of his voice was like a splash of cold water in her face. After a moment she went on, more calmly; "Tru knew about this. I'm sure he did. He must have been behind it. He would do anything to hurt us. You know he would." She started for the house.

"Where are you going?"

"To phone Tru."

"No."

"I'm going to tell him—"

"No." He stood up, dropped his napkin on the table. "You will not phone Tru or harass him in any way."

"But Casa Vale?"

"My allowance from Vale Enterprises is more important to me just now, darling Alex." He gave her a cool kiss on the cheek as he passed. "I'll see you this evening."

He had a woman. In Nice. Alex was sure of it.

Norman Williamson, the private investigator who was on permanent retainer to Vale Enterprises, cabled his report to Tru Vale in Hong Kong only a day later than the cable from Noel. He read the report and then reread his nephew's cable. Whatever had possessed Giselle to buy Casa Vale? Tru wondered.

For a moment a brief hope flared inside him, but was just as quickly damped down. He had never been at the Palm Beach house while she was there; she would not think of it in connection with him.

Tru added the report and the letter to the bulging file that was always with him in his briefcase.

1977

ONE

Zandra had expected an objection from her mother, but not outright refusal. "I won't let you send Lilli away like this," Giselle said.

"It's time. You've indulged yourself with her enough."

"She's just a little girl."

"It's time she went to boarding school. She's twelve years old. How healthy is it for her to live with her grandmother and old Halloran doting over her? She needs friends her own age."

"She is in school. Here. I think it's a perfectly adequate arrangement."

"I don't, and if you'll recall, I'm her mother," said Zandra as Halloran entered the drawing room.

Halloran sat the tea things down with a rattle. "The girl is happy here," he said, without the slightest attempt to pretend he hadn't been listening to every word.

"Get out," Zandra told him.

He remained, an expression of distaste on his face, until Giselle herself told him, "That will be all, Patrick."

"Why don't you get rid of him?" Zandra asked her mother, not caring whether or not the old man heard her.

"He's been with me since you were a baby."

"Isn't that a good enough reason?" Zandra didn't wait for a reply. "There's something else we need to talk about." She braced herself; this was a subject she hated to bring up. "You need to get out more socially, to mingle more, to have your name in the press. While you've been playing doting grandmother, our image has been slipping."

"Don't you think you have your name in the press enough for both of us?" Giselle asked, amused.

"You're the one the company is identified with and we both know it. Your name and your photograph mingling in international society again; that's what it will take to revitalize the company."

"I thought that was what Camilla was supposed to do."

Zandra had the grace to blush. Camilla Pace, the Giselle Durand woman, had been her idea, and the company had spent a great deal of money on it. "Camilla isn't enough."

"So my punishment for being right is that you're going to take Lilli away from me."

"Really, Mother, that's not it at all. I'm trying to do what's best for Lilli. She's no longer a baby."

Giselle shook her head. "She's not like you, Zandra. She's shy. She needs—"

"She needs to grow up. That part of it's settled. Now I want you to think about what I've said. Henri Laud is having your Paris apartment renovated. You can use that for your European base. Jessie told me you had let your passport lapse. She's taking care of that."

"Really, Zandra, this isn't what I want to do."

"You'll enjoy it," Zandra said briskly, her mind already on the hundreds of other things she had to arrange this week. "And it will be good for Giselle Durand Cosmetics. That's what's important."

If the mistress hadn't sent him out of the room, Halloran would have had more to say. Poor little Lilli. Such a good, quiet child, and yet her mother would ship her off to boarding school without a second thought. He knew the mistress would not be able to stop her, not when Zandra had the ultimate authority of being the child's mother. And as for Bryan Rawlings, that pantywaist never bothered to see his own child as far as Halloran knew, not that Halloran wanted the likes of him hanging around the mistress again.

Now his great-nephew Francis was a child who could have done with boarding school, Halloran thought. Doreen's boy was eighteen now, but he had been in one scrape or another ever since he could toddle, each progressively worse. Keefe had given up on the boy long ago. Sheila would let not let him punish the lad when he was small and he was far too big for that now. She was the problem, not Francis. She thought her grandson a misunderstood saint, and not even the visits of the juvenile authorities could change her mind. The thought of Sheila made his frown darken. He would put off tonight if he could, but if he didn't make the trip to Brooklyn Heights, she would be calling him here.

Halloran waited until the nasty bitch had left before he went back to check on the mistress. He found her still seated on the drawing-room sofa. "Can I get you anything, mistress?" he asked, knowing a stiff whiskey would do her a world of good.

"No, thank you." She glanced down at her watch. "Patrick! You should have left by now. Your family will think I'm a slave driver." That small bit of thoughtfulness on her part made him feel worse than anything.

"And where is Keefe?" Halloran asked as Sheila pulled him toward the bedroom.

"Out drinking somewhere, with no thought for either of us, I can promise you."

"And young Francis? Do you know where he is?"

"Can't you put them out of your mind?"

"Not as easily as you."

"Perhaps this will direct your thoughts in the proper direction." She guided his hand to her breast.

A pounding on the door, as loud as God's judgment come upon them, made them break apart. "Mrs. Halloran!" a woman shouted from the hall.

Sheila answered the door. "What do you want, Maureen?" she demanded of the pasty-faced woman who stood there.

"A call has come for you."

"And why didn't it come here on my own phone?"

The woman ducked her head. "Because it's bad news and they thought you should hear it from me."

Sheila shrieked and clutched her chest. "My Francis? Something has happened to my Francis?"

"No," Maureen told her. "It's your husband."

After the funeral, Sheila's glittering eyes told Halloran that not even the presence of young Francis would keep her from his bed that night. Though he knew he would bed her again, he had no stomach for it the day Keefe was put in the ground. Against Sheila's protests, he went back to the mistress's apartment. That evening was the worst of Patrick Halloran's life. He tossed and turned, remembering with crushing detail each time he had bedded his brother's wife.

After the night he'd had, he was not surprised to learn from Cook that the mistress would leave the country as soon as young Lilli was packed off to school. God's punishment upon him for his adultery. He deserved no less.

Giselle thought her heart would break when she saw Lilli standing in the entry hall beside her suitcases. It was all she could do not to sob aloud. Zandra insisted it was what her daughter needed to make her grow up self-reliant and independent, but Giselle saw the frightened little girl inside Lilli's big blue eyes.

Then, although she could feel her heart like a leaden ball in her chest, she made an effort to comfort Patrick Halloran, who was crushed by her decision to go abroad. "I haven't even been to Paris in—what—twelve years now. Our European offices have forgotten who I am." She could see her travel plans caused him pain, but she was glad Zandra had urged her to go to Paris. So much of Giselle's life had revolved around Lilli these past few years. Perhaps too much. A change of scene might make Lilli's absence easier to bear.

"You'll need a car there."

"You have better things to do than drive me around Paris. Lilli will want to spend her holidays here in New York. And you'll open the Palm Beach house in October."

"You'll be spending the season there?"

Giselle smiled at his eagerness. "I plan to, yes. You love that house as much as I do, don't you?"

It was the thought of Casa Durand that gave Halloran the idea. "It would be good for you and the boy both," he told Sheila.

"I see no advantage for Francis."

"You want him to keep running with gangs and such? It's the city's bad influence on him."

"And West Palm Beach is not a city?"

"It will be different. Yank the boy up and transplant him. You'll see. His evil associations will fall away."

"I'll not deny the climate would be a better one. And I've an old friend there already."

That look in Sheila's eyes gave Halloran an uneasy feeling. "What old friend?"

"Friend is all you need to know. How often will I be seeing you if I allow myself to be shipped off to Florida?"

"When the mistress is there, I'll be with her."

"Fine," Sheila said.

"So here you are, returned from the dead," Orlena cried when she arrived for lunch at Giselle's Ile St.-Louis apartment. The last few years had not treated the countess kindly. Orlena's skin was aging badly, and her puffy face and thick waist were no doubt due to her taste for wine.

"But you," Orlena cried, as though she could read Giselle's mind. "How lovely you look. How youthful. Why don't your products do this for me, darling?"

"You look wonderful," Giselle said, kissing the countess on both cheeks. That was more diplomatic than telling her some women were born with good skin and some—those who were born with bad—abused even that.

Someone coughed delicately, and Giselle realized Orlena had not come alone. The man who stood in the doorway of Giselle's drawing room was not one of Orlena's *minets*, no baby-faced gigolo, but a distinguished-looking man of perhaps forty. Orlena waved for him to come forward. "The famous beauty Giselle Durand," she said, and for some unaccountable reason Giselle found herself blushing under the man's steady gaze.

"Romain Michaud, at your service." He bowed over her hand, and his lips sent a tingle up her arm.

"My husband's cousin. When he heard I was meeting you for lunch, he pestered me to come." Orlena glowed at him like a proud mother. "He'll be joining us on the yacht."

Giselle looked into Romain Michaud's dark eyes and found she was very glad of that.

Halloran ignored the chattering of the women in the backseat as he pulled up to the gates of Casa Durand. He unlocked them and stood beside them for a moment in the warm October sunshine. His first glimpse of the mansion always made his heart glad the mistress had bought the place, pricey though it had been.

". . . like a slave driver," Ruthie, the maid, was saying as Halloran strode back to the car. Both she and Joyce, the cook, looked a little alarmed as he stood for a moment looking at them.

"If it's me, you're discussing, Ruthie, you're entirely right. I'll drive you till you drop. You and those worthless females arriving tomorrow."

"You always make us do twice as much as the others this first day," Joyce complained.

"I'm sorry for that," Halloran told her. "And I'll try to make it up to you. I'll drive those poor wretches all the harder tomorrow to even out the score." The smiles that had blossomed on the women's faces as he spoke died abruptly.

When he had set the two of them to work, Halloran's first action as always was to make his way to the great tiled loggia and slide open the plate-glass walls so the brisk wind from the ocean could blow through the arches. When he had shoved all the walls open, he gazed across the terrace, to the aqua-marine waters of the swimming pool—an unneces-sary expense with God's free ocean only a few steps away.

It was a grand old house, he thought as he retraced his steps through the loggia. There had been a blowup, so Halloran had heard from other servants in Palm Beach, when Truman Vale willed the house, not to his own daughter, but to her sons. Anything that troubled that bloody bitch, Alexandra Mainwaring, made Halloran's own heart glad.

"Phone call for you," Ruthie called from the hall.

Halloran followed her back to the kitchen, a mis-take, he realized as soon as he lifted the phone and heard Sheila's voice on the other end of the line. "Come at five," she told him, and he could not argue with her, not with those two worthless females watching him with wide eyes as they washed glassware.

"At five," he said, though his wish was to be here this evening, in his own dear room over the garage, thinking about the mistress's arrival next week. Surely Keefe was looking down from heaven now, and saw the truth of his brother's lust for his wife. But Sheila wouldn't release her hold on him, nor was Halloran sure he wanted her to.

It was a snug little house he had found for Sheila and young Francis, Halloran thought as he pulled up in front of the West Palm Beach bungalow. There was no life insurance when Keefe's heart gave out on him, more's the pity. But what had a bachelor like Halloran to spend his money on besides his family? So he'd helped them find the place, and paid the deposit and the rent and would continue to do so.

Sheila met him at the door, and before he knew how it was going, they were in the bedroom together.

"Young Francis," he said, almost gasping from the feel of her hands on him.

"He'll be here later, but we'll be done by then, won't we, my fine stud."

Dressed again, Sheila dished up the stew for dinner. "Your prissy mistress has a new man, the papers say. A Frenchman. Did she ask you to fix up a separate bedroom for him or will they sleep together?"

"It's none of our business, now, is it?"

Sheila laughed. "Now don't go all moral on me, Pat. You know she's been with him, like me with you. She's no better than me, and maybe now you'll be admitting it."

The knock on the door was not young Francis but Mick Taggart. Normally Halloran would not be glad to see the man, for he had a suspicion this was Sheila's bedmate when he was not there. Add to that the man's bragging about his exploits in the IRA, a thing that—if it were true—Halloran thought best kept silent. Each time the man got a few drinks in him, he wanted to talk explosives and timers and how best to make bloody bits of bodies fly about. But tonight Halloran surprised both Mick and Sheila by welcoming Mick with open arms and practically forcing a whiskey into his hand.

"What's made Pat so friendly now?" Mick Taggart asked Sheila as they were climbing into bed together after Halloran left.

"He fears I'll give him the rough side of my tongue about his mistress. He thinks she's a virgin, you know."

"He doesn't think that about you, does he, old girl?" Mick asked with a slap to her fanny. "Does he know how many years you and I have been bouncing on the mattress?"

"He does not, and you'll keep your mouth shut about that when he's around."

"Oh-ho. So he's your sweetie, too."

"He pays the bills here, doesn't he? That gives him certain privileges."

"And what about when poor old Keefe was alive and paying the bills? Did Pat have privileges then, too?"

"None of your bloody business," she told him.

"So it's the both of us you've had for all these years, then? And how many more besides, I wonder?"

"You've never had another woman? St. Mick, is it?"

Mick grew serious. "Did he ever suspect the other thing?"

"No, nor how bad you bungled it."

"Did I know the wee thing would die like that?"

"We could have been millionaires except for your clumsiness," Sheila scolded, not for the first time.

The front door creaked and steps crossed the living room. "Young Francis?" Mick asked in the dark. "Will you tell him his uncle was here?"

"That's why he stayed away. He wanted no sour-faced lectures from our Pat." She ran her hand over him. "Will you get to the business at hand now?"

"With young Francis in the house?"

"What has that got to do with anything?"

TWO

Camilla Pace reminded Giselle of nothing so much as a large doll. If you dressed her, groomed her, and set her in place, there she would stay, a wistful smile on her lovely face, a blank look in her beautiful eyes, until someone collected her and moved her somewhere else. "I don't want her at Casa Durand," she told Zandra flatly over the phone when her daughter's call caught her on her brief stopover at the New York apartment on the way to Palm Beach. "One of the joys of seven months abroad has been that I don't have to see Camilla anywhere except in a glossy photograph."

"Really, Mother, I can't understand your attitude. She's not just anyone. She's the Durand Girl."

"She's an idiot. Not a brain in her head."

"But a very expensive idiot," Zandra countered. "If we wine, dine, and entertain her, her price won't go up."

"How can it go up? We have her under contract."

"And if she suddenly announced in a press conference that in spite of the contract, her doctor feels she should give up her position as the Durand Girl because the cosmetics are too harsh for her delicate skin?"

Giselle's heart fluttered. "She wouldn't do that?"

"She hinted as much. Besides, you know that her taste in men is execrable. And this last one . . . We simply must get her out of New York for a while."

Giselle glanced up as Romain Michaud entered the drawing room. In a moment she signaled with a wave of her hand. He nodded his understanding, and Giselle turned her attention back to the phone. "You're the one who insisted we hire Camilla."

"I insisted we hire someone. Every time we want to expand, the financiers all complain the company is too closely associated with you in the public's mind. If something should happen to you—"

"But nothing has. And in the meantime we have beautiful, brainless Camilla to contend with."

"I'm sure you'll manage," Zandra told her mother. "Oh, and have someone meet her at the airport. Camilla would never be able to hire a car and get all the way to Casa Durand by herself."

When Giselle hung up the phone, she closed her eyes and leaned back, massaging her temples.

"Headache?" Romain asked softly.

Giselle opened her eyes to find him standing before her, a drink in his hands. "Bless you," she said.

"Is there trouble?"

"Just aggravation." Giselle smiled up at him. "I had hoped to have you to myself. That was why I put off my granddaughter's visit. Now I find we're to be stuck with a houseguest for at least a few days. Camilla Pace?"

He shook his head. "The name is not familiar."

"Perhaps the face is." Giselle flipped through the magazine she'd bought at the airport. "Here," she said when she found the ad for Giselle Durand Cosmetics.

Romain looked at the photograph. With her angular, high-cheekboned face and huge, lash-framed eyes,

Camilla looked as delicate as a fawn. "But, of course. I've seen her face everywhere. I will enjoy talking to her."

"I doubt it," Giselle said dryly. "Unless you enjoy endless discussions about her face, her skin-care routine, her diet, her manicures, her pedicures, her waxes."

"Ah," Romain said as her meaning penetrated. "She is not mature like you."

His glance was still fastened on the glossy image on the page. He failed to catch the little shudder of distaste Giselle gave at his word choice. "No," she said after a moment. "Not mature at all."

The tone of her voice caught his attention. He looked up and then dropped the magazine. "Not that again," he said as he took her in his arms.

"I'm nine years older than you are, dear Romain. It's impossible to turn back the clock."

"What will it take for me to convince you that the clock has no meaning where we are concerned? This?" He kissed her lightly on the forehead. "Or this?" He kissed her on the chin. "Or this." He took possession of her mouth in a way that promised dinner would be delayed.

In fact, they never got to dinner at all. After Romain drifted off to sleep, Giselle rose quietly and went into the guest's bath to shower. Then, carefully, meticulously, she cleaned her face of makeup and put on the moisturizers she had chosen for maximum effect with minimum oil so that if Romain touched her cheek in the night, he wouldn't think she was coated with mayonnaise.

When she returned to bed, Romain was still asleep, but nevertheless, he reached for her and drew her to him. Giselle snuggled close and lay there thinking how lucky it was that Orlena had introduced them. Not that Orlena had thought so. "A *minet* was what you needed, not Romain. He is my husband's cousin, but by marriage. Though he calls himself a count, one cannot always be sure of these things."

"What difference does it make? He's fun to be with."

"But he lives in rather high style. You will soon see that. He'll begin asking you for money. If you don't give it to him, he will drift away."

"If he's so bad, then why did you introduce us?"

"Because, dear Giselle, I forgot you were an American. So serious, American women. They think of marriage and being supported by a man for the rest of their lives."

"And European women?"

"They think of the pleasures of the bedroom. And at that, my dear Giselle, Romain is a champion."

So he was, Giselle had learned. But now, to her chagrin, she was becoming more and more the American woman. Even if he were nine years her junior, she wanted him to ask her to marry him. In fact, she had planned to bring up the subject herself, as soon as they reached Casa Durand. That was the reason she had asked Lilli to delay her visit until December, much as she wanted to see her granddaughter. Now Camilla Pace had spoiled it all.

Patrick Halloran disliked Romain Michaud and made no bones about it. For the first time in their long association, Giselle found herself longing to fire her chauffeur on the spot. Romain, on the other hand, made it into a joke. "Ah, the faithful watchdog," he called Patrick behind the chauffeur's back.

"It's not funny, Romain," Giselle protested. "He's barely civil to you. I won't have him acting like this."

"But, my darling, don't you see. It's because he, too, loves you. Even an old fool like Monsieur Halloran cannot fail to be touched by your beauty and charm."

"Don't tease about that," Giselle pleaded.

"You've known for a long time, haven't you?"

She looked down.

Romain put his hand under her chin and tipped her

face upward. "Don't worry, dear Giselle. I won't make fun of him. I know true love when I see it."

It was Romain who volunteered to go to the airport and pick up Camilla Pace. "Really," he told Giselle. "I must see this phenomenon in person as soon as possible. To be so beautiful and so ignorant . . . I can't believe it unless I experience it for myself."

To Halloran's fury, Romain took the white Rolls she had purchased the year before, the twin of the one she kept in New York. When Romain failed to return in a reasonable amount of time with Camilla Pace, Halloran was inconsolable. "He's wrecked it for sure. Let me call the police, mistress."

Giselle waved him off, but she, too, had begun to worry before she heard Camilla's tinkling laugh in the loggia, echoed by Romain's deeper bass. She hurried down the hall and found them there, staring out over the swimming pool, toward the beach. "There you are," she said, relieved.

Halloran pushed past her and, before she could restrain him, demanded, "What did you do to the mistress's car?"

Although Romain assured him that it was perfectly all right, Halloran stomped off to reassure himself. Giselle turned to Camilla. "How good to see you," she told the Durand Girl.

"I didn't want to come," Camilla blurted. "But Zandra said I must, and now that I've met Romain I really don't mind. Who are those men at the front gate? The ones in uniform? They look ridiculous."

"Security guards." Orlena had talked Giselle into the guards. "Think of what happened to Madame Rubinstein," the countess said. "And in her own apartment, too. I provide the guards while you stay with me, but now that you have your own home in Palm Beach, you should have the guards, too." Giselle had carried the notion a step forward. Why have the guards simply blend into the landscape? If they were to serve as a deterrent, let them be dressed in crisp white uniforms with snap-brimmed caps. Now they had become a symbol of her residence at Casa Durand. If the guards were out, Giselle Durand was at home. "They're better than an advertisement in the Shiny Sheet, Camilla."

"What's that?"

"The newspaper here, dear. *The Palm Beach Daily News.*"

"If it's a newspaper, then why is it shiny."

"It's printed on paper that's specially treated."

"Why?"

Talking to Camilla always made Giselle feel as though she were talking to a three-year-old. "I believe it's so the newsprint wouldn't rub off on white gloves."

"Why would anyone wear white gloves to read a newspaper?"

"I really don't know, Camilla. Why don't you call the newspaper office and ask them that?"

Camilla glanced around the great tiled loggia. "Where's the telephone?"

Exactly like a three-year-old, Giselle thought. "Wouldn't you like to go up and change first?"

When the maid Giselle summoned led Camilla upstairs, Giselle turned to Romain and took his hands in hers. "I'm truly sorry. I'll speak to Halloran about his manners."

"I know he has your best interests at heart."

"That's generous of you. Sometimes he takes his role as my bodyguard too seriously."

Romain brought her hand to his lips. "Don't worry yourself, darling. As a European, I am familiar with the tyranny of old family retainers. What you really should apologize for is letting me languish for over an hour in that idiot woman's company."

"Isn't she awful? I truly don't believe she has a brain in her head. But she photographs beautifully. She's had a decided impact on sales."

"How long does your daughter intend to make us suffer Camilla's presence?"

"I'm sorry, darling. At least a month."

"She's a sadist, your Zandra. I don't look forward to meeting her."

"You won't, for a while. She's on her way to the Orient. The whole idea of having Camilla here was to keep her out of trouble while Zandra is out of the country."

"Trouble? What kind of trouble could that empty-headed creature cause?"

"You'd be surprised."

The oleanders were barely visible in the darkness. Halloran stepped further back into the shadows beside the hedge. He had known for almost a month that one of the maids was using the changing rooms by the pool to meet a man. Tonight he would catch them in the act.

Sheila had made it easy enough, calling as she had a few minutes ago and demanding Ruthie pass along the message that he was already late to dinner. He had driven out of the garage as though he were in an all-fired hurry and then parked the car at the end of the drive and made his way back to the rear of the house on foot. Now, as he heard the sound of footsteps crossing the terrace toward the changing rooms, he knew that the maid had believed his departure. The mistress was a softhearted soul, refusing to allow Halloran to fire even the most incompetent female if she had been with the staff for long. However, if he caught the maid in the act, he knew the woman, which ever one she was, would resign rather than have her mistress learn the truth.

The door of the changing room swung open just as

the footsteps reached it. A man's low-voiced greeting floated across the lawn to where Halloran stood, and for the first time that evening, Halloran hesitated. He recognized that voice. After a moment he shook himself like a dog and crept closer to the changing room. As he neared he heard the murmur of voices more clearly and he knew he was not wrong. It was that damned Frog! Not fit to hold the hem of the mistress's skirt, yet there he was in her bed each night.

And which of the maids was meeting Romain Michaud night after night? Halloran would have thought the lot of them either too old or too unsophisticated to interest the Frenchman. He moved closer, until he stood just outside the changing room, until he heard the laughter of the woman and realized who Michaud's playmate was.

"Really, Pat!" Sheila cried. "I might as well have cooked an old shoe for all the notice you've given dinner."

Halloran looked up to find her regarding him, hands on hips. "Could I have a drink?"

"The way of the Halloran men," she grumbled as she went to fetch the whiskey. "They take to the bottle whenever they can." When she brought the whiskey back, she gave him a searching look. "What's wrong, Pat?"

"Nothing," Halloran muttered. He poured himself two fingers of whiskey and tossed it down like water.

"Nothing, my eye. That's the rotgut Mick Taggart left here, and you drank it down without a shudder."

"Can't you leave me alone, woman!"

Sheila looked at him for a moment and then poured him another glass of whiskey and one for herself. "So it's something to do with your precious mistress, isn't it?"

Halloran stared into his glass. "Not her," he said. "Him. The fancy Frog. She looks at him like he hung the moon and all the time he——" Halloran broke off and downed the whiskey. This time the rawness of it penetrated his consciousness and he shuddered.

Sheila refilled his glass again. "He's done something to hurt her, then?"

"He's sleeping with that idiot model Camilla Pace," Halloran blurted. "The mistress knows nothing of it and when she finds out . . . When I tell her . . ."

"Look at me, Pat." When he raised his glance to her face, Sheila said, "Your mistress must not find out. Not from your lips. If God is merciful, from no one else's either. No woman's ego could survive a blow like that."

"I'll teach that damned Frog a lesson with my fists. With a fine woman like that who loves him, why does he want that featherheaded idiot? When I get through with him——"

"You'll stay out of it Pat. Besides," Sheila said, and her voice softened, "she'll not thank you for meddling. Think how it would embarrass her to find out you knew. Every time she met your eyes, she would think of it, and it would become a barrier between you. You see her little enough as it is."

He had misjudged his Sheila, Halloran thought as she continued to soothe him out of his shock and rage. He had thought she hated the mistress and here she was counseling him as to what was best for her. The warm glow of Mick Taggart's cheap whiskey helped calm him as well—until the question of why Mick Taggart had left a bottle of whiskey at Sheila's house rose to trouble him.

When Sheila finally bundled him off to bed at last, he fell heavily onto the mattress and then reached for her. "None of that now, Pat. You'll be glad of every minute of sleep tonight when you face tomorrow's hangover."

"And if Mick Taggart was here? Would you leave him like this?"

"Oh, jealous, are we? Go to sleep, Pat."

And he did, tumbling into a sleep so deep no dreams of fancy Frenchmen troubled him.

Sheila Halloran stood outside the bedroom door until Pat's even snores assured her he was out for the night. She walked down the narrow hall to young Francis's doorway and peeked inside. The bed was empty yet, even though it was almost 1:00 A.M. At least Pat hadn't thought to ask about his grandnephew or there would have been a scold for her. The boy was eighteen now, not a child anymore, yet Pat thought he should be in by ten.

Sheila smiled in the darkness. Her Francis was a wild one and the girls thought so, too. Once Pat had been like that, she remembered. Before he turned into a prudish old maid. Before he met his Mistress Giselle.

Sheila went on down the hall to the kitchen, pulling the door shut behind her. For safety's sake, she wedged one of the kitchen chairs under the knob, although she doubted Pat would stir again before morning.

It took her half an hour to get through to France and another ten minutes to be connected with Alexandra Mainwaring's villa in Nice. "Tell her it's Sheila Halloran," Sheila said as loudly as she could without rousing Pat in the bedroom. "Tell Mrs. Mainwaring I have a piece of news about her sister-in-law she'll like to hear."

Giselle was breakfasting with Romain on the terrace when the maid summoned her inside for a phone call from Jessie Fiedler. But when Giselle identified herself, there was only silence on the other end of the line.

"Jessie?" she asked her secretary. "Are you there?"

"I don't know how to tell you this," Jessie cried.

Giselle felt the crazed galloping of her heart. "Is it Lilli? Has something happened to her?"

"It's not Lilli. It's the *National Enquirer*."

Giselle laughed. "My God, Jessie! I thought it was something serious."

"They have photographs. All over the front page. Nude photographs," Jessie said hoarsely. "Oh, they've blotted out the strategic parts with black rectangles, but that only makes them look more naked."

"Nude photographs of whom?"

"Camilla Pace."

"Oh, no! And the new campaign just beginning." Giselle thought furiously for a moment. "Well, we'll just have to say that our cosmetics have made her irresistible."

"It's worse than that. The man . . . It's Romain Michaud."

Giselle swayed, clutching the phone with a suddenly bloodless hand. Not Romain, who had pulled back the sheets only this morning and kissed her all over her body in the pale dawn light. Giselle had a sudden vivid picture of her fifty-four-year-old body compared with Camilla's. Shame rushed over her.

"Giselle? Are you there?"

"I'm here," she said grimly. "Go on." For she knew there was more. She could tell from the hesitant quality of Jessie's voice.

"The headline, it says, 'Cosmetics Queen Loses Youthful Lover.'"

"Youthful! He's forty-five!"

"Yes? But . . ." Jessie said to someone there with her. "Just a moment, Giselle," Jessie said, and then put her hand over the receiver.

After a moment Jessie came back on the line. "That was Zandra's secretary. Zandra's seen the paper, too.

She's having this call switched to her office. Oh, Giselle, I'm so sorry."

A click and then Zandra said, "Mother? Are you there?"

"I'm here." Giselle looked out toward the terrace. Romain still sat at the breakfast table, but now he had been joined by Camilla. He leaned over and said something to her and she threw back her head and laughed. What a beautiful neck she has, Giselle thought.

"I've just checked with our lawyers. Camilla's out. This violates her contact, so there's no problem on that score. If you want to keep your phony count, that's your affair, but personally, I would dump him."

"What makes you think he's a phony?" Giselle asked, her curiosity overriding even her pain for a moment. "He's the cousin of Orlena's husband."

"Silvain's a ringer, too. I thought you knew that."

"But Orlena's title?"

"She kept it after she buried her first husband. Really, Mother. I don't have time for all this. We're besieged by reporters. I'm surprised you don't have them at the front gates by now."

"Perhaps they are," Giselle said vaguely, watching Camilla butter a role for Romain.

"Jessie's making the reservations for your flight back. We'll have a press conference tomorrow afternoon."

A press conference? And what would she look like after a rushed flight back to New York and the kind of sleepless night she knew she'd have? Giselle suppressed a shudder. "No press conference. And have Jessie make my reservations straight through to Paris."

"You can't leave the country! We have to choose the new Durand Girl."

"You do that, Zandra." Giselle hung up without waiting to hear her daughter's protests and walked out to the terrace. As the sunlight struck her face she thought how old she must look next to Camilla.

Romain and Camilla looked up as she reached the table. "Giselle, darling," Romain said. "We were just discussing our plans for today."

"I'm afraid all our plans have changed." Giselle had grown quite perceptive suddenly. She was aware that the slight shift of Romain's body, the quick intake of Camilla's breath, meant that he had placed his hand on the model's upper thigh. "I've been called to Paris on business."

"So abruptly?" Romain asked.

She nodded.

"Then I must go and pack. Although I hate to leave this lovely place."

"You're not going with me, Romain." Her voice was perfectly calm, but she found that she had to grasp the back of her chair for balance. "You and Camilla will have to make your own arrangements. I'm afraid you can't stay here, though. I'll be closing the house as of this afternoon. The hotels are crowded this time of year, but I'm sure you'll find something. If not here, perhaps in West Palm Beach or Miami."

Romain laid his napkin on the table. "Of course I'm coming with you."

She ignored him and turned to Camilla. "You had better get in touch with your lawyer, Camilla. I'm sure you'll want their advice on how to proceed now that your contract with Giselle Durand Cosmetics is canceled."

"She knows, Romain," the model said flatly, the first intelligent words Giselle had ever heard her utter.

"Yes, I do," Giselle said before the Frenchman could say anything. "Be out of this house by this evening." She started back to the house.

She heard Romain's footsteps behind her on the terrace, but she did not slow or turn. "My dear strait-laced American," he said. "You have let yourself become upset over nothing. This is a small thing. A private thing between two people. Perhaps you would find it interesting for the three of us to enjoy love together. Camilla is much more experienced than she looks, both with men and with women. No one else need know."

Giselle turned on him then. "Everyone knows, Romain!" She left him standing there on the sunny terrace while she went into the house to pack her bags for Paris.

Giselle was far over the Atlantic, and quite drowsy from a combination of sleeping pills and vodka when she finally opened the folder Jessie had thrust into her hand during Giselle's layover at Kennedy. She leafed through the papers idly, her mind on her lovely Paris apartment. Romain's things were there. She would stay at a hotel for a few days while she had every sign of him removed and the rooms repainted.

Giselle turned another page and saw her daughter's face looking up at her. In the glossy photograph, Zandra looked feline and dangerous and far younger than thirty-five. The caption beneath the photograph read, "The Durand Girl Becomes a Woman." Zandra had taken her at her word. Giselle laughed aloud, a harsh, painful sound that brought the stewardess to her side.

She ordered another drink, and while she waited for it to arrive, Giselle continued to study the photograph. At least the Durand Woman looked as though she had a few brains in her head. Unlike Camilla. Unlike herself.

1981

ONE

Giselle, dressed now, waited while the doctor scribbled a note to himself. She had chosen him at random under *médecins* in the Yellow Pages of the phone directory.

"I think you know what the problem is," the doctor said in heavily accented English. "You have known a long time."

Giselle laughed as she turned to face him, dismissing his diagnosis with a wave of her hand.

"This is no matter for amusement. Your condition must be monitored. I will give you *une ordonnance*." He reached for a pen and scribbled out the prescription, and then handed it over along with the bill. "Next week you will return for tests. The important thing to remember is not to exert yourself. You are no longer a young woman."

"I'm so sorry, Monsieur le docteur Adlard," Giselle said, reaching for her purse. "I'm afraid I won't be in Paris next week. But I'll be certain to see a doctor as soon as I return to the United States." He shrugged, but she saw in his eyes that he knew her lie for what it was.

As soon as she reached the street, she tore the prescription into tiny pieces and dropped it into the first trash receptacle she passed.

Her concierge spoke as Giselle crossed to the elevator of her Ile St.-Louis apartment, but Giselle didn't even nod at the woman. All the way up in the elevator, she kept clenching and unclenching her fists. When she reached her apartment, she dismissed the maid for the rest of the day and went directly to her bedroom. Kicking off her shoes, she threw herself onto the bed and began to sob.

She had no idea how long she lay there, but when she came to herself, the pillow was damp against her cheek and her fingernails had dug holes in the silk coverlet. Giselle listened to the hollow sound of her heart beating in her empty chest and wondered why she had never heard it before.

Henri Laud spent the longest Friday of his life following Giselle Durand through the building that housed the Paris branch of her company, staying just at her elbow, ready to step forward with any information she might desire. He ran a damp nervous palm over his shining bald head. The unruly curls his staff used to claim gave him the look of a poodle had vanished long ago. He sometimes joked that he had given his hair in his service to Giselle Durand. Today it felt like no jest.

What in the world was happening? he wondered. He had assumed—everyone had assumed—that Giselle Durand was no longer involved in the day-to-day operations of her cosmetics company. For three years she had been back in Paris, and yet this was the first day she had come to poke and pry through the Paris operation.

They finished the tour in his office, where Giselle Durand spent two hours going over the books. When she closed the last of them with a snap, she looked up and smiled. "Well done, Henri."

He waited, shifting his weight from foot to foot like a nervous boy, for some further indication of the purpose of this visit, but she was already gathering up her purse, her light silk jacket. When it seemed she would depart without another word, he could stand it no longer. "Isn't there anything else, madame?"

She patted his hand. "Just keep me informed, Henri."

She was already at the door before he could speak. "But, madame . . . You wish reports sent to you?"

"Of course, Henri."

Merde! What a nightmare! "I . . . at your apartment?"

"No, Henri," she said with the first hint of impatience she had shown the entire day. "To my office. In New York. I'll be there bright and early Monday morning."

When the door closed behind her, Henri sank back into his chair, feeling the damp sweat in his armpits. Instinctively his hand reached for the phone. Then he paused. Who in New York deserved more warning than Henri himself had gotten? Had they alerted him last year that the Dragon Lady was flying to Paris? No, Zandra Rawlings had arrived unannounced and spent two weeks on the same inspections that had just taken her mother the space of one day to accomplish.

Henri took a deep breath and leaned back, enjoying himself for the first time that day, as he imagined the havoc ahead for the New York office of Giselle Durand Cosmetics.

Patrick Halloran picked Giselle up at the airport. It would have been simpler to take a taxi, but she knew his feelings would have been hurt by that. How old was he now? Sixty-nine? Seventy? He should be thinking of retirement. Of taking it easy. That thought brought the French doctor's words back to her: *You are no longer a young woman.* Giselle's fingers tightened on her bag. She leaned forward. "Don't take me home. Take me to my office."

"But, mistress . . . After this long trip? Surely you need a rest first."

"To the office, Patrick."

She leaned back, feeling the miles she had traveled. Tonight she would rest. Tomorrow she would arrange to see another doctor. Someone who didn't think of her as an old woman simply because she was fifty-seven. Someone who knew how to keep his mouth shut. But today she planned to take back what was hers. It had taken a shock like the moment in the doctor's office in Paris to remind her that she was not ready to give up on life—or on the company that bore her name—just yet.

Halloran glanced in the mirror and the smile on the mistress's face made his heart glad. When he pulled up in front of the Giselle Durand building, he hopped out of the car and rushed around to open her door. "Like old times, mistress," he said. The doorman had recognized the car and was already advancing. Halloran watched the mistress sweep into her kingdom.

The phone rang on Jessie Fiedler's desk. "Looks like you're employed again, Jessie," said Barbara Sheraton from Bookkeeping. "I just passed Giselle Durand on her way to the elevator. Look sharp, girl. You don't want the Boss Lady to find you doing a crossword puzzle."

"I owe you." Jessie hung up without waiting for a response, stuck the crossword puzzle she had indeed been working on, into a desk drawer. She snatched up the vase of fresh flowers she had arranged that morning on her own desk and hurried into Giselle Durand's office.

Thank heaven she always checked to see that the janitors had done their duty in here, she thought as she set the vase on Giselle's desk. Then she rushed over to the credenza and snatched up Giselle's favorite cup and one of the linen napkins with *GD* embroidered in the corner.

In the outer office, she filled the cup with black coffee and set it on a tray with the napkin. She took the remaining croissant from her own desk—still fresh, as the one she just ate had been—placed it on the napkin, and thrust the rest of the remains of her own midmorning snack into the wastebasket.

When the door to the outer office opened, she was standing there, tray in hand. "Good morning," she said to Giselle Durand. "I was just taking your coffee in for you."

"Jessie, you never fail to amaze me. You must have ESP." Giselle paused in the doorway of her office and gazed at her desk. "Fresh flowers, too. How much do I pay you?"

"Not nearly enough," Jessie told her as she set the tray down on her desktop. "Especially if I'm going to have a boss-in-residence for a change."

"I'm afraid you are," Giselle told her.

"Wonderful!" Jessie meant it. She was tired of Lori Segal, Zandra's snippy secretary, lording it over her.

Giselle laughed. "Pour yourself a cup of coffee, too, and tell me everything that's been happening."

What wonderful timing, Jessie thought as she hurried to the outer office for her own coffee. Zandra Rawlings was in Los Angeles all this week. Someone would call her with the news that her mother was back, but by the time she returned, the coup would be over. Too bad it would probably be bloodless. Jessie would love to see Lori Segal's head chopped off.

By 6:00 A.M. Monday morning, Zandra was in her office. Jet lag was nothing compared with her worry over why her mother had suddenly decided to return to New York. Add to that the missing folder. She had pawed through the litter on her desk twice and gone through all the file drawers, but she couldn't find the file on the Zandra line. By the time her secretary arrived, she was in a fury. "Where's the Zandra folder?" Zandra demanded as soon as Lori walked in.

"Mrs. Durand has it," Lori Segal told her boss.

"You stupid little bitch. Why did you give her that?"

"I didn't give it to her. She took it."

"What?"

"She spent all day Friday going through your files."

"You let her go through my files?"

"How could I stop her? It's her company."

Zandra looked at her for a moment. "You're fired."

The girl's face went white. "Mrs. Rawlings! How could I—"

Zandra marched back into her office and slammed the door. All she wanted to do was weep. Abruptly she realized that the phone in the outer office was ringing and ringing. She opened the door. Ignoring the ringing phone, Lori was going through a desk drawer. "What are you doing?" Zandra demanded.

"Cleaning out my desk. You just fired me, remember."

"Don't be stupid. Answer the damned phone, will you?"

The girl slammed the drawer and reached for the phone. "Of course," she said, to whomever was on the other end of the line. When she hung up, there was a trace of satisfaction in her otherwise pale face. "Your mother wants you in her office. At once."

As soon as she stepped into the hall, Zandra could feel the difference. Giselle Durand was back. Everyone knew it. Each face she passed registered that fact. Some were loyal to her. Others . . . Zandra dug her nails into her palms. What was it about Giselle Durand that made everyone love her? And why hadn't Zandra inherited that particular quality along with her mother's flawless skin?

"Hello, Zandra," her mother said when Jessie waved her on in. Giselle Durand came around the desk and pecked at her daughter's cheek.

Zandra pulled away from the polite gesture. "Why did you go through my office? You had no right!"

"Hello, Mother. Good to see you," mocked Giselle. "I had every right. This company, this"—she spread her arms wide—"everything still belongs to me."

"You walked away four years ago."

"I'm back."

"It's too late."

"It's not." Giselle sat down on the edge of her desk. In spite of her anger, Zandra couldn't help marveling over how well her mother looked. How beautiful her skin was in the light that fell through the window facing the desk. "Sit down, Zandra. We need to talk."

Zandra sank down in the nearest chair. "If you were unhappy with the way I'm running things, why didn't you let me know?"

Giselle ignored the outburst. She reached behind her, on the desk, and picked up a folder. Zandra recognized the tab. "I want you to know that I've read through this with a completely open mind. You've done some excellent work in developing the concept of a Zandra line. But I'm afraid I don't agree that a new line is necessary at this time."

"You're wrong." In spite of her conviction, Zandra could hear the shrill edge in her own voice. "It's a logical extension. I've been the Giselle Durand Woman for four years. People identify the line with me. This will expand our market."

Giselle tapped the folder against the edge of the desk. "I don't agree."

"The sales projections—"

"I am the company. I. Giselle Durand."

"Women have identified you with the company for over thirty years. But now it's my turn."

Giselle tossed the folder on the desk. "No. There will be no new line."

Charles Vale was looking out over the harbor when the small quick man with a terrier's face joined him. "Don't think of it as blackmail," the man said as he handed the envelope to Charles. "Think of it as a fine for damaging the merchandise."

"They deserved it." The breeze whipped his words away.

"Deserved that?" The man spat. "They were pretty boys, able to earn a great deal of money. Now because of your fists, they are no longer pretty. They will be no better than beggars for the rest of the their lives."

"They called me a homosexual!"

"And what are you, if not that?"

Hands clenched into fists, Charles took one step forward before he saw the 9mm automatic the man held. He halted.

"Why does this label anger you? It is the reason why we do business in the first place, is it not?" The man looked at Charles's face carefully. "Perhaps you deny it to yourself. That is all right with me. But I know the truth about you and so did those boys. Just as I know you will want my services in acquiring other young friends." He nodded at the envelope. "Examine those photographs at your leisure and then call me."

"The negatives?"

"The negatives will remain with me, insurance against the loss of any other valuable assets."

When the terrier-faced man walked away, Charles opened the envelope. The boys had been good. Looking at the photographs, he remembered the precise feel of those small quick fingers on his penis. The way the boys used their mouths and tongues to bring him to an erection. The probing pleasure he had felt kneeling over the smaller boy while the larger one knelt behind him. But then afterward, one of them had giggled and called him a homosexual.

His hand closed, crushing the photographs. The salt breeze whipped his hair from his face as he gazed out toward the horizon. Finally he turned and walked away from the shore. He knelt behind the shelter of a rock and touched his lighter to the edge of the envelope. When the whole thing had been reduced to a pile of ashes, he scattered the ashes with his foot, watching the breeze lift them like small gray butterflies. Then he went down to the sidewalk café he frequented every afternoon and ordered a drink.

Alex woke to the echoes of a thunderclap. She lay there, conscious of the depression in the sheets left by Charles's body. She turned on her left side and snuggled her face into her pillow. With her right hand, she stroked the warmth he had left behind him.

Somewhere in the silent villa, she heard a door creak, and then the shuffle of soft-soled shoes against a tile floor. What time is it? she wondered. It must be nearly morning if Charles was already up. Closer, another door creaked, and then a shrill scream sounded.

Alex rose, grabbing her robe, and hurried out of

the bedroom. The screaming stopped, cut off like water from a tap. Other doors were opening now, and other feet, bare like hers, made soft, slapping sounds against the tiles. "Charles?" Alex called, but received no answer.

At the door to the library, a maid tried to block the entrance with her body. Alex shoved her away. The housekeeper was already inside. She looked at Alex with huge dark eyes. "Madame. Don't." She wrung her hands.

Alex looked beyond her, toward Charles's desk. The chair was shoved back, all the way against the wall. And on the wall itself—Alex stared. Someone had dashed red paint on the cream of the wall. "Who did this?" she cried, turning to the housekeeper. "What vandal dared do this?"

The housekeeper grabbed for her hands, but Alex snatched them away, turning back to the desk. "Please, madame. Come away from there."

"We mustn't let Monsieur Charles see this mess. You know how he hates ugly things." Alex brushed her hair back and was surprised to find her cheeks wet with tears. "Bring buckets of water. We must clean this before he sees it."

This time the woman caught Alex's hands and clung to them. Alex was surprised by the warmth of the housekeeper's hands against her own. "The police, madame. They will not want anything touched."

"Of course," Alex said, nodding her head with exaggerated movements. "They will want to catch the culprits. They will need every clue." She jerked her hands free and grabbed the housekeeper's shoulders. "Monsieur Charles will understand? Won't he?" She shook the woman. "Won't he understand?"

"Madame, please. Come out of here. We must call the authorities."

Alex had turned back to the desk. The splash of

paint on the wall looked like a crude outline of Africa. A thick runner of red had sluiced down from Cape Town and pointed like an arrow at what lay between the chair and the desk. The housekeeper's hands plucked at the sleeves of Alex's robe. She batted them away as if they were insects and took a step forward.

Now she could see the seat of the desk chair, and a man's arm—odd how much it resembled Charles's arm in his favorite robe—flung across the leather. She stepped closer. The body was caught between the desk and the chair, crumpled into a heap, like a small boy hiding there behind the desk, hoping to escape Father's punishment. Charles was always hoping to escape Father's punishment. "It's all right, Charles," she said as she had a million times before. "You can come out now. I won't let Father hurt you."

But Charles remained still, slumped over in that awkward position. Why, it made her bones ache to look at him. "It's all right," Alex said again, coming around the desk. She reached over and patted his shoulder, shoving against the chair as she did so.

Charles slumped sideways, and fell, the flat of his back striking the floor with the thud of a piece of beef on a butcher's counter. His head turned, so that he appeared to be staring at the legs of his desk, and Alexandra saw the bloody mess where the back of his head had been.

TWO

Tru's man picked them up at the Nice-Côte d'Azur airport. "You have a suite at the Negresco, Mrs. Vale," he told Giselle. "And Mrs. Mainwaring has a room ready for you at the villa, Mrs. Rawlings."

"No," Zandra said. "I won't stay at the villa."

"Right," Tru's man said with a smoothness Giselle would have found amusing under any other circumstances. "Perhaps there's another suite available at the Negresco. Or—"

"You can't stay in my suite, Zandra." Giselle forced an amused tone into her voice. "I need my privacy."

Zandra ignored her as she had all the way across the Atlantic. "I'll sleep in a maid's closet if I have to," she told Tru's man. "But I won't stay at the villa."

As soon as she reached her suite at the Negresco, Giselle hurried into the bathroom with her purse and took out her heart medicine. She emptied one of the pills into her hand and put it under her tongue. Then she closed the toilet and sat down on the lid. The strain of keeping her condition to herself was beginning to tell.

She shouldn't have made this trip. At first she had told herself she was coming because she owed it to the company. What would the media think if she failed to show up at her husband's funeral? she had asked the department heads of Giselle Durand Cosmetics. No one had been rude enough to mention that their founder and her husband had been separated for over thirty years. Everyone crowded around, showering her with sympathy.

Giselle laughed harshly at the memory. She owed Charles nothing. He had ruined so much of her life, taken so much from her, that she had been glad to hear he was finally dead. No, the real reason for this trip had been the airline tickets hand-delivered to her office, her name on the envelope written in Tru's handwriting.

Somewhere a door crashed open. She heard Zandra call her name, and then someone banged furiously on the bathroom door. "Mother? Are you in there?"

Giselle stood just as Zandra threw open the door. Realizing she still clutched the prescription bottle, she stuffed it back in her purse.

Zandra clutched a newspaper in her hand, her face a white mask of shock. "Did you know about this?" she asked, waving the newspaper. A large picture of Charles was on the front page. "It says he killed himself."

All the anger that had consumed Giselle as she crossed the Atlantic turned to joy in that single instant. She grabbed the newspaper and reached in her purse for her reading glasses. "Benjamin," Giselle breathed softly as she read the first paragraphs. "He did it because of Benjamin."

Zandra snatched the paper back. "It's always

Benjamin with you, isn't it? You loved him more than you loved Father. More than you loved . . ." She choked and then went on. "More than you loved me. Everything goes back to Benjamin, doesn't it?" She screamed that last.

Giselle reached for her. "You don't understand," she cried, but Zandra rushed from the bedroom, taking the newspaper with her. In a moment Giselle heard the door of the suite slam. She sat down on the bed, feeling the uneven palpitations of her heart.

"Zandra?" Alexandra Mainwaring cried when she reached her niece's suite at the Negresco. "Why are you there? You're supposed to stay here with me."

Zandra cradled the phone against her shoulder as she zipped her dress. How easy it was to slip back into the old patterns. They might have spoken only yesterday. She refused to let herself think of the awful morning she had walked into her aunt's bedroom. "No one mentioned I was to stay there. Perhaps it was Mother's idea to get me a suite here." Zandra grinned at herself in the mirror.

"That woman! I won't have her at the funeral!"

"Uncle Tru wants her there, so I'm afraid you have no choice. She was my father's wife."

"Only because he never went through the formality of divorcing her."

"How would it look if she stayed away? The papers might dig even deeper for the reason Father killed himself."

"He didn't kill himself! It was a terrible accident."

"Then you don't want the press printing innuendos about his relationship with my mother."

The silence on the other end of the phone told Zandra she had chosen the right words. "Will you be here tonight for dinner?" Alex said at last.

"Mother and I both?"

A longer silence. "Of course," Alex said finally. "Charles would have wanted that."

"What about Uncle Tru?"

"Oh, he'll be here. He's taken charge of everything," Alex added bitterly. "He's even insisting that Charles be cremated. If he had wanted that, he would have left instructions."

"Aunt Alex, try to—"

"I'm not staying here, you know. Tru has no further hold on me now. I've my own money and I don't intend to stay in exile."

"You're moving back to the States?" In spite of herself, Zandra felt a little thrill of joy. After she hung up, she stood there for a moment, realizing just how much she had missed her aunt these past few years.

If it had not been for Noel and Wesley's presence at dinner that night, it would have been a completely silent meal, Zandra thought. It was her cousins who carried on the conversation at the table. None of the others spoke directly to each other. She noted that her mother, not normally a heavy drinker, accepted several refills of wine. When Aunt Alex rose after dinner, Uncle Tru said, "Why don't we forego the after-dinner brandy and send Giselle and Zandra back to the hotel? Giselle is out on her feet."

"Not very flattering, Tru," Giselle said, the first words she had directed to him that evening.

Zandra took a closer look at her mother and realized her uncle was right. She had never seen that pale drawn look on her mother's face before. "Are you coming down with something?" she asked.

"I'm fine!" Giselle snapped. "If you want to worry about someone, worry about Alex."

"How generous of you, Giselle!" Alex cried, and then burst into noisy tears.

Zandra was aware of her uncle and cousins exchanging glances across the table, and then suddenly both she and her mother were being bundled toward the dining-room door by Uncle Tru and Wesley while Noel moved to his mother's side.

"Wait!" Aunt Alex called through her tears. "Zandra's things are here. I had the hotel send them over."

"Very well," Uncle Tru said. Before Zandra quite realized what was happening, Uncle Tru had transferred her to Wesley and exited with her mother.

"But I don't want to stay here tonight," she whispered to Wesley.

"She needs you, kiddo. We'll play poker after she hits the sack. If you behave, Noel and I'll let you win a couple of hands."

Outside Alex's villa, Tru waved off his man and took the wheel of the car himself for the drive to Nice. When they reached the Promenade des Anglais, he pulled over and parked. He helped Giselle out and then, taking her hand, he led her down the steps to the public beach. Behind them, the palms that lined the avenue rustled in the night wind. The waters of the Baie des Anges were black velvet in the moonlight, sparked by the lights of the luxury hotels that followed the gentle curve of the bay. "I've always regretted banishing Charles here," Tru said, the first words he had spoken since they left the villa. "Nice is one of my favorite cities."

"You've missed it?"

"I've missed you," he said, and took her in his arms. When they kissed, it was as though all the years rolled away.

"Come back to the hotel with me," Giselle said when they broke off to look into each other's eyes.

"I intended to."

As they walked through the lobby of the Negresco, hand in hand, Giselle felt like a schoolgirl. So many wasted years, she was thinking. And it took Charles's death to bring us back together. But she wouldn't allow herself to think of Charles now. He had no place in this wonderful night.

"Oh, Tru," she said as the door of her suite closed behind them and he took her in his arms once more. "Why did we wait so long?"

The phone rang just as the sun rose. Tru raised up on one arm and stroked her face tenderly with his other hand. "You'd better answer it," he said.

"I'm sure my reputation is already in tatters after the way we paraded across the lobby last night."

He slapped her lightly on the rear. "Answer it, woman!"

She did, only to find Alex on the other end, demanding to speak to Tru. "Put him on at once. I know he's there! Don't try to deny it, Giselle!"

She didn't. She said nothing, simply passing the receiver over to Tru and watching the various emotions wash over his face as he listened to his twin.

When he finally hung up, the joy had gone out of his face. "I have to go back to the villa this morning." He rolled out of bed and began to dress. "I'll send someone to pick you up for the service."

Giselle rose, too, wrapping the sheet around herself. "Tru? What's wrong?"

He stopped dressing for a moment. "Blackmail. Someone sent Alex some rather nasty photos of Charles with some young male friends."

Giselle sat down on the edge of the bed.

"You didn't know?" Tru asked her.

She shook her head. "Orlena tried to tell me, but I didn't believe her."

"With Silvain for a husband, the countess should know."

"What are you going to do?"

"I've already had a long talk with the authorities here—and made a generous cash contribution to several of them. I don't believe I'll have any trouble getting rid of this scum." He grimaced. "It's the other I'm worried about. The servants could talk and I'd rather the boys didn't find out. I need to get Alex back to the States as soon as possible."

"What 'other,' Tru?"

"You must know after all these years what a close relationship Charles and Alex had."

"Why, of course, I do. He was her younger brother, almost like a son to her. He—"

"No, Giselle. Not like a son. Like a lover."

His words came from so far away that she suddenly believed that they were in two different rooms, two different worlds. In her world, people didn't say things like that.

Tru sat beside her on the bed. "Now you know the worst about my family, Giselle." Her hands were in her lap. He covered them with his own. "Now I can ask you something I've wanted to ask you for years. Will you marry me?"

She raised her head and looked straight into his eyes. "Oh, yes, Tru! Yes!"

They returned to the villa after the service. Giselle could still remember how Alex had looked after she received word that Neville Mainwaring had been killed in the war. Beautiful and stoic. Now she was a haggard wreck, as if she had lost some vital part of herself.

Giselle clenched her hands together. She and Tru had agreed back at the hotel this morning that they would keep their engagement a secret from the rest of the family. She could see by Alex's distraught face that this had been an excellent idea. Alex was a woman on the ragged edge. Anything might tip her over.

Many government officials had come to pay their respects at the villa, as well as a large cross section of the jet set—so many people, all of whom seemed to know Giselle's name. As the afternoon wore on she began to feel pawed at, bruised from too many hands grasping her arms. She made her way through the throng to her daughter, who was nursing a large drink. "Zandra? I think I'll go back to the hotel now. Do you want to come or will you stay here?"

"I've just heard the most amazing thing," Zandra said, as though her mother hadn't spoken at all. "Someone is trying to blackmail Aunt Alex."

Giselle patted her arm. "Don't worry about it. Tru is taking care of everything."

Zandra jerked away from her mother's hand so abruptly that her drink spilled. "It's true, then?"

"I don't have any personal knowledge of it," Giselle said swiftly, hoping to forestall any further questions. "You'll have to ask your uncle."

"He brushed me off. So did Noel and Wesley. But something's up. I can tell from what Aunt Alex let slip."

"You should try to get her to bed."

Zandra took another sip of her drink. "Not my job."

"Zandra, the poor woman is—" Giselle broke off, realizing that something behind her had brought an unaccustomed glow of happiness to her daughter's face. She turned to see Bryan Rawlings crossing toward them.

But when he reached them, it was Giselle's name he uttered, Giselle he took in his arms, although she stiffened and tried to step away. "I'm sorry I couldn't have been here earlier." He nodded to his wife. "Hello, Zandra." A swift glance at her daughter told Giselle that the light had gone out of Zandra's eyes.

"You!" Alex Mainwaring shrieked from across the room. "What are you doing here?" She rushed at Bryan like a madwoman, her hands extended.

Bryan stood where he was, until he realized at the last moment that she intended to claw his eyes. "Alex! For God's sake," he cried as he caught her arms. "What's wrong with you?"

"I know what you did!" Alex screamed. "You and her." Tru and Noel moved swiftly to Alex's side.

"Get a doctor here," Tru told Zandra. She hurried away to phone while he and Noel half led, half carried Alex to the nearest sofa.

Giselle and Bryan were left alone in a small silent space in the middle of the crowded room, every eye upon them. Giselle walked away. Outside the villa, she found Tru's man lounging against Tru's car. "Take me back to the Negresco," she snapped at him.

"Certainly, madam. As soon as I check with Mr. Vale."

"Now!" Giselle told him, opening the door for herself.

Tru's man looked back at the villa, and then said, "Certainly, madam," and slipped behind the wheel.

Alexandra Mainwaring lay in the darkness of her bedroom staring up at the ceiling. She had never realized a room could be so lonely. The door opened with a creak. She glanced that way. A familiar male form was silhouetted in the rectangle of light. She sucked in her breath. Before she could call Charles's name, her twin said, "I'm going back to Nice, Alex. I just wanted to make sure you were all right before I left."

All right? She would never be all right again. And he was on his way back to that whore. She shifted her glance to the ceiling once more.

"Alex? Noel and Wesley will stay on and help you pack. I'll do anything necessary to get you settled in New York."

"Thank you, Tru." She kept her eyes on the ceiling. If she turned her head, she would see the empty spot beside her on the bed.

"If you don't need anything, then . . ." His voice trailed off. After a few moments she heard the creak of the door closing once more.

Back to New York. Yes. Perhaps that was best. She turned on her side abruptly and let her hand drift down the faint hollow Charles's body had worn in the mattress beside her. "Don't worry, darling," she whispered in the darkness. "I'll take care of everything."

She continued to stroke the mattress, but her mind was already far away. Zandra had come back to her once more, and Alex planned to make the most of that. Last night she had listened to her niece telling her sons about her plans to launch a new cosmetics line and how Giselle prevented it.

Next August Zandra would be forty years old, and it was a birthday Alex intended to help her niece celebrate. She would remind Zandra that because of the sacrifices she, Alex, made years ago, Zandra would come into ownership of enough of Giselle Durand Cosmetics to launch a new cosmetics line if she so chose. Or perhaps even force Giselle out of the company entirely. Alex smiled in the darkness, like a wolf baring its teeth.

* * *

From the window of her suite at the Negresco, Giselle watched the vivid blue of the Baie des Anges darken to black as the sun set. When the phone rang, it was not Tru on the line, but Bryan. "Will you have dinner with me? I'm downstairs. I already have reservations at the Chantecler. I'll meet you there in half an hour."

"Bryan, I'd rather not—"

"I have to talk to you, Giselle. If you won't meet me at the restaurant, then I'm coming up."

At the desk Giselle stopped and left word where she would be in case Tru called. What was keeping him? He couldn't know how badly she missed him at this moment.

"Giselle!" Bryan called as she reached the Negresco's main restaurant. Before she could fend him off, he took her in his arms.

She pulled away. "What did you want to talk about?"

"Over dinner," he said, reaching for her arm.

She stepped back. "No, Bryan. Here."

"If you're worried about Zandra—"

"You're the one who should worry. She's your wife."

"You know we don't love each other. We're never in the same city. We might as well be legally separated."

"She's still your wife."

"It was a mistake. I've made a lot of mistakes in my life. Like letting you pass my child off as Charles's."

"Don't!" she cried.

Heads turned their way. Bryan stepped closer and took her by the shoulders. He pulled her to him, so that her head rested against his chest. "I think I understand why you did that, but—"

"Did you understand that Charles would have killed me otherwise?" Giselle demanded as she jerked away from his arms. "Or you?" She could feel the tears beginning to trickle down her cheeks, but she made no move to brush them away. "As it was, he stole my daughter's love from me."

"Giselle, don't—"

"Go back to her, Bryan. You and I have nothing to do with each other now."

"That's not true," he called after her as she walked away, but she didn't slow her pace.

At the hotel desk, she stopped to inquire if there had been any word from Mr. Vale. "Yes, madame," the clerk said. "I told him you were dining in the Chantecler. He went in search of you."

"But he didn't . . ." Giselle's voice trailed off as an awful fear took hold of her.

"That's right, Mother," Zandra said.

Giselle turned to find her daughter standing by the desk. Behind Zandra was a porter with her luggage. "My bill, please," she told the clerk. Then, to Giselle: "We saw you and my husband cuddling outside the restaurant."

"That wasn't what we were doing!"

Zandra shrugged. "It made no difference to me, of course. But Uncle Tru seemed a little agitated."

"Where is he?"

"On his way back to New York. Just like me." Zandra looked at her as though she were a perfect stranger. "Good-bye, Mother."

Giselle watched her cross the lobby.

"Mrs. Durand? Mrs. Durand?" The voice seemed to come from far away, and she heard the dinging of a small bell. Someone put an arm around her and she realized that the clerk had summoned one of the bell-boys. "Do you require a doctor, Mrs. Durand?"

"No," she said hoarsely. "Just—get me to my room."

"But the doctor—"

"No! No doctor."

Alone, finally, in her room, Giselle lay in bed listening to the uneven rhythm of her heart. Tru wasn't coming, she realized. He really wasn't coming.

LILLI

1982

ONE

When the moon rose, the party moved from the indoor pool to the outdoor pool. Some of the teenagers drifted off in pairs down the beach. Even the rowdiest of the boys stayed out of the ocean; three Portuguese men-of-war had washed up earlier.

Lilli Rawlings had showered and changed back into her blue jersey dress and sandals. When she joined her friends on the ocean terrace, Annette Crown took one look at her and moaned. "You're not leaving already?"

Lilli sat down on the tiles beside Annette and Sarah Dodd, whose parents' house it was. "Halloran will be here in a little while to pick me up. I don't like to keep him waiting." Although, she acknowledged to herself, she wasn't looking forward to being alone at Casa Durand tonight. Her grandmother had left for New York this morning because of something to do with her company; Lilli only stayed over because of tonight's party. She would be leaving tomorrow.

"Tell the corpse you've got other plans," Annette urged.

"Don't call him that." Lilli found Halloran's crusty bossiness hard to bear sometimes, but he had been a permanent fixture in her life for as long as she could remember. In spite of his gruffness, she was fond of him.

"That's what he looks like," said Sarah. "Tell him you're spending the night. We can stay out here as long as we want. Mother always takes a sleeping pill at eleven."

"Maybe." Lilli wanted to, but she hated to worry Halloran.

"Wow!" Annette said suddenly and sat up. "Who is he?"

The dark-complexioned man in his twenties was the most handsome male Lilli had ever seen. He moved through the teenagers on the beach with a feline grace and a natural arrogance. He looked at each group he passed as though he were searching for someone. Some lucky girl, Lilli thought.

"Devil Cardenas!" said Sarah as though she were pronouncing sentence. "I can't believe he's here. My father said he'd shoot him if he ever saw him again."

"Shoot something as gorgeous as that?" Annette said. "Your dad must be crazy."

"It cost my parents a fortune to get my sister out of his clutches," Sarah said glumly. "That's why they're trying to keep me under lock and key. I'd better go and tell my dad he's here again." She rose to her knees.

Annette grabbed her arm and pulled her back down. "Don't you dare!"

He knows how good he looks, Lilli thought, just as Devil Cardenas looked right at her. The smile that lit his face sent a shiver of emotion through her.

"He's coming over here." Annette grabbed Sarah's arm. "If he asks me to leave with him, I will.

You'll cover for me with Mom if she calls, won't you, Sarah?"

"Don't be stupid," Sarah said. "She shouldn't leave with him, should she, Lilli?"

Lilli shook her head absently, her eyes still caught by the stranger's glance. Devil Cardenas walked up the terrace steps and stopped in front of them.

"Hi," he said to Lilli. She was aware of Annette suddenly slumping beside her. "What's your name?"

"Lilli. Lilli Rawlings."

"'Consider the lilies of the field . . . they toil not, neither do they spin.' Are you a rich little girl, Lilli? In this town mothers warn their rich little daughters about guys like me."

"My mother's not around to warn me about anything."

"So are you coming for a ride with me?" he asked her, and held out his hand.

Like someone in a dream, she took it and let him pull her to her feet. Annette said something, but Lilli didn't hear it.

"I'll bet you've never done anything like this before," Devil Cardenas said as his red Trans Am pulled out of the drive of the Dodds' house. "Mother's little angel, right?"

No, my grandmother's little angel. My mother barely knows I'm alive. "Is your name really Devil?"

He rolled up the sleeve of his T-shirt enough to show her the tattoo on his shoulder, a grinning devil's face. "I'm his namesake." He flashed her a white-toothed grin. "How long before the police show up?"

"What?"

"You twelve? Thirteen?"

"I'll be seventeen in April."

"No breasts," he said. "Makes you look like a kid."

She blushed in the darkness. "If that's all you're interested in, Annette wears a C cup. Drop me back at the Dodds' and take her. She was dying to go with you."

"Spicy," said Devil Cardenas. "I like that better than breasts." Suddenly he frowned.

"Is something wrong?"

"This car," he told her. "I'm tired of it."

"How long have you had it?"

"About three hours."

Dread shot down her backbone. "You didn't steal it?"

"I borrowed it. Just like I'm going to borrow the next one." He looked at her. "Game?"

That look would make her follow him anywhere. Lilli nodded. He stepped on the accelerator.

"I'll be leaving now," Halloran told Sheila. It hadn't gone the way he liked anyway, with Mick here all the time. Away from Sheila, Halloran thought he was free of lust for her, but he had only to see her for that unused part of him to stir to life again.

"Surely, you've got time for another drink," Mick said.

"I've had enough. I have to pick up the child from her party."

"It's a nursemaid our Pat is now," Sheila told Mick.

"My job keeps you and young Francis well enough," Halloran said more roughly than he had intended. It was the way she said "our Pat." It reminded him too strongly of Keefe. That, and the way Mick kept sipping his own drink as though he were a permanent fixture at Sheila's kitchen table.

Halloran's temper did not improve when he reached the Dodd house. Two giggling girls told him Miss Lilli was spending the night there, but was changing clothes and could not be bothered to give him her message in person, which was not like the child at all.

"And what time shall I pick her up, then?" he asked the girls. "She has a plane in the morning."

They exchanged a glance and then said they would see she was delivered to the house by the Dodds' driver in plenty of time for her flight.

He left them to their party, but he stood beside the car for some minutes in the drive. That exchange of glances worried him and left him with half a mind to go back and investigate. Not that Miss Lilli ever gave the mistress a moment's worry. She wasn't a hell-raiser like young Francis. The thought of Francis brought back his need for Sheila like a sharp ache. If Miss Lilli wasn't coming home this night, then he could go back to West Palm Beach and bid his nephew good-bye. And see Sheila one more time.

As he turned on to Sheila's street Halloran could see the porch light still on and a car in the drive. But as he drew closer he saw that it was not young Francis's auto but Mick's still parked there.

He stopped, engine running, halfway down the block, considering whether to go and have a drink and come back later after Mick had left. Otherwise the man might overstay his welcome, talking of his exploits in Belfast. Mick still disappeared for long intervals and, when he returned, claimed to have struck telling blows for Ireland. He talked of booby traps in the loving tones other men used for women.

The porch light went off, followed by that of the living room. Halloran released the brake and glided forward. He was two houses away when the kitchen window on the west side went black as well, leaving the only light still burning that in Sheila's bedroom. Then it went out also.

Halloran stared at Mick's car still in the drive, and

then stepped on the accelerator. "So there we are, Keefe. She's cheated on me as well as you." The thought did nothing to lessen his guilt for bedding his brother's wife. Nor his desire to do it again.

Devil spotted the Porsche in the parking lot of a restaurant on Worth Avenue. He ditched the Trans Am a block away and he and Lilli hiked back on foot.

She stood in the shadows watching as he levered a bar of some kind into the well of the Porsche's window. Her breath caught in her throat when she saw a valet hurry through the parking lot, car keys in his hand.

Devil heard the scrape of the boy's heels on the pavement and ducked down beside the Porsche until the boy drove past in a BMW. Then he went back to work on the Porsche's window.

When he suddenly turned and waved, Lilli thought she was going to faint. She must have been holding her breath without realizing.

"Come on," Devil called as he opened the door. "Move your pretty tail!"

"You ever been where the servants live before?" Devil Cardenas asked Lilli as he pulled into the parking lot of the West Palm Beach liquor store. "That's why they built this place, you know. For the servants who took care of the pretty little rich girls like you over in Palm Beach." He got out and she started to follow. "What do you think you're doing?"

"Going with you."

"Not if you want any booze, you don't. Wait here."

While she watched him through the window of the liquor store, Lilli told herself she should get out of the car and find a telephone. She should call Halloran to come and pick her up. She wasn't the kind of girl to go joyriding with someone like Devil. That was something the Durand Woman would do. What her mother would do.

Devil came back with a large paper sack. Bottles clinked as he put the sack in the back of the Porsche. "Now to find a quiet place for just the two of us," he said, and leaned over to kiss her on the lips.

He broke off the kiss before she was ready. "Wow," he said. "Spicy all the way through."

As the Porsche sped away from the liquor store Lilli asked, "Have you ever gotten caught?"

"Afraid you're out with a jailbird?"

"I'm not afraid."

He flashed her a grin. "What would your daddy think if you got caught joyriding in a stolen car?"

"I live with my grandmother when I'm not at school. I don't see him much. Or my mother." She opened the glove compartment. Inside were a pair of sunglasses, a woman's gloves, a pretty compact. What would the woman think when she came out of the restaurant and found her car gone? Lilli had a sudden awful feeling. What if the owner were someone she knew. "Afterward what do you do with the cars?"

"Leave them for the cops to find."

Lilli leaned back. That was all right, then. No one would be hurt. The owner of the Porsche would get her car back in a day or two minus a few gallons of gasoline. She looked at the passing landscape in the darkness and realized they were not returning to Palm Beach. "Where are we going?"

"A place I know."

"I can't," Lilli said, pulling back.

The wine had made her warm and receptive to Devil's wonderful kisses, but when he tried to pull her panties down, reality came back.

Even though their faces were only inches apart, she couldn't see his expression in the gloom. The tide had come in so far that the surf was almost at their feet, but to have retreated farther up the beach, out of the sea breeze, would have exposed them to a cloud of mosquitoes.

When Devil didn't say anything, Lilli stood up and slipped off her sandals. She lifted her dress and waded out into the surf. As the waves roared in they were all the way to her upper thighs.

Devil kicked off his shoes and came in after her, not bothering to roll up the legs of his jeans.

When he reached her, he pulled her back against him and nibbled at her neck with his lips. She could feel the hardness of him against her hip. "You didn't tell me you were a virgin." He turned her around to face him. "Sweet little Lilli. You're not at all what I expected."

The breath caught in her throat. "Does that mean you don't like me?"

"That means I like you very much."

When Devil Cardenas pulled up to his grandmother's house, another car was in the drive. He parked on the street. Not right, he thought. He should have a place of his own. When he got his money, that's what he intended to do. His grandmother opened the front door before he could reach for his key. "Francis Devlin?"

"Gran? You up already?"

"Still. You took a long time getting back."

"Had a car to drop at the chop shop." Devil's grin matched the mocking face on his arm as he remembered what he had told Lilli Rawlings. Like hell he'd give back a beauty like that Porsche. By now it was a pile of parts and he had a wad of bills in his pocket.

"How did it go?"

"She had to leave this morning?"

"I know. But will she dream of you in that fancy school of hers."

"She will," he said, and flashed a smile.

"You almost sound like an Irishman, my boyo, for all your heathen father's blood."

"Whatever I sound like, she approved. She'll want more." He opened the paper sack he carried to show Gran his bottle.

"Come in the kitchen, then," she said.

Devil sat down at the table and watched as she poured them each a water glass full of whiskey. "Your health, Gran," he said, and took a healthy swallow.

"Next you'll write her," his grandmother said.

"Call her." Devil reached for the bottle and poured himself another drink. "Then I'll be driving up there."

"And I'll find out from our Pat when the house will be opened in the fall."

"I don't see why we have to wait," Devil said.

"Because that's the way I want it." Sheila Halloran smiled to herself. "He and Mick were drinking to each other's health last night."

"Does he know you sleep with Mick when he's not here?"

"Keep your dirty thoughts to yourself," Gran said, and drained her glass. "Keep your voice down, too. I don't want Mick guessing what we're up to. He'd want a share." Her glance turned inward. "He's bad luck in a thing like this."

Devil turned the glass in his hands, staring into it. "She's a pretty little girl."

"Don't get too fond of her. She's just a rich little bitch, same as all the others." He and Gran had made a healthy pile of money with their blackmailing. Gran's idea. She was the brains. But he was the one who could attract the girls.

"It's money I'm fond of," Francis Devlin Cardenas told his old gran.

"And we'll be having plenty of it at last," said Sheila Halloran. "Now you'd better shower and get over to the hotel. She'll be wanting you there when she wakes."

"You know a lot about her habits."

"After all these years, I should."

Mick Taggart was still asleep, tangled in the sheets. And how had he gotten to be an old man so fast? Sheila Halloran wondered when she looked down at him. Just like Pat. And maybe herself, if she was fool enough to look in the mirror, which she was not. "Wake up, Mick."

He stirred and groaned. "Let me sleep, Sheila. I have a terrible head on me this morning from Pat Halloran's cheap whiskey."

"You drank enough of it," she said. "If you want better than that, buy it yourself. And while we're on the subject of money I need cash for the rent."

"I'm tapped out, old girl."

"You're not. You have a money belt around your waist." She stuck out her hand, palm up.

"I'm surprised you haven't already had your hand in it," he grumbled as he threw back the covers.

"Knowing your fondness for booby traps, I wouldn't dare. Why two old fools like yourself and Pat Halloran would sit talking about bombs and such until all hours of the night is beyond me."

Mick loosened the belt, unzipped it, and counted three hundred dollars into her hand.

"And a bit on the grocery bill," she said.

He laid a fifty on the pile.

"And there's the liquor," she said, her hand still extended.

"Pat furnished that."

"So he did, but not what you drank after he left."

Mick added a twenty to the stack. "Why don't you let me move my things in here? There's no use my paying rent two places."

"Our Pat wouldn't like that."

"Pat's a fool if he takes you for more than you are."

"And you're a bigger one if you take me for less." She stood. "Get on your things and clear out. I won't have you lying around all day long."

"Why don't you get that grandson of yours to contribute to the kitty?" Mick asked as he rolled out of bed and reached for his pants.

"My life's my own," she told him. "I won't be needing your advice on how to run it."

"I don't suppose you'd furnish breakfast to a man with a hangover big enough to float a battleship."

"There's a diner two blocks over that's not so bad."

"I know the one," Mick said as he put on his shoes. "Eggs floating in grease and bacon burned to cinders."

"It will remind you of your dear old mum's cooking," Sheila told him.

After he left, Sheila stood looking down at the impression his body had left in the sheets. He was no good in bed anymore. Neither was Pat, for that matter. She put up with their fumblings because she needed them. But come next fall, she wouldn't need either of them again.

Devil Cardenas ignored the hard-eyed glances he garnered as he entered The Breakers. Come 7:00 P.M., no one would be allowed to cross the hotel's lobby unless he was wearing a jacket and tie. Devil knew he looked out of place in his jeans among the frescoes and gilt, the marble and chandeliers. When he reached the suite, he knocked softly and then opened the door. The roar of the shower told him where to find her.

He shucked his own clothes in the bedroom and paused for a moment to look at himself in the mirror, a workman examining his best tool. Satisfied, he went into the bathroom. Just before he stepped into the shower, he had a momentary recollection of Lilli Rawlings's firm young body. He stopped, his hand on the shower curtain, and forced it out of his mind before his body could betray him. The shower spray, warm and hard, hit him as he reached for her and pulled her to him.

"Hello, darling," said Alexandra Mainwaring, and kissed him on the lips.

"Aren't you going to ask me how it went?"

"How could any silly little girl resist you, darling? I know I can't."

He held her back so that he could look into her face. "I think you and Gran are crazy to wait. Why not go for it now? Why not pluck her out of that fancy school of hers?"

"You don't understand, darling. I'm not really kidnapping her. I just want to frighten her grandmother into making a certain business concession."

"Why not now?"

"Because all the pieces won't be in place before next fall." She rubbed a finger across his lips. "Don't pester me about it anymore. Sheila understands and I don't see why it should make any difference to you. You get paid for doing what I want. Now, let me have a little of what I'm paying you for, darling."

She pushed his shoulders, urging him to his knees, and as the water cascaded onto both of them he leaned forward and kissed her between her legs.

Afterward, a towel around his waist, he sprawled across the bed and watched her pack. A silly woman, he thought. But useful, all the same. She thought it was her idea to frighten Giselle Durand by kidnapping her granddaughter. The silly bitch even thought they would give the money back.

"You're smiling, darling," Alex Mainwaring said from across the room. "Was it good for you, too?"

"Come here and I'll show you how good," Devil told her.

TWO

Giselle was surprised to see the meeting room packed with the heads of all the departments on this late-August morning. Even Henri Laud was there. When had he arrived from Paris? she wondered. And why was he there? A lavish buffet complete with champagne and caviar had been set out. Who had authorized all this expense?

At the front of the meeting room, a table was draped so that its contents were hidden. Everyone looked at Giselle as though she should know what was going on. She caught Zandra by the arm as her daughter rushed by. "What is all this?"

"A surprise party, Mother. A belated birthday party for myself. You'll see." Zandra continued on to the front of the room. Conversation ceased abruptly when she reached the draped table.

"I can hear you all asking each other what's up," Zandra told the group. "The easiest way to answer your questions is to show you the prototype commercial for a new line of Giselle Durand products."

Giselle managed to keep her own face carefully expressionless, but inside she was fuming. With the rest of the group, she turned to the monitor.

For a long moment only swirling mists filled the screen. Then the mists dispersed enough that a small clearing became visible in the midst of towering pines: a green, quiet place at the base of a ridge. One side of Giselle's brain admired the beauty of the scene before her, while the other side ticked off the cost to film what she was seeing.

Just as Giselle was about to turn from the screen and gauge the reaction to the commercial on the faces of the others in the room, a roar erupted in the silence of the forest. A motorcycle hurtled off the ridge and became airborne over the camera. It landed in the center of the clearing and drew up with a flourish. The black leather-clad figure who rode it looked like an evil knight out of some medieval legend.

Then the figure took off the helmet and shook out long, lustrous black hair. The camera drew closer and focused tightly on Zandra's face, and Giselle realized with an ache of loss for her own beauty, just how lovely her daughter was. Even though Zandra had turned forty earlier this month, she looked as though she were still in her late twenties.

The camera drew back to take in her entire figure as Zandra removed her lipstick and compact from the pocket of her black leather jacket and reapplied her lipstick. Then there was a close-up of the lipstick as Zandra replaced the cap on the tube. Her scrawling signature engraved on the cap enlarged to fill the screen: *Zandra*. Then came the voice-over, the only spoken words in the entire commercial: "Zandra. For the real woman in you."

There was a moment of stunned silence in the room, then a babble of voices. Giselle realized her fingernails were biting into her palms.

"And here is our new line," Zandra said as she whipped the cloth off the draped table.

Giselle stood with the rest of them. As she moved toward the table the group parted before her, giving her a clear passage. Each item on the table—all the lipstick cases, bottles, and compacts—was inscribed with Zandra's distinctive signature. Ad layouts were arranged at one end of the table. Each glossy page carried Zandra's face. To her name, they added only, "For the real woman in you."

"But they don't say anything about Giselle Durand Cosmetics?" Henri Laud pointed out after a moment. "How will people recognize this as ours?"

"It's a new direction, Henri," Zandra said.

"We don't need a new direction," Giselle said abruptly.

"I'm afraid you're going to have it whether you like it or not," Zandra told her mother. "As of my birthday, I'm now one of the major stockholders, and I think it's my duty to see that the company doesn't lose ground."

"No," Giselle said. "The answer is no." She turned and walked from the room.

The meetings started that afternoon. Zandra did little of the arguing herself. She didn't have to. Everyone from the department heads to the financiers did it for her. Each time Giselle glanced across the room, she saw the triumph on Zandra's face. She would lose; Zandra would win. The best she could hope for was to drag it out.

As she sat in her office and listened to the arguments against her, she could feel her heart racing. At least she'd had the good sense to keep her physical problems to herself. If her heart condition were known, that would be used as one more reason the company should not continue to be identified so strongly with her.

Why didn't she just give in? Giselle asked herself. It was not that Zandra's idea was a bad one. Market surveys showed that the product tested well.

It had nothing to do with the products or Zandra, she realized as the drone of voices continued, but with something deep inside herself. She had lost so many other things. Only this, her company, still gave her any identity. It was all she had left, and she intended to keep it just as it was.

"I almost feel sorry for her," Zandra said as she kicked off her shoes and curled up on her aunt's sofa. "She didn't expect it at all. You'd think she had completely forgotten about the stock. It was like watching a boxer take a body blow."

"She's not as forward thinking as you," Alex told her niece as she poured them both another glass of champagne. "To the Zandra line," she toasted, not for the first time.

"Right," Zandra said absently. "Now that the money men are on her case, she'll cave in soon enough."

Alex frowned. "Don't underestimate her. She could still win."

"How?"

"Money."

"I told you that the money men—"

"She could agree to everything and then underfund the launch. The line would sink without a trace. She'd have been proven right. You'd have been proven wrong. You'd never get another chance." Alex shook her head. "How can you have forgotten what she was like when you were a child? All those promises broken. All the times she said she was coming to get you and never arrived. That's the kind of person she is. She'll capitulate completely, agree to everything, and then—somehow, someway—she'll contrive a problem with the money that will make it impossible to give the Zandra line the launch it needs to be a success."

Arriving for her doctor's appointment, Giselle felt like an actress in a cloak-and-dagger movie. She had dismissed Patrick Halloran for the day in spite of his protests. She actually found herself looking forward to his leaving for Palm Beach to open the house. He had turned into a nagging nursemaid, as though he sensed something was not quite right with her.

After the exam, Giselle dressed and the nurse showed her into the doctor's office. He entered in a moment and sat down to look through her file. He glanced up. "You've been under more of a strain than usual lately?" She nodded. "We don't need that," he said.

"We have a business to run," she retorted.

"Isn't there someone who can take part of the load off your shoulders?"

"Is that what I need?"

"Yes, it is."

The silence continued for a moment. "But I don't feel like an old woman," Giselle wailed suddenly.

"Fifty-nine isn't old," the doctor assured her. He held up a hand before she could say anything. "And you don't look that. But my goal is to see you live to be an old woman. A very old woman. The only way to do that is for you to take much better care of yourself. Ease off a little. Smell the flowers."

"Give up my work," Giselle said bitterly.

"If that's what it takes, yes. Why not? But that's not what I'm saying. Easing off is not the same as giving up. Think about it, Mrs. Durand. And I'll see you again in a month."

* * *

It was the call she had been waiting for all of her life, Zandra thought as she listened to her mother capitulate completely. No, not completely, she realized with fury. As Aunt Alex had predicted, money was the problem. Her mother gave in on every point but that.

"You can't strip the company of all its operating capital in order to launch a new line," Giselle protested.

"But we can't launch the Zandra line unless it's properly funded. You know that."

"I'm afraid that's your problem, Zandra," her mother said before she hung up.

"You haven't won a thing," Aunt Alex said when Zandra phoned to give her the news. "I told you she would use the money to trip you up."

"She seems changed somehow, Aunt Alex. She sounded very low, not herself at all."

"A ploy. She'll make you feel sorry for her and you'll stop fighting for what you need to launch the Zandra line. You'll send it out into the marketplace underfinanced, she'll win, and you'll look like a fool. After all these years, why can't you understand how her mind works? You have her on the run now, but don't give in on the money." Alex chuckled. "She'll tell you how she started on a shoestring, but Tru financed the whole thing."

"How is Uncle Tru?" Zandra asked in an attempt to head off Alex's diatribe.

"The same as always. Rich and selfish. Don't forget about the money."

After she talked to her aunt, Zandra paced around her apartment trying to decide who to call next. She even went as far as to look up Lilli's phone number at school, but then she snapped her address book shut. Lilli wouldn't understand at all. Her daughter would think that Zandra was somehow striving to punish Giselle herself.

Maybe she was, in a way. But there was more to it than that. She had lived and dreamed this line for years and she had the sure knowledge that she had stumbled upon a winner. The advertising campaign had turned out even better than she had hoped. Just the thought of it made her bubble with excitement. She didn't want Lilli or anyone else to bring her down to earth.

Almost against her will, she thought of Bryan. He was the one she would like to tell. But although they still shared the same apartment after all these years, there was almost no communication between them. Between the traveling Zandra did for Giselle Durand Cosmetics and that Bryan did for Rawlings, Ltd., they were seldom in New York at the same time.

She should have ended the marriage years ago, Zandra thought. But she was afraid. Afraid that just as finally besting her mother wasn't what she had dreamed it would be, neither would divorcing Bryan Rawlings.

The morning after she called Zandra, Giselle dressed for the office and then decided at the last minute not to go. It was earlier than she had planned, but she decided to leave for Casa Durand that evening. Patrick was already there opening the house. Let Zandra chase her to Palm Beach if she wanted to continue the discussion about finances. Giselle had given in all she intended to.

She was packing her bags when the phone rang. She picked it up and heard Patrick Halloran's voice on the other end. "Patrick? What's wrong?"

She could hear him, more than a thousand miles away, begin to weep. "Mistress," he said through his tears. "Giselle. It's happened again."

As surely as if he had spoken the words, the knowledge cut through her like a knife. "Lilli?" she breathed. "Oh, no. Not Lilli!"

But the tears on the other end of the phone told her it was true.

THREE

"**A**ny word?" Giselle asked as soon as she and Patrick Halloran were alone in the study of Casa Durand. She had taken a taxi from the airport so that he could wait at the house for the kidnappers' call.

"Not yet, mistress. But they'll be calling soon enough for their blood money. Begging your pardon, mistress," he added with a look at her face.

"Who knows?"

"Only those useless females in the kitchen. They're weeping still, the both of them. But they won't say anything. I've seen to that. I've called and canceled the rest of the staff from coming in as yet. I said there was a flu bug about and you didn't want the whole lot of them coming down with it."

Giselle nodded. He had done well, but she didn't have to tell him so. They were thinking with the same mind now, and that mind had but a single thought: Don't let Lilli meet Benjamin's fate.

"And when will you tell her mother?" Halloran asked. "Or have you already?"

"No. We don't know the ransom yet." But that was not the real reason and they both knew it. Both of them feared that Zandra, like her father before her, might do something that would end with Lilli's death. A horrible thought to have about your own flesh and blood. But every time Giselle had reached for the phone while waiting for her flight to leave New York, the memory of Benjamin had made her draw her hand back again.

"And her father?" Halloran asked after a moment.

Giselle shook her head.

"Good. The man would be no use at all in this."

Giselle spent a sleepless night. Half a dozen times she almost nodded off, and then the memory of Charles, of Benjamin, would intrude, and yank her back into the awful reality.

When the sun rose, she got up and dressed. Her face in the mirror was pale and drawn, with huge black smudges under her eyes. Downstairs, Halloran was already stirring in the kitchen, making her coffee. His face was a reflection of what Giselle had seen in the mirror.

"I told those useless females to stay out of our hair," he told her. "Besides my coffee is as good as Joyce's." He handed her a mug, strong and black. When she sipped it, she found he had laced it liberally with brandy.

"You'll need it," he answered her raised eyebrow. "They'll be calling this morning."

The phone rang at 8:00 A.M. Giselle answered it herself, grasping the receiver so tightly her knuckles turned white.

"Giselle Durand?" It was a man's voice, muffled by something, perhaps a handkerchief.

But men didn't use handkerchiefs anymore, she thought, and then realized her mind was wandering, close to breaking. "This is Giselle Durand."

"We have your granddaughter."

In spite of the muffling and the traffic sounds in the background, there was a haunting familiarity about the voice. "Who are you?" she demanded.

He laughed with real amusement, and she realized it was a young man on the other end of the phone. In his twenties perhaps. But his voice, when he spoke, was hard. "The ransom is ten million dollars. Cash." He ignored Giselle's gasp. "I'll call you back tomorrow evening with the instructions."

"I can't raise that much money by tomorrow."

"If you don't, she dies."

"Please don't hurt her!" Giselle's voice broke. "I'll get the money. I promise you I will. But you have to give me some time to get that much cash."

"No cops, you know that."

"Of course not. But I have to tell her mother. I'll need her help to raise the money."

"Okay. Tell the mother. Nobody else."

"Let me talk to Lilli," Giselle pleaded, but the kidnapper had already hung up.

Alex watched her niece's face undergo a kaleidoscope of emotions as she talked on the phone. "But I don't understand why Lilli was in Palm Beach," Zandra said. "She was supposed to be in school."

Alex started to ask something, but Zandra waved at her to be quiet. "Halloran said what?" Zandra said into the phone. "Ten million! But we can't! Not that quickly!" When it ended, Zandra didn't so much hang up the phone as drop it. She turned to Alex and her face was pale.

"I expected this," Alex said before Zandra could speak.

Zandra laughed harshly. "That Lilli would be abducted?"

"That something would happen to drain the money away from the launch. That's what she's asking, isn't she? That the company put up this so-called ransom."

"For God's sake, Aunt Alex! My daughter has been kidnapped. I don't have time to think about the launch. Not when Lilli's life is in danger."

"Is it in danger? What proof do you have that this 'abduction' really happened? And if money is needed, why doesn't she call your moneybags husband?"

"The kidnappers said—"

"And why was Lilli there? How could anyone have known she was to show up at that particular time?"

"Alex, this is not an intellectual game of some kind. We're talking about Lilli's life!"

"Are we?" Alex leaned back and lit a cigarette. "Where did this so-called kidnapping take place?"

"Mother's house in Palm Beach."

Alex ignored the little flare of anger that she felt every time she thought about Giselle changing the name of Casa Vale. "And why was Lilli there? Isn't she supposed to be in school?"

"Halloran doesn't know. He had just arrived to open the house for the season and she showed up without warning."

"Halloran? Your mother's creaky old chauffeur?" Zandra nodded. "Who else was there?"

"A couple of maids."

"And Giselle hasn't reported this to the police?"

"What is this third degree!" Zandra said angrily. "Of course she hasn't reported it. The kidnappers said they'd kill Lilli if she did."

"What if there are no kidnappers?" Alex asked her niece. "What if this is a ruse dreamed up by Giselle to tie up the operating funds of the company so that she can destroy the launch? Just as I predicted."

"I know you don't like my mother, but—"

"I know her, Zandra. I remember how she treated you over the years. I would put nothing past her. Not even this."

"But Lilli—"

"Lilli idolizes Giselle. She would do anything that woman asked." Alex could see from the expression on Zandra's face that she had succeeded in raising doubts.

"But it's Lilli's life," Zandra said. "I can't take a chance on that."

"Then don't take your mother's word. Go to Palm Beach yourself. Look into this in person. After all, Lilli is your daughter."

"But Mother wouldn't do something like this!" It was the cry of a desperate child.

"Wouldn't she? That woman would do anything. She ruined my brother's life, didn't she?" Alex took a deep breath. She couldn't let her own rage defeat her. "All I'm saying is that you should go to Palm Beach yourself. Now. Tonight. I'll go with you." She could tell from Zandra's face that she had won.

"But what about Bryan?" Zandra asked. "Shouldn't I let him know what's happening?"

That was another one she'd like to see suffer, Alex thought with a vicious little thrill of pleasure. "You told me he has nothing to do with Lilli as it is. If this turns out to be a hoax by Giselle, I think it would be better that he didn't know about it. Don't you?"

Zandra nodded slowly.

"Don't worry, darling," Alex told Zandra. "I'll stand beside you. Everything will be all right. You'll see."

It was a nightmare, Giselle thought. She had done without the guards at the entrance to Casa Durand. Halloran had protested that omission, but she had no intention of doing anything that might frighten the kidnappers. But even without the guards in evidence, word had already spread throughout Palm Beach that she was in residence and now the invitations were flooding in.

She left the phone to Halloran, knowing that it would be tomorrow before the kidnapper called again. Still, every time it rang she flinched as she sat at the desk in the study, filling sheets of paper with figures, trying to think how in the world she could raise so much cash so quickly. Sitting there, she fought the hopeless feeling that it was already too late. That just like Benjamin, Lilli was already dead.

Patrick Halloran only reinforced her fears when he brought her another cup of his strong, black coffee. She could see by his slumped shoulders and the expression in his eyes that he, too, feared for Lilli's life.

Giselle looked at the rows of figures. Damn the advisers who'd had her invest everything! Yes, on paper she was worth at least $200 million. But that included her share of the company's billion-dollar annual revenues. The only source of ready cash was the company itself. She opened her little black book and looked up the number of Harold Milton, the treasurer of Giselle Durand Cosmetics.

"But I don't understand," Harold said when she reached him.

"Just do it," Giselle told him.

"I can't. Not without something in writing."

"Call Zandra, then. She'll give you written authorization."

When Giselle hung up, she breathed a sign of relief. She had many things that could be sold and the money put back in the company. Nothing could replace Lilli's life. Tonight she would sleep soundly, knowing that she had found the cash for the ransom.

*   *   *

"Are you sure you won't eat something, mistress?" Halloran asked the next morning when she came downstairs to the kitchen. He looked ridiculous with an apron around his middle. Another time Giselle would have been forced to hide a smile. Now there was no laughter in her.

"I can't eat," she told him.

"We'll be calling the doctor for you, then."

"No!" she cried. "No doctors," she added more softly, aware she had startled him with her outburst. The heart pills were in her purse, ready, only inches away from her hand if she should need them. Halloran was right, she thought. She mustn't fail Lilli by becoming ill or worse. "I will eat a piece of toast, Patrick."

He made it, but in spite of her good intentions, she found herself unable to swallow. The sound of a door slamming somewhere in the house distracted Halloran before he could scold her. "Those stupid women. I'll go and ask them to be quieter."

But before he could leave the kitchen, they heard Zandra's voice call, "Mother? Are you here?"

Giselle rushed out into the hall. "Zandra!" She started forward to embrace her daughter, but something in Zandra's posture made her hesitate. "When did you arrive?"

"I flew in last night," Zandra said. "Aunt Alex and I have suites at The Breakers." She looked at Halloran. "Can we talk privately?"

"Patrick knows everything," Giselle said. "He was the one who called me. If you want him to go through the whole thing for you—"

"Later," Zandra said. "Bring us some coffee in the study, Halloran."

Her curtness made Halloran bristle. "And will you be wanting a full-course meal as well?"

"Just black coffee," Giselle answered quickly, unwilling to watch them dig at each other.

She followed Zandra down the hall. In the study, Zandra stood looking at the window for a moment. Giselle obeyed her impulse this time and walked over to hug her daughter's shoulders. "Don't worry. Harold will have the money here by this afternoon. We'll get her back safe and sound."

Zandra stiffened and pulled away. "Harold caught me before I left New York last night. He asked me to authorize the transfer of ten million dollars to the bank here. I refused."

Giselle's heart began to race and she realized she had left her purse in the kitchen. "Why would you refuse? It's the only way we can raise so much cash so fast."

"And strip the company? That will stop the launch of the Zandra line."

"What difference does that make? We're talking about Lilli's life."

"Are we? Aunt Alex thinks we're talking about you taking one more opportunity to torment me like you did all the time I was growing up. Promise me something and then jerk it away."

"I never did that!" Giselle cried in astonishment.

"Aunt Alex thinks this is something that you and Halloran and Lilli cooked up between the three of you."

"How could she—"

"I don't know if she's right or not. But until I'm sure, there will be no transfer of funds from the company into your hands."

Halloran lingered over the coffee. He had no desire to hear that nasty bitch shouting at the mistress. She was like Mrs. Mainwaring, like her father, evil to the core. Tormenting the mistress almost beyond bearing. And to think she would care so little about her own daughter.

He sat down at the table and stared at the tray he had arranged. Not that it made any difference. He had known as soon as he picked up the note that Lilli would never be returned alive. Now he knew by the lack of feeling in his own heart that she was dead. Dead and left on some trash heap like poor little Benjamin.

He slumped forward, his head in his hands, and began to weep. For Benjamin. For Lilli. For poor dead Keefe and all the other failures of his life. Why couldn't he have done something to prevent this last misery from coming upon the mistress? The slamming of a door roused him. He rose, wiped his eyes, and picked up the tray.

In the study he found Giselle, white and trembling, dealing out a hand of solitaire on the desktop. "She thinks it's a trick," she told Halloran when he set her coffee beside her. "She thinks it's something that I've engineered to keep her from launching her new line."

"But her own daughter's life?"

"She thinks Lilli was a part of it. And you."

That last did not surprise him. Never had there been any love lost between him and Zandra. But to put a child as sweet as young Lilli to risk was more than he could understand. "The ransom?"

"She's kept me from getting it from the company for now. Maybe I can go around her, but I don't know if there will be time."

"And is there no other way to get the money?"

"There's all this," the mistress said, waving her hands. "But it takes time to turn things into cash." She swept the playing cards into the floor. "How could she do this? How? How? How?"

Aunt Alex had arranged for adjoining suites at The Breakers. Zandra stopped off at her own suite first. As she stared at herself in the bathroom mirror she admitted the panic she felt. What if she was wrong? What if Lilli's life were actually in danger? The thought made her so faint with fear that she turned on the tap full force and splashed her face with cold water.

Her aunt knocked on the door between the suites and then opened it. "Zandra? I thought I heard you in here," she said as Zandra toweled her face dry and came out of the bathroom. "I don't suppose you learned anything from that woman."

A few weeks ago, Zandra would have found her aunt's reference to "that woman" amusing. Not now. What if her aunt's hatred of her mother—for hatred was exactly what it was, she admitted to herself—was blinding Alex's perception of Lilli's danger. "What if we're wrong?" she asked Alex bluntly. "What if Lilli's life is really at stake?"

Alex nodded to herself. "She's frightened you. I was afraid she might. That's why I did some checking while I was waiting for you. Lilli's school said she made several calls to Florida just before she left. Without the school's permission," she added archly.

"You're saying that she set this up?"

"I'm saying again that the timing is just too perfect. Your mother has done everything she could to keep you and Lilli apart. Now she can kill two birds with one stone. She'll destroy your launch of the Zandra line and she'll convince Lilli that you care more about control of the business than you do about her."

"And how do I convince Lilli that last statement is untrue, Aunt Alex? By sitting here and doing nothing."

"You don't have to prove anything to Lilli. She'll fall into line quickly enough when you face down your mother."

"How will I do that?"

"By refusing to be stampeded into doing anything stupid." Alex patted her on the arm. "Now change into

something charming and we'll have lunch downstairs."
She went back into her own suite, leaving Zandra alone
with her rising sense of panic.

Alex closed the connecting door behind her and
leaned against it, smiling. After a moment she went
over and poured herself a drink and hoisted the glass
in a silent toast. It was over, she thought. When Zandra
confronted Giselle over withdrawing the ransom
money from the company, Alex knew she had achieved
her purpose. After that show of strength on her daughter's part, Giselle's days as head of the company were
numbered.

Alex took a healthy swallow and then picked up the
telephone and dialed Sheila Halloran's number.

"You did well," she said when Sheila answered, not
bothering to identify herself. "Have Francis give her a
big kiss and send her back where she belongs. It's
over."

Mick, sitting at the kitchen table, gave the cards a
quick shuffle as Sheila hung up. "And who was that?"
he asked her, when she sat down again.

"No one." Sheila reached into her apron pocket
and pulled out a wad of dollar bills. "Deal, you old fool.
I feel lucky this afternoon."

The phone rang.

Halloran met the mistress's glance for a moment,
seeing his own dread reflected in the brilliant blue of
her eyes, then picked it up. "Durand residence."

"Giselle Durand." The voice was so muffled he
could barely understand it.

Silently, he passed the phone to the mistress. He

stood there, his hands in his pockets, listening to her plead with the man for Lilli's life. Listening to her shame as she confessed that the girl's mother would not help her raise the money.

At last she hung up. "Forty-eight hours," she told Halloran. "That's all he'll give us."

But Halloran thought of that poor sad bit of human flesh that had been Benjamin and he knew that the girl was already dead.

FOUR

Devil Cardenas took a cigarette from the pack on the nightstand and lit it. Any other time he would have taken out two cigarettes, lit both of them, and handed one over to the woman with him in the motel room. He and Gran had made a lot of money out of his looks and his ability to charm both younger and older women. But Lilli Rawlings was different. Her freshness and vulnerability stirred something deep inside him he hadn't known was there. No one who knew Francis Devlin Cardenas would believe that he had been alone with Lilli as much as he had over the past year and had never made love to her. Least of all his old gran.

Lilli, beside him on the bed, looked at him with her sad eyes. "Don't worry," he told her. "It's almost over."

"You should have let me get my swimsuit top," she said, not for the first time. "What will my grandmother think?"

"The truth. You're so ravishing that the mean old kidnapper couldn't keep his hands off you."

"She'll be worrying about me. And so will Halloran. Oh, Devil! I'm sorry we decided to do this!"

"Hey!" He sat down on the bed beside her and put his arm around her. "You're not sorry we're engaged, are you?"

Lilli sniffed audibly. "No," she said, so softly he barely caught the words. "But . . ."

"But what?" He tipped her face up and kissed her on the lips. She answered back so passionately that it sent a tremor through his groin.

After a moment she pulled away. "I don't see why we have to upset my grandmother. Why couldn't we have just sent the note to my mother like we talked about?" A note of bitterness crept into her voice. "She wouldn't have been upset at all. She doesn't even acknowledge I'm alive."

"Because this is the way I planned it." Devil frowned as he pulled her head to his chest. Actually it was Gran who had done the planning. Gran who decided it was Giselle Durand who would get the ransom note. Gran who decided when and where the fake abduction would take place. Devil himself had been all for setting it up at Lilli's fancy boarding school and getting it over with. He knew, if Gran did not, that the less time he spent in this girl's company the better. Gran was pulling his strings too energetically this time. Once it was over, it would be over between the two of them as well. He would leave his grandmother a bit of the money to get by on—how much did an old woman need anyway?—and use the rest to give himself the kind of life he'd always dreamed of.

He pulled Lilli close and kissed her more deeply this time. With one hand he reached up under her dress.

She pulled away. "No, Devil," she said. "Not till after we're married. You promised."

"You're a funny girl," he said.

"I'm a good girl," she retorted.

He lay back on the pillow, and she snuggled beside him, her head on his shoulder. He thought, Here I am, the biggest stud in Palm Beach, alone in a hotel room with a virgin, and no action at all. Women fucking beg me for it, and she's having none of it.

Lilli traced the smile on his lips with her fingers. "What are you thinking about, Devil?"

"About you," he told her. "About us."

"When we're married?"

"Yeah," he said. "When we're married."

Then, to his great surprise, that was exactly what he began to think about. And wouldn't his old gran think him a fool for that?

Halloran listened from the door of the study, his heart quivering, as the mistress pleaded with a banker to help her turn something into cash. Hopeless, he thought. The girl was already dead. He could feel it in his heart. Just like he had felt young Benjamin's death. If only he had been more alert. He might have prevented the taking of her.

Dead, he thought. Dead as young Benjamin.

And the bastards would go unpunished again.

Nothing he could do here, Halloran thought. He had no brain where money was concerned. Not on the mistress's scale. But there was something else he could do. He waited until the mistress hung up the phone. She crossed another name off the list before her. "And will he cooperate?" he asked her.

"Yes, after holding out a stiff penalty." Giselle rubbed her forehead. "But not soon enough, I'm afraid."

"I have to leave for a little while. Will you not let me arrange for the guards?"

"No guards. But hurry back, will you, Patrick?"

The sweet smile she gave him touched his heart. "You know you're the only one I can trust now."

And I'm the one who let them take her, he thought as she reached for the telephone once more. The knowledge that he had failed the mistress cut him right to the bone.

For once Halloran would have been glad to find Mick Taggart's car parked in Sheila's drive. But it was not there, and neither was young Francis's automobile. He frowned as he parked in front of the house. He had not seen Francis yet this trip, but when things settled down, he intended to give the boy a piece of his mind. Jumping from job to job as Francis did was no way for a man turned twenty-three, as Francis had this month, to earn a living. High time he learned some trade, and Halloran intended to tell him so. But later. When this thing was over. He'd give young Francis a scold that would set him straight.

Sheila answered his knock. "Why, Pat. I didn't think I'd see you so soon. Not with your precious mistress here already. Why didn't you tell me she was coming so soon?"

"And how do you know she's here?" Halloran demanded.

"Even a poor old woman in West Palm Beach can read the Shiny Sheet. What's happened to her guards? Has she lost her money, then? That's what the paper's hinting."

"What do you care?" he asked her bluntly.

"If she's got no money, then you've got no money," Sheila answered back just as bluntly. "And you know we depend on you, young Francis and me."

"Time young Francis depended on himself. I plan to tell him that when—" Halloran stopped in midsentence, aware he'd almost said more than he intended.

"When what?" Sheila demanded. "When you're not hanging on to your precious mistress's skirts, then?"

"Keep your tongue leather off the mistress," Halloran said by habit. "Where's Mick?"

"And why do you want that old reprobate?"

"He owes me a drink."

"At this time of the day? What's gotten into you, Pat?" Sheila reached out and grasped his arm. "Something's not wrong, is it?"

It was all he could do not to tell her. To share the burden of his worries with someone else. He fought the impulse back. "I'm off for the afternoon, and I've a mind to spend it drinking. What's wrong with that?"

Sheila gave him a suspicious eye. "I think there's more to it than you're saying, Pat Halloran. But if drinking with Mick is what's on your mind, you'd better have the cash to pay. The good Lord knows he does not." Halloran thought she might argue more, but to his relief she gave him a list of bars where he might find Taggart, and then watched, hands on hips, as he went back to his car.

When he slipped behind the wheel, he sat there for a moment looking back at her framed in the doorway of her house, but it was Keefe he had on his mind. I miss you, big brother, he thought. Though you must hate me now that you're in heaven and know all about Sheila and myself.

Sheila stepped out on the porch. "If you've changed your mind about drinking with Mick, I've a bottle in the kitchen we can share."

And then end up in bed while the mistress made call after call to an uncaring world.

Halloran shook his head and drove off in search of Mick Taggart.

As soon as Pat drove away Sheila went straight to the kitchen and poured herself a shot of whiskey. "Here's to it," she said aloud, and drank it down.

Then she poured herself another shot and dialed the number of the motel and asked for Francis's cabin. When he came on the line, she said, "It's working well, boyo. Your uncle Pat was just here."

"No names," Francis warned. "Did he say anything?"

"He didn't have to. He looked like death warmed over."

"I hope you're right."

The element of doubt in his voice angered her. Alone in the motel room with that young girl, he was having second thoughts. "I'm right and you know it," she said harshly. "You do what I tell you, and we'll both be rich." She slammed down the receiver and stared at the shot of whiskey for a moment, thinking of how Pat's face had looked when he walked up to the porch. He was hurting for his Mistress Giselle. That memory warmed her more than the whiskey. More than the thought of the money.

Sheila Halloran stood up in the middle of her kitchen, a broad smile on her face, and lifted her glass in a salute to herself. It had taken more than thirty years, but at last she was getting her own back from that hoity-toity bitch Pat worshiped.

"Who is this?" Bry asked impatiently. "Is this some kind of prank?"

"I . . . I'm sorry," a woman's voice said. "I asked for Bryan Rawlings. Who—"

"This is Bryan Junior." Damn that new switchboard operator, Bry thought. This was the third time this week she had made the same mistake.

"This is Giselle Durand. I must speak to your father at once."

Bry, who had just leaned forward to transfer the call, instead settled back into his chair. "I'm sorry, Mrs.

Durand. That's impossible. Perhaps I could help you."

"I must speak to him. Today!"

"If you could just tell me what this is in regard to, then perhaps I could—"

"His daughter. Lilli. My granddaughter. Tell him that. But please, don't mention this call to anyone else."

"Is there a problem?"

He heard her ragged breathing over the line. "Just tell him that I must speak to him. Today. I'll be at this number." When she rattled it off, he recognized the area code as Florida.

He repeated the number back. "I'll give him the message as soon as possible," he told her.

After she hung up, he stared at the number on the notepad for a moment. Lilli. His half sister. The daughter of the bitch who made his mother try to kill herself. Someone knocked on the door of his office. "Come in," Bry called.

"Did you know your secretary's taken flight?" Bryan Rawlings asked his son.

"She's out with the flu," Bry said absently as he crumpled the sheet of paper with Giselle Durand's phone number and tossed it in the wastepaper basket. "It's hell with no one to screen my calls, Dad."

"I suppose I'll have to tell you about the times I had to answer the phone myself after I walked five miles through the snow to school. Ready for lunch?"

"Sure thing," Bry said. "Let's make it a long one while some other poor bastard mans the phones."

Giselle hadn't been surprised to learn that Alexandra Mainwaring was in Palm Beach at The Breakers. Nor that Zandra had told her everything in spite of Giselle's begging her to remain silent. But Giselle was running out of people to call for money, and for Lilli, she would even phone Alex.

"Don't you think you've carried this farce on long enough?" Alex demanded when Giselle reached her.

"It's not a farce, Alex. It's the truth."

"No, it's a trick to keep Zandra from launching her line of cosmetics. And I've told her so." Alex broke the connection.

Giselle slumped back in her chair. "Damn you Vales!" she said aloud in the study. "Will you kill another child?"

She stood up and walked to the door. "Ruthie," she called. When there was no answer, she went in search of the maid. She found Ruthie in the kitchen with the cook. "Has Halloran come back yet?" she asked them.

"No, ma'am," Joyce told her. "Would you like something to eat now?"

Giselle shook her head. "I want to know as soon as Halloran gets back."

She could feel their eyes on her as she left the kitchen. She couldn't stand much more of their sympathetic glances and coddling, Giselle thought. They were fretting over her when it was Lilli they should be worrying about. Lilli who had been gone for three whole days.

She had to get the money. Somehow. Someway.

Giselle took a deep breath and went back into the study to call the number she had known all evening she would finally have to call.

"Of course I'll loan you any sum you need," Tru said into the phone. "Just call me at the office tomorrow and I'll have my bank transfer—"

"You don't understand, Tru. I need the money here. In cash. By tomorrow afternoon."

"Eight million dollars in cash? By tomorrow afternoon? Don't you want to tell me what this is all about, Giselle?"

.

"The expansion of my business. I told you that. But if you prefer to support your niece in this—"

"I knew Zandra had different plans for the company than you, but I fail to understand why you would need cash."

"It's my company. If I say I need cash, I need cash."

"And you wouldn't mind giving me some sort of collateral?"

"Anything," Giselle agreed hurriedly, and Tru's heart thudded in panic. "Just get the cash here by tomorrow afternoon."

"I'm not sure I can raise eight million in cash that quickly, but—"

"Anything," Giselle said quickly. "Whatever you can raise. My goodness," she added with a brittle laugh that told him she was lying. "Won't Zandra be surprised to find out I've managed to come through with the money after all?"

"Giselle, don't you think you should tell me what's really going on?"

He heard her gasp, and then she said, "I've told you everything you need to know. Just get me the money!"

She hung up before he could say anything else.

Tru considered for a moment and then dialed Norman Williamson's home number and told him about the call he had just received.

"Let me check around," the private investigator said.

All these people alive, Halloran thought as he entered the last bar on Sheila's list. All these worthless wretches, drinking their lives away and whoring around, while a sweet, pure girl like Lilli lies dead. Her life snuffed out too soon. Like Benjamin. Like Doreen.

He stared around the room, but Mick was not in sight. Sheila had given him a bum steer and kept him away from the mistress's side on a day when she needed him there the most, Halloran thought with a flash of rage.

When a man bumped in to him, Halloran turned with his fists at the ready, only to find it was Mick Taggart himself. "The very man I've been looking for," Halloran said by way of greeting.

"Shall we have a drink?" Mick asked hopefully. "I'm tapped out myself."

"We'll stop and buy a bottle on the way to your place," Halloran said, steering Mick toward the door. "I've a business proposition for you, my man."

"And what would that be? You know I don't like regular work, Pat. I can't wear the harness day in and day out like you."

"No, this is something else," Halloran told him. "I'm in need of one of your tricks."

"You in the bomb business? Don't make me laugh, Pat."

"Any man can be a patriot," Halloran told him. "It's a free country, isn't it?"

FIVE

"**I**n cash? The best I can do is . . ." On the other end of the line the banker paused. "I can have three million dollars in cash in Palm Beach by this afternoon, and the rest there tomorrow, Mr. Vale."

"Do it," Tru told him.

"Will you require Mrs. Durand to sign anything?"

"No. Just get the money there as soon as possible."

Tru broke the connection and dialed Norman Williamson's office again. "Mr. Williamson still doesn't have any news for you," the private investigator's secretary said. "He'll call you the moment he does."

It was 7:00 P.M. before the private investigator finally returned Tru's call. "Giselle Durand has called everyone she knows trying to raise cash. Everybody I've talked to thinks it's because of the clash with her daughter over control of the company."

"And what do you think?" Tru asked Williamson. "You must have some insight into her character after all these years I've had you watching her."

"For starters, I think the amount she's trying to raise is ten million dollars. She's got part of it already."

"But why?"

"Possibly an extortion attempt. Or maybe . . ."

"Yes?"

"A kidnapping. You got anybody missing in your family, Mr. Vale? Anybody Mrs. Durand would care enough about to pay ten big ones?"

Zandra burst into Alex's suite, her face pale. "I thought you said this was a hoax. Uncle Tru just called me. Mother phoned him last night and asked him to loan her eight million dollars. She never would have done that if Lilli hadn't actually been abducted."

Alex looked at her niece with a calmness she didn't feel. "She asked me for money, too, darling. Don't you see? She has to make it look real."

"But what if you're wrong. We're talking about my daughter's life."

"I'm not wrong."

Zandra picked up the phone and dialed a number.

"Who are you calling?" Zandra ignored her. Alex clenched her hands into fists. She'd given Sheila Halloran the word to have Francis send Lilli home. Everything she had hoped for had been accomplished. So why was Giselle still trying to raise cash?

Zandra slammed down the receiver. "She's not there! She and Halloran left with two suitcases. She's gone to pay off a kidnapper!"

"You don't know that. Perhaps she's returned to New York."

Zandra looked at her aunt coolly. "Do you hate her enough that you'd risk Lilli's life?"

"What she did to your father—"

"What my father did to himself!" Zandra turned toward the door.

"Where are you going?"

"To Casa Durand to wait for my mother. And to pray I haven't cost my daughter her life."

Halloran pulled the white Rolls-Royce off the road. "We're in the Everglades," he grumbled. When there was no reply, he glanced in the rearview mirror. The sight of the mistress's face nearly broke his heart. "It'll be done with soon." He patted the suitcases beside him. "As soon I hand this over."

"Don't you think I should carry the money to him?"

"Of course not," he said quickly. "He'll know a woman's too frail to carry this load."

"But if he should be frightened off—I can't bear to think of it, Patrick."

"He won't be. Not with the scent of cash in his nostrils. There." Halloran pointed. "See those headlights. I'll wager that's our boyo." He started to slip from behind the wheel.

"Wait," Giselle Durand told him. "I'm going, too."

"No. I'll not risk his snatching you as well."

"You don't really think he'd do that?"

"Who knows? But you'll stay in the car and let me handle this." God was merciful for once. She fell silent and leaned back. Halloran slid out and then reached back for the two suitcases he had carefully packed with all the cash the mistress could raise so quickly. Five and a half million was all she'd managed, but during his last call the kidnapper had agreed to that, to her great relief.

But the boyo's easy acquiescence had told Halloran he was right in his suspicions; they had done Miss Lilli in. And your trick had better work, Mick Taggart, he thought. Or I'll be paying you back as well.

The approaching headlights swept past him, and then came back to shine directly on Halloran as the kidnapper parked, motor running, a hundred feet away.

Halloran strained his eyes against the glare of the headlights. Was that two figures getting out of the car? Merciful Mother of God, it was!

"It's Lilli!" he heard the mistress cry out with joy.

"I see her." But after the first ripple of joy, Halloran concentrated on the man beside Miss Lilli, gripping her arm, a woman's panty hose hiding his evil face.

The kidnapper and Miss Lilli came forward slowly into the lighted area between the two cars. "Have you got the money?" the villain shouted.

"Let the girl go first."

"No way."

"Then we stand here for eternity, because I'm not giving you the cash until you release her."

"Patrick!" the mistress cried from the car.

"Be patient," he told her softly. "The boyo will want the money more than anything else." Then he raised his voice so the kidnapper could hear. "Look at this, my fine fellow." Kneeling, he unsnapped first one suitcase and then the other. "Did you ever see so many green-backs in your miserable life? Let the girl go and it's all yours." Closing the suitcases, he picked them up again.

"I have a gun," the kidnapper called. "I'll shoot her if you try to leave without handing over the money."

"I'll not do that. But you have to release her before you get the cash."

"Come halfway and put down the money. Then I'll let her go."

A young man's voice, Halloran thought as he fingered the switch Mick had installed in the suitcase in his right hand. A shame about that, but the boyo should have chosen a different line of work.

"Well?" the kidnapper yelled.

"I trust you to do the right thing," Halloran shouted.

"Patrick," the mistress called to him. "Be careful."

"Don't worry." He started slowly across the bare

space between the two cars. His arms protested the weight of the heavy bags and a tight hand of emotion closed on his chest, making every breath ache. He could see Miss Lilli's face now in the glare of the headlights, but it was no longer her he was thinking of, but that poor baby so long ago, his life cut short before it had even begun.

Halfway between the two vehicles, Halloran halted. "Let her go now," he called to the kidnapper. "You could shoot us both before an old man like myself could hobble back to the car with all this money."

"All right," the kidnapper said after a moment. "Go on," he told Miss Lilli. She stood there for a moment, like a fawn transfixed in the headlights of an approaching car, until the kidnapper gave her a firm shove. "Go to your grandmother, little rich girl."

She started forward, one hesitant step after another. Halloran held his breath until he saw she was truly clear of any last lunge on the part of the kidnapper.

"All right, old man," the kidnapper called. "Put the suitcases down and back away."

Lilli was almost even with him now. "It's all right," Halloran told her. "He can't reach you now. You're safe. And here's the boyo's money."

He stooped to set the suitcases on the pavement. As he did he felt beneath the handle of the right one for Mick's switch. As he straightened Halloran felt a fierce thrill of sheer blood lust shoot through his body. There, Benjamin! he wanted to cry. That is for you, poor little babe.

Miss Lilli was right in front of him. He held out a hand. "Come to Halloran, darlin'."

She halted, staring at his outstretched hand. Then, before Halloran understood what was happening, she grabbed the two suitcases and ran back toward the kidnapper, the heavy leather bags banging against her slender legs.

"No!" Halloran cried. "Come back!"

But Lilli didn't slow. The kidnapper raced forward to grab the suitcases from her.

Halloran ran toward the kidnapper's car, ignoring the pain in his legs, his chest. Lilli glanced back at him from over the top of the car, a mingling of fear and excitement in her face. Then she yanked open the door and climbed into the car.

"No!" shouted Halloran. But the kidnapper's car sped down the highway into darkness.

Halloran dropped to his knees in the dust, and then fell forward, gasping for air. The pain in his chest was nothing compared with that in his heart.

Behind him, he heard the soft sound of footsteps on the highway. Then the mistress was bending over him. "Oh, Patrick," she cried. "Are you all right?"

"Help me up," he said, and she pulled him to his feet. "We have to get after them," he told her. With her hand on his arm, he stumbled toward the Rolls.

She grasped his arm, trying to stop him. "Zandra was right, Patrick. It wasn't a real kidnapping or Lilli wouldn't have run back to him. She'll be all right."

"You don't understand!" Halloran screamed at her.

She backed away from him. "What—"

"I put a bomb in the suitcase! To pay them back! For Benjamin! For killing the baby! I thought she was dead. And then I thought she was safe. We have to get her back or she'll die along with him!"

Sheila was in the bedroom, throwing the last of her things into a suitcase, when she heard Mick Taggart calling her name from the front of the house.

When she didn't answer, he came in search of her. "Packing, are you?"

"A change of climate will do me good, I thought."

He sat down on the edge of the bed and began to look through her suitcase.

"What in the world do you think you're doing, Mick!"

"Habits die hard. I was wondering if your packing had anything to do with my visit from Pat last night."

"And what would make you think that?"

"Something's in the air. I'm not sure what. I was wondering if you'd decided to go into the kidnapping game once more, but this time cut out old Mick."

"We said we'd not talk of that again."

"It was a lot of risk for no money. If the baby hadn't died—"

"You're getting senile, Mick. Your mind's wandering."

"It wasn't the baby dying that got your goat. It was the lack of cash. I remember that part well enough."

Sheila turned back to her suitcase and closed the lid.

Mick glanced around the room. "You're not leaving much. Not planning on coming back, are you?"

"And what business is it of yours?"

"I'll miss the occasional tumble, but not your sharp tongue. Our Pat, though, he'll be cut up."

"Will he? I doubt that. He'll have more time to worship at the altar of his lady."

"It's not worship he had on his mind last night, but booby traps," Mick said as Sheila hefted her suitcase.

She let the case fall from her suddenly nerveless fingers. "What kind of booby traps?"

"The kind a man could fit in a suitcase with a timer attached. I was into my cups last night when he offered to pay me for one of my specialties. And I'm a man who can rig a bomb drunk or sober. But this afternoon when my head cleared, I began to wonder why a man like Pat would pay so well for a booby-trapped suit-case."

Sheila grabbed his arm. "You bastard! You didn't?"

Mick pulled free of her grasp and stepped back. "Ah, so you did do it, old girl. Yes, I did the job for cash. A good thing, too. It'll buy my ticket out of here before things get too sticky." He started for the bedroom door.

"Where are you going, Mick? We have to stop them. Francis . . . Nothing can happen to Francis!"

"I hope not, Sheila. But maybe God's decided to make you pay for the other one. If not, I'm afraid Pat has."

He started for the door again.

"Mick!"

"If I can figure it out, Pat might. I'll not be having him after me for that old crime. I've a lot of dead men on my conscience. One baby more or less won't make any difference when I get to hell. But I'm not anxious to go before my time, and Pat would see to that if he knew."

Sheila sank down on the bed. After a moment the front door slammed behind Mick. She flung herself flat on the mattress and began to weep for her Francis.

"Are you sure this is the place?" Alexandra Mainwaring asked the taxi driver. Somehow she had never considered what kind of house Sheila Halloran might live in. This was a slum!

"This is the address you gave me," the man said.

"Wait for me," Alex said as she opened the door.

The driver got out before she could leave. "Pay me for this trip first," he told her. "Then we'll talk about the next."

"All right. But wait for me," she said, when she handed over the bills.

"Sure," the taxi driver said.

Alex was halfway to Sheila Halloran's front door when he took off with a squeal of rubber. She watched his taillights disappear in the gloom.

The porch light was off. Alex felt for a doorbell. Finding none, she knocked.

"Who is it?" Sheila Halloran called.

"It's Alexandra Mainwaring. Let me in, Sheila."

When the door opened a crack, Alex pushed her way inside. Sheila Halloran stared at her and Alex wondered if she would ever look as old as this ruined old woman. "Where's Lilli, Sheila? Why didn't you have Francis send her back like I told you to do?"

"Who cares about the girl now? He's booby-trapped the ransom."

"Who?"

"Pat. Pat Halloran. He's killed my Francis. His own nephew." A crazy light danced in the old woman's eyes.

Alex took a step backward, reaching behind her for the door.

"No," Sheila Halloran said. "Don't be leaving just yet, Mrs. Mainwaring."

"I'm afraid I have to—"

"No," Sheila said, and that was when Alex saw the revolver in her hand.

SIX

Lilli twisted around to glance through the rear window. "They're not following us!"

"It'll take Uncle Pat half an hour to hobble back to his car," Devil said, and then cursed himself when he realized what he had said. Instead of concentrating on the business at hand, he had been thinking that he should have left her back there with Uncle Pat and her grandmother. Sweet little Lilli. Gran had warned him about getting fond of her. But Lilli was different from the other rich bitches he and Gran had preyed upon.

"Halloran is your uncle?" Lilli asked, amazed. "I don't believe it."

"My mother married a Puerto Rican. Big scandal. My granddad almost threw them out of the family. Then when my parents were both killed, he and my grandmother raised me."

Lilli put a hand on his thigh. She was too innocent to know what the pressure of her hand did to him and

331

that made the sensation all the more powerful. "How did they die?"

"They—we—lived on the edge of Spanish Harlem. New York City. Some junkie killed them for their cash. Left me there—I was two years old—left me to scream my head off for a couple of days. New York. Great place."

"Won't Halloran be mad at you when he finds out what we've done?"

"How will he find out?"

"When we give the money back."

But we're not giving it back, sweet thing. You'll find that out soon enough. And what was Gran going to say when he showed up with the money *and* Lilli?

Devil glanced in the rearview mirror. Far behind him on the lonely highway, he could see a pair of headlights. Maybe it was Uncle Pat; maybe not. He really was the great fool Gran was always calling him. Here he was, about to dump Gran for five million bucks and a life better than he'd ever dreamed of, and he was bringing another anchor to the party. Did he really think Lilli would agree to live happily ever after on his ill-gotten gains? "Damn!" he said, and slammed on the brakes.

"What is it?"

"Something's wrong with the front tire." He left the motor running, and opened the door. "Come look at this," he said when he reached the front of the car.

Lilli got out and came around the car to stand beside him. "I don't see anything wrong."

To hell with Gran, Devil thought. He grabbed Lilli and kissed her.

Her lips were so sweet. So good. Too good for him. I wish I'd fucked you, baby, he thought. But that wasn't the truth. He wished he had made love to her, slow, sweet love. He pulled back and looked at her face.

Lilli stared over his shoulder. "Devil! Someone's

coming!" She tried to pull away. He caught her by the arm and pulled her back. "Devil! We've got to go!"

"You're staying here."

"No! I'm going with you!"

The headlights were closer now, silhouetting them against the night.

Devil hit her on the chin. She sagged into his arms. He half dragged, half carried her behind the car, and let her down into the weeds beside the road. "Goodbye, Lilli," he whispered. "I think I love you."

Then he scrambled to his feet and ran back to the car. The other car was closer now, but he knew they'd stop for Lilli. He jumped behind the wheel and shifted into gear. As he floored the accelerator he could see in the rearview mirror that the other car was slowing.

Ahead of him, the headlights pierced the lonely darkness. Behind him, in the backseat, something made an audible click.

"Praise God!" Halloran cried, when he saw the two figures struggling beside the car. Then the man struck Lilli and carried her behind the car.

From the backseat, he heard the mistress's moan.

"It's all right. He's leaving her. Now he's only thinking to get away. We've won!"

Sure enough, the boyo leaped into the car and left Lilli beside the road. As Halloran braked, the headlights of the Rolls picked out her defenseless young figure in the grass beside the roadway.

"He's hurt her," Giselle cried as she reached for the door handle.

"He's knocked her out," Halloran said as he threw open his own door. He watched the kidnapper's rear lights as the boyo's car sped away. Then the twin points of red vanished in a great fiery ball as Mick's time bomb went off.

"My God!" Giselle stumbled back against the side of the Rolls, her hand clutching at her chest. "You did *that*! What were you thinking of, Patrick?"

"The baby," Halloran told her, not sorry at all he had taken the man's life. "Young Benjamin. Them that did that were never punished. This one was."

Giselle scrambled across the road to where her granddaughter lay. Halloran stood beside the Rolls watching the blaze of the blackmailer's car. It gave him a feeling of satisfaction deep in his soul. He had made them pay. Years too late, but they had paid at last.

The mistress was sitting on the ground beside the road, the girl's head in her lap. Just as Halloran reached them Miss Lilli moaned and came around. "Oh, Grandmother," she cried, and buried her face in her grandmother's chest.

"Are you all right?" the mistress asked her granddaughter. When Lilli nodded, Giselle asked, "Why, Lilli?"

"I thought . . . He said it would be fun. He said we'd give the money back. I thought . . . The money was supposed to come from my mother . . . Not you . . ." Lilli clutched her grandmother's arm. "You won't send him to jail, will you? It was just for fun. Like the cars. Just for fun."

"He'll have no more fun," Halloran said somberly. He took them both by the arms and helped them to their feet. "That's the last of him," he told Miss Lilli as he pointed toward the blazing remains of the kidnapper's car.

"Devil?" she cried. "That's Devil?"

"That was his name?" Giselle asked her.

"Devil Cardenas." Lilli turned to Halloran. "He said he was your nephew, Halloran."

Halloran got the two of them into the Rolls as fast as he could, ignoring Miss Lilli's protest that they should try to do something for poor young Francis, as if there was anything to do for him now. Then she wanted to know if they should call the police. "No police," Halloran told her gruffly. "You don't want your grandmother's business in the newspapers, do you?"

He could not meet the mistress's eyes. She knew as well as he that he was guilty of murder. Of killing his own nephew. Pale and drawn, she sat in the rear of the Rolls with her arm around her granddaughter.

"Where are you taking us, Patrick?" the mistress asked when he slipped behind the wheel.

"Home. And then you're getting on an airplane back to New York. The first flight out."

"But Devil?" Lilli cried. "Won't someone want to know what happened to him?"

"I'll take care of that," Halloran said grimly. "But whatever happens, the mistress and you will be out of it."

Giselle hugged Lilli close while Halloran drove. She shouldn't let him sweep everything under the rug, she thought. Yet to do otherwise would only hurt Lilli.

"Your money, Grandmother!" Lilli cried suddenly, a stricken expression on her face. "It blew up, too."

"That's not important."

"And Devil's dead." She leaned against her grandmother and Giselle could feel the sobs racking Lilli's slender young frame. But Giselle's own heart was glad. I've got you back, she thought as she held Lilli close. Alive. That's all that matters to me.

The Rolls pulled up in front of Casa Durand and Halloran hurried around to open the passenger door.

Giselle was startled to see Zandra emerge from the big front doors. For a moment Giselle thought her daughter would race on down the steps and take Lilli in her arms, but Zandra hesitated.

"She's safe," Giselle called to her daughter. "And she won't break. Come and give her a hug."

"Oh, Lilli!" Zandra cried, and ran down the steps.

Behind her, Giselle heard the car door close. She turned to look at Halloran. "I'll be leaving now, mistress," he said, his face sober.

"Patrick—"

"I have to tell Sheila myself. My God! Young Francis! That he would do a thing like that. That I would!"

"Don't be too hard on yourself. You didn't know—"

"I didn't think, and it's cost me something I loved dearly." He motioned at the mother and daughter hugging at the top of the stairs. Giselle looked up, just as they went inside. "Get them on the plane, too," Halloran told her. "Don't let it touch them, mistress. You deserve better than that for you and yours."

Then he hurried around the Rolls and got in. She watched as he drove it toward the garage. In a few moments he drove off in the station wagon he used for household errands. She watched until the station wagon's taillights disappeared at the end of the drive.

Inside Casa Durand, Giselle found that Lilli had already gone upstairs. "We have to leave," she told Zandra. "Take a plane to New York as soon as possible. There could be"—she searched for the right word—"repercussions here, and I don't want Lilli involved."

She expected an argument, but Zandra, as always, surprised her. "I've got a rental car. I can drive us to the airport. That is, unless you want Halloran to drive us in the Rolls?"

"No." She gave Zandra a spontaneous hug. "I'm glad you're here."

When she would have turned away to go upstairs and pack, Zandra grasped her arms. "Are you going to tell her?"

"Tell her what?"

"That I wouldn't lift a hand to save her life."

"You were right. It was a trick. She and the boy—"

"She told me. But he's dead. And she could be, too."

Giselle stood perfectly still, feeling her heart clanging in her chest. "Yes, if he hadn't put her out."

"It was Aunt Alex who convinced me it was a hoax, but she believed you were behind it. That it was just a ploy to stop the launch of the Zandra line."

"Alex!" The beat of Giselle's heart accelerated, and she took a slow, careful breath. "Your aunt and I have always been at odds over you. I think you've had plenty of chances to observe that over the years. The games she played with me . . . refusing to let me see you . . . she's a very cruel woman, Zandra."

"But she was always there for me. While you . . . All I remember of my childhood are the times that you said you would pick me up and never arrived. The times that you had me dress and wait for hours before you finally showed up."

Giselle shook her head wearily. "I'm afraid I don't know what you're talking about, Zandra. But even if I did, that was a lifetime ago and we have Lilli to consider now. We must pack and leave as soon as possible."

Zandra halted her with a hand on her arm. "You haven't answered my question. Are you going to tell Lilli I didn't care enough about her to come to her aid?"

"I love you both very much. What you tell, or don't tell, your daughter is up to you. Now, don't you think you'd better get back to your hotel and pack your own things."

Zandra shook her head. "I'll have my things sent here if there's time before we leave. If not . . . Lilli is more important than anything I've left at ·The Breakers."

Giselle embraced her daughter. "You have no idea how many years I've waited to hear you say that, darling."

SEVEN

In her bedroom, Giselle threw a suitcase on the bed and repacked the few things she had brought with her from New York. As she moved around the room she could feel her heart beating faster and faster. She hadn't felt this tired since she flew to Nice for Charles's funeral. Tru, she thought. The last time I saw Tru.

She sat down on the edge of the bed and dug through her purse for her heart medicine. She emptied one of the pills into her hand and put it under her tongue. After a moment, still clutching the medicine bottle in her hand, she lay back on the pillow beside her open suitcase.

Three men in my life, she thought. Charles, Bryan, and Tru. And each of them loved something else more than they loved me. Charles, that image of himself, which was more important than the reality of me. And Bryan, an idealized lady that wasn't me at all. And Tru. Tru loved his family. She heard the door open, but she was too tired to rise, or even turn her head in that direction.

"I've made the arrangements for our flight," Zandra said. When Giselle didn't answer, she came over to the bed. "Are you all right? You look so pale."

"It's late and I'm tired."

Zandra sat down on the edge of the bed and took Giselle's right hand in her own. "Your hands are clammy. Is something wrong? Should I call a doctor?" Giselle shook her head. "But are you sure? You don't look at all well."

Giselle looked into her daughter's face and made a decision. Slowly she raised her left hand and opened it to show Zandra the prescription bottle.

"What's this?"

"Something I've been keeping from you. From everyone. Last year in Paris I found out that I had a heart condition. The doctor there told me I needed to slow down, but I wasn't ready to give up the company. To give up life."

"So you came back and waded into a full-scale war with me." The amusement in her daughter's voice lightened the weight in Giselle's chest. "You really are amazing."

"Not as amazing as your grandmother Lillian."

"I've always remembered the first time you told me about her. I think I was four or five. That's why I wanted to name Lilli after her." Zandra looked down at the prescription bottle. "I understand why you kept this from me. But why are you telling me now?" Sudden alarm flashed across her face. "You're not having a heart attack?"

Giselle patted her hand. "I'm all right, Zandra. Just bone weary." She looked up into her daughter's face. For the first time since Zandra's birth, she could see beyond the "Vale look" of which Alex had been so proud to the piece of herself in her daughter. The part that was a legacy from the Durand women. "I'm telling you because I don't want there to be any secrets between us again. Because I love you and I trust you."

Lilli came in while they were embracing. "Is Grandmother all right?"

"I'm fine," Giselle told her.

"We'll leave at six. That will give us plenty of time to get to the airport." Zandra patted her mother's hand. "Try to rest," she told Giselle. "It's all over now."

It was past midnight when Halloran pulled up in front of the house. Before he reached the porch, the front door opened and Sheila emerged from the dark room beyond. "My Francis?" she said as he mounted the steps, and he could hear the ragged sound of tears in her voice.

He took her arm and walked her into the living room, but as soon as they were inside, she jerked away. "Tell me!" she demanded.

He held out his arms to her, but she backed away, toward the lighted rectangle of the kitchen doorway. "I swear, Sheila! On my sainted mother's soul! I didn't guess it was Francis playing a prank. I could only think of the other time and how they got away free. I was certain Miss Lilli was already dead. And so I thought of Mick and all his talk of booby traps and bombs."

"The two of you murdered Francis." A sob escaped her.

Halloran reached for her, but once more she backed away, toward the kitchen. Through the kitchen doorway, over Sheila's shoulder, he saw someone seated in a straight-backed chair. Then, to his utter astonishment, just as it registered that the figure was a woman, bound and gagged, he recognized her:

Alexandra Mainwaring, her eyes wild and terrified above the gag. "Sheila? What in the—" Halloran started toward the woman, but Sheila grabbed his arm and spun him back to face her.

"No. Leave her be."

Halloran pulled away and knelt to examine the ropes that bound Mrs. Mainwaring. "Get me a knife," he said as he reached for the gag. "Did Mick do this?"

"Mick doesn't have the brain for planning. I found that out when we tried the game before. This time I mean to have what's mine."

Her words barely registered as Halloran worked the knot of Mrs. Mainwaring's gag. He could feel the woman trembling. "It's all right," he soothed. "We'll have you free in a snap of the fingers."

"The gun," Mrs. Mainwaring gasped as soon as the gag left her mouth.

Still kneeling, Halloran turned to follow her glance. Sheila held a snub-nosed .38 pointed at the two of them. "Move away from her, Pat," she told Halloran. "I'm not letting her go until I get the ransom."

"And who would be ransoming her?" he asked to gain time. A horrifying thought began to trouble his brain.

"Her brother. Her sons. Even your hoity-toity Giselle. She's a softhearted fool. If she would try to raise ten million for that granddaughter of hers, she would cough up a few million for this one. I won't take the risk and come up empty-handed for the third time."

Halloran stood slowly. "Tell me it's not true," he said hoarsely. "Tell me you weren't the one."

"The one what, you old fool?"

"The one who kidnapped little Benjamin. The one who let him die and dumped him in that vacant lot like a piece of garbage."

"And what was that child to me? You may have worshiped the ground your mistress walked on, but there she was seeing that man behind her husband's back and trying to pass off that bastard as her husband's child. She was no better than any woman in our tenement. No better than me. Yet you thought she hung the moon."

"My God, Sheila! It was an innocent babe you killed!"

"That was long ago, Pat. Now you've killed my Francis. I'll put that behind us if you'll help me get the ransom for this one." She pointed with the .38 at Mrs. Mainwaring.

Halloran was far away, his mind's eye focused on a piece of soft and fuzzy blue cloth stained with long-dried blood. "You!" he roared at Sheila. "You killed Benjamin! You took him away from the mistress and me!"

He lunged forward and grabbed her by the neck. There was an explosion so close to him it made his ears ring. A sharp pain shafted through his chest, but his fingers clamped mercilessly around Sheila's throat as his momentum carried them both backward onto the floor.

The gun roared once more just as Sheila's head hit the floor, and Halloran cried out with the pain. He fell heavily on top of her, but he did not lose his grip on her throat. She wasn't struggling now, but still he grasped her throat, his fingers tightening and tightening and tightening.

When Halloran came to himself, it could have been moments later or it could have been hours. Someone was calling his name from far away and he could feel his own life's blood draining out onto Sheila's lifeless body beneath him.

"Halloran!" Alex Mainwaring cried. "Do you hear me? You have to untie me!"

Leave off, you nasty bitch, he thought. Can't you see I'm busy dying.

But she went on calling his name until at last he heaved himself up off Sheila's body and dragged himself across the floor to the chair where she was bound.

His numb fingers worked to loosen the knots. There were knives, sharp and shiny, in the kitchen drawers, but they might have been in another country for all the good they would do him now. It took an eternity to loose the rope enough for Mrs. Mainwaring to slip her hands free.

Halloran flopped back against the wall and watched her bend forward to untie her own feet. A great bloody swath of a trail led from Sheila's body to him. The gun lay just beside her on the floor.

When Alex Mainwaring freed the last of the ropes and stood up, she came and knelt beside him. "Don't worry, Halloran," she said. "I'll call an ambulance." She stepped daintily across the trail of blood and left the kitchen.

She had not noticed the phone on the kitchen wall, he thought. Then he heard the sound of the front door and knew she had not used the phone in the living room either.

Halloran heaved himself away from the wall and grasped at the chair, trying to raise himself. The chair toppled and left him sprawling in the pool of his own blood.

It was only a few feet to Sheila's body, but it took him the rest of his life to crawl there. When he reached her, he bent over her and whispered, "She's not calling, Sheila. She's left us to die." Only Sheila was already dead, and he had killed her. "My darling Sheila," he said aloud. How long ago that had been. Before he met the mistress. Please, Mary Mother of God, he prayed. See the mistress safely away from all this.

Sheila's dead face with its wide staring eyes rebuked him. Even now, it's her in your head, and not me.

That was his last conscious thought.

EIGHT

Giselle woke to the wonderful aroma of freshly brewed coffee. Lilli stood beside the bed, holding a cup. "Mother said you would like this. She made it herself. She told Ruthie and Joyce they could have a few days off."

Giselle sat up and took the cup. "Are you all right this morning," she asked her granddaughter.

Lilli began to sob.

Giselle put her cup aside and pulled Lilli into bed with her. "This reminds me of when you were a very little girl and I used to climb into bed with you to read you bedtime stories." She held Lilli close until Lilli's shoulders stopped shaking.

"Oh, Grandmother," Lilli said at last. "I didn't mean for all this to happen. I didn't mean to hurt you."

"I know," Giselle said softly. "I know how easy it is to forget about everything and everyone else and simply try to grasp a little pleasure for yourself."

Lilli stared at her wide-eyed. "But no one died because you did that. Devil *died*."

346

"Yes, someone did die. Your uncle Benjamin."

"But he was really kidnapped, Grandmother. That was different."

"Was it?"

"You're blaming yourself for something you couldn't control."

"And so are you. Devil died because of the way Devil lived."

"But what about the way I hurt you?"

"You came back to me safe and whole, darling. That's all I care about."

A soft knock at the door made them both glance up. "May I come in?" Zandra asked, a puzzled expression on her face.

"Is something wrong?" Giselle asked her.

"No, it's just—I called The Breakers and had them send my things here. They also sent a note Aunt Alex had left for me. She's gone back to France. To Nice." Zandra shook her head. "I don't understand it. She told me a dozen times since Father died how much she hated Nice. And she didn't even wait to make sure Lilli was all right." Zandra shook her head and then glanced down at her watch. "You'd better dress, Mother. We need to leave."

Giselle dressed hurriedly and carried her suitcase downstairs. Lilli rushed forward to grab it from her. "You shouldn't be carrying that, Grandmother!"

Giselle looked at Zandra accusingly. "You told her."

"Of course I did," Zandra said calmly. "But I won't tell anyone else and neither will she."

"When does our plane leave?"

"As soon as we get to the airport. It's one of Rawlings's corporate jets. Bryan sent it." Zandra blushed slightly. "I called him last night. Lilli is his daughter. He has a right to know."

"Of course he does." But why, she wondered, if

he cared that much, hadn't he even bothered to get back in touch with her after her message concerning Lilli?

Almost as if she could reach her mother's mind, Zandra said, "He didn't know any of what happened until I called him. Your message must not have gotten through to him."

"What about Patrick?"

"Halloran? What about him?"

"Has he come back yet?"

Zandra shook her head. "Not yet."

"I'll leave a note for him." Giselle sat down at the hall table to scribble a few words. Then she paused for a moment, pen in hand, and glanced around Casa Durand. "I wonder if we'll want to come back here after all this."

"Oh, Grandmother!" Lilli cried. "You love this house. Of course we'll come back."

"You won't have any bad feelings about it?" Giselle asked her granddaughter.

Lilli smiled shyly and leaned down to hug Giselle. "I'll remember the good things about it," she said, and then turned to hug Zandra as well.

When Giselle turned back to her note, she could hardly focus on the paper for the blur of tears in her eyes. *Dear Patrick,* she wrote. *I'm sorry to leave so hurriedly. I'll call you as soon as I get to New York and let you know what my plans are.* She paused for a moment and then added, *I'm sorry for your loss, Patrick. But thank you so very much for helping me get Lilli back safely.* She signed it and then stood and smiled at Zandra and Lilli. "That's everything."

On the way to Palm Beach International, Zandra said, "Bryan's meeting us when we land in New York." Neither Lilli nor Giselle said anything. After a moment Zandra continued. "I'm sure you and Bryan will have a lot to talk about, Mother. I won't stand in your way."

Bryan's child snuggled closer to her. Giselle looked down at Lilli's fresh, untroubled face and understood, if Lilli did not, that Bryan's wife had just given up her claim on him. She had the entire flight to New York to think about herself and Bryan, together again after all these years.

Giselle walked down the airport corridor between her daughter and her granddaughter. She was weary after the flight from Palm Beach, but the sound of Lilli's chatter lifted her heart.

Ahead of her, down the corridor, she caught sight of a familiar face. "There's Bryan." Lilli fell silent. Giselle glanced at her daughter. Zandra had gone pale.

Lilli pointed further down the corridor. "And Uncle Tru."

Giselle paused and set down her luggage.

"What's wrong, Mother?" Zandra asked anxiously. "Is it too heavy for you?"

"I don't want it to slow me down," Giselle told her daughter. She almost laughed at the look on Zandra's face at that moment. Then, swiftly, before she could change her mind, she walked down the corridor toward Bryan Rawlings.

As she approached him she remembered those wonderful, stolen hours they had spent together in another life. The hours that had produced Benjamin. As she drew closer she could see the dawning expression of hope in his eyes.

She glanced past him, farther down the corridor, to where Tru had halted, hands jammed in his pockets, watching her with a neutral expression. How well I know you, Tru, she thought. If I pause for one moment, you'll melt away into the crowd and I'll lose you again.

"Your wife is waiting for you," Giselle told Bryan as

she passed him without slowing her pace. She felt, rather than saw, his surprise.

And then she forgot Bryan, Zandra, even Lilli, as she began to run down the long corridor to Tru.

After Lilli had gone to bed, Zandra joined Bryan in the living room. "Do you think she'll be all right?" he asked as he handed her a brandy.

"I think so," Zandra said as she took the glass. "Do you know how pleased she was that you stayed to dinner?"

"'Stayed for dinner,'" he mused. "That's an odd way to put it. This is my apartment. My child."

"You haven't always acted like it," Zandra said, but there was sadness, not accusation, in her voice.

"I know I've been a stranger in her life. I'm not happy with that anymore." He sipped his own brandy as he studied her face. "I found out why Giselle's message didn't reach me."

"Oh?"

"Bry took it."

"He still hates me, doesn't he?"

"Yes."

"You don't mince words, do you?"

"Not anymore. I've decided that I've wasted a lot of my life by not saying what I really wanted to say."

Zandra glanced at him mockingly. "And what do you really want to say tonight, Bryan?"

"That I want to spend the night in your bed."

She looked at him in astonishment and then, as he opened his arms, she threw herself against his chest. "Oh, Bryan. I'm so glad you said that."

"Does that mean I'm invited?"

"Yes."

*   *   *

Giselle glanced up as Tru came into the bedroom. "You look tired," she told him.

"Getting married for the first time is rough on a man my age." He sat down on the bed beside her and pulled her over for a kiss. "I've been on the phone to the West Palm Beach police."

"Anything new?"

"Not yet."

"This theory the police have is ridiculous, Tru. I knew Patrick for thirty-six years. He wouldn't have killed his sister-in-law. And what would have been his motive? He went there to tell her that her son was dead."

"But we can't tell the police that. There was one piece of interesting news, though." Tru paused, staring off into space as though something had just occurred to him.

Giselle nudged him. "What news?"

"The police think someone was there, gagged and bound to a kitchen chair. They say that the physical evidence at the scene indicates that after Halloran was shot, he released the person."

"Who, for heaven's sake?"

"They don't know. But if they did, I imagine they would want to question that person quite thoroughly."

She looked up into his face. He still had that far-away look in his eyes. "Tru? Do you know something?"

He shook his head. "I was just thinking how odd it was that Alex decided to go back to Nice so suddenly."

"You don't think there was a connection between her and this business with Patrick and his sister-in-law?"

"How could there have been? But . . ."

"But what?" Giselle demanded.

"Did you know that Sheila Halloran was Alex's maid at one time?"

"No. But what significance would that have?"

"None that I know of, but still . . ." He smiled suddenly. "I believe there's a trade-off here. We may have lost Nice once more, since Alex is buying herself another villa there. But I wouldn't be surprised if we've gained Palm Beach. Especially if I drop my twin a note saying that the West Palm Beach police inquired about her connection to Sheila Halloran."

"Did they?"

"No, but Alex won't know that. You know twins share a certain closeness, and I can't shake the feeling that she was involved in all this mess somehow. If I'm right, that note will be enough to keep her far away from Palm Beach for years."

"Oh, Tru, you're as bad as the rest of the Vales!"

"Devious and underhanded," he agreed. "It was a trait I inherited from Father." He looked at her seriously for a moment. "You won't be upset if we don't give the police that piece of information? Even if she was involved with Sheila Halloran in some way, I don't see Alex as a murderer."

Giselle pulled his head down to hers and kissed him. "I don't want to think about it anymore," she told him.

"The police said we could go ahead and make the burial arrangements for Halloran."

"Good."

"Do you want to be there for the funeral?"

"I think I ought to."

"And then?"

"Oh, Tru, would you think I was crazy if I told you I wanted to rename the house?" Tears sprang to her eyes. "Did you know that Patrick helped me rechristen it Casa Durand when I bought it from your nephews?" She smiled through her tears. "We smashed a lovely bottle of Dom Perignon on the front steps."

He kissed her damp cheek. "I just happen to have a bottle of Dom Perignon we can take to Palm Beach with us for the ceremony." He paused. "And what will you name the house this time, darling?"

"Casa Vale."

"That sounds logical, since you've become Mrs. Vale again."

Giselle sighed happily and snuggled closer to Tru. "Finally, after all these years, the right Mrs. Vale."

Dona Vaughn is the author of four published books. She and her husband live in the greater Houston, Texas area.

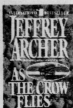

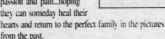